When you hit a man with a sword, it can go clean or ugly. A clean hit and you barely even feel the impact. Oh, your opponent feels it. Trust me. But for the swordsman, your blade travels through skin and muscle as if it is parting water. Arms can come right off. Legs are tougher, but a good strike will cut clear to the bone and leave them crippled. A katana will shear a rib like paper, and their guts will fall out like a butchered pig. Then with a snap of the wrist the blade has returned and the swordsman is prepared to strike again. Simple. Effective. *Clean.* I'll spare you all the flowery talk the perfumed sensei spout about rhythm and footwork that inevitably make killing sound like a formal court dance, but when you do everything just right, I swear to you that I've killed men so smoothly that their heads have remained sitting upon their necks long enough to blink twice before falling off.

However, an ugly hit means you pulled it wrong, or he moved unexpectedly. The littlest things, a slight change in angle, a tiny bit of hesitation, upon impact you feel that pop in your wrists, and then your sword is stuck in their bone, they're screaming in your face, flinging blood everywhere, and you have to practically wrestle your steel out of them. Whatever bone you struck is a splintered mess. Usually the meat is dangling off in ghastly strips. Some men will take that as a sign to lie down and die, but a dedicated samurai will take that ugly hit and still try to take you with him, just because in principle if a samurai is dying, then damn it, he shouldn't have to do it alone. It can be a very nasty affair.

The tax collector died very ugly.

—From "Musings of a Hermit"
by Larry Correia

FORGED IN BLOOD

EDITED BY

MICHAEL Z. WILLIAMSON

FORGED IN BLOOD

"The Tachi," © 2017 Zachary Hill; "Musings of a Hermit," © 2017 Larry Correia; "Stronger than Steel," © 2017 Mike Massa; "He Who Lives Wins," © 2017 John F. Holmes; "Souvenirs," © 2017 Rob Reed; "Broken Spirit," © 2017 Michael Z. Williamson and Dale C. Flowers; "Okoyyūki," © 2017 Tom Kratman; "The Day the Tide Rolled In," © 2017 Michael Z. Williamson and Leo Champion; "Ripper," © 2017 Peter Grant; "Case Hardened," © 2017 Christopher L. Smith; "Magnum Opus," © 2017 Jason Cordova; "Lovers," © 2017 Tony Daniel; "The Reluctant Heroine" ("The Reluctant Heroine" appeared in slightly different form in the novel Freehold, copyright 2004, Michael Z. Williamson), © 2017 Michael Z. Williamson, "The Thin Green Line," © 2017 Michael Z. Williamson; "Family Over Blood," © 2017 Kacey Ezell; "Choices and Consequences," © 2017 Michael Z. Williamson.

All additional material © 2017 by Michael Z. Williamson

A Baen Books Original

Baen Publishing Enterprises
P.O. Box 1403, Riverdale, NY 10471
www.baen.com

ISBN: 978-1-4814-8353-7

Cover art by Kurt Miller

First paperback printing, October 2018

Library of Congress Catalog Number: 2017023384

Distributed by Simon & Schuster
1230 Avenue of the Americas, New York, NY 10020

Pages by Joy Freeman (www.pagesbyjoy.com)
Printed in the United States of America

For Cassandra Hazel,
whose timely arrival
changed my life immeasurably.

Contents

FORGED IN BLOOD

—⚡—

There was awareness.

She knew she'd existed, but where and in what form wasn't clear.

She remembered the fire, and the water. There had been tension and pain, but now she was a hearty beast, ready for battle.

Hopefully.

She stood on a polished stone floor, against a panoply of armor, on duty as a sentry. Small wars raged around the province, but none came close, so she waited, as was her duty, her only option.

It was a long, long time before she felt the hands of a fearful but determined warrior.

—⚡—

The Tachi

Zachary Hill

Hatsu Kitanosho watched the severed head sail through the air. Its wide eyes stared at her in silent judgment. It alone knew that she was a lie.

The head hit the wooden floor with a wet, heavy sound before rolling down the stairs and out of sight.

Struggling to maintain her calm, she placed the butt of the naginata on the floor and stared at the men and women that surrounded her.

"No one else will bring up the subject of retreat. Understood?"

Retreat would be the wise course of action. The enemy was coming and there were more of them than she could muster. Looking around her she saw old men and young boys that weren't fit for her husband's campaign against the Taira Clan.

Her family's old retainer, Seimu, stood straight and proud while his white beard poured over his red armor. He nodded to her as he had in her childhood training sessions. It meant that she had done well.

She didn't glow with pride like she usually did at

his rare approval. She had not done well. She had killed a man to silence her own misgivings. It had been done out of weakness, not strength.

Yet she couldn't flee. This was her family's manor and had stood for over two hundred years. She couldn't leave it to be burned and desecrated by the Taira's brigands. Her ancestors would never forgive her if she let their shrines be burnt without a fight.

In front of her were her men, loyal soldiers and retainers. They stood in a semicircle around her in the audience chamber. She stood on the raised platform with silk screens behind her that had been brought over from China.

It wasn't as grand as their summer home in Kyoto, but it was a beautiful room. The dark stained wood was darker from age, and window shutters were propped open so she could listen to the cicadas outside. A banner of her calligraphy hung on the wall next to a rack of spears.

"Seimu, gather every able-bodied man and boy and organize our defense. Man our walls. Get archers ready."

"Yes, Lady Hatsu."

He gave a deep bow.

Kitanosho nodded her head.

She then turned to the captain of the guard, the closest thing to professional soldiers she had.

"I need you to follow Seimu's instructions. You are now under his authority. Open up the armory and get a spear into every hand you can."

"Yes, my lady."

She then looked at the body of the man. Blood pooled over the dark wood of the floor. A glance to the two servant women was enough to get them to drag the body away and return with brushes and buckets.

"We will not retreat or surrender," she said more to herself than to them.

She walked to the narrow window that looked over the courtyard and the fields that radiated out from the small village. Beyond her sight was the enemy and they were coming closer by the second. They were cowards to attack this place while the lord was out. They expected a quick and cruel victory against unarmed women and children. They would not find their victory quick nor their enemy unarmed.

Her slender hands gripped the window sill.

I wish Kotaro was here.

Her husband would know what to do.

It was all bluster. Like a raging sunset she put on a magnificent display but affected nothing.

I'm no general. I'm no brave warrior. I'm just a spoiled noblewoman with too few years to know much of anything.

She spoke in a controlled tone to hide the weakness in her stomach. "When will they be here?"

"Before nightfall, Lady Hatsu," Seimu said.

She nodded and acted as if she were thinking. Really, she was only trying to get the whirlpool of her thoughts in some kind of order.

Seimu approached and stood just behind her.

"And the peasants?" he asked in a near whisper.

"Arm them? I think they would more be in the way," she whispered so the others wouldn't hear. Seimu knew who and what she was. There was no point in hiding anything from him. But the others needed to see her as an infallible goddess of war.

He said, "Then we need to evacuate them now or they'll be killed."

She knew the enemy would kill any peasant they saw. They were a part of her duty. They belonged to her family and had to be protected.

"Very well. Send some of your men and get them out of the village. Hide them at the temple near the river."

"Yes, Lady Hatsu."

He bowed and left in his stride that hadn't slowed down after all these years. Many heroes fade as they grew older. Seimu only grew brighter.

Down below she heard her men shouting orders in that sharp cadence the military men spoke. If she hadn't been raised around it, she would never have understood what they were saying.

The manor came alive with running people. Some carried bundles of spears, others carried water or food. The village on the other side of the field rang their bell. She could hear the familiar hollow sound. The bell had been a gift to her grandfather from a temple on a nearby island. She couldn't see them but she imagined the peasants gathering in that dusty town square of theirs and listening to one of Seimu's ashigaru telling them to pack their things and leave.

The peasants would continue to do their duty to her ancestors no matter how this night ended. The same ancestors that looked down at her with disdainful glares.

Kitanosho went down the narrow stairs that were more like a ladder to where the shrine of her ancestors stood. In a small alcove rested the armor that her grandfather had worn into battle. Every scratch and indent on it was known to her. Her grandfather's straight-bladed tachi lay in its scabbard with the hilt pointing out. It had killed many foes in Korea. She had never been allowed to touch it and knew she still wasn't worthy of it. The older-style sword had been forged by a master sword maker, a prize worth more than the manor and the village combined. The lacquered face under the wide-brimmed helmet stared down at her with its angry grimace. Another silent judgment.

She lit sticks of incense and bowed to the floor in front of the armor and her grandfather's sword.

In silence she begged their forgiveness. She was an unworthy servant and could not meet the challenge before her, but she was all her clan had and so they all had to make do.

She listened but there was no answer. Either she was beneath their attention or they were ignoring her.

Outside she heard more shouting. It disturbed her thoughts but it meant the defense was underway.

She looked to the doorway and saw two of her ladies in waiting. They kneeled just outside, waiting for her permission to enter.

They were pampered ladies that weren't important to their families. They could not help in the manor's defense and would only be in the way.

"You two. Gather your things and leave. Go to my uncle's fort in Maruoka."

She noticed the relieved glances they gave each other. They bowed and left in too much of a hurry.

They didn't think the manor was a safe place to be. At least they were smart enough to realize that.

Kitanosho dusted her knees off and went outside.

Her hair trailed behind her, almost touching the floor. She squinted into the brightness of the noon day and waited for the pain to recede.

She didn't go outside unless she could help it. The men liked pale women, and she'd do anything to please Kotaro. Also, her books and poetry were inside. What good did it do to be outside where the burning sun, insects and hot weather were? It was better to be inside with some good tea and better poetry.

She stepped down from the covered porch and as she walked out she looked back to the manor. The tiled roof filled the sky above her and sloped down to the windows of the second floor. It was a collection of buildings that all flowed together into one whole. Some were attached directly to the main house and others had covered walkways leading to them. The space underneath the raised house had been wonderful for hiding when she was a child.

There would be no hiding now.

Men filled buckets of water from the well and stacked them around the manor. If the Taira Clan wanted to burn her home down, they would have to step over the bodies of her men to do it.

Kotaro, I'll protect our home for your return. If I don't, please forgive me.

It had been a political marriage to keep the clan together and nothing more. At least, to everyone else. To her it was breath itself.

All her life she had stood off to the side, watching Kotaro. She had written countless poems about him and faded into dreams thinking of him. At first she had been afraid that it was one of her dreams when her father told her that she would marry him.

The manor was her family's home, but he lived here now and so it was his home as well. She would protect his home for his return.

As she walked around the courtyard pretending to inspect the ongoing work, she wondered if Kotaro would miss her if she died this night. How long would it take for the clan to give him another wife? Perhaps not long. She had not given him a child yet and so would not be remembered.

One of my many failings.

When she escaped from her thoughts she realized that Seimu was standing next to her.

She cleared her throat and straightened her shoulders. "How goes the preparations?"

"Well. Or as well as can be expected, my lady."

The white and blue walls of the fortified manor had been her life for the past twenty years. Only twice had she ventured beyond her family's lands. The red tiled roofs would soon have arrows pouring down on them.

It was such a poor time to have a battle. The first pricks of cold had seeped into the air. The leaves would be changing soon and it would be a great pity to miss writing poems about the beauty that would surround her.

"You have that look in your eye again, my lady."

"And what look would that be?" she asked.

"The one where you wish you were somewhere far away. I haven't seen that look in a long while."

"I'm not a child anymore."

"I know. You don't have to be a child to wish for better times."

"Seimu, can we win?"

He replied, "I don't know. I'd have to see what

they brought. But if what our scouts say is accurate, then few of us will live through the night."

"For once you may lie to comfort me."

"But then I'd fail at my duty," he said.

"Is that what I'm doing?"

"Hardly." He straightened his back and stuck out his chest. "Tonight you will lead us in battle. Live or die, you will do honor to our clan."

For once, she didn't believe him.

As the soldiers did their duty and prepared the manor for battle, she went back up to her room and sat down with hot tea and Chinese poetry.

The day passed with the sound of yelling soldiers. She tried to ignore the fact that the light outside grew gray and then orange. Her time was drawing to a close and soon her fate would be handed to her like a message from the capitol in Nara.

As the light blazed red outside, Seimu came in. He had polished his armor for what could be the last time. His beard and mustache went into perfect points. He seldom had time for such niceties, and the last time she had seen him so prepared was on her wedding day.

"It's time to get ready, my lady."

She put her book down and closed her eyes.

Ancestors, give me strength.

She stood as a lady should and followed Seimu downstairs where soldiers stood with her equipment. One held her naginata. Another held her breastplate and another held her headband and straps to keep her robes tight and out of the way.

Kitanosho stood as they worked around her, getting her ready for battle. Her sisters had learned the bow, but she had never shown promise with it.

"You lack patience," her father used to say.

But with the naginata she had found her path. It made sense to her and flowed with her like a cool mountain stream. There were many similarities between poetry and the naginata. Both required her to know when to pull back, when to wait, and when to strike with everything she had. Despite being a large weapon, it required the subtlety of a poet to make its power effective.

Shouting came from outside.

With her robes tightened and her hair up in a bun, she gripped her old naginata and followed Seimu out. The soldiers by the gate were sliding the heavy beam into place. The other soldiers in simpler versions of Seimu's armor stood by with their spears held tight in both hands. They cast looks to each other in silence.

"Report," Seimu said as they approached the gate.

He didn't shout but his voice carried like thunder.

"Our scouts reported armed men in the village heading our way."

"Numbers?"

"I don't know. Many. Some were seen moving in the woods, and a column of spears coming down the road."

Seimu grunted and turned away.

"I suppose it doesn't matter. There are as many as there are."

"When will they be here?" she asked.

"Any moment."

She glanced over at the men standing in the courtyard. They gripped their weapons like a life line in a raging river.

"Are we ready for this?" she asked.

"As ready as we can be." He turned to the men

and stepped toward them. "String your bows. Fight with all your strength and you may live. But more important, you may die with honor. No enemy soldier gets into the manor. Not one!"

The men raised their weapons into the air and shouted out, "Die for honor!"

He turned back to her.

"Now, my lady. It's time you get inside."

"No, I'll stay here. This is my home and I will fight for it."

"But, my lady—" He hadn't meant for her to take "lead" literally.

"No. I will not change my mind. I can't do any good hiding like a frightened girl."

Seimu let out a long breath and shook his head.

"Very well, but stay close to me. Very close."

In another setting she would reprimand him for daring to give her an order. But now, as she felt her heart pounding inside her chest like a taiko drum, she knew she would need to follow every order he gave like she used to do during training.

As a girl she would hide in the wardrobe, listening to Seimu and her father telling stories of their past battles. So many seemed hard to believe, but even the lesser ones told her that this man had seen more fighting and death than almost anyone else. He knew what he was doing, and he knew how to kill.

She hoped she would learn. She knew how to spar. That was different than an actual fight to the death. Killing a servant or retainer wasn't the same either. They wouldn't fight back. She was about to face many men that wanted to kill her.

Her naginata grew slick from the sweat on her

palms, and she tried to wipe them off on her robes without anyone seeing.

People are coming to kill me.

She stood there, trying to appear calm while everyone buzzed around her preparing for the fight.

A faint red glow over the walls marked the sun as it went out for the night. Torches and lanterns appeared as the stars mirrored them above. Now a comforting soft glow of flickering lanterns filled the courtyard.

She stood with her naginata in both hands and Seimu right beside her. She had done all she could. Now it was for the kami to decide.

A hundred voices yelled out at once. They were muted from floating over the fields and over the walls, but it was enough to shake every bone in her body.

"Get ready!" Seimu ordered.

Something flew past her head and landed with a loud slap. She turned to see an arrow sticking out of the wall.

Then arrows came down like hail, pelting everyone who hadn't run for cover.

Seimu crushed her in his arms and threw himself into the doorway. More arrows rained down outside as she lay on the wooden floor with him on top of her. He scrambled off her and got to his feet. His sword was already in his hand.

His helmet had come off in his rush to save her and she picked it up as she got off the ground.

The shouting only grew closer as more arrows came down. One went through the wood slots of the window and stuck into the polished floor.

Someone would have died for that in peacetime. Someone will die for it tonight.

"Here they come," one of the soldiers at the gate shouted.

Something heavy struck the gate with a force she felt in her feet. Her archers shot through the narrow slots in the doors. They kept loosing shafts without pause.

More arrows came down into the courtyard. She heard the harsh *thunks* of the ones that hit the roof.

The gates moaned under another violent impact. She assumed they had some kind of ram. *Perhaps a cut-down tree.* The pounding continued as people shouted orders and glinting arrows filled the dark sky.

Already cracks appeared in the gates. The wooden doors that had stood for over a hundred years were being broken down in so short a time. It felt as if her life were measured in the life span of that gate. Once it broke the enemy would swarm in like a flood.

Seimu shouted and waved his arms. Spearmen got into position in a half circle around the gate. Archers took up position between each spearman, ready to unleash a volley as soon as the doors gave way.

There wasn't long to wait. The hinges of the mighty gates broke away from the walls and the heavy doors slammed to the ground kicking up dust around them. Arrows flew from bows into the dark and open gateway. Before they could loose another round, dozens of men, followed by dozens more, poured through the gate. Spears were leveled out as they rushed in.

Seimu shouted and his men charged forward. In an instant the courtyard filled with the furious sound of men trying to kill other men. Spears plunged into exposed necks and arms. On both sides bodies fell down to be trampled by their brothers.

"Hold the line! Don't let them break through!" Seimu called out over the chaos.

The push of men moved toward the gate. It was a tide like the shallows near Oshima island. A heavy, unstoppable force surging forward at an almost lazy pace.

"We're holding," she said.

He didn't respond. His eyes remained locked on the fight. There was no happiness in his eyes. They weren't winning. He saw something she didn't.

"I must move in. Follow but do not engage," he said.

Without waiting for her response he charged forward with his sword in the air. Hefting the naginata that now seemed twice as heavy, she followed after him. In front of her was a mass of lethal spears where death could come at her from any angle.

Seimu rushed into the fray without slowing down. His long, curved blade moved in short, fast movements. No effort was wasted. One swift downward swing and an enemy soldier's face split open. Another swing and a man's arm fell to the ground.

She stood and watched, not knowing what to do. This was nothing like sparring in the dojo.

Kitanosho readied her naginata in an offensive stance and looked for an opening. He had told her not to engage but she couldn't stand there and watch while the enemy attacked her family home.

An enemy soldier wearing dark blue armor broke through the mob. He held his spear at his waist while he looked for a new target. The flickering lanterns cast half of him in an orange glow and the other half was dark shadow.

This is my chance.

She charged with the curved blade of the naginata just below her eye level. He looked up from under his wide-brimmed hat and saw her. With a shout showing all his yellow teeth he charged right at her.

In the dojo this had happened before but always in the back of her mind was the knowledge that the other person wasn't trying to kill her. This man was. He had broken in here with the intent to destroy her home and slaughter her.

It was war, but it felt sharper than that. It felt as if this man wanted to kill only her.

"How dare you," she shouted back.

His spear leveled at her head. In one motion she knocked the spear aside while bringing the butt of her polearm up to smash the side of the man's face. The heavy wood shaft connected, sending blood and teeth flying.

The man stumbled and fell to the ground. He looked up in time to see her blade come down onto him. The bones of his spine offered a faint resistance as she severed his head. The momentum of the naginata did most of the work.

She stood there for a moment looking down at the headless body. Her first kill in real battle. That man had tried to kill her and she killed him instead. It was that simple.

I shouldn't worry about this. It's what I was raised for. Don't look. Pay attention to the battle, fool.

She forced her eyes away from the corpse and back to the gate. Her men were being pushed back. Soon they wouldn't be able to hold the gate and the enemy would break through.

Kitanosho charged in again and started swinging.

Every opening she saw she swung at. An exposed arm, a face, a knee. Standing just behind one of her men she was able to reach in and cut the inner thigh of a blue-armored man. He howled in pain just before her soldier speared him in the face.

A half second later an enemy spear thrust into her man's shoulder. She slashed the head off the spear but couldn't get at the enemy.

A strong hand gripped her shoulder and yanked her back. Seimu stood over her. In the fire and darkness of the courtyard his face was a black shadow with red, flickering eyes.

"My lady, you must fall back to the house. Stay inside. It's now too dangerous for you out here."

"But I can . . ."

"No! Do as I say. Go inside."

She tried to think of something to say, but there was nothing. He understood the situation better than she ever could. It wasn't a cowardly act. It was part of the defense. She was too exposed out there, but inside she could defend with more efficiency.

She nodded and squeezed his arm before rushing inside. After sliding the door closed she stood and waited. She didn't move in order to hear everything happening outside.

There were shouts, grunting, the sounds of metal on metal and screams. She didn't know how long she stood there. It could have been a few minutes but it felt like all night. Every moment that passed she knew she was closer to death. Death wasn't what worried her. It was if she earned enough honor to redeem herself in her ancestors' eyes. Time was running out and she hadn't done enough.

Blood splattered against the paper screen of the door. The jagged, staccato stain was unmistakable. The battle was now at her door.

Something heavy slammed into the wall. She felt the thud.

After taking deep breaths to calm herself, she readied her weapon out in front of her.

The door slid open with a sharp *bang*.

A figure stood in the doorway, backlit by the fires still burning in the courtyard. In one hand it held a long curved tachi. In the other was a severed head.

The figure tossed the head at her and it came to a rolling stop by her feet.

It was Seimu.

There wasn't judgment in his eyes, only pity. The strongest man she knew was dead and all was lost. She couldn't protect her home without him. Her ancestors would be disappointed and her husband would be shamed. Perhaps he would never speak of her and move on to a new wife with no more thought of her.

She looked up at the man who had killed Seimu. He was a large man in yellow and blue armor. His thick panoply seemed to cover every inch of him. Only his eyes stared out from the grimacing face mask.

Blood poured down his left arm. Seimu had at least wounded him. Even in death, Seimu had served her. The man that could kill him could kill her with little difficulty. But perhaps a wound could give her the chance to kill him as well. Her own death was assured. She would die regardless, and she would take him with her.

"I am Hatsu Kitanosho of the Hashiji clan. And I will end your life today."

"You sound as though you lack conviction," he replied almost casually.

She looked down at the head of Seimu that stared up at her. The sounds of fighting continued outside.

"You have conviction. But what you lack is honor," she said.

"Honor is what grants me victory."

"Then your honor will fall short tonight."

He raised his sword in an overhead stance and shifted his weight on his feet. His stance made him ready to move forward to strike. It was pure offense with no regard to defense.

One lesson she learned from Seimu was that with the naginata, she couldn't afford to be defensive. The sword was too fast. She had to take the offense and keep him at a distance. He was larger and better trained. She didn't have a choice.

Ancestors, guide my hands.

Kitanosho made a quick slash to put him on the defensive. He bashed her blade to the side and moved in closer. Closer was where she didn't want him, and he knew it.

She swept the butt of her naginata up but he blocked that as well with little effort. With her blade still moving she swung it down in an overhead chop that wouldn't be so easy to brush aside.

This time when he deflected the blow he used both hands. She noticed the hesitation in his left arm. It was still bleeding.

No amount of training could compensate for lack of blood. If she could hold off and wait for him to grow weak she had a chance.

He struck, knocking her back. Her foot shot back

to maintain balance, but just barely. There was a chink in her blade where his tachi had struck.

The man reached up and took off his grimacing mask. He was smiling.

"Life isn't like the dojo where your father's servants are too afraid to hit you in training. I just want you to know that there is no dishonor in dying by my sword. Many better warriors have been bested by me."

"Seimu was a better warrior," she said.

He looked down to the head on the floor.

"Apparently not."

"He had honor," she said.

"Honor is found in victory. Dying and failing to protect his mistress is not honorable."

She returned, "Neither is attacking the home of a noble warrior while he is away. Killing women and children is a suitable test of your abilities?"

"Don't mock me, girl. My honor is in doing what my lord tells me. Do you always get to do as you wish? Did you choose your husband or did you marry him out of duty to your clan? Duty. That is the only real honor."

"Then it is your masters that have no honor." She should have felt angry. She felt nothing.

"For that, I will make you suffer before you die."

"You won't live to see that," she assured him.

He laughed. It was a loud and genuine laugh and she couldn't blame him. He was wounded but he didn't seem concerned at all. He thought he could beat her with only one arm and he was most likely correct.

Then he raised his sword and crouched slightly into an offensive stance. She leveled her naginata out in front of her, waist high in a stance to counter his.

Survive and let him bleed out.

Even if she did manage to kill this man, her manor was lost. She didn't hear anything from outside. The fighting was over, and all that was left was to let their leader gain the glory of killing the mistress of the manor.

All her life she had read stories about warriors drawing on the strength of their ancestors to beat superior foes.

She felt nothing. There was no score of ancestors watching over her. All she felt was the deafening sound of being alone. There was no Seimu to come rescue her. Her husband was weeks away fighting near Edo. In all likelihood, her men lay dead in heaps in the courtyard.

She was left alone to face this man who outclassed her in every way.

"Ancestors, guide my hand," she pleaded in a whisper.

She jabbed with her blade and he stepped to the side.

He was fast. Faster than Seimu had ever been.

Using one arm he made two flashing strikes that she just managed to block. His third attack locked blades with her and pushed her back toward a support pillar. She couldn't risk being pressed against it. It would give her nowhere to go.

Kitanosho sidestepped to avoid the trap and kept retreating away from him to gain distance.

The man kept pace and wouldn't let her get out of reach.

He struck again and the blow was so hard that she felt the bones in her hands ache. As her curved blade veered off to the side from the violent impact, he stepped forward and chopped downward in a light but quick motion.

She brought her naginata's shaft up to block it and angled it so it wouldn't be a direct hit.

Still, his sword sliced halfway through the haft of her weapon.

He yanked his sword out and readied into another offensive pose.

Before she could settle into her own defensive stance he attacked again. His sword came down and she raised to block it, but in midswing it shifted direction and came down onto the same spot of the haft.

There was a crack and her weapon split in two.

She stumbled back as her balance was thrown off.

He didn't hesitate and moved in closer.

With one last straining effort she swung with the broken naginata. The heavy blade was now clumsy and off balance. It was a desperate move and little more.

He swung his sword up. But instead of blocking he aimed lower and in one blinding motion he slashed up into the air.

A trail of blood, and her left hand, went sailing into the air. The pale, thin hand still clung to the broken haft of the naginata. For a moment she saw it for what it was, a weak and soft hand of a poet. She was no warrior and this man knew it.

She had failed. The hand sailing through the air in a lazy arc was the final judgment of her ancestors. She had failed and their home would be desecrated and burned. She had been too weak to prevent it.

Then the pain shot through her body and she stumbled backward, falling to the ground.

Kitanosho looked down at the bleeding stump. The blood was dark, almost black in the faint light of the lanterns. It was silly but she thought about how much trouble it would be to have it cleaned. And her silk clothes were ruined. Blood splattered all over her pink and blue summertime robe.

She scooted away from the man who stood over her, sword down in a relaxed pose. He could let his guard down because she was no longer a threat.

Kotaro, I'm sorry. I'll never see you again, so please forgive me for failing you. I did what I could, but it was not enough.

"Praying to your gods? They won't help you."

He stepped forward and she backed away further until she hit the wall. There was nowhere else to go.

"I'll bring your head to my lord. I'll wrap it in your finest silk."

"May I ask one thing?"

He nodded.

"Please have a poem written about this."

"I don't have time for such things."

He stepped closer, raising his sword in his good hand.

Death was standing over her and there was nothing she could do. The blade over her head would end her life. She looked around for something, but the only thing nearby was her grandfather's armor sitting in its shrine.

He was the last person she wanted to see. Her shame burned her worse than the jolts of pain from her missing hand.

"I'm sorry, grandfather."

Then a figure burst into the room. It was one of her ashigaru. He was covered in blood and his wide-brimmed hat was in tatters. He panted as he struggled for breath. He raised his spear and yelled a wordless cry at the man.

The warrior turned to see the new spectacle.

Her soldier would die and the warrior would decapitate her. It was inevitable.

Soon, all I see will be in flames as the manor crumbles around my headless body. I'm a failure. Grandfather, forgive me.

She looked to her grandfather's armor for any signs of forgiveness or reproach. Any scorn he had for her had now been earned in full.

The armor's mask stared down at her with its shadow-filled eyes.

In that moment she knew he saw her. She couldn't tell if it was with anger, disappointment or regret, but he noticed her.

"I've failed," she said.

Her eyes fell on the hilt of his old sword and stayed there. It was as if he was offering his sword to her.

"I'm not worthy," she said.

Still, the handle offered itself to her.

The warrior above her still looked to the stumbling ashigaru. Her soldier was no threat and was no longer a distraction. If she had any chance to do this, it had to be now.

With her remaining hand she reached out and gripped the sword she had never dared touch. The hilt felt cold and hard beneath her grip.

The warrior turned back to her, raising his sword in the air.

She grimaced in pain and yanked the sword out of its bamboo scabbard. It was heavier than she thought it would be and she swung with her whole body and all the strength she had left in her.

As the blade sliced through the air she got her first

look at it. It was dark metal with rippling textures all along the surface. Growing up she had heard many tales of where it came from. Seimu had said it was forged from a rock that fell from the sky. Another one of father's warriors said that it had been forged by a witch and was thirsty for blood. Her uncle said the metal was from a normal mine in Shikoku.

Wherever it came from, she was shocked by its beauty.

She didn't have long to admire the delicate patterns before the thick blade struck the warrior's side. It didn't so much as cut through the warrior but tore through him. It smashed through his armor and carved deep into his belly. Pieces of lacquered bamboo scales flung through the air.

He staggered back, pulling her and the lodged sword with her.

His face went pale and his eyes went wide. He stuttered something she didn't understand and raised his sword. Blood gushed out of the tear in his armor and covered her hand in warm, sticky liquid.

Despite dying, he would still kill her.

It didn't matter now. She had killed him in return and avenged the desecration of her home.

No! I'm not going to let this honorless dog kill me.

She rose to her feet, pushing forward to drive the sword deeper in. He grunted and fell backward to the ground. She crashed on top of him as she kept pushing. As they struck the ground together, the blade of her sword snapped.

It was a singular sound like the funeral bell from the village. She fell off him and rolled to the side.

She lay there, panting for breath, staring up at the

ceiling. In her hand was the hilt of the broken sword.
A gift from her ancestors. *Acceptance.*

It was no longer cold. Now covered in the warrior's
blood, it seemed warm and alive.

There was no doubt that the ancestors hadn't helped
to spare her. She was just one of many. But they had
used her to save the family home.

She had been honored. Despite all her failings,
they felt her worthy of being a tool in their hands.

"Soldier, help me up," she called out.

Her voice came out weak and unfamiliar.

The bleeding soldier stumbled over to her and
helped her to her feet. Once she had wrapped a
cloth tightly around the stump on her left, she went
outside to the courtyard, leaning on him for support.
She could admit to needing help now.

Bodies were everywhere. Blood splatters covered
the white walls. A few fires burned, casting the whole
scene in flickering orange.

A few of her men were still alive. They checked
on the wounded and put out fires. It was a scene of
devastation but one she knew they could come back
from. The manor still stood and her husband had a
home to return to.

"Get a spear ready. I want to mount that man's
head on the gate as a present for my husband," she
said through a wave of nausea.

"Yes, my lady," one of the soldiers said and rushed
inside.

The rest of them stopped and stared at her with
wide eyes. Her hair was undone and she was covered
with blood.

I must be quite the sight, she thought to herself with a laugh.

"Also, find me a sword maker. This sword will be reforged."

It wasn't just a weapon. It was a symbol. It was her ancestors' will made manifest. It was a symbol to all that her family would always fight for honor.

I'm the weapon of my ancestors. Like this sword, I am wounded but will be reforged into something greater. Doubt no longer clouds my mind.

"Clean this mess up and prepare the manor for my husband's return," she shouted out with greater strength.

> That forthwith Hatsu Kitanosho is to be jito over Sadakiyo Manor and Shigetsugo Manor within Katakata District, Ise-no-kuni.
>
> The aforesaid person is appointed to the steward's revenue of these two manors as a reward for defending her Lord Hatsu Kotaro's castle in the tenth month of this year. Authority is to be exercised in accordance with precedent. In pursuance of the command, it is decreed thus.

—∾—

The fires caressed her again, then tortured her. Hammers and scrapers made her shorter and slimmer, but she felt her balance improve. Cold water shocked her and forced her into a new, gracile curve.

Once properly dressed in skin, wood, horn and cotton, she resumed her watch. Her keepers called her "The Handless Poet," and practiced with her against tatami, and the bodies of condemned felons. They developed a tradition of practicing with the right hand alone, as well as with both hands properly matched.

And she fought. The battles were small and large, over petty territory and to protect the very islands themselves. Once blooded, she was respected and treated. She did her best to imbue her bearers with her thirst and strength, so they could present themselves with honor.

—∾—

Musings of a Hermit

Larry Correia

When you hit a man with a sword, it can go clean or ugly. A clean hit and you barely even feel the impact. Oh, your opponent feels it. Trust me. But for the swordsman, your blade travels through skin and muscle as if it is parting water. Arms can come right off. Legs are tougher, but a good strike will cut clear to the bone and leave them crippled. A katana will shear a rib like paper, and their guts will fall out like a butchered pig. Then with a snap of the wrist the blade has returned and the swordsman is prepared to strike again. Simple. Effective. *Clean.* I'll spare you all the flowery talk the perfumed sensei spout about rhythm and footwork that inevitably make killing sound like a formal court dance, but when you do everything just right, I swear to you that I've killed men so smoothly that their heads have remained sitting upon their necks long enough to blink twice before falling off.

However, an ugly hit means you pulled it wrong, or he moved unexpectedly. The littlest things, a slight change in angle, a tiny bit of hesitation, upon impact you feel that pop in your wrists, and then your sword is stuck in their bone, they're screaming in your face, flinging blood everywhere, and you have to practically wrestle your steel out of them. Whatever bone you struck is a splintered mess. Usually the meat is dangling off in ghastly strips. Some men will take that as a sign to lie down and die, but a dedicated samurai will take that ugly hit and still try to take you with him, just because in principle if a samurai is dying, then damn it, he shouldn't have to do it alone. It can be a very nasty affair.

The tax collector died very ugly.

I only wanted to be left alone.

Kanemori was sitting by the stove, absorbing the warmth, debating over whether it was too early in the afternoon to get drunk, when there was a great commotion in his yard. Someone was calling his name. It wouldn't be the first time in his long life that someone with a grudge had turned up looking for him, but this sounded like a girl. He rose and peeked out one of the gaps in the wall that he'd been meaning to repair, to see that it was the village headman's daughter trudging through the snow with determination.

"Go away!" he shouted.

"Kanemori! The village needs your help."

The headman always wanted his help with something, the lazy bastard. A tree fell on old lady Haru's hut. Or Den's ox is stuck in the river. Or please save us from these bandits, Kanemori-sama! And then he'd have to go saw wood, or pull on a stupid ox, or cut down some pathetic bandit rabble. He knew it was usually just the headman trying to be social, but it was a waste of his time. He didn't belong to the village. He'd simply had the misfortune of building his shack near it.

"What now?" he bellowed through the wall.

"The new Kura-Bugyo is going to execute my father!"

"What did your imbecile father do to make the tax collector angry this time?"

"The last official was honest, but the officials this year are corrupt. They take more than they're supposed to. They take the lord's share, and then they take more to sell for themselves! Father refused to give up the last of our stores. If we do we'll perish during the winter."

Of course the officials were corrupt. That's what officials were for.

The girl was about ten, but already bossy enough to be a magistrate. When she reached the shack she began pounding on his door. "Let me in, Kanemori!"

"Go away."

"No! I will stay out here and cry until I freeze to death! Your lack of mercy will cause my angry ghost to haunt you forever. And then you will feel very sorry!"

Kanemori sighed. Peasants were stupid and stubborn. He opened the door. "What do you expect me to do about it?"

"You are samurai! Make them stop."

"Oh?" He looked around his humble shack theatrically. "Do I look like Oda Nobunaga to you? I am without clan, status, or even basic dignity. Officials aren't going to listen to me. Do you think I moved to the frozen north because I am so popular?"

"You are the worst samurai ever!"

In defense of the clumsy butchery that passed for a battle against the corrupt tax collector and his men, my soldiering days were over. It had been many seasons since I'd last hit a man with a sword, so I was rusty. When your joints ache every morning, the last thing you want to do is practice your forms, so my daily training consisted of the minimum a retired swordsman must do in order to avoid feeling guilty. Why do more? I had no lord to command me, no general to bark orders at me—The only person who'd done so recently was my second wife, and I'd buried her two winters ago—and if I spent all my energy swinging a sword who was going to feed all these damnable chickens?

It isn't that peasants can't fight. It is that they're too tired from working all day to learn to fight. A long time ago some clever sort figured that out, traded his hoe for a sword, started bossing around the local farmers, said you give me food and in exchange I'll protect you from assholes who will kill you, but if you don't, I'll kill you myself, and the samurai class was born. From then on, by accident of one's birth it determined if you'd be well fed until you got stabbed to death, or hungry and laboring, until you starved... or got stabbed to death.

Spare me the history lectures. I actually do know where samurai come from. I was born *buke*. I slept through the finest history lessons in Kyoto. You would not know it to look at me now, but I was once a promising young warrior. It was said that handsome Hatsu Kanemori was a scholar, a poet, and the veritable pride of my clan, and high-ranking officials were lining up to offer me marriages to their daughters... until one day I finally told my lord I was sick of his shit. Then I promptly ran away before he could decorate his castle wall with my head.

Now, the life of a ronin is a different sort of thing entirely. Samurai live well, but they're expected to die on behalf of their lord. Ronin live slightly better than dogs, and are expected to die on behalf of whichever lord scraped up enough coin to hire us. Being a wave man retains all of the joys of getting stabbed to death, but with the added enticement of being as miserable and hungry as a peasant, up until when you get stabbed to death.

But at least you are your own master.

After he closed his door in her face, the headman's daughter had sat down in the snow, started wailing, and seemed petulantly prepared to freeze to death in his yard in protest. He'd known mighty warriors who had committed seppuku to protest a superior's decision, but this was a new form of protest to Kanemori. He thought about throwing rocks at her until she left, but even a curmudgeon has his limits. So he put a blanket over his head to muffle the noise and took a long nap instead.

When he woke up, the girl was still there. Kanemori was surrounded by stubborn idiots.

"Does your family know you walked all the way here?" he shouted through the hole in the wall.

"No! I snuck out. They will think that I was devoured by wolves. They will perish with sadness! You are so cruel, Kanemori! My ghost will wail like this forever!"

He opened his door. When the orange light of the stove hit the girl, she quit her fake crying.

"You will save our village?" she asked.

"The Kura-Bugyo is an important man. If I report him, it is his word against mine, and I am without status in this district. There isn't much I can do." Before she could start crying again, he hurried to add, "But I suppose I could try."

"Thank you, noble samurai!"

It was a very long walk to the city, and the local governor's representatives would probably just turn him away, but he'd traded with these villagers, at times he'd chosen to help them, and they'd chosen to help him. It was remarkable how well folks got along without being ordered around.

"I will leave in the morning and travel to the city. I can request an audience with the Mokudai about this corrupt tax collector and—"

"There's no time. They're coming for father tomorrow morning. If we walk all night we can get back in time to save him."

Well, that complicated matters. That meant engaging with the tax collector personally, and since Kanemori had no place in this province, the petty official would probably take an interruption as an insult, and the girl's father wouldn't be the only one executed in the morning.

But she had started crying again. And as far as Kanemori could tell, it looked real. Those tears were probably going to freeze her eyelids shut, and then he wouldn't have to just walk all the way down to the village, but carry a blind girl too.

Kanemori sighed. "Stop that awful noise. Fine. I'll try to save your stupid village. Let me get my sword."

❖   ❖   ❖

I have never been good at taking orders. Petty authority annoys me. I have always had a surly, contrarian disposition. These are not desirable traits in a samurai. A good warrior is supposed to have unquestioning loyalty to his lord, no matter how ridiculous he might be. My problem was that I always questioned everything. When I was a boy, my individualistic attitude helped me collect an inordinate number of beatings. That was good. It made me tough. Because if you are going to make it on your own wandering a world that is all about surviving as part of a group, you'd better be tough.

Luckily, by the time my family sent me off to training, I'd learned when to keep my mouth shut... mostly. I had enough natural talent with a sword that my sensei usually overlooked my flippant attitude. It turns out you can afford to give some inadvertent insults when everyone else is scared to duel you. But that only applies to equals—insult a superior, and you had better have a fast horse nearby.

In this world, every man has his place. You know it, you live it, and you pretend to love it. A good samurai would rather let his superior make a foolish decision unchallenged than bring dishonor to his name. Yes, your leader could be an imbecile giving orders that are sure to lead to ignominious defeat, but you'd better take those orders and die with a smile on your face. That is the way of things. So when you slip up and anger your betters, you need to be very valuable on the battlefield—which I was—for them to overlook it. Sadly, when peace finally came to my home province, my painful honesty outweighed my value with a sword.

Stupid peace.

I remember the day when my father gave me my sword. It had belonged to him, and his father, and his father's father's father, so on and so forth, back to tales of glorious battles long ago, and a family legend of a one-handed matriarch, all accompanied with a proud genealogy that was probably half forgery, and half wishful thinking. But regardless, it was an excellent sword.

I suspect he knew I was unworthy of such a legacy, but every father hopes for the best.

At sunrise the village headman ran down the steps of the storehouse, slipped through the packed snow, scooped up his little girl, and swung her around in his arms, before holding her tight. "Iyo! You're alive! We woke up this morning and you were gone. Where have you been? We were so worried about you."

"I went to fetch the samurai so he can save you from the officials," the little girl declared proudly.

"What?"

"Defiant Kanemori! Hero of Sekigahara!"

Kanemori cleared his throat so the headman would notice him. Personally, he hated those titles, but bored peasants like to tell stories. The little girl's head had been filled with nonsense exaggerations about his exploits. During their journey down the mountain, she'd asked him about *all* of them.

Kanemori had walked all night, in the dark, in the miserable cold, lucky he hadn't fallen off a narrow trail to his death, and now he was tired, hungry, and annoyed, and probably about to anger another official who could order him killed with so much as a nod. At least it had been a clear night, and he'd always enjoyed gazing at the stars. His father used to say he was too much of a dreamer in that respect.

"You?" The headman was shocked to see him there. He quickly regained his composure, and went into a deep bow. "Apologies for my daughter disturbing you, noble samurai." Then he realized he probably wasn't showing enough deference to his better and began to grovel. "So many apologies for this inconvenience."

"Stop it. Just..." Kanemori waved his hand. "Stop all that." He'd never been much for etiquette or social niceties.

"It was not Iyo's place to—"

"She says you're about to get executed for not paying your taxes and you need help. This isn't any different than when you needed an extra man to drag that dumb ox out of the river. Today you're the ox. Where are these officials? I'll try and talk some sense into them."

"Thank you! Thank you, samurai!"

"I can't promise anything." Over the years he'd found that any given official's reasonableness and mercy was in direct proportionate opposition to their inflated sense of importance and level of corruption. Since they'd been assigned to administer a northern pig hole like this, he wasn't expecting much.

"The Kura-Bugyo should be here soon. I am willing to be executed. It is better they take out their wrath on me, than steal the last of our rice from the mouths of our children." Again, a good man was prepared to lay down his life for others. Too bad he was so poor nobody would bother to write a poem about it. He looked up, hopeful. "I would rather not die. They will listen to you."

"Maybe. More likely they'll still kill you, then take the rice anyway. Either way that means you have time to make me breakfast first."

When I was young, they called me a dreamer. I suppose that is true. I imagined a world different from this one. Where a man could be free to do as he wanted, without legions of officials standing in his way. Where a man could own things without his superiors taking them away on a whim. A world where someone bold enough to make his own way could do so, and not be bound by the status of his birth. Where you could decide for yourself how to live, rather than be spent on a bloody field by a shogun.

I still imagine a world where a man could marry the woman he loved, rather than having her lord give her to another man for political expediency. A world where a samurai could protest this unfair decision, but not lose face and be condemned for his emotional outburst, and have to run away in shame . . . only to find out years later that she cut her own throat in protest, rather than be wed to a cruel, barbaric man instead of him.

These are silly ramblings. That is not the world we live in. Not at all.

The four men rode into the village not long after breakfast. Only Kanemori and the headman walked outside to meet them. The officials seemed amused that the rest of the peasants were hiding from them. Their haughty attitude was not so different from bandits.

Unfortunately the Kura-Bugyo was a young man. An older, wiser official might have let the slight pass. The callousness of noble youth, coupled with the unrivaled arrogance of a tax collector, meant that Kanemori had his work cut out for him. The official also had three samurai escorting him, who were acting more like friends than guards. That was another bad sign. An official would feel no need to show off for soldiers, their opinions would be beneath contempt, but the same official would strut like a rooster to save face in front of his friends.

"Where is my rice, headman?" the official shouted, not bothering to give any introduction. "I said to have it waiting. There is a wagon not far behind. Why do you waste my time?" His friends snickered.

The headman bowed so hard he nearly buried himself in the snow. Kanemori was ashamed for him. This wasn't the emperor. This was probably some minor noble's third or fourth son, given a job intended for a clerk, probably to get him out from underfoot, but having power over these poor people had clearly gone to his head.

Only Kanemori had promised little Iyo that he would try, so he needed to speak up before the headman's blubbering caused this pack of dogs to get too riled up. When a deer ran, a dog's instincts were to chase it down. Likewise, a peasant's weakness would make a bully eager for violence.

"Greetings, honored officials." Kanemori gave a very proper bow, showing the right amount of deference, and for the correct amount of time. He hadn't slept through *every* lesson.

They didn't even bother to get off their horses. Sitting up there must have made them feel tall.

"Who are you supposed to be?" the tax collector sneered.

"I am Kanemori. I am merely a humble friend of

this village, and have come to beg for leniency for them today."

The officials exchanged confused glances. "Who?"

"These kind people have called on me in the hopes that I might be able to appeal to your mercy. Their harvest this year was not very good, purely due to weather beyond their control and not from laziness, yet they still met their obligations. If you examine their stores, you will see that if they meet your new demands, they will not have enough food to survive the winter. They're already eating millet only fit for livestock."

"That's a sad story, only it isn't my problem," the tax collector said.

"But if these villagers sicken and die, then next year there will be no harvest at all." Thus far Kanemori had kept his face neutral and his voice polite, but he could feel that starting to slip. What was it with shortsighted fools? Officials who had nothing personal at stake could never see beyond their immediate gratification. "Please think of the next season, honored representative. Will your lord not be disappointed?"

"Next year I will have a better appointment."

"You talk like a samurai, but you wear no mon," said one of the young men. His own family signal was proudly embroidered on his sleeve with golden thread. "I think I've heard of this old man. He's that ronin hermit that lives up on the mountain."

"Ha! From his ratty clothing, I took him for another peasant!" said one of the other fine young examples of Bushido. "Have you been rolling around in the dirt to look like that?"

"He has dirt under his nails. He's more farmer than samurai."

"You are obviously a long way from home, old man. Step aside. You have no say here. Now where is my rice, headman?"

This was not his place. Kanemori had done all that he could. He had no further legal recourse. It was his duty to step aside. This was the world they lived in.

Enough.

They'd started calling him Kanemori the Defiant for a reason. Nobody had ever accused him of being Kanemori the Eloquent.

"It isn't *your* rice, boy."

"How dare you, old man?"

"Did you grow it? Did you harvest it? No. These people did. I didn't see your pampered ass sweating in the fields."

It was plain the bullies were not used to that kind of response.

"This land belongs to your lord, and he appointed you to administer and defend it. From the look of you songbirds, you've never defended a thing. The last few times these poor saps have been menaced by bandits, they didn't even bother calling for you. They came and got me instead. Your lord has already collected his taxes. This is about your greed. Spare me the sanctimony. I know how it works. That wagon coming down the road is probably some merchant paying you on the side."

"Such impudence! I'll burn this whole place down!" the tax collector bellowed.

The headman squeaked in fear, but the sound was still muffled by the snow. "Please no, young master! Have mercy." Kanemori had forgotten about him there.

"I was feeling merciful until you got some ronin

fool involved. Now you will discover what happens when you disobey your betters."

Kanemori was old, tired, and too damned grouchy to get out of the way. His order-taking days were over. "The only difference between the government and bandits is that the bandits are at least honest about it."

"Kill him, Shingen," ordered the tax collector. One of them kicked his horse and it started forward. Kanemori watched him rapidly approach. It was obvious the young man wasn't a trained cavalryman, and that was certainly no war horse, but the animal seemed used to the idea of running down peasants.

Kanemori reached for his sword. Out of practice or not, a soldier kept his instincts, and not getting pulverized by hooves was among them. He drew his blade as he smoothly stepped aside, and the cut went very deep. The animal's front leg collapsed, the other hooves slipped, and the unseated rider flew over its head to land in the snow.

The tax collector was obviously shocked. This wasn't what normally happened when you rode down a peasant at all. His friend was thrashing about in the suddenly red snow, trying to figure out how he'd gotten there. The horse was screaming. The other horses began bucking, terrified, at the sudden smell of hot blood, which just went to show the value of a horse properly trained for war.

There is nothing in the world quite so unnerving as the scream of a horse. Kanemori had killed a lot of men in his day, and none of them really kept him up at night, but the wide-eyed thrashing of a terrified wounded horse always bothered him, so he struck again. This time at the neck. *Clean*. It died quickly.

Worst-case scenario, once this was over the hungry villagers could eat the horse. Peasants were efficient like that.

It was not so much a battle, as a slaughter.

If any of those young samurai had a brain in his head, he would have stayed on his mount and ridden for help. The authorities would have come, and I would have died a criminal. But no. Fury made them dumb and pride demanded that they had to put me in my place. They were better than me. That's just how it was. That's how it always has been, and always must be. They don't understand any other way. That's how it is with these people. It's like they're compelled to meddle.

Such is the nature of man. We must join together to survive, but then somebody has to be in charge. Somebody always has to be in charge. And we let them. At first because we need them, but even when we really don't anymore, they're still there. And their power grows, and grows, and grows, until it consumes everything.

I dream of a world where a man can make his own way, but I suppose there will always be samurai and peasants.

I just wanted to be left alone.

The horse was the only clean death that morning. The rest were ugly. Damned ugly.

No honorable samurai would ever sink to the level of doing manual labor, but Kanemori had often lowered himself to help the local peasants, whether it was cutting trees, or dragging an obstinate ox from the river, or in this case, digging a shallow grave in the frozen ground.

"This must never be spoken of," the headman told

the handful of peasants who were standing around their hastily filled hole. The ground was so hard that it had taken a long time, and they'd broken a few valuable shovels in the process, but if there was one thing peasants knew how to do, it was work. By the time the sun had gone down, there was no sign the tax collector, his friends, or their merchant crony had ever come to the village at all.

"If the governor was ever to discover what happened here today, our village would be razed, and every single one of us would be beheaded as criminals." The village headman really wanted to keep his. "We never saw our tax collector. He simply never arrived. Is that understood?"

All of the peasants agreed. Even though none of them had lifted a finger against the tax collector, those in power would never tolerate even the hint of rebellion. If there was something else peasants understood, it was how to keep a secret.

"It is unfortunate, but such things happen when there are so many bandits in these mountains," Kanemori stated flatly. "Perhaps they will send more officials to protect you better in the future."

Of the peasants, only young Iyo was truly glad he'd done what he had. To the rest, he'd simply complicated their already difficult lives. That's because like him, Iyo was a dreamer. She was still naïve enough to think that one person could change things.

After the somber and terrified villagers returned to their huts, Kanemori had remained standing by the grave. Men of such stature were due a proper funeral ceremony, and a small shrine. Instead, they got a shallow pit that no one would ever speak of.

Some of the villagers had thanked Kanemori, but it had been a dishonest thanks. Those who were incapable of defending themselves were often frightened of those who fought in their behalf. He saw there was fear in their eyes, directed at him, and he did not like it one bit. If he had enjoyed such things he probably would have made a fine tax collector.

It was time to move on, to find a new place, to try and make a new home again, where he could just be left alone. Where he could be free.

But there was no place like that in this world.

Kanemori gazed up at the stars, and wished for another way.

Far up the hill, past an old hut, three villagers built a pyre for the body of an old man. The corpse had mummified, and the wiry muscles of the man underneath showed through the shrunken skin.

The youngest said, "Shouldn't we just put him in a hole? He was only an old hermit. This is costing the village money."

"No, we must do it this way."

"Why? He was a ronin."

"But his kami was that of a samurai. It deserves this. You do not know what he has done for us before."

The boy looked at the stone which was to become a discreet monument over the urn. "It's a lot of work."

"Just make the carving neat."

The inscription was simple.

The Defiant.

Even a ronin could fight with honor. Preventing peasants from being abused and starved was not a grand act, but it was still a great act. While she wished for more action, his life was a worthy one she was proud of.

She understood why she was hidden away. Peasants were not allowed swords, and the chief's daughter was no warrior. She waited in her saya, inside a silk case, in a trunk while time ebbed endlessly past. The samurai themselves faded away. That saddened her, and she hoped there would be another culture that respected her, not let her age away for naught. Eventually, the red blight of rust bloomed on her skin.

Then one day, she was taken from the trunk, and hands passed her to another.

Stronger than Steel

Mike Massa

February 1904
Jena, Germany

The duel wasn't going well for Armsman Pavel Ustikov's charge.

By the end of the first beer, the brothers had picked a fight at the new bar. Georgi had asked his older sibling about the heavy facial cicatrices exhibited by the preening Germans. The country's universities often hosted fencing academies, the main point of which seemed to be gathering scars to demonstrate students' courage in battle and impressing the ladies. Pyotr, by then more than a few drinks into the evening, replied loudly that it was a dubious distinction to proudly wear your enemy's superior swordsmanship on your own face. Finally, his brother's sniggers had provoked the *studentkorps* cadet from Jena into demanding satisfaction.

"The FEET!" bellowed Ustikov again. The boy wasn't bad, exactly, but he was overconfident. The armsman was scowling as he critiqued the elder Melishnikov's movement across the carefully uneven floor of the *salle d'armes*. The duel was only until the first touch, but even a duel to first blood didn't mean that your opponent mightn't "accidentally" open an artery. Still, Ustikov was compelled to criticize his student.

"Even steps, the same distance, until you lunge!" he thundered.

Looking to the edge of the dueling space, he observed Georgi standing with his right arm behind his back. Glancing down, Ustikov's eyes narrowed as he spied the unbuckled flap of the younger brother's holster. He couldn't spare more than a glance, however.

Pyotr's opponent feinted with a series of lightning passes, seeking to make the young noble over commit with his longer blade. The German's speed was tremendous, and his weapon seemed to be everywhere, testing Pyotr's wrist.

The *studentkorps* fencer continued to dazzle with quick slashes toward the face. Even as Pavel yelled "He repeats!" Pyotr beat his opponent's blade, disengaged on the low line and lunged quickly, scoring a clear touch to the German's side. Though he struck without drawing blood, the poke was unmistakable to all, and Pyotr began to withdraw, relaxing. Ustikov saw the referee begin to raise his scarf to signal the end of the duel.

Quick as thought the German closed again and made a creditable attempt to run Pyotr through. In his haste, the older Melishnikov threw himself backwards, tripping over his own feet and falling, his sabre out of position. Pavel swept his own blade out and took the first step too late, too late.

The German drew his *schlager* back for a lethal thrust and a gunshot cracked, arresting the action.

Pyotr ignominiously scooted back on his hindparts and spared a glance for his younger brother, who was now aiming his revolver quite precisely and obviously at the German's face, whose sword arm was still cocked.

"You wouldn't dare!" said the academy referee, scowling fiercely at the young pistoleer.

"The duel was over. My brother clearly won, even if he wrongly assumed that your man would honor the point. My role as his second is to intervene if someone breaks the rules of the duel—as was clearly about to happen."

Sounding much older than his pink and unlined face suggested, Georgi had thumb-cocked his Smith & Wesson No. 3 in order to permit an accurate single-action shot. Ustikov knew it was a hair-trigger weapon. After watching the boy fiddle with it for weeks, he'd shown him how to carefully polish the sear so that a slight pressure would release the hammer, improving the accuracy of the heavy revolver.

The frozen tableau continued for a moment, the German panting and his supporters poised on the cusp of action. Georgi's eyes glittered in the gaslights.

Ustikov sheathed his sword and bellowed laughter. In rough German he called to the group. A little distraction was needed.

"Come, honor is satisfied! There are women, there is wine, there is my younger master with his finger on the trigger of a fine Russian pistol just hoping that he finally gets to shoot someone with it! I am too eager to keep drinking your fine beer, and how you say, schnapps! I will buy the drinks with honest Russian gold!"

At least their father had seen the wisdom in bank-rolling his armsman with an eye to buying instead of cutting their way out of trouble. Free alcohol provided the excuse needed for the Germans to hustle forward and pull their man back, patting him on the back and congratulating him on his superior form. Everyone could clearly see that he would have won had it gone on, right?

Georgi decocked and lowered his pistol, his eyes cold. "Get up. You look stupid sprawled on your ass."

Pyotr might be eldest, but his younger sib was ever the serious one. He scrambled to his feet, glaring as Georgi holstered his weapon.

"I had it in hand, I was about to show you!"

He received a snort in reply.

Pavel gathered up a few of the German's support-ers and swept most of the crowd toward the bar, yelling for the bartender. Looking over his shoulder at Georgi, he met the young noble's eyes and jerked his own toward the door.

Once they had safely exited, Ustikov could sigh, and reflect on how well he had predicted exactly this danger when he had argued, politely mind you, with "the-count-their-father."

"Ustikov—it will be no problem. They will accom-pany Minister Lamsdorf and observe how the negotia-tions are conducted. They will get to see something of the world. You will temper their enthusiasm and provide them the wisdom of your counsel."

"Lord, it isn't my counsel that I will need to use if they take the bit in their teeth!" The First Arms-man to the House of Melishnikov had enjoyed his time teaching the lads to ride, fence and shoot. He had "worked" with these two throughout their young lives, and even come to love them as his own. That didn't mean that he relished the prospect of serving as "eyes behind" and general babysitter to two active, intelligent and independent young noblemen seeking their first adventure in a foreign country.

The count waved his hand in dismissal.

"It is decided. They have learned when to heed your counsel, and when to be Romanovs. Long have you borne your family's blade in my service. I have no fear that you will suddenly fail."

Count Melishnikov didn't have to look; his armsman wore the sword everywhere. If Ustikov was storied in his fearlessness, his sword, handed down from father to son for as long as they had served his own family's line, was legend. The Cossack version of a sabre, or shashka, it mounted an unnaturally long hilt, and the pattern of watered steel shone differently than the regulation weapons that most carried.

"I know that you can keep my sons safe with your weapon's keen edge. And if needed, you can keep them in hand with the flat."

Ustikov winced. He took his duties as the martial instructor to the boys very seriously. The elder, Pyotr, had ever been entranced with the romance of the sword and the thrill of a cavalry chase. Even as a tyke, if he saw a strong charger for sale, he would grab Ustikov to "show him something!" Generally, that one listened, perhaps too well, to the armsman's stories of tradition, battle and honor. His younger brother was more interested in the technic arts. This cannon, or that rifle cartridge, or some new artisan's contraption held his imagination far more than the traditional ways.

He recalled exactly his promise to the count. "On my honor, Lord, I shall do as you command."

Several rounds of German beer later, Ustikov carefully navigated the hotel's front stairs. Through the door opened by the bellhop he saw the brothers gesticulating in conversation with a Russian officer—an embassy staff courier by the mud on his trousers and boots.

Not good.

Spying their armsman, the brothers pivoted.

"Pavel—the damned Japanese have attacked!" shouted Pyotr.

Ustikov instantly sobered.

"Where, when?"

The staff officer clicked his heels. Though technically not an officer, the armsman of an Imperial House warranted respect from any mere lieutenant. Or perhaps the young courier knew of Ustikov's reputation.

"Port Arthur, two days ago now. The fleet was attacked but repulsed the Japanese. General the Count Melishnikov has sent instructions. His sons are to entrain with the horse artillery as soon as they reach Moscow and report to General Kuropatin's staff at Chita. You will accompany them and keep the count informed of your progress by telegraph."

"Chita is nearly two months away!" lamented the older brother. "We will never get there before the *yaposhki* are beaten!"

"Artillery!" enthused Georgi.

Watching after two demi-noble brothers in Germany wasn't enough. A war was needed, apparently.

"Well, shit," was all Ustikov had to offer. The curse didn't seem to warm him very much.

April 1904
II Corps Rail Assembly Area
Chita, Russia

Cold. Really cold. Southern Siberia in late winter. The trip had taken longer than expected. Between the incompetence of the *kanonir* who struggled to load their batteries onto the train in St. Petersburg and the effects of the weather on the new rail line east of Irkutsk, they were arriving ten weeks after their departure from Germany.

The brothers, stiff in their newly minted rank, clomped to a halt in front of their uncle's desk and saluted in unison.

"Lieutenant Pyotr Melishnikov, reporting to the general with a party of two!"

Their uncle received their salute with gravity, and then rose from behind his desk with a wide grin under his beard.

"Boys, you made it! And in time to help me teach those little yellow fuckers what it means to attack the Empire of all the Russias! And you brought Ustikov— how are you, old horse soldier? Still finding the worst in everything?"

Ustikov stomped and saluted in best parade-ground style.

"Your High Excellency."

"Please, so formal! Alexi, some vodka for our newest additions."

As the aide poured, Pyotr interjected.

"Thank you for the promotion, Uncle Mikhail, we will make you and father proud!"

"What do you think Georgi?" the general directed at his other nephew.

"Uncle, I think that your regular artillery had better be in a condition higher than the pieces that we brought. The horse batteries are disorganized, their training inadequate and their carriages and caissons in poor condition."

Lieutenant General the Count Mikhail Zasulich laughed aloud, and quickly smothered it in his fist.

"I sometimes wonder if you two are truly related to each other. Hmm. What say you, Ustikov?"

"Lord, the b— the lieutenant may have a point. I am no master of hardware, but the artillery officers seemed to spend more time at the bottle than keeping their troops in hand. The entire group was a gaggle of handless cows when it came to getting their pieces on the train."

Zasulich tapped his desk.

"Alexi, take a note. You three, come take a look." He gestured toward a large map.

"The Japanese landed at Inchon about the same time as their surprise attack on Port Arthur. That did more damage than you will have read—our battleships are trapped by sea mines now. The Japanese army will move north and threaten Port Arthur and Vladivostok directly. Kuropatin insists that we need six months to build our forces. However, I will need to delay them while we assemble and exercise the corps—the damned train and the weather is slowing everything.

"To do that, I need information on where they are, which means more telegraph lines and more likely, gallopers between the armies. I am appointing you both to the staff, to be my eyes, and carry messages of the highest priority. You will report to me both on what you see and what you hear."

"Uncle, surely our troops are more than a match for the Japanese? What can stand before our charging Cossacks and the Czar's troops?" asked Pyotr.

"Boy, I like your style. I do. The reality is that this is a different sort of war now. We need the infantry to get more time with the new *avtomat*, the Maxims. We need to exercise the great guns and get better coordination between the cavalry and the main army. We can't just walk up to the Jap and start beating on him, as you might think we did in the old days when I rode with Ustikov, here."

"Sir, the Japanese still have officers who took archers to war against the Chinese four years ago!" protested the newly made officer.

"Boy, listen!"

The general was no longer smiling.

"The Japanese are damned good soldiers, some of them. They carved up the Koreans that made the mistake of opposing them. They likewise crushed the Qing during the Boxer Rebellion, and yes, they did bring some archers—but only because the damned things were faster and quieter for night work than the Berdanka rifles which we carried then, and still have for most of the corps!"

"Sir, what of the Mosins? Why are troops still using the single shot Berdan?"

"Well, Lieutenant, we are at the end of a very long supply line after all. But, with the arrival of newest batteries, we can move what we have accumulated here and head south. Captain"—the general gestured again to his aide—"show the lieutenants to the gallopers' tent and introduce them. Ustikov, stay a moment."

After the others filed out, the general hitched one leg up on his desk and perched.

"Oh, I said relax, Pavel. When did you start being so regulation?"

"If the general will permit, I am still trying to adjust to the crawly feeling on my spine that this is going to be a *pizdetz* of the first order. Worse than the feeling I had when you and I crossed the Danube and the Turks had double our numbers."

"As bad as that, Pavel?"

"Sir, since my last visit to the colorful frontier, I have seen exactly this camp and the train, but as the lads pointed out, our troops are mostly equipped the same as they were when we rode against the fez-heads. And no one failed to notice that you trust your own staff so much that you want to use family to double-check the reports."

Zasulich frowned, but poured more vodka.

The outwardly stolid armsman paused before speaking again. The general, no matter what familiarity he invited, still held the ear of the man who wielded plenipotentiary power east of the Urals. He was not a man to irritate lightly.

"Your pardon sir, but when I was seconded to help defend the legation in Tianjin, the Japanese had regular troops inside as well. Not many, but they were well led. Their spirit was as strong as any Cossack, and their officers worked hard to learn all they could from the English, the French and us. When the Manchu came over the wall in the hundreds, the Japanese repulsed them using rifles, bayonets, swords and as you pointed out, arrows. The Japanese couldn't conceive of defeat."

The general listened carefully.

"And some call you a simple troll with the heart of a Cossack and the sword of a demon. When did Melishnikov send you to the staff officers school? Some of my advisers can't sum up our opponents as neatly."

Zasulich stood up and turned around to look at the map again.

"It isn't complicated. We have to get as much as we can into place on the Yalu and prevent the Japanese from moving their artillery within range of the port. Come full spring, we are joined by Kuropatin and push them all the way back down Korea, and into the sea."

He glanced up at Ustikov.

"What do you think of that?"

Ustikov considered his words carefully.

"Excellency, it isn't our equipment, our superior numbers or even the supply lines. Our army is made up of much more than just the Cossacks that you led into that cursed Turkish fortress. The regulars are uneasy—you will have heard of the unrest back at home. The Japanese are made of fighting spirit—their officers call it Bushido—and those two boys that I brought can't wait to get into the fight. And in the middle of this, Count Melishnikov expects me to return his heirs to him hale."

"Drink," ordered the general. "We will keep the boys out of overmuch danger, but they are men now, in the Czar's service—my nephews will take their chances like any other galloper. And I do need their eyes, damn it. I may need you to help me stiffen the spine of a few of my officers, much as you helped me in Vilin," he said, naming the Ottoman fortress they had stormed together. "Fuck their Bushido. I have you, my troll! You keep your family's *Kladenets* handy," he said, referencing a legendary magic sword. "We have need of the old ways."

May 1904
Yalu River, Korea
Forward elements of the Japanese Third Army

"These new guns are a pain in my ass."

"What was that, sir?"

Major Tanaka Heihachiro looked over at the platoon leader and shook his head. He had been muttering more to himself than for any audience.

The Russians, inexplicably, had let the forward elements of the Japanese army infiltrate all the way through the town of Wiju completely unopposed. Unmolested, they had advanced their forces north into the hills which guarded the Manchurian border. Then they attacked.

The enemy Maxim ahead of 1st Company continued to fire, traversing slowly. The gunner seemed to know his business, tapping out conservative bursts to economize his ammunition and slow heat buildup. The cost to gain the first few hundred meters had been high—they had already lost dozens of men from the lead company.

A tremendous crash just the other side of the dirt rise he was sheltering behind took his breath away and replaced the sounds of battle with a deafening ringing. One of the Russian field guns had dropped a shell perilously close. He turned to address the lieutenant that had asked him the question and stopped.

The young officer was still kneeling next to him. He must have tried to peek over the top at just the wrong moment, because not only was his helmet missing, but most of his head above the eyes. The corpse slumped against Tanaka, splashing him with blood and . . . other things. Refusing to look at the mangled corpse, Tanaka spied the whistle still clenched in the officer's bloody hand. Yanking it free, he looked back around at the next company assaulting toward the first. Already men were falling to the damned machine gun above.

Staying here was suicide. They had to have the shelter of the trenches, or they wouldn't have enough men left to hold them against a counterattack. Victory lay ahead and upwards—and their lives were the emperor's, as duty demanded.

He gathered up the dead lieutenant's men by eye, and drew his sword. In response, they fixed bayonets and with a visible mixture of savagery and fear, awaited his command. Raising the whistle to his lips, Tanaka blew the staccato blast that signaled an all-out attack—all companies to advance at a charge. That done, he drew his pistol with his free hand and plunging over the top screamed, "Attack!"

Pyotr ducked under the whirring sound of shrapnel. *Too close, Georgi, me lad! The idea is to kill the fucking Japanese, not me!* he thought. At least Georgi was safely out of the way. He had drawn duty with the divisional artillery, relaying spotting information if the telegraph lines to that critical support were cut.

The general was using his gallopers to back up the telegraph to the front lines as well. When the

command post lost contact with the 13th Imperial
Guards, likely due to a Japanese shell cutting the
line, Pyotr had been ordered out and he sped to the
defending battalion's command post to deliver the
general's message and await a reply.

In the distance, he saw the Japanese line briefly stutter as one of the two remaining Russian machine guns
killed the troops crossing between lines of barbed wire
and trenches. He heard one, and then many Japanese
whistles start to blow, and all over the facing sector
what appeared to be thousands of Japanese troops rose
screaming and began running toward Russian lines.

He carefully aimed his modern Mosin downhill at
the Japanese. All along the trench, Russian soldiers
took advantage at the lull of inbound fire and began
shooting at the rushing men.

He squeezed the trigger with exquisite care, just as
Pavel had taught him, and the moment of recoil was
a surprise, just as it should be. Only a few hundred
meters away he saw a figure fall. He aimed again.
Miss. Again. Miss. Again. A hit? Another shot and
the rifle ran dry, so he inserted a charger clip into
the breech and rammed the rounds into the rifle.

Resighting, he was shocked at how close the Japanese
appeared now. Firing was continuous, the sounds of
massed rifle fire stabbing at his ears. Even as artillery
burst on the Japanese, he could see the leveled bayonets
driving into the first line of defenders. Looking for a
target, he heard the company commander screaming
at him, inches from his ear.

"Back, get back you fucking git! Take this to division. We need more guns and troops, or we will lose
this line in ten minutes, fifteen at most! Tell them!"

He pulled Pyotr backward and shoved a waxed dispatch folder into his jacket.

"Ride, damn you!"

With another horrified look downhill, Pyotr passed his personal rifle to the commanding officer and bolted for his horse, tied in a trench behind him. The Japanese were consolidating. Again the whistles blew.

This was going to be a close thing.

Tanaka observed his companies conducting the cleanup of the first set of Russian trenches. From his vantage above the western hills over the Yalu, he could see most of the battlefield, including the causeways that his battalion had used to cross the river.

Despite very heavy casualties during the attack, discipline held and the assault had succeeded. His men were moving briskly, despite the strain of the march to date, and the losses which they had suffered for the first time. The new ways of instilling traditional samurai spirit into regular soldiers had been something of an experiment even ten years ago, but the practice had truly ignited a martial spirit even among the lowest of his men.

Tanaka Heihachiro believed in the code of the warrior. Austerity in life, prowess at war, honor and duty to the emperor—this was the soul of the army now. Men were judged not by noble birth, but by their service. Japan should be judged not by where it started, but by what it had become. It deserved a place among the great powers, and if such a place would not be given, then Japan would take it. Tanaka had arrived too late to serve against the Russians during their annexation of Manchuria a decade or so earlier. The occupation blocked Japan's route west, and more importantly, allowed a European power the ability to directly threaten the shipping that was Japan's link to the modern world.

Intolerable.

He examined the Russian position below him more closely and looked back at the approach his troops took. Scores in his command had died, and more would succumb to their wounds. Even though many of the Russian artillery batteries had been reduced early in the battle, the rain of Russian shrapnel caused horrific wounds. He had ordered the dead covered to avoid demoralizing the survivors. The neat lines of tarps outnumbered the number of dead Russians littering the emplacements. Yet his troops had maintained discipline, instantly ceasing their pursuit when commanded. His weapons, both the issue revolver and his personal, more finely balanced katana that he preferred to the mass produced gunto carried by most officers, had remained unused.

"Easier than I thought, Tanaka."

Heihachiro stiffened to attention and saluted as the brigade commander spoke.

"Stand at ease, Major. What is your assessment?"

"Sir, the enemy didn't hold as long as I had expected. Casualties were very heavy, but we have the field. The enemy survivors fled before we committed our reserve. Their spirit is weak."

The colonel grunted. His field staff remained below them, out of earshot.

"Maybe. It is early yet and these look like frontier troops—not the fresh units that we know are coming east. We must move ever faster before the Russians can field a larger force."

"And our navy, sir? What if the Russians sortie?" Tanaka dared the question.

"We are still keeping the Russians bottled up in Ryojun—Port Arthur, as the enemy calls it. If their fleet had any more spirit than their sorry infantry, they could harry our convoys and prevent our resupply. They did catch some transports—we lost an entire battalion, but that's not for other ears. Fresh troops are behind us now, and the whole of the Second Army behind them. We will advance north across the Yalu to begin the conquest of Manchuria. Soon we will retake what was ceded to the Russians by European treaty—and make our own peace."

"The new artillery proved its worth, sir."

This time the senior officer laughed.

"Yes, Krupp sold us good guns, but the guns are not enough. Did you see how the men pushed into the Russian's fire? Their eagerness to press the attack with steel shocked the enemy—and the *Russki* fled in sheer disbelief!"

"As you say, sir. I was too busy at the time to appreciate it, let alone draw my own steel."

The colonel chuckled a bit more. "There will be a time to wield your sword for the emperor. For now, you are done here. We are hiring laborers to finish the cleanup. I am detaching your command for independent duty—take your battalion west, and skirmish to contact. I want to get a feel for how far the Russians will run and where they will reconstitute their front. We must have their ships under our guns by summer."

May 1904
Nanshan, Manchuria

"I expected you to be proud of me, Ustikov! Instead, you hound me like woman, worried about risks!"

"Master Pyotr, you covered yourself in glory, and not a little of your own blood. Taking on necessary risks in order to serve the Czar is a hussar's job, sure enough. You, however, have been actively hunting your own death in a ditch since we lost that battle more than a month past. That may be brave, but it is also fucking stupid."

Pyotr had picked up a promotion, courtesy of a shrapnel wound during the retreat of the Guards from the nightmare at the Yalu. Despite the wound, he had continued to run messages between the surviving commander and the division. He had also helped to rally retreating men, reestablishing something that resembled a formation west of the battle, attracting the attention of a general staff desperate for any good news.

"Stupid is waiting in a trench to be attacked. We should be taking the fight to the enemy—we have numbers and mobility. Haven't you always told me that the cavalry's main weapon is its ability to be where it is unexpected? Instead our lancers are gathered in stinking, wet holes—and every third man is down with the squirts."

The shack to the door flew open.

"Every goddamn Japanese private has a better rifle than the best of our ranks!" Georgi yelled, slamming a rifle onto the tabletop. "Arisaka Type Thirty. Five rounds in the magazine and one more in the barrel, can be rapidly reloaded with a spring clip and accurate past six hundred arshins. And we still don't have enough Mosins for a single battalion, let alone the entire army. And if we did, where would the ammunition come from!?"

Georgi's pithy observations about the management of the divisional artillery during the loss at the border had reached the ears of the nobleman who commanded the guns. Despite the accuracy of Georgi's comments, this resulted in his assignment to the logistics section to speed the flow of men, new equipment and supplies from the west. Even now, only a trickle was reaching the front.

Ustikov looked up from his cold food, his expression mild. The boy was working himself into a fine rage.

"So? Did you expect the Japanese to attack with their oldest equipment?"

"That's not the point, Pavel!"

"I know, lad. Believe me, I know."

"And they are indifferent to casualties! We lost the Yalu despite months of preparation. Mines, pre-sited artillery, wire, three lines of trenches, searchlights . . . we had fucking searchlights for a night battle!"

Ustikov kept his voice low, but his eyes were hard, and replied.

"It is almost as though the finest technological creations that our czar buys for his army have not guaranteed our victory, no?"

Pyotr interjected, "We lost Yalu because we didn't use our forces to attack—we sat on our ass and gave the Japs the initiative!"

"*NO!*" Georgi nearly screamed. "We lost because that pig fucker of an artillery commander expended half his ammunition shooting at fake bridges. Then, before we had to retreat, he caught a case of cold feet and blew the ammo dumps. HE. BLEW. UP. HIS. OWN. AMMUNITION!"

"Both of you shut up and listen." Ustikov stood, his hands on his hips. "Pyotr, you have bravery, but no judgment." He turned to the younger officer. "You know a lot about weapons, Georgi, but you don't know much about men."

The stripling drew himself up, his face red with anger.

"Armsman, I am Lieutenant Melishnikov and not the boy you tried to teach to fence with an archaic blade! And I mastered that to your satisfaction, eventually!"

With a grunt, Ustikov made a long arm over his lunch and grabbed the Japanese rifle.

"I am not too impressed with rank, boy, so save your spittle. All those facts, and yet you missed the most important detail about this weapon." He worked the action to ensure it was empty, and spun it so that the breech first faced Georgi, then Pyotr.

"Do you see this design, the flower stamped into the metal?"

"Of course. The Japanese mark their rifles with a chrysanthemum. Some armory inspector's mark."

"No, young master. Listen carefully. That flower is the special symbol of the Meiji emperor. It is the chop of his house, used to mark personal property. That rifle, in fact every weapon that the Japanese issue to their men, is so marked because it means the emperor has placed his personally owned weapons into the hands of his soldiers. They believe that he trusts them, individually, you see?"

Georgi took the rifle back and looked at the mark.

Ustikov continued. "It doesn't even occur to them to give up, to stop an attack—to fail. They are each holding what amounts to a holy relic that links them to their lord, and they are bound to each other by a code of honor foreign to most of our army—self-sacrifice, discipline and aggression. Their new weapons help, but the power is the men. How many did they lose charging our Maxims, under our artillery barrage, when they took the promontory at Wiju?"

"Hell, I don't know. A lot." Georgi slumped in his seat, deflated.

"A shit ton," offered Pyotr.

"The best estimates are that their lead divisions lost six thousand—about five times what we lost, even during the retreat. And they won. It wasn't a newer, better rifle, it wasn't the larger army—it was the army that believed that they couldn't lose."

Both young officers looked up disbelievingly.

Ustikov continued. "That is what we are up against. Their soldiers believe in their victory even more with each battle that they win. We are trying to stand and fight against an enemy that isn't merely trying to occupy a point on some general's map—we must stand against this foe who wants to eat our army whole."

Pyotr stood, insulted. "Are you saying that we can't win! A defeatist in our house?"

Ustikov stood as well. He was no taller, but his bulk forced Pyotr back half a step.

A scarred, hairy hand drew a foot of shining Damascene steel from the scabbard that he wore.

"No young master. Long has my family borne our *Kladenets*. I don't know how many times we have replaced the scabbard, the leather on the hilt. My own family's sigil is etched here. As long as it is drawn in honor, it can never break. As long as you believe in your victory, you will fight with honor."

He looked at both of the young men, for truly, if they could learn this lesson, their boyhood was done.

"If we can help our army believe that it can win, they will fight with honor. As long as honor lives, our army won't break."

He stared at them both.

"So—Pyotr. You must fight smarter, not harder. And you, Georgi, think about how we can win with Russian soul, not the newest German or French inventions."

Pyotr looked hopeful. "I'm still going to see action, right? I'll show you!"

Ustikov sighed.

Outside, the occasional rifle fire they had been hearing from the trenches failed to mask a distant series of booms that presaged Japanese artillery. All three looked up as a trumpet sounded.

"To arms, lads. Let's see what the little *yaposhki* are up to now."

The attack had been delayed two weeks while larger stocks of shells were accumulated. Tanaka's depleted battalion had been folded into a rump regiment with two other understrength units, and overall command given to Tanaka. This campaign had been hard on the army across all ranks, and experienced officers and sergeants were being moved up, promoted into battlefield vacancies.

Three hundred *cho* ahead, the Russian defenders were lashed by the Japanese artillery. The hills in the distance protected the landward gateway to Port Arthur. Further in, they would also provide the elevation needed to deliver plunging fire into the port itself. Both sides understood what that meant.

This time, the Russians had aggressively pushed back on the patrols which Tanaka had ordered forward to find the best routes through the minefields, wire and machine guns which protected the outer works. Russian sharpshooters were active, limiting how often he peeked forward. However, the last snatched glance showed the central defending earthworks enveloped in dust and dirty gray smoke, being ground into paste by the Japanese guns. At this point, Tanaka had only permitted a third of his guns to fire. Still, the accuracy was all that he could hope for.

He had organized his unit with alacrity and driven the men hard. Training replacements, preplanning artillery fires, weeding out any officers that showed the slightest hint of reluctance—all of it necessary staff work and properly the job of the commander... and yet. His yearning for personal battle remained unfulfilled.

You couldn't argue with the efficiency of modern implements of war, however.

"The artillery is actually getting better at this..." muttered Tanaka.

The new junior officer that he now rated as his aide asked, "What was that, Major?"

Tanaka began to reply, but caught himself even as he heard the sound of a melon being split open with a cleaver. He felt a weight across his legs. A quick glance over confirmed that his former aide must have addressed his superior even as he looked directly over the top of the shelter. The lieutenant's corpse sprawled gracelessly.

Profoundly annoyed, Tanaka continued, "—but maybe I should stop talking to myself."

He waved his hand behind him in a come-hither motion. Another officer scurried up to his side, assiduously staying as low as possible.

"Sir!"

"Message to the artillery: shift fires. And to the assault groups: advance now as planned."

"Sir, the artillery is still..."

Tanaka jerked a handspan of his katana into view. "Was my order not clear?"

"Lieutenant, the damned Japs attacked into their own artillery barrage! They rolled up the first trenchline in twenty minutes, and now their artillery is dropping all over the cavalry staging areas."

The regimental commander's eyes showed white all around the iris. Apparently, he had been in the trenches on an inspection when the first artillery fell, and had hastened back to the command post short by a couple of unlucky staff officers. Ustikov had accompanied Pyotr to the command tent once they heard the enemy artillery, and then they had ridden hard for the central sector where the pressure seemed highest, while Georgi headed to the southern lines.

"I need to know how many are coming at the middle so I can time the commitment of the reserve. Observe the center, assess the condition of the battalions that have withdrawn to the second line, and bring word back."

His job was already more or less what the commander was directing, so Ustikov mentally shrugged.

Some minutes later, they reined in as the battle came into view. The Japanese artillery had paused, and the enemy infantry had stalled against the last trench line and was busily getting chopped up by the Russian Maxims. The Guards reserve infantry had filtered into the rearmost trenches and their fire denied the invaders any additional gain.

Maybe this is going to work out . . . Ustikov thought. He had time to snort at his own optimism.

With a tremendous crash that redoubled, and doubled again, the Japanese artillery, which had been focusing entirely on the center, exploded across the Russian lines again, but exclusively on the right flank. So many shells were exploding that from two versta away the defending trenchline was entirely obscured.

"Pyotr—ride to the command post, tell them to shift everything south. The real push is south! Go!"

Ustikov felt his heart tighten. He had sent the youngest into the lion's mouth.

Georgi pressed his face as hard as he could into the filthy trench floor. The explosions overhead were less than a second apart. Overpressure from each close shell felt like a hot, tight fist around his chest, battering him. Other defenders lay with him, some quite still. He had gone out of his way to regularly visit the forward regiments and build relationships with their commanders, as his man Pavel had suggested. To his surprise, he was learning something. He was beginning to appreciate some of the differences between efficiently managing the technicalities of a battle and leading the men that fought it. There was in fact a "Russian soul" to the army. He wasn't going to learn much more from the friendly major in this regiment. His open but motionless eyes were collecting dust from the nearby explosions.

After what felt like hours, the fire slackened. His stunned ears rang, and it was the shaking of his arm that brought him to his senses. He looked up into a dirty bearded face and saw the man's mouth working, but heard nothing.

Yanked to his feet, he first saw that the Maxim in his trench wasn't manned. A quick look through a gun port showed the Japanese troops in full view, their bayonets glinting outside long rifle shot. He could also see a clear path to the rear—his horse was another hundred yards that way.

But.

He knew these men now. If the gun was up, they could hold the line until supports arrived. He leaped to the machine gun and started firing.

A dusty corporal slid in beside him and straightened the ammunition belt.

"Feed me!" Georgi yelled.

This time he wasn't going to ride away.

Formerly quiet, the Russian machine gun decisively halted his line of troops. The new weapons were shockingly effective, and again Tanaka's lead elements had paid heavily to close with the Russians. The regimental commander had started in the rear, coordinating individual battalion-sized attacks. He was down to the reserves now. Much further behind, he could see the next regiment forming to reinforce him. They *had* to hold their gains long enough to deny the Russians a chance to throw the attack back, and catch the Japanese reinforcements in the open.

Initially suppressed by the intense shelling, the defenders were pulling themselves together. The Maxim fired continuously, pausing briefly every ten seconds as the gunner reloaded. He watched more Japanese fall. Above, a screen of infantry appeared to be shaking itself together, adding their fire to the thickening resistance.

That machine gun would have to go. There was no time for a clever strategy or a courier to the guns in the rear. He felt his heart lift.

Tanaka ordered his two courier officers and his guidon bearer to come with him.

"Follow me now! Do not slow, do not hesitate."

Not waiting for their response, he drew his revolver and sprinted through the tears in the wire. As he jumped down into the trench, he stumbled on a Japanese body and nearly fell. A shot cracked over his head as three Russians ran toward him yelling. His own pistol came up and he emptied it into the press, dropping the first man and wounding another.

The next closed with his rifled clubbed overhead. Discarding his empty sidearm, Tanaka drew his katana and struck using the iaijutsu, or draw strike. The blindingly fast sword cut forward directly out of the scabbard and the shocked private stumbled as his arms, still holding his Berdan, fell to one side. Without pausing, Tanaka screamed and charged the Russians, more now in plain view. He parried a bayonet with the flat of his katana, and then opened his enemy's throat with his backswing. Still another Russian charged him as he did so, stumbling over the dying soldier. His bayonet scored Tanaka's calf, but Tanaka ignored the burning, and reversing his wrists, drove his blade downward at the Russian, who was nearly kneeling at his feet. Blood flew from the massive wound, and the severed head fell off.

Behind him, he heard a warning, "Down!" and he dove to the trench floor as a fusillade of "friendly" fire killed the next Russians to come around the angled trench.

Yells of *"Bomba!"* accompanied a pair of grenades that flew over his head and exploded.

He levered himself painfully to his feet, as more Japanese filled in behind him. Ahead, the machine gun was quiet again.

Despite leaving windrows of their dead behind, the Japanese had gained the trench line.

Georgi's hearing had returned sufficiently that he could hear the crunch of the grenades that his assistant gunner had just thrown. Despite the cooling water jacket, waves of heat rose from his smoking gun. Worse, the ammunition for the Maxim was exhausted.

He risked a look past the firing position, but only a few Japanese were visible.

Shots sounded down the trench and he turned, filling his hands with revolver and sword.

The corporal lifted his single-shot rifle and gut shot the first Japanese to turn the corner in the trench. He fumbled his reload and looked up at Georgi's hoarse yell, but caught the next man's bayonet in his chest. Georgi's revolver barked twice, three times, dropping the enemy even as he jerked his bayonet from the fresh Russian corpse. He heard feet scuffling behind him and finished the ammunition in his pistol as another Japanese threw himself backward out of sight.

Still another Japanese stepped into view, limping as he raised a bloody sword. His pistol holster hung empty above even bloodier trousers.

Georgi moved forward fluidly, stepping evenly across the mud. He stopped outside of lunging distance, blade forward in sixte. The Japanese used British-style insignia—the crown on his collar marked this one as an officer, a major. The major's eyes searched the trench, taking in the empty Maxim, the bodies and finally rested on Georgi's sabre. His posture straightened, and he inclined his head fractionally. The young Russian returned the movement and settled into guard.

The major took his sword in a two-handed grip and slowly raised it above his head, the weapon held nearly parallel to the ground.

The blades flashed.

The cleanup this time had taken longer than the battle at the river. Tanaka's regiment was too exhausted to participate, and Tanaka had withdrawn the survivors to the assembly area, where they stumbled to their meal.

Tanaka knelt in his tent. Bushido was clear. First, the mission. Next, the equipment and his men. Done.

Now he was free to care for his own equipment. The pistol, recovered by one of his men, was simple. Punch the bore, wipe down with oil, reload. He had used his father's katana heavily this day, and despite wiping it on the Russian officer's coat, coagulated blood saturated the silk cord wound about the grip and showed in the seams between the guard and the other fittings. As it served him, he would properly clean and return the sword to perfection, to fighting condition.

He arranged his tools, a small mallet and bone needle, and his parts, including a selection of replacement pegs, or mekugi, for fastening the sword handle to the blade. He allowed himself to relax, even as his hands methodically disassembled the katana. A blend of ritual precision and reverence marked his movements, but his thoughts drifted.

The sword dated far back in his family's history.

The blade originated before the Tokugawa regime and the spirits of his ancestors had surely guided his hand this day. Yet, the old path dating to the time of the shogunate would never have gotten the empire this far. The European methods, the new army organization and the new weapons, were required, but the old ways—strength, honor, the Code—these were still needed.

He felt a warm wash of conviction. His father had passed knowledge and tradition to his son, not merely a sword. The katana reminded him of his father's lessons and he added to that store his own hard-won understanding. The useful old ways were not discarded, but preserved. The useful new ways were not idolized, but evaluated and added to sum of what already was.

As he completed each step, he cleaned and set successive pieces of his weapon to one side. Finally, he tapped the old mekugi out. The handle came free, and he used powder and oil to clean and polish the blade.

The Russians had fine soldiers. The young lieutenant that he had fought today had been skilled. A very fine incision the length of his forearm marked one swing of the Russian's sabre.

Their artillery was hellishly accurate. He frowned

slightly as he worked uchiko powder into the blade. It took time to finally polish a faint shrapnel scar from the metal.

They could be brave. None of his opponents had shown him their backs. The fine stone he used to hone the edge required many strokes to restore an edge dulled by repeated strikes to bone.

But...their conviction as a group was weak. Did they believe in the final victory? Did their officers understand their men? Did each know their duty and place?

No.

His emperor relied on General Kushiro to defeat the Russian empire. The general ordered his regiment to gain a foothold to take the port. The regiment would have failed if Tanaka hadn't personally taken the trench and denied the Russian's their forward guns. It had come down to one man.

He selected a plain, straight-grained mekugi. The bamboo was almost white. He sanded it very slightly, increasing the taper enough to improve its grip on the blade. The entire sword relied on the one bamboo peg that connected the blade to the hilt, and therefore the sword to the man.

The peg slid home under the patient tapping of the mallet, and he carefully sighted down the edge, before completing the reassembly. Once finished, he noted that the light was dimming. His eyes had adjusted as twilight fell. He gripped the hilt and performed a basic *suburi* form. The weapon was satisfactorily tight, the many pieces now a single living thing again.

Gleaming, it shone in the red evening light.

August 1904
The Foot of 203 Meter Hill, Port Arthur

Ustikov watched the new reinforcements moving into camp. Their uniforms were in much better condition than those of the veterans of the campaign. Mostly they were garrison johnnies from the port itself, and a few were scarce infantry whose transports had slipped the early Japanese blockade. He ducked his head back into the tent. In between intermittent Japanese artillery fire, he could hear the rattling breath of the surviving Melishnikov.

Another massive howitzer shell shrieked overhead and burst in an empty field to the rear. The Japanese had brought up huge ship-killing guns. Each shell weighed a third of a ton and made a horrible, distinctive sound. Troops called them "roaring trains," attendant with the macabre jokes about going on a "train trip."

They were under canvas now, at least. The first weeks after the retreat west had been a nightmare. If the Japanese had maintained momentum after Nanshan, they could have advanced nearly unopposed west to the port and north all the way to the railroad that was keeping Russian hopes alive. Ustikov, already suspecting that he had lost one of his charges, had rallied broken units by force of will, and on a few occasions, by threat of force. Pyotr had stayed close, quietly hysterical with grief, but ready to explode at a touch. A captain of engineers who wouldn't halt his retreating column narrowly avoided execution at his hands, saved only by Ustikov's intervention. Shortly thereafter, likely as a result of fatigue, exposure and sorrow, Pyotr had been driven from horseback by typhoid.

Nearly one in three would die from typhoid, and Ustikov forsook his duties to nurse the remaining Melishnikov. As the weather worsened, evacuating Pyotr became inadvisable. The Russian fleet had lost another battle, and with the loss of many of their screening ships, the big battlewagons were confined to harbor, and the blockade tightened.

Unconscious, Pyotr exhaled weakly. So far, Ustikov's care and the young man's natural resilience had staved off the disease when many others lay buried in the mud.

Another shell roared overhead, this time exploding close enough to make the ground shiver. The Japanese had tried an initial all-out assault, but had been thrown back. The defending Russian general experienced a rush of blood to his brain and ordered the river at the foot of the defenders' lines to be dammed, creating a swamp which the Japanese infantry had to cross under fire.

Ustikov didn't really care at this point. He was desperate to get Pyotr fit to travel. He had to return the sole remaining heir to his father, and redeem what remained of his own honor. Though Georgi's body was lost, the story of his ward, a young hero, manning a machine gun and slowing the Japanese attack was carried back to Ustikov by those that fled as the defense crumbled. The entire month had been a series of probing Japanese attacks in company and battalion strength. Slowly, Russian lines were split— one front pushing them back into the port proper, and another chasing survivors as they withdrew to the Russian railhead. The perimeter defending Port

Arthur shrank back, reaching the bottom of the hill where he now sat, less than a mile away.

Before Pyotr was felled by the disease, Ustikov had suggested that they withdraw north. The suggestion had not been well received. The slow but burning rage in Pyotr face's would have frightened a lesser man. New lines crossed Pyotr's face, and his eyes burned in Ustikov's memory.

"Leave? Retreat now? Leave the Japanese with their victory? Are you mad?"

Ustikov had expected resistance, anger even. Pyotr had simply refused every subsequent discussion. Too big to carry, too senior to command and now too experienced for Ustikov to overawe, Pyotr sought revenge for Georgi.

The casualty lists had certainly reached Moscow by now. Georgi had been listed as missing, which in battle conditions, was effectively the same as "dead, but mutilated so badly that we can't tell which body fragments belong to which person." An old soldier like the count would know that, yet create the kinder fictions suitable for the family.

In order to return with any honor at all, he must get Pyotr ready to ride and escape this rat trap.

He looked over at the cot again. His old soldier's eyes already knew a truth that his heart denied. If Pyotr didn't rouse soon and start to eat, he would die.

The Russian defenses in view were the most formidable of the campaign. Tanaka used field glasses to scan the layered series of trenches, gun pits, obstacles and cleared fields of fire. There was no approach possible that wasn't under direct observation. During

the months since Tanaka took the first line of defense
for Port Arthur, the Russians had worked very hard
to get ready for the inevitable attack. They had even
moved some ship's guns ashore, improving the depth
of their gun line.

This was proving to be a very tough oyster to open.

Recuperating, Tanaka's command had provided a
screening function against nonexistent Russian patrols.
Other regiments had attacked the lines defending the
two prominent hills whose crests commanded the entire
field of battle, as well as the harbor. More than two
thousand soldiers had died so far. At one point, the
Russians had sortied a cruiser which pumped shells into
the Japanese positions from nearly point-blank range.

It was only a matter of time before his regiment
was back in the fight.

He nearly thought out loud again, when he heard
scrabbling next to him, obviously his aide trying to get
a better view of the enemy. Keeping his eyes forward,
Tanaka ordered the young man back.

"Keep down, fool! The reason that you have this
job is that the last two decided to offer their heads
for Russian target practice!"

"What was that, Major?" Tanaka heard the division
commander speak at his side.

Jumping down from the observation port Tanaka
saluted his commanding officer.

"Sir!"

Kushiro was apparently in an expansive mood.

"What was that about then, Major? Are your aides
anxious to die for the emperor?"

Tanaka allowed himself to mentally relax for a
moment, but his features remained impassive.

"No sir—but despite my effort to keep these young lieutenants alive long enough to be of meaningful service to the Heaven Born, they insist on offering themselves as targets. I thought that you were my third such officer, about to find his fate and leave me to train the fourth."

Tanaka saw the general smile. He understood officers like himself were a big part of the general's success during the campaign. Tanaka had kept his men moving forward despite frightful casualties. Like all the surviving line officers, he knew that the casualty numbers were so high that a few Japanese units had refused to advance, which news had been omitted from public reports.

General Kushiro looked over. "We have cadre to train the new men. The heavy losses have been mostly made good, and the units with the most replacements are shaping nicely." Tanaka's contacts on the staff had remarked that entire additional regiments were available since the Russian efforts to regain access to the Yellow Sea had failed. Heavy equipment, vast stocks of ammunition and more men were ready for the imminent effort to seize a few more kilometers of the peninsula. At that point, the new Krupp 28 cm howitzers would range the entire Russian anchorage. Once the port was theirs, the Japanese Second Army would march north to help the forces even now trying to push the Russians further out of Manchuria. In short, their logistics was all that they could hope for. The Russian logistics situation was simpler.

They didn't have any.

"I have more news for you, Tanaka. Your performance in this campaign, and the performance of your regiment in the attack on Nanshan, was exemplary in all respects. As a result, I am confirming your permanent appointment to First Regiment. I am adding another battalion of infantry and best of all, you are promoted to lieutenant colonel. Congratulations, Colonel!"

Tanaka was simultaneously enervated and concerned. By now the soldiers who had won at the Yalu and Nanshan knew how to estimate the enemy's strength. While he had mentally prepared himself for another attack, he knew that the men were not anxious to throw themselves against the intimidating defenses lying ahead. The promotion and extra men was a clear sign that his unit would not be sitting to the rear when the next assault was ordered.

And yet, duty.

"General, do we attack soon?"

The general stepped up onto the observation point. Tanaka winced as an enemy bullet made a snapping sound as it passed overhead.

Unconcerned, the general tossed over his shoulder, "Soon enough, Tanaka. And your regiment will have the honor of leading."

Though he had regained consciousness a few days earlier, Pyotr hadn't been able to take any nourishment beyond a little water.

This night, Pyotr had seemed to stop breathing several times. Each time, Ustikov's heart nearly stopped too. He had dragged the divisional surgeon from his tent after midnight, but the exhausted and overworked man looked at Pyotr and pronounced him beyond the doctor's ability to help.

"There are hundreds like him right now. If truly you care about him, try to get him to take some water, and some broth."

He sat on the bed next to Pyotr, trying to get him to take some thin, warm soup. The young man's lips moved and Ustikov leaned closer to hear a whispered "Sorry. I am sorry, Pavel. Tell father that I am sorry."

Ustikov had heard death-bed confessions before. He knew the tone of a man who, feeling his death near, needed to shrive his soul. The nearly inaudible words were plain and he understood what this meant. He felt his heart tear inside his chest as he at long last began to accept the impending loss of Pyotr.

"Nonsense, lad. You'll tell him yourself when you see him."

"No, Pavel. I can feel it." The words came slowly. "I am paying the price for not protecting him."

"Please, Pyotr, take a little soup. Once you are better, we can ride to your family's home, and we will bring Georgi's things with us. Please, take a little."

Pyotr turned his head.

"Need to rest some more."

"Lad, you must eat, or you will die. You've listened to me all your life, please listen now. Take some soup, please!" Ustikov begged.

The figure on the bed didn't answer, but continued to breathe laboriously.

In the distance, Japanese artillery began to rumble.

September 1904
203 Meter Hill, Port Arthur

The "train" landed only fifty yards away, within the circle of Russian defenders. The damp ground rolled away from the point of impact like water, throwing men from their feet. Shrapnel sledged into the side of the bombproof where Ustikov squatted, waiting for the enemy infantry. His expression didn't alter.

The adjoining hill had fallen. Pyotr was dead. Georgi was dead. Ustikov's heart was an empty hole in his chest. The port defenses were being destroyed, and Port Arthur would fall.

His given duty was lost, unrecoverable.

After Pyotr had died, Ustikov had thrown himself into his duties as a galloper for the general commanding the final resistance. As the lines continued to shrink inward, pressed by the attackers, he carried fewer messages and fought more often. The Japanese infantry had gained the edge of the summit four times in six days. Each time, Ustikov had led a charge into the teeth of the attack. His heedless advances, the fearsome toll collected by his long sword and his absolute lack of any serious wound had made him the soul of the defense.

It seemed to his fellow defenders that Ustikov wasn't courting death with his action, he was slapping Death across the face and demanding to be heard. Magically, shells that fell at his feet failed to detonate, and bullets passed closely enough to turn his garments ragged.

The ground shook again. Next to him in the shelter was a small group of orphaned hussars who had adopted him as their leader. Men instinctively seek strong leaders, and absent a cavalry officer, the famed armsman of the House of Melishnikov wasn't a bad second choice. A nervous man shifted his weight and shot a glance at Ustikov from under his busby. The hussars were in awe of his record and a little scared of him, so this one didn't stare overlong.

If any victory was possible, it would surely be because of this demon of a Cossack, whirling the shashka with such power that he parted arms and legs from trunks, and souls from their bodies.

Yet another shell landed, closer.

More glances at Ustikov.

Impassive, he stared at the door, waiting for the whistles.

Tanaka blew his whistle, and the next company surged forward to gain a few more yards of muddy, bloody trench.

His regiment had gained the hill on the morning of each of the last two days. The defenders fought like demons. Their casualties had to be high, but the Japanese, crossing open spaces in full view of scores of machine guns and several hundreds of rifles, fell in numbers so high that attacks didn't fall back.

They simply ceased to exist.

The 1st Regiment was little more than a thousand men now. One of three assaulting 203 Meter Hill, it had established a lodgement on the side of the prominence. The trajectory of Russian guns wasn't steep enough to drop on the reverse side of the hill that they defended, without risking hits within the Russian lines.

The company of Japanese infantry crashed into the enemy line. Rifle fire and machine guns harvested more of the attackers, but they actually filled the trench at several points and began to spread laterally, as they had on previous semisuccessful advances. One soldier horsed around a Maxim, and turned it on the defenders.

With a firm beachhead established, Tanaka waited for the company commander to push a little more, making room behind them for another company. Sending more men right away would leave them milling in the open space, exposed to machine guns from points slightly higher in the defenses.

They needed just a bit more space.

The shells had stopped falling, and the Japanese infantry was coming again. The short squad that sheltered with Ustikov waited for his instructions, even as he cocked his head, judging where the volume of fire was heaviest.

There were several places, so he picked the closest and waved his cohort along with him. The hussars all bore the more modern Mosin rifle, as well as sidearms. With these, they could maintain very heavy fire for a short time. Once the ammunition was expended, or if there wasn't time to reload, the fight would revert to the old ways.

Entering the trench, they immediately joined the confused fight. Defenders and attackers were intermingled, preventing the little band of reinforcements from simply shooting indiscriminately. They carefully emptied their rifles at the Japanese, who, belatedly recognizing the threat, returned the favor. In moments, the cacophony of fire subsided. All of the Japanese were down in this section, but the original defenders were mostly dead or severely wounded.

Ustikov bellowed, "Reload!" They charged down the trench line toward the next section.

The burly armsman pushed through the narrow aperture and emerged in a gun pit full of more struggling men. He slipped a bayonet thrust and shot that Japanese twice. His men flooded into the space, squeezing combatants so closely together that rifles couldn't easily be brought to bear. Dropping his Mosin, Ustikov unholstered his Broomhandle Mauser, a battlefield pickup from a dead Japanese officer in an earlier attack. The German weapon held ten rounds and was quicker to reload than the standard Russian revolvers.

He felt a searing burn on his side. Looking down, he saw that another Japanese bayonet had scored his ribs, but the wielder was unable to pull his rifle back for a second thrust. Ustikov shoved the Mauser against the man's chest, and pulled the trigger several times. The Mauser had a decent round, but he didn't trust pistols and he wanted to ensure that the man stayed down.

Again, the battle seemed to pause suddenly. Ustikov breathed heavily, almost choking on the thick propellant residue that was confined inside the large trench. Men lay scattered so thickly in the gun pit that he had to watch the ground as he strode. Most bodies were still, but a few figures groaned. He saw a Japanese sergeant lift his head and shot him twice in the back. They couldn't afford to leave any live ones behind them.

"Reload!" he ordered, again.

Stuffing the Mauser with cartridges, Ustikov heard a new sound—a Maxim, but firing over the encampment. He immediately realized that some enterprising Jap was using a Russian gun against its owners. He gathered the last hussars and once more stormed to the sound of guns.

Kneeling below the military crest fronting the assembly point of his second company, the new colonel watched his leading assault company filter into the adjoining trenches and called for the commander of 2nd Company. He could hear the now-friendly Maxim still firing, but couldn't make out any of the critical details of the action. Tanaka knew that duty and therefore his place was ahead. He couldn't lead what he couldn't see. He also couldn't keep his head up indefinitely.

That's long enough, he thought.

Ducking his head, Tanaka remarked aloud, "Our place is forward. We will plant the regimental colors on that position."

His aide started suddenly, but Tanaka's iron grip prevented the young officer from raising his body even an inch just as a burst of fire swept the lip of their trench. Tanaka smiled.

"Sooner or later you will learn *not* to stick your head up. It is practically a prerequisite for promotion, you know."

The lieutenant shouted, "Sir!"

Without time for more professional development, Tanaka turned to the newly arrived, panting captain who led 2nd Company.

"I will reinforce First Company. You are to take your remaining force and assault the section of trench immediately on the right flank. I will direct Third by messenger to reinforce you, if necessary."

Tanaka overrode the automatic objections to the concept of risking himself and dismissed the captain. The objections might have been a *trifle* pro forma. He hadn't even had to show steel to get the company commander to accept his order.

Tanaka turned to his aide. "Have this platoon follow me, and you will follow with the color bearer, *behind* them. Is that clear?"

"Sir, please allow me to come with you!"

"Enough! To your place!"

The lieutenant slunk back as Tanaka, the platoon commander and twenty men ran forward the hundred yards or so, nearly reaching the place where 1st Company had disappeared into the now-silent trench.

Why is the trench quiet? Did the Maxim we captured run out of ammunition?

Tanaka's unspoken question was answered in a moment as the gun's fire shredded his group. Next to him the platoon's officer simply fell headlong, his face torn away.

Tanaka felt bullets pluck at his cap and trouser legs as he dove in the dirt. His right calf throbbed.

Always with the legs! Can I at least make it to the fight with both legs, ever?

The Russians had regained the trench. If the new Russian gunner was allowed to keep his position, the assault would falter, again. His duty was to take the hill. The cost wasn't material. Their lives belonged to the emperor.

He could claim that storming a trench was a lieutenant's job, or a captain's job—and he would be right. He could claim, with some justification, that his regiment needed him to stay alive, to direct the attack. He could even just hold still a moment and let the gun move on.

Every army and navy cadet was required to memorize and recite on command the Imperial Rescript. The five precepts contained therein were engraved in the brain of every officer, indeed, on every soldier and sailor at any rank. Loyalty, Respect, Valor, Faithfulness and Simplicity. These precepts bound each man to the emperor. Loyalty was the essential duty, and the text of the rescript was clear. "Duty is heavier than mountains. Death is lighter than a feather."

The code was clear. Duty was meant to be heavy.

Tanaka felt the weight bearing down and gripped the hilt of his father's sword, finding strength.

He yelled. "Grenades, now!"

Then he charged the gun, pistol drawn.

The Maxim had changed hands yet again.

Ustikov's heart had finally lightened. The situation was so impossible, so unlikely to be survivable, that he could finally let go of his worry, doubt and guilt. He exulted as he traversed the machine gun across the file of advancing Japanese. Ustikov watched them fall, or dive to cover, then became aware that he was screaming the entire time.

The sharp fight for the gun position had left the Russians with only three men.

One hussar was poised next to the armsman, the next belt of ammunition flaked out neatly, the brass feed tab held ready to be guided into the action. The other was in defilade behind him, binding a deep cut on his arm.

Several enemy rose to charge his position and he finished his belt, hitting most of them.

Small objects flew into his trench.

"Grenades!" came the call, too late. One exploded close enough to kill or wound his assistant.

The gun was askew and his vision was a little blurry, but he was otherwise fine. Three Japanese leaped into fighting position as he stumbled to his feet. One was shot by the wounded hussar and the other finished him in turn.

Ustikov drew his Mauser again, and head-shot the

second man, a private, before pivoting to shoot the other who wielded a pistol and one of the funny looking Jap swords.

He squeezed the trigger but nothing happened. The slide was locked back on the empty gun, and he looked down the impotent sights at a bloodied Japanese officer who looked as surprised as Ustikov felt. The Japanese raised his own pistol and squeezed the trigger as Ustikov felt his guts tighten, waiting for the impact of the bullet.

Effectively deaf, Ustikov watched the hammer on the Jap's gun snap forward.

Nothing.

His was empty too.

In a detached corner of his mind, Ustikov wondered if he could actually hold this bit of trench long enough for...what?

With a ringing of steel, Ustikov drew his shashka and dropped the useless Mauser. The Japanese, looking hard and fit, discarded his pistol as well, and took his sword in a two-handed grip. With a shout, Ustikov closed the distance and lunged, and as the Japanese sword flashed in a parry, he began a remise with passes to his opponent's face, neck and shoulders.

Quick flickers of the chisel-tipped Japanese sword deflected his strikes left, right and left again and then it licked out, scoring a bright red line on Ustikov's wrist. Still, the Japanese seemed to have problems, clearly favoring his right leg.

The big Russian paused, and gauged the dimensions of the planked trench. He looked into his opponent's dark eyes a moment. There was no magic or message there, save determination, or perhaps desperation to match the feelings in his own breast.

He lunged again and again, but the Japanese swordsman expertly parried his attacks, using the flat of his blade, protecting the fighting edge. In turn the Japanese risked an overhand chop at Ustikov's leading leg. He didn't seem to have full use of his right leg, and his lunging attack was a bit short, but he still managed a cut across the middle of the Russian's thigh.

Great, thought Ustikov, *Thirty thousand Japs to fight, and I get the fencing master.*

He cautiously tested his leg without moving his eyes from his opponent. It began to burn like fire, but he seemed to have full strength, still. Panting, he attacked.

He needed to end this soon, and playing dirty, he began to force the officer to back to his right, punishing the leg injury. All he needed was a slip, an opening, and he could open this one's throat. He pushed, paused and pushed some more. His target stepped on a body and for just a moment, the Japanese overbalanced.

In that moment, Ustikov put everything that he had left into attacking his target. Without sure footing, the timing of the parries let some of the strikes through. Within two seconds, Ustikov scored cuts on the Japanese, bloodying his shoulder, his temple and ribs. The Japanese fell to a knee, holding his sword up, one-handed in a useless defense.

This will end it, thought Ustikov, and with a yell he brought a two-handed strike down, straight through the Jap's sword.

Kladenets struck right at the little round guard that protected the hilt, splitting it.

And shattered.

The shashka broke at the point of impact and Ustikov, shocked, overbalanced and stumbled a little past his intended victim. Staring at the jagged stump of his sword for a moment, he whirled back to finish the officer, turning just in time to catch the Japanese's thrust directly into his heart, slamming him back against the trench wall.

He felt the fire and ice of the wound, and his hands stopped obeying, dropping his ruined weapon. Somehow, he was still upright.

Pavel Ustikov took in the dead, the smoke and the filth. He could see his broken *Kladenets,* so far below him, and above it, an oddly shaped sword hilt projecting from his chest.

He had broken his vow, and never redeemed his honor. Vision dimmed.

He looked up and saw the Japanese officer staring at him, a sheet of blood covering most of his face.

Then Pyotr appeared, obscuring the Japanese.

"Pavel, there you are! Let me show you something!"

His katana pinned the big Russian to the wooden trench wall. Tanaka slumped to the muddy floor of the trench, and watched the light leave the dying man's eyes. At the very end, the Russian smiled, gently.

A beautiful death. Tanaka would honor that.

He took the Russian's broken sabre and tried to regain his feet, using the sword as a prop, but slipped in the blood and muck and decided to stay down for a moment.

Because he wanted to. Nothing to do with blood loss.

His thoughts came slowly, single file.

His vision blurred from the blood running from his scalp wound. The Russian had been faster than Tanaka could believe. *If the sabre hadn't shattered...*

Looking at the katana still impaling the corpse, he

could see that the tsuba was split, and the blade notched. *Have to see to that. Needs fixing.*

He glanced at the sabre in his hand. The pattern of watered steel was evident. The Russian sword was made using the same techniques as his own.

It had been an honorable fight, where two men—not distant cannon or machine guns—decided the victor. In such a fight, he could almost feel a kinship with his opponent.

Slowly, he became aware of the battle still being fought around him. He didn't have much time before one side or the other interfered with his reverie. He would retain the broken sabre to remember this fight, and this man. Maybe use some of the broken blade to mend his own.

Rifle fire and artillery obscured the hammering of feet on the duckboards until they were quite close. Rough hands hauled him upright, and he winced.

Allies then.

"Sir, are you alright?"

"*Bakayaro*! Do I look alright, fool?"

The cluster of men fell back respectfully, and Tanaka swayed a little, still clutching the ruined sabre.

"Fetch my katana."

As a sergeant turned to tug the sword free Tanaka added, "Gently! My brother died with honor."

Incredulous, the soldiers exchanged glances.

But they did as he said.

For meritorious conduct during wartime the Emperor bestows the Eighth Class Order of the White Paulownia Leaves and the sum of 250 yen...

—⚉—

That battle had hurt her. Her tang hadn't broken, but it was bent and cracked, and her blade edge damaged near it. But what a battle! It had been a most worthy duel between her and a foreign sword, their bearers both men of honor and courage.

She sensed that metal again, as the smith heated them both and forged it into her body and tang. Its accent was strange, but it, too, knew of past battles of greatness, and she welcomed its presence.

It was not so long before she was again called to serve, this time even further from home.

—⚉—

He Who Lives Wins

Sergeant First Class (Ret.) John F. Holmes

It was either the sand on the beach getting into everything, your gear, your clothes, your hair; or the bugs and the heat in the jungle, dried sweat and insect bites gnawing at you. Either way, you were always itching and scratching, till you dug raw bloody sores in your skin and your uniform was ragged. The only times you forgot about the constant misery was when the Japs opened up on you. Sometimes the whistling *BANG* of a near miss shell from a destroyer that had come down the Slot, red-hot shrapnel mixed with chunks of coral; other times the zipping pieces of copper-jacketed lead that came to a stop lodged deep in your buddies' flesh. Or your own.

Today was the latter, first time under fire for the Americans. There was a Nambu Type 92 Heavy Machine Gun bunkered somewhere ahead, pointed down the trail at them, spitting rounds at a furious rate. All thought of misery and discomfort were forgotten, except for one, the one you never seemed to forget. Water, always water. Killing was an exhausting, dry business. Powder residue caked into the lines on the faces of nineteen-year-old soldiers, making them look like someone from the old folks' home back in your hometown in West Virginia, or the tenement you all shared in Chicago. Some of the GIs had taken to drinking rainwater collected in old shell holes, and most of them had ripped the crotch out of their fatigues to let the dysentery run free. They had only been there three weeks, relieving the Marines, the 132nd Infantry Regiment thousands of miles from the plains of Illinois and the slums of the Windy City.

"FLAMETHROWERS UP!" came the call from the front of the column, and a grimy, sweaty man picked himself up from where he had been leaning with the heavy tanks against a tree. It was one they had borrowed from the Marines, and Private Tony Montero was glad it wasn't him carrying that big target on his back.

"So long, sucker!" he called out after the man, who shot him a dirty look. Montero took another swig of gin from his canteen. Not enough to get drunk, but enough to take the edge off his fear. Montero was scared, scared right down to his bones, like all the rest of them, and he covered it with a straight-up obnoxious streak. He caught his squad leader, Sergeant Anderson, looking at him and grinned.

"Montero, are you going to be an asshole your whole life?" asked Anderson. The NCO had told the Italian to his face that he was a "Goddamned selfish son of a bitch who would get other good men killed."

"Just till we get off this shitty island, Grandpa," answered Montero. Anderson scowled at him, and turned away waiting for the call everyone knew would come.

Sure enough, word soon passed down the line of resting, nervous men. The repeated call, "ANDERSON!"

"You, smartass," Anderson said, pointing to Montero and another man, his BAR gunner, Private Nilsen, "and you. Come with me." Nilsen, a big Norwegian kid from a farm in Wisconsin, said nothing, merely picked up his gear. Montero started to protest, then shut his trap when Anderson glared at him. The three of them started out, with Montero trying to hide his body behind Nilsen's huge form.

"Jævla fitte," muttered the platoon's newest commander, Sergeant First Class Johansson, at the head of the trail. The regiment was committed to this attack, and this platoon was on the sharp edge. The unit had started the day with thirty-seven effectives, and was now down to maybe thirty. He looked down the trail and a few dozen pale, sweaty, fearful faces stared back at him. Most were hunched down, even though the rounds were zipping high overhead due to the draw they were in.

In front of him lay the body of their battalion commander, Lieutenant Colonel Wright. Johansson looked down at the poncho-covered form of the officer, and Johansson saw in his mind again the bullets exiting from the man's back; the man who had been like God to his troops for the last year. Beside him, under another poncho, lay their platoon leader, Johansson's cousin Karl, who had been, up until a few minutes ago, showing the battalion commander suspected Japanese positions. A burst of machine gun fire from a hidden bunker had cut down both officers.

Between the bodies, their company commander

sat, helmet off, staring blindly into space. He was completely shell-shocked.

"Dammit, Karl!" the NCO cursed under his breath. What the hell was he going to say to his aunt and uncle back in Wisconsin? He tried hard to put it out of his mind and concentrate on the problem at hand, unconsciously slapping at a mosquito that was sucking on his neck.

"ANDERSON UP!" he yelled at the top of his lungs. The firing had stopped, but his ears were ringing from the sounds. Johansson looked down at his captain, sitting there, disgusted with the man's cowardice, angry that all the decisions now lay with him.

That's why I have the rockers, he thought. After a minute, three soldiers detached themselves from the crowd and hustled forward, hitting the dirt next to him. He looked them over, considering his plan. Going up the trail was suicide against that gun, but if they flanked either to right or left, the jungle would be wide open. Someone needed to watch that flank. It seemed that Anderson had already anticipated this, bringing his BAR gunner.

Looking at his watch, Johansson said, "Sergeant Anderson, I'm going take the platoon on an attack down the right side of the trail in ten minutes."

The rest of the guys called him Grandpa Anderson, since he was in his forties, and a veteran of the Great War. The grizzled NCO chewed steadily on a cigar, blowing the smoke at the mosquitoes that surrounded them, and looking impassively at the younger man, saying nothing. Up until a month ago, Anderson had been the platoon sergeant, but he had punched out another NCO from a sister platoon in a drunken brawl.

Johansson had given him his stripes back yesterday, because he desperately needed the steady presence the older man exuded.

"I want you to take these two out on the right flank and provide some security. Once you hear the firing stop, you can come back in."

Anderson grunted, and spoke in a raspy, smoke burned voice. "I'm going to want your BAR and a lot of ammo. Some extra grenades too. Getting dark in a few hours; kinda late to start an attack, Sven."

Johansson shook his head, even though he knew the older man was right. "I want that machine-gun nest." Unspoken was the silent voice of his cousin. A pool of blood had grown under the body, and a trail of ants were already finding their way under the poncho. He kicked at them idly. In the jungle, nothing was wasted.

"Okay, your call." Anderson drew deeply on the cigar and exhaled, turning to the two younger men. "You heard him. Go back along the line and get as many magazines for that Browning as you can. Six grenades each." Neither one moved, realization dawning on them that they were going to be out in the hostile jungle, separated from their friends and the comfort of numbers.

"Well? What in the Sam Hill are you waiting for? An invitation from the goddamned nips? MOVE YOUR ASSES!" He said this all without even taking the cigar out of his mouth.

"Wait a minute," said Montero. "You want us to go out there?" He waved a hand at the overwhelming green jungle. "I ain't so sure that I'm okay with that."

Anderson took the cigar out of his mouth and barked, "Nobody ASKED you, Private Montero. Now get your ass moving and go get some more grenades and ammo. Got it?"

Montero and Nilsen retreated back down the line, Montero looking back once. Anderson kept his glare on him and he hurried along.

"Thanks, Johnny. I'm glad I can count on you," said Johansson.

"Yeah, well, don't you be getting some other boys killed just for revenge. It always tastes like crap in your mouth, kid."

"Gotta do it regardless. The captain wants this approach cleared. He's losing it now that the colonel is dead. Thinks it's his fault somehow. Don't forget the sign and countersign when you come back in." Anderson said nothing, merely held out his hand. Johansson took it and they gripped each other hard. Behind them, their company commander still sat between the two bodies, frozen. His first brush with combat, and he had been standing between two men who were shot dead. The captain had not moved or said a word throughout their whole conversation.

Privates Montero and Nilsen were waiting about fifty yards down the trail, where there was a small break in the undergrowth. Nilsen, a fair-haired, tall young kid who was one of the original National Guardsmen of the 132nd, had the Browning automatic rifle resting on one shoulder, a musette bag with extra magazines slung over the other. Beside him stood Montero, a short, dark Chicagoan who had been assigned to the regiment to bring it up to strength. Hanging off his shoulder was a 1903 Springfield, the bolt-action rifle that had been standard issue for the Army before the war.

"Where the fuck, Private Montero," growled Anderson, "is your goddamned *Garand*?" He had paid little attention to the Italian in the proceeding day, concentrating on the more useful members of his squad, and only noticed now that Montero was carrying the thirty-year-old bolt-action rifle.

"I traded it with a Marine for a quart of gin, Grandpa," he answered, with a grin, cigarette hanging lazily off his lip.

"You gave someone your rifle for some gin?" exclaimed Nilsen, drawing back in amazement. He had grown up on a farm in Wisconsin, and still thumbed through his Lutheran Bible every chance he got. To him, they were on a God given mission to rid the world of evil. All Montero thought of it was a way out of the Italian ghetto of Little Sicily in Chicago.

"I needed a drink. You can't imagine what I would trade for a woman! I ain't been with a woman for way too long. Hell, I'd even trade *you* for one of them native girls with a bone through her nose!"

"Quit messing with the kid," barked Anderson. "Go swap that peashooter for a Garand, NOW!"

"Okay, geez. I'm movin', Grandpa." He returned in a minute carrying the semiautomatic rifle, tucking eight-round ammo clips into his pockets. The three set out into the jungle, quickly leaving the relatively bright trail to move into the gloomy, green hell.

"Hey, Grandpa, you ever see any shit like this before?" asked Montero, looking up at the gigantic trees that towered over them. Once away from the undergrowth that rose on either side of the cleared trail, they actually had an easy time of it. The ground was covered in small, fernlike scrub, while overhead birds chattered in a layer of foliage about ten feet up.

"Yeah, Philippines. I went into the jungle a time or two, hunting spic monkeys like you, Montero."

"Hey, Pops, I'm not a spic. I'm Italian." Anderson ignored him, looking for a good place for a defensive position.

"Did you really trade your rifle for alcohol?" said Nilsen, who seemed horrified, and fascinated, by some of the decadent Chicagoan's stories.

"I told you, farm boy. I needed a drink. Which, if you stay in the infantry for a lot longer, you will find out, takes precedence sometimes over equipment."

Anderson stopped them and said, "Montero, quit messing with the kid. You probably *did* trade it for some gin, but I know you ain't drunk now. Just your usual slacker self. And if we get in the shit, don't even *think* about running away. I know you're all about yourself."

Montero started to halfheartedly protest, but Anderson cut him short, and they continued on into the jungle. They had come to a spot where the trail rose up and dipped down to a small stream, and Anderson held up his hand for them to stop. Both of the privates fell silent. Nilsen set the BAR down, first folding out the bipod on the barrel.

"Okay," said Anderson. "Montero, start digging. Nilsen, you make sure that BAR is clean."

"Where are you going?" asked the young farmer, a look of worry on his face.

"Up ahead to see what's around that bend in the trail. Don't worry, I'll be back in a few minutes. Then we wait here until the shit hits the fan."

He left them sitting there, with Montero reluctantly unstrapping the entrenching tool where it hung from the back of his pack and Nilsen furiously breaking down the heavy automatic rifle. In the jungle humidity, some of the steel parts seemed to rust even before you put the weapon back together. Still, thought Anderson, it was good to have the firepower, and he knew the teenager was a good, steady soldier. Montero, on the other hand...

He walked slowly up the trail, the heavy Thompson slung across his chest, raised slightly. To be honest, he just wanted to get away from everyone for a bit. He had been in the Army for more than twenty years, as a scared sixteen-year-old fighting hand to hand with Germans in Belleau Wood with the 3rd Infantry Division, later spending years in China on garrison duty. He had been thinking of retiring, finally getting out, when they had pulled out of Tientsin, but Mi May hadn't wanted to go with him to a strange land, and had taken their kids with her back to her village. Then this shit with the Japs had put him back in the whirlwind of mobilization and training, followed by shipping for this godforsaken place. He just needed a few minutes, some peace and quiet to think about his kids, lost to him now. The submachine gun in his hands was heavy, heavier than he would have found it even five years ago.

"Yep, Johnny, time to hang it up and leave this to younger men," he muttered to himself, sitting down on a dead branch, just out of eyesight of Nilsen and Montero as they bickered. Ahead of him, the jungle waited, quiet and oppressive.

❖   ❖   ❖

Two hundred yards away, behind a small ridgeline, Corporal Yamada Katsuro watched a bug crawl up the tree in front of him. He took a bayonet from its sheath and speared the insect through its shell, pinning it to the bark. After it stopped moving, he carefully cracked it open and sucked out the insides.

"I wish," said Lieutenant Shizuka, "you would not do such things in front of the men."

Yamada glanced around at the twenty ragged figures who were hunting for food, digging at roots or catching their own insects. They were all that remained of the second company of the 2nd Battalion, 124th Infantry, Imperial Japanese Army, after weeks of combat and, even more deadly, disease and starvation. They had been assigned to patrol down the flank of what the Americans called Mount Austen on captured maps, which were better than their own, and their progress had been painfully slow. Now they were taking a break, ignoring the sounds of machine gun fire that come from over the far ridge. One man had been sent forward to scout the area, and Yamada was taking the time to try and fill his growling stomach. He grunted and hacked at another insect, turning his back on Shizuka.

The young officer had only been on the island for a few weeks, and had yet to show the effects of the starvation rations the men had been subsisting on. He himself had barely escaped drowning when his transport ship had been struck by American airplanes. He'd clung to a raft of supplies as the sharks feasted on his men. So far, nothing had been as they had told him back home. For example, this *gocho,* this corporal, had ignored him at every turn, making only token efforts to respect his authority. True, the man had fought from China to Singapore, and had been on this hellish island for months now. Last week, he had been commended for leading a night raid behind the American lines at Henderson Field, destroying one of their planes. Still, he was *Kasō kaikyū*, of the lower class, while Shizuka was descended from a long line of samurai. Shizuka fingered the hilt of the sword at his waist, thinking of how he would like to show this commoner his place. Once, he knew, his family had been high in the councils of the emperor, but now the sword was the only thing his father had been able to pass down to him.

"You know, if you played with your dick more than you played with the hilt of that sword, Lieutenant, you would probably be much happier," said the corporal.

Shizuka rose, starting to pull the sword from its scabbard as the men around him laughed. His face turned red with anger as he shouted at the enlisted man. "Corporal, you WILL treat me with respect! I AM AN OFFICER OF THE IMPERIAL ARMY AND YOUR EMPEROR'S REPRESENTATIVE!"

Yamada stiffened, dropped, and bowed deeply to the lieutenant, but said nothing. He was no doubt experienced, and such talk likely helped keep the men in line, but Shizuka had to maintain discipline and proper deference to his class. Shizuka mentally composed how he would demand a proper apology, and opened his mouth.

The tension was broken by the high-pitched crack of a rifle shot, followed by the stuttering burst of an American tommy gun, a sound the veteran knew all too well.

✧   ✧   ✧

The bullet, fired from high in a tree, entered Sergeant Anderson's chest in a downward angle, just below his collar bone, puncturing his right lung and exiting out his lower back, shattering a rib as it did so. He felt no pain at first, just a hammer blow that knocked him down off the fallen tree he was sitting on. Adrenaline pumping through his body, the old soldier jumped back up, fired off a full magazine in the general direction of where the shot had come from, turned, took two steps and fell flat on his face, sprawling headlong. He rolled over, feeling the life drain out of the large hole in his back, soaking his blouse. The pain started, then quickly dulled as his vision faded. Overhead, the sun was a glitter of individual spots seen through the jungle canopy, and he tried to reach for it, before his arm fell lifeless in the dirt. Anderson had fallen just in view of his two soldiers, and his last sight was of the two of them staring, dumbfounded. Then the world blinked out.

"HOLY SHIT!" yelled Montero, who had only begun to scratch the ground in front of him with the shovel. "WHAT THE HELL!" he yelled again as he dove for cover behind a fallen log. To his amazement, he heard Nilsen pull back the bolt and then fire off a full twenty-round magazine in short, disciplined bursts in the general direction of the enemy. Montero yanked hard on his pants leg.

"Jesus Christ, kid, we gotta get the fuck outta here!" the smaller man hissed.

"What do you mean? The sarge is out there! I'll provide some covering fire, go get him!"

"Are you out of your farm-boy MIND? That sniper zapped him, and he's just waiting for one of us to go get

him. We gotta get out of here!" The Italian was white with
fear. This was the first time that either had been under
fire, having been at the rear of the column when the
colonel was hit and killed. Now, their NCO lay just visible
to them, the red blood showing black on his fatigues.

"Go, damn you. All those shit-talking stories you tell,
Montero. I always knew you were full of crap!" Nilsen
inserted another magazine into the BAR and slowly
lifted his head, scanning the area in front of them for
any sign of the enemy. The older man looked at him for
the briefest second, then started running back the way
they had come. There was a huge difference between
getting in a rumble with some other wops or Irish in
the city and facing high powered rifles and machine
guns in the jungle.

Behind Montero, the BAR started firing again,
intermittent muzzle flashes lighting up the trees around
him as he ran. Return fire echoed back, sharp cracks
of Japanese Type 99 rifles. Spent bullets ricocheted
overhead, and he heard Nilsen give a yell, followed
by the flat *BANG* of a grenade. Ahead of him, a sustained, muted roar sounded as the platoon made their
own attack. Montero stopped in his tracks, slipping
on the mud of the jungle floor, and fell. He lay there
for a moment, staring up at the green jungle canopy,
then got up and turned back the way he had come.

Lieutenant Shizuka ducked as a round zipped high
over his head, then was ashamed of himself. Corporal
Yamada stood rock solid, a look of disgust on his face.
Shizuka ignored him and stood straighter, grasping the
hilt of his sword tightly.

Their scout had climbed a tree, and fired on the lone

American, then scrambled back to report as rounds tore limbs from trees and scattered bark. He had bowed low and reported, not to the officer, but to Corporal Yamada. Even as he bowed and spoke, the firing stopped.

"You damned fool!" shouted the NCO, and he struck the scout across the shoulders with a piece of bamboo. "Where there is one, there is always more!" He proceeded to kick the prostrate soldier, landing several more blows across his back with the cane, then turned back to Shizuka.

"What are your orders, sir?" the NCO asked, without even the hint of respect in his voice.

"Why, we advance forward, as we intended!" exclaimed Shizuka. Then he paused for a second. Inexperienced in combat he might be, but the officer was also a very intelligent man. "What . . . would you do, Corporal Yamada?"

The smallest of smiles played on the veteran's lips, and the officer felt a bit of gratitude to the enlisted man. "I suggest, sir, that we find out what is in front of us before we rush headlong to our glorious deaths. YOU!" he barked at the still crouching scout. "GO!"

The private jumped to his feet, turned and rushed back up the trail. Yamada motioned for three others to follow him, and the men ran forward with him. He slapped idly at a mosquito, then placed a hand on Lieutenant Shizuka's arm as he started forward. "Wait," he said.

The shooting erupted again, this time accompanied by return fire from his own troops. "An outpost, nothing more. One automatic weapon, an automatic rifle from the sound of it. There were many of them at Singapore. You can tell by the sound, and the pauses as the gunner changes magazines."

There was the report of another grenade, then the firing stopped, and two of the men returned, dragging a third, who had a growing blood stain on the leg of his tattered uniform. They dropped him on the ground and attempted to bandage him. The fourth man also appeared, the original scout. He again threw himself on the ground, but this time Corporal Yamada pointedly stepped aside. The man looked up, and quickly turned to face the officer.

"SIR! There seems to be only a small outpost, perhaps a listening post." Behind him, the wounded man started to scream, and Shizuka blanched, then tried to cover it. *This* was a problem that he had learned of in school. They may not have taught him to win the respect of his men, but they *had* taught him the simple aspects of fire and maneuver.

"Then, we advance. Corporal, take five men and provide covering fire. The rest will move to one side and flank. Once the listening post is destroyed, we will continue on to the main trail and see what we can see."

Yamada efficiently directed the men to form in a skirmish line, and they moved forward into the jungle. Shizuka watched them go, then motioned for the rest of the men to follow him. He felt a cold nausea in his stomach, and tried to put it aside, thinking of his ancestors who had faced battle for the first time. He gripped the hilt of the sword even more tightly. Perhaps, like them, he would even get to use it. The feeling of nausea was replaced by a growing excitement. He would finally get to lead men into battle like his samurai ancestors!

✧   ✧   ✧

Montero slid back into position next to Nilsen, who said nothing, merely glanced at him and then looked forward again, resuming placing BAR magazines and grenades in front of him.

"You're going to get me killed, you stupid yokel," panted Montero. He was shaking inside, and his stomach felt like ice. Every part of him screamed to run back to the safety of the platoon, back to the trail. He didn't even know why he had come back.

The other side of the clearing erupted in rifle fire, the bullets aimed in their general direction. Several struck the log in front of them, and Montero crouched lower. Nilsen hammered back with the BAR, the heavy rounds tearing into the trees where the firing was coming from.

"Goddammit, shoot!" yelled the big Norwegian. Montero, stung into action, raised the Garand and fired off a whole clip. He didn't even hear the distinctive *ping* of the empty rifle, just kept pulling the trigger. Then he realized it was empty and slid back down behind the log as Nilsen reloaded. He fumbled with a clip, pushing another eight rounds down into the well and letting the bolt ride forward. It caught on his thumb and smashed it. Montero cursed and put the injured tip in his mouth, spitting out the blood and mud that was on it.

Bringing the BAR back up into its bipod and starting to pull the trigger, Nilsen suddenly grunted and fell back against the tree, clutching his shoulder. Blood began to flow freely from beneath his hand. He stared at it quizzically, then hissed with pain. "Ow, this shit burns, Montero. Patch me up!" The ex-farm-boy's teenaged face suddenly seemed a hundred years older.

"Sure thing," answered Montero in a quavering voice, trying to steady his own shaking hands, and pried Nilsen's fingers away from the wound, then ripped away his sleeve. A small hole was leaking blood at a furious rate. Montero, trying to remember his first-aid training, ripped open a sulfa packet, poured the contents on the wound, and then placed a large bandage over it. Nilsen said nothing, though the Italian thought it must hurt like hell. Over their heads sporadic rifle fire still cracked.

"Think we should pull back?" asked Nilsen. Getting hit had seemed to bring the reality of their situation to him. Bits of leaves and twigs rained down on them, and both flinched as a round stripped bark off the fallen log just over their heads.

"What are you, some kinda chicken, farm boy?" was the reply, but Montero grinned, a terrible rictus that did nothing to hide his fear. He was shaking like a leaf.

"No," the teenager answered, trying to cover his own fear, "I mean we should move our position. They know where we are."

Montero peeked over the top of the log, to where Sergeant Anderson's body was stretched out on the ground. In front of him lay the Thompson submachine gun. That was far better than the Garand for this type of fighting, but it was out in the open. Only thirty feet way, but it might as well have been a mile.

"Screw it," he said, and to Nilsen's amazement, and his own, he jumped over the tree and sprinted for Anderson's body. The rifle fire fell silent as he ran and grabbed the Thompson. For a split second, he saw the dead white face staring up at the sky, and he stopped. Right out in the open. Then he reached down and slung the sergeant's body over his shoulders, heaving

him up onto his shoulders, and started to stagger back
to the tree.

"NO! You fool," shouted Yamada. The Japanese soldiers had stopped shooting, watching in amazement as
the American ran out and stopped by the body of his
comrade. One lifted his rifle to fire, and Yamada slapped
it away. He watched in admiration as the man, obviously
outweighed by his companion's corpse, struggled to
heave it onto his back. The American staggered, then
turned to head back. Another of Yamada's men raised
his rifle to his shoulder, but his fear of his superior kept
him from firing.

The corporal had been a soldier for many years, and
had first seen combat in Manchuria, against Chinese
bandits and Nationalist Army soldiers. They were scum,
not fit to live, but he had learned, over the years of
brutal combat, to respect courage in any enemy. This
American was showing it "in spades," as they said in
American movies.

His admiration and thoughts were interrupted by the
Browning opening fire again, bullets slamming into the
jungle just to their right, and walking toward them in
short, three round bursts. They returned fire, but one
of his men, Private Hashimoto, was flung to the jungle
floor, the back of his head exploding and showering his
comrades with blood and bits of brain. The corporal's own
blood began to boil, and he took careful aim at the American, still struggling to reach safety, honor and courage
be damned. He fired, but the bullet only slammed into
the corpse. Even as he worked the bolt to load another
round, his target disappeared behind the fallen tree.

✧   ✧   ✧

Montero dumped Anderson's body on the ground and collapsed himself, laughing hysterically. Nilsen, having emptied another magazine, again fell down behind the log and started to reload.

"You know, that was pretty stupid. Three minutes ago you run away, and now you go get the sarge's body, for what? He's dead!"

"For this, farm boy." He unslung the Thompson, then started pulling thirty-round box magazines of .45 cartridges out of Anderson's ammo pouches. Stopping for a second, he muttered a quick Hail Mary and closed the corpses' eyes.

"Do you even know how to use that?" asked Nilsen, amazed by his companion's turnabout.

"About the same as you, only familiarization in basic," said Montero, looking in the chamber to see a fat, shiny copper-jacketed slug sitting at the top of the magazine well. "But it can't be that hard."

"So why did you come back?" His question seemed halfhearted, though. The loss of blood, combined with the shock of the wound, was probably making the world recede a little bit.

"For the life of me, I have no idea," answered Montero.

"Why aren't you running away now?"

Montero's answer was drowned out by the crack of rifles less than fifty feet *behind* them, the bullets thudding into the dirt, the tree, Anderson's corpse. One sent the grenades flying, and another round split the dirt beneath Nilsen's feet. He turned and fired off an entire magazine of the BAR, and beside him, Montero did the same with the Thompson. Both had acted more out of surprise and instinct, rather than any kind of training, but their quick reaction caught the attackers off guard, causing them to drop for cover from the sustained burst.

Nilsen pointed left and they crawled away from the log, further into the jungle. Neither stopped until they had reached the base of a veritable giant of a tree, and crawled around it to get something between them and pursuit. Montero started feeling himself all over, amazed that the bullets, fired at almost point-blank range, had missed him.

"HEY! HEY YOU STUPID NIPS! YOU MISSED ME!" he yelled out from behind the tree, a note of hysteria in his voice. He rolled back around and then noticed his pants. There was a bullet hole through the fabric, just below his crotch. His pants were also soaked, and for a horrified second, he thought that he had been shot. Then the smell wafted up to him, and he realized he had pissed himself.

"Farm boy, if you tell *anyone* back at the platoon I pissed myself, I'm gonna kill you." Nilsen just shook his head.

A sense of gloom started to descend over the jungle. Lieutenant Shizuka crouched behind another tree, close enough to hear the Americans yell at him. Behind him, the six remaining men huddled, dispirited. One clutched his leg where a bullet had torn through his calf, but stoically said nothing.

The Americans' quick reaction had come as a surprise to him. The flanking movement had been perfect, and Shizuka had his men *stand* to deliver a volley, drawing his sword and yelling *"Ute!"*—or Shoot!—at the top of his lungs, while slashing dramatically downward.

Maybe his shouting the command had warned them; in any case, standing to deliver the volley had been a mistake; one he felt sure Corporal Yamada would not have made. His face burned with shame, and he looked at his men.

They first looked back with the impassivity of the Japanese peasant. All of them had been on Guadalcanal for long enough to know that they were not making it out alive, and had given in to their fate. The second look they gave him though, was one of fear and contempt. Two of their comrades lay dead on the jungle floor, hidden by the undergrowth. Another was somewhere between them and the Americans, pitifully screaming for his mother. After a few moments of this, one of the soldiers took a grenade and pitched it out into the brush. The explosion silenced the wounded man.

Shizuka looked down at the sword in his hands, the heavy katana-length blade shining dully in the gloom. He thought of his grandfather, who had carried the sword in battle against the Russians at Port Arthur, and his grandfather's father, who had fought to restore the emperor, serving under the great Saigo Takamori. The sword had been used by his grandfather's father when Takamori had defeated the rebel forces, killing a hundred of the shogun's men. So much history, and he knew that, although the hilts had been replaced more than once, the blade was far older than that.

Still, here it sat in his hand, unbloodied, and his men lay dead on the ground in front of him. His shame threatened to overwhelm him. Shizuka knew he must do something, but what? He could make his way back to where Corporal Yamada waited with the rest of his men, and overwhelm the Americans with a banzai charge. Somehow, though, he felt that the practical Yamada would recommend against it. The man seemed bitter and did not seem to care about their mission all that much. Also, returning would bring dishonor to his family, something he could not face. No, better to go forward, and attempt to flank the Americans again. He motioned to Superior Private Kuroki to come forward. The man reluctantly ducked and walked over to him, trying to keep his head down.

"Kuroki, take two men and fire toward where we saw the Americans go. I will take the others and we will go to the right. Between our fires, and that of Corporal Yamada, we shall have them in a box."

The man, older with a scraggly mustache, just looked at him. The death of his fellow soldiers had crushed any faith he had in the young officer, but finally he nodded, the habit of obedience beaten into him by the harsh discipline of the Imperial Army. He crept back and motioned for three men to go with the lieutenant, and sent the wounded man to tell Corporal Yamada. Together they started off, Shizuka leading the way this time, sword unsheathed. Behind them, a desultory fire had started, random shots cutting through the underbrush.

Montero looked over at Nilsen. The big teenager was paler than normal, and he could barely lift his left arm. They were both coming down from the shock of their close brush with death, and Montero felt gross as the urine cooled on his pants. *If only the guys back in Chicago could see me now,* he thought. He had joined the Army to get out of rough tenement life in the Italian section of the Windy City, and here he was, bullets and grenades flying around him. He had hoped to get a job as a mechanic or something, but somehow wound up as a filler in the 132nd as it prepared for war. The Italian laughed at the thought. *Momma Montero's baby boy, finally getting out of the bad city to wind up in the bad jungle.* Why the hell he had come back to fight alongside this big dumb Norwegian farm boy, he would never know. It was as if his body had ignored the scream in his brain to run away.

"Okay, Erik, what do we do now?" he said, using Nilsen's name for the first time. They had been in separate fire teams, only grabbed by Anderson at the last minute, and had never worked together before. Still, couldn't hurt.

"Well, uh, I don't feel so good." Montero glanced at Nilsen's bandage and was shocked to see it soaked through with blood.

"Damn, you look like crap, too. Hang on, let me tie that bandage a little tighter." He handed Nilsen some water, and the man gulped it down thirstily. "As for what we should do, well, maybe we can head back to the platoon."

As if to answer him, the muttering roar of small-arms fire rose from the east, and they heard the *crump* of mortars going off. "On second thought, it sounds like they have their own problems."

"We gotta stay here. At least until dark," said Nilsen, somewhat revived by the water. "Not too much longer now. Two hours maybe."

More firing broke out in front of them, scattered rifle shots that zipped by, the closest hitting some trees a few yards away. Both soldiers hunched together, back to back, facing out from either side of the tree. Nilsen took a grenade, the only one he had managed to save from their old position, and stuck his finger through the ring, pulling hard. The spoon popped off and he counted one, two, and threw the grenade as hard as he could, high up in the trees. It detonated with a BANG after disappearing into the lower canopy, and they were rewarded with a chorus of yells and a shriek, causing the firing to stop.

"Damn good throw! You looked like the Babe throwing a pitch over home plate!" said Montero, but his companion seemed to have sunk back into a stupor. It was time, thought Montero, to get the hell out of Dodge. "Come on, buddy, we gotta get you back to the docs." He grabbed at Nilsen's harness, pulling him. The man responded instinctively, getting to his own two feet, and picking up the heavy BAR.

They made their way cautiously through the brush, paralleling the small-game trail they had used on the way in. Montero was in the lead, glancing worriedly at a compass he held in his left hand, his right hand tightly around the pistol grip of the Thompson. He knew that due east would take them back to the main trail, somehow, and they had to avoid the Japs. Nilsen followed, one hand on Montero's shoulder, almost leaning on him as they walked.

Ahead, a stand of bamboo blocked their path, and Montero pushed his way through it. The stiff stalks clacked together, and Montero stumbled, tripping over a fallen branch. A flashing glint of silver, and something slashed over his head, burying itself halfway into a stalk of bamboo, and all hell broke loose.

It was a sword. A Jap officer pulled hard at the blade, scrabbling desperately for the Nambu pistol at his belt with the other hand. Nilsen fired the BAR directly into the chest of the next Japanese soldier who had been using the bamboo stand as cover to creep up on them. The man's rifle fired reflexively into the air as the burst threw him backward. The next man leveled his bayonet tipped rifle, screamed at the top of his lungs, and rushed forward, driving the blade downward into Nilsen's already wounded shoulder. Nilsen screamed with pain, a brutal, animal yell and leapt to his feet, swinging the heavy weapon like a club, crushing the Jap's skull as the wooden stock shattered. The last soldier dropped his rifle, turned, and ran into the gloom.

Montero grabbed the officer around the waist and tried to throw the man to the ground, but the Japanese had better footing and stood firm. Still trying to wrench the sword from the bamboo, he fired once without aiming. The bullet sparked off Montero's helmet, and he clasped his hand to his head, letting go of the man as his ear drum burst. The Jap fired again, and the round struck the Thompson, then plowed into Montero's shirt, ripping through his pectoral muscle. He fell to the ground, clutching his chest.

A fierce look in his eyes, the descendant of samurai wrenched the sword from the bamboo, dropping the pistol and taking the long hilt in a two-handed grip. He raised it for a decapitating blow, but the barrel of the BAR intersected the strike as it came down, sending a ringing tone through the jungle and carving a sliver of steel from the barrel. The impact numbed

Shizuka's hands and the force of his swing drove him to his knees. Nilsen tried to grab for the blade, but he had exhausted his strength and fell to the ground, eyes fluttering closed.

The Italian dove for the sword, and Shizuka tried to get back up as Montero grasped the bare blade in his hands, grunting as the razor-sharp steel cut into his palm. He held on as hard as he could, and kicked Shizuka in the crotch. The Japanese doubled over, but didn't let go, and he pulled the sword from Montero's hand, neatly severing one of the fingers. It fell to the ground, lifeless, but the American didn't seem to feel it. He slammed the butt of the Thompson forward, catching Shizuka in the jaw with a brutal cracking sound. The two fell to the floor of the jungle, wrestling and throwing punches at each other. Finally they wound up with Shizuka on top, his hands wrapped around the other man's neck, squeezing like iron bands. A darkness started to creep into the edges of Montero's vision, and though he scrabbled madly to try and pry the fingers off him, he felt himself growing weaker by the second. He placed one hand on Shizuka's face and tried to gouge out his eyeball, to no effect. *Twenty years of life,* he thought, *that's all I fucking get. I should have married Marie.* His thoughts grew scattered and Shizuka started slamming his head on the jungle floor, screaming with rage. The Jap reached behind him and grabbed at the sword, swinging wildly with one hand, even as he continued to choke the nearly unconscious American. The blade hammered down, making a long cut on Montero's face, and Shizuka stood to deliver a final blow.

The shot caught him under the arm and punched its way through his ribs. Nilsen fired again, the Colt 1911 sending another heavy slug into Shizuka's back, and the sword faltered and tumbled. Montero grabbed the hilt and stabbed upward, driving the sword through the man's body. Nilsen's eyes closed again, and the .45 dropped to the jungle floor. The only look on Shizuka's face was one of puzzlement as he weakly pulled at the sword, then fell over.

Montero woke to the sounds of the jungle. Monkeys yelled at each other overhead, and birds called. His face felt like it was on fire, and he pushed Shizuka's body off him, sitting up. In front of him, Nilsen lay stretched out on the ground, arm still extended, with the Colt nearby He lay without moving, and Montero stumbled over to to the body. A pool of blood had collected under him, soaking the blond hair. Montero fumbled around at his neck, feeling for a pulse, but the corpse was already cooling and still.

He took the .45 and looked at the Thompson, but the bullet had shattered the mechanism. Montero felt for where the pistol bullet had struck him; the blood there had coagulated into a sticky mess, closing the wound. His chest, too, felt like it was on fire, and the heavy pistol felt like a brick in his hand, so he shoved it in his belt. He stumbled over to where the sword lay next to the Japanese lieutenant. He picked up the sword by the hilt, and used it to poke at the Japanese, getting no response.

Montero let out an exhausted sigh, and pulled his canteen out, taking a long drink of gin. He had just drained it when a harsh voice barked in Japanese. He dropped the canteen and turned to face Corporal Yamada and two other soldiers, rifles raised.

"Piss off," he said, and tried to raise the pistol in a shaky hand. Yamada stared at him. Taking in the scene, the Japanese NCO glanced at the bodies lying all around, stopping on the lieutenant, then looked up, past Montero. Through the trees, he heard the harsh yells of an American patrol coming up the trail. He barked an order to his men, and they raised their rifles, taking aim. Yamada held out his hand, and motioned for Montero to give him the sword.

"No way, Tojo. Come take it from me, and you die first." He raised the sword to point it directly at Yamada.

"Hai!" said the corporal, and he stepped forward, drawing his own fighting knife from his belt. The voices were getting closer, and Yamada knew he had little time, but he respected this warrior, and would give him a warrior's death.

The men from the 132nd found the wiry Italian sitting there, his back against a tree, smoking a Camel cigarette, naked steel across his lap. The .45 was still clutched in his hand, slide locked back. In front of him lay the body of a Japanese corporal, arm hacked off and body run through. One of the other Japanese lay on the edge of the clearing, shattered by heavy pistol rounds. The last man was sprawled behind the dead corporal; a slash through his torso had spilled his guts on the ground. He moaned feebly until one of the men shot him through the head.

"Sweet Jesus," said the medic as he looked at Montero's face, the long sword cut still dripping blood, "what happened here, Tony?" The Japanese corporal's knife was buried in his shoulder, and a vicious cut had opened up Montero's forearm. The medic whistled at the damage he had suffered.

"Well," Montero said, wincing at the medic's attentions and looking at Nilsen's body. "I didn't run."

Across his legs lay the reddened steel of the officer's sword. The mix of American and Japanese blood seemed to turn the shiny edge into a wavering flame as the sun set, and Montero grasped the hilt tightly in his hand, not letting go even as the stretcher bearers carried him back down the trail and away from Hell.

The Emperor of Greater Japan, having come to the Imperial throne in an unbroken Imperial line with divine guidance, confers the Order of the Rising Sun Third Class...

The President of the United States takes pleasure in presenting the SILVER STAR MEDAL...

—◆—

Her new home was strange. The warrior was exceptionally brave, though he lacked any graces in manners or form.

He cherished her, but didn't know how to care for her. He scoured her delicate skin with an abrasive cloth, and a heavy, mechanical oil. He used coarse tools to grind out nicks, and turned her whisper sharp edge into something resembling an axe.

Then she went on a shelf above a fire, where she was regularly drenched with smoke. From time to time, she was taken down and passed around to be admired, while the bearer drank heavily. He reminisced honorably about his companions, but there were no battles, nor even practice.

The guests had even less manners, and fingered her blade and edge. From time to time she was rubbed with the same thick oil, as her skin acquired rust and age.

Years passed, until she was handled by a youth.

—◆—

Souvenirs

Rob Reed

01 September 1990 C.E.

Andy Montero was getting ready to head to Saudi Arabia as part of the ongoing Operation Desert Shield when his dad guilted him into visiting. His deployment had been delayed pending his completion of a specialty school and, now that he'd graduated, he only had a few days of "normal" life left before his orders sent him overseas. He was trying to settle all his affairs but his father convinced him to fly in to Chicago to spend some time with him.

His father, Erik Montero, picked him up at the airport. They went out to dinner, got caught up a bit, and then headed back to his dad's house in the traditionally Italian Melrose Park neighborhood. The Craftsman bungalow was the home Andy had grown up in. It was familiar and comfortable, but visiting was never the same since his mom died a decade earlier.

"There's a reason I wanted you to come out now," the senior Montero said as the two men sat at the round kitchen table, beers in hand.

Andy's stomach went cold: "You're dying," he said, fearing the worst.

Erik laughed. "No, not yet, not that I know of at least. Sorry, didn't mean to scare you. Just a minute."

He left the room and returned with a long wooden case. As soon as Andy saw it, he knew what it was: the sword. His grandpa's sword.

Erik set the case on the kitchen table, opened it, and pulled out the curved samurai sword in its lacquered wood scabbard. "You know what this is, right?" he said, holding it out to his son.

"Of course. It's Grandpa's Japanese sword he captured in the Pacific."

Andy took the sword from his father, grasped the silk-wrapped handle and pulled the blade clear. The polished metal shone and sparkled as he rotated it to catch the overhead kitchen light. He could see a wavy discoloration, like a dark smudge, that ran the length of the blade. He wanted to touch it, to see if it would wipe off, but knew better.

"I bet this sword has some stories," he said, pointing out some nicks and gouges on the blade's edge and a chip near the tip.

His dad winced. "I'm sure it has many, but I only know two, and only one that is mine to share with you."

"Your story? You didn't take this to Vietnam, did you?"

"No, your grandpa gave me the sword after I returned from my first tour. My story goes back to when I was a kid."

"A kid? What kind of story would a kid have with a sword?"

"A life-changing one, as it turns out," Erik said. "Let me tell you about it."

Thirty-Three Years Earlier

"Dad, can I take the sword to school for show-and-tell tomorrow?" I asked as we sat in the living room after dinner while Mom did the dishes.

It was October 1957 and I was in Mr. Coleman's sixth-grade class at Fairplain Northwest Elementary school. All the kids would try to bring in their best stuff for every Friday's show-and-tell. Our dads' war souvenirs were near the top of the list and Billy Thompson had been the envy of all the boys last week. I could bring in something better, if Dad would let me borrow it.

"I don't know, Erik, why do you want that?" Dad asked.

"Billy Thompson brought in a Nazi SS dagger last week," I said. "He said his dad got it off a German officer he captured. I think your sword is better."

"Captured German officer, huh?" Dad said. "I know Mr. Thompson. He was a supply sergeant. He more likely traded a bottle of hooch for it than got within a hundred miles of a German officer, dead or alive. He's a braggart and so's his kid. Yeah, you can take the sword in."

He left and returned with a bundle of cloth. He unwrapped it to reveal the curve of the scabbard and the cord-wrapped handle. "Be careful, it's very sharp," he said as he pulled the blade free and rested it on his sleeve.

"Dad, can you tell me how you got it, so I can tell the class?"

He looked at me, looked at the sword, and pushed

the blade back into the scabbard. "No. Maybe when you are older, maybe . . . Just say I was a soldier."

"Did you kill a lot of Japs?"

"Never ask that. Ever. The war was . . . the war. They were killing my buddies and trying to kill me. That's all I'll say."

"Mr. Coleman talked about the kamikazes in school. He said one almost hit his ship. How could they deliberately crash like that knowing they would die?"

"The Japanese pilots thought hitting one of our ships was worth dying for."

"But, why didn't they jump out right before they hit?"

"They could have, I suppose, but then they might miss the ship. They were committed to doing their duty as they saw it and if that meant dying for the emperor, then they died for the emperor."

"But it was stupid. They had to know they were going to lose. They couldn't beat us, so why die when they were going to lose anyway?"

Dad sighed. "I don't expect you to understand. The Japanese wouldn't give up, no matter what. We thought we'd have to kill them all, every one of them, to end the war."

"Mr. Coleman said we could have blockaded them and starved them out. He said their navy was gone by the end of the war and they couldn't have done anything about it and would have given up eventually. He said we didn't have to drop the atomic bomb."

"He says that, does he? Well, he was in the Navy, but he never saw them face-to-face. The Japs never quit. I hated them for that, but respected them for it too. They were just too stubborn. To get someone to quit you have to break their spirit. You have to show that your will is stronger than their will. The only thing that could do it was the bomb. They realized they couldn't fight the bomb and our willingness to use it. Sometimes it takes using overwhelming force and doing whatever is necessary to win before someone will admit they're beat. That's what happened with the Japanese when we dropped the bomb. Maybe you'll understand when you're older."

He handed me the sword. "Be careful with this, Erik, it's not a toy. Take care of it."

The next day the sword was the hit of show-and-tell. Even Mr. Coleman was impressed. I thought Billy Thompson was jealous of the attention and that made it even better.

At the end of the day as we were leaving school Billy came up to me. "That sword is cool. I've got something else neat too, but I couldn't bring it to class. Let's go to the woods and I'll show you."

Billy and I weren't exactly friends but we weren't enemies either. He was the biggest kid in class, and it wouldn't hurt to be on his good side, so I went along.

There were several acres of undeveloped woods nearby where a bunch of us would sometimes play army. We used surplus military shovels and Boy Scout hatchets to dig foxholes and build small bunkers out of tree branches. It was a great place to be out of sight of parents and other adults.

Billy led me through the red and gold autumn woods to an area I hadn't been before. We stopped at a makeshift shack of scavenged bricks, lumber, and plywood. It had three sides, a roof, and an old army blanket for a door.

"This is my headquarters. Wait here," he said as he

ducked into the shack. He came out a few seconds later with one arm behind his back. "Ta-da," he said, like a magic trick, as he brought his arm out to reveal a dark green object nestled in his fist. I instantly recognized the distinctive shape of a "pineapple" hand grenade, complete with pull-ring on the pin and safety handle, from the movies.

"No way. That's not real," I said.

"Is too," Billy replied. "I found it in the garage with some other army stuff my dad brought home from the war."

"It has to be a dummy," I said.

He held it out to me. "If you think it's a dummy, take it, pull the pin and throw it, I dare you."

"No way!"

"Watch this," he said, as he held the handle down with his fingers and carefully straightened the ends of the pin, put his finger through the ring, and pulled the ring and pin from the grenade. "As long as I hold the handle down, it's safe," he said.

I froze in place, too stunned to move. He held it that way for a few seconds and then just as carefully replaced the pin back into the small hole in the fuse housing and bent the loose ends down.

"Now you do it," he said, handing it to me. I took it and grabbed the handle without thinking as he reached out and took the sword from my other hand. I was not going to pull that pin.

"No way!" I repeated.

"Chicken."

"That's just nuts," I said. Billy smiled.

I tried to hand him the grenade but he wouldn't take it back so I kept a death grip on it as he played with the sword. He did a fast draw and dropped the scabbard on the ground, swung the sword around in the air with both hands, and then started chopping the smaller tree branches and saplings with it.

"Hey," I yelled, but he didn't stop until he finally thrust it into directly into a tree trunk. I thought it would stick but when he let go it drooped down until it pulled free under its own weight and hit the ground.

Billy picked up the sword. "I'll trade you the grenade for the sword," he said.

"No, give it back."

"Make me," he said, holding the sword away from me.

I reached for it, but he pushed me away with his other hand, dismissively. He dropped the sword behind him and stood there waiting. I dropped the grenade and charged him. He took my charge, shoved me away again, and punched me in the stomach, hard. I went down again. He outweighed me by thirty pounds and was stronger as well. He watched as I gagged and tried to catch my breath.

"Thanks for the sword," he said, picking the sword and the scabbard off the leaf-covered ground. He shoved the sword into the scabbard and walked away, leaving me alone.

As I recovered one thought kept running through my mind. What was I going to tell Dad?

By the time I got home I was crying. I didn't know what to do. I called to Mom that I was home and then went to my room before she saw me. As I waited for Dad to get home I wondered what I was going to say. How could I have lost his sword? How would I get it back? I thought until I realized the answer: I didn't have to get it back. Dad would.

He'd just have to go to Mr. Thompson, explain what happened, and ask for the sword back. I'd have to avoid Billy, but I could do that.

I had it all worked out in my mind when I heard Dad's car pull up. I waited until he'd greeted Mom and she returned to the kitchen to finish getting dinner ready. I went downstairs to face him, feeling like I'd throw up.

"Hey, how was show-and-tell?" he asked when he saw me.

I didn't know what to say so I just blurted it out. "I lost the sword. Billy Thompson took it from me. I tried to get it back but he's bigger and I couldn't. I'm sorry."

"What?" he said, trying to follow as the words tumbled out of me.

"Billy Thompson took the sword from me. I tried to fight him but he won. I can't get it back. You have to go to Mr. Thompson and get it back. I'm sorry, I'm so sorry."

Dad told me to slow down, so I explained it for the third time, slower, and he understood what had happened, mostly. I left out the part about the grenade because it seemed like I shouldn't say anything about that for some reason.

"So, will you talk to Mr. Thompson and get the sword back?" I finally asked him.

"I could, but I won't. Erik, when I gave you the sword it became your responsibility. You get it back, or you don't, but it's up to you. I trusted you with it and I'm very disappointed."

I broke out crying again and tried to convince him, but Dad would have none of it. Mom came over to see why I was so upset and Dad explained what happened. She asked him to intervene but Dad just repeated that it was my responsibility. "I'm not going to fight the kid's battles for him," he said. He then sent me to bed early without dinner as they started to argue. In my room I could still hear them through the walls, but couldn't tell what they were saying. It sounded like Dad had the last word though.

I was in bed awake for hours. I kept thinking about how I lost the sword and let Dad down. I wanted, no needed, to get it back, but how? Billy Thompson was bigger and stronger than me. I could try to go to Mr. Thompson myself, but would he even believe me? Or would he just side with his son anyway? I could tell Mr. Coleman, but that didn't seem to be the right answer either. Dad said it was my responsibility, so I needed to do this myself. But how?

As I drifted in and out of sleep my mind turned over and over. My dreams were of the sword, my dad, the Japanese, and Billy Thompson. As I came to in the morning I had a plan. I was so tired I didn't know if it was a good plan or a bad plan. But, it was a plan. The only question was whether I could carry it out.

As dawn broke I got out of bed, quietly dressed, and sneaked into the hall. It sounded like Mom and Dad were still sleeping so I headed for Dad's workshop in the basement. I went through the stuff on his workbench until I found what I needed and then slipped out of the house. I headed toward the woods and Billy Thompson's headquarters. I figured that was the perfect place for Billy to play with the sword this Saturday morning and I had to get there first.

After getting turned around a bit I found the spot.

I could see where we scuffled and searched in the leaves until I found the grenade where I'd abandoned it. I then went into the small headquarters shack and settled down to wait for Billy to show up. I reviewed my plan in my mind and resolved to make it work.

I must have dozed off for a while because I awoke to the sound of wood chopping and Billy's voice as he yelled, "Take that, and that, you dirty Nazis." I waited for a few minutes as he tired himself out attacking the trees with the sword.

As I came out of the shack he was facing away from me, hands on his knees, as he caught his breath from his exertion. The sword was stuck in the dirt and the scabbard lay nearby.

"Hi, Billy," I said. As he turned I continued, "I want the sword back. Here's your grenade."

I held the grenade out in front of me, holding the safety lever compressed with both hands. Billy looked at me and laughed. "Keep it. It's a fake anyway. I like the sword better." He pulled the sword out of the dirt and made a show of knocking dirt clods off the blade.

I pulled the pin with one hand while holding the safety lever down with the other. I made it a point to show him the ring hanging off my finger. "You don't understand. Either give me the sword or I'll let go. If you run, I'll throw it at you. If you rush me, I'll drop the grenade. I don't think either one of us could get out of range."

I met his eyes as he leveled his gaze at me. "You must know it's a dummy," he said.

"I don't know. Is it? We could find out pretty quick. Do you want to play catch?" I said as I mimed tossing it to him.

He visibly flinched. "I'll just wait until you put the pin back in," he said, with menace in his voice. "You were a chicken yesterday and you're a chicken today."

In response I held the pin out toward him at arm's length. When he stepped forward and started to reach for it I turned and threw the pin as far as I could. He tracked it as it fell somewhere into the leaves and was instantly lost from sight. When he turned back toward me his eyes were wide. The acrid smell of urine filled the air as a wet spot appeared on his pants.

I held the grenade in one hand over my head. "Put the sword in the scabbard and toss it over here," I said.

Billy didn't say anything as he picked the scabbard off the ground and carefully inserted the sword. He tossed it toward me in a gentle lob and it landed near my feet.

"Now run," I said. "My arm is getting tired."

Billy turned and took off down the path. As I watched his back recede I tried to control my breathing. My heart was racing a million miles a minute and I could feel, and see, my hands shaking.

As I calmed myself I kept a firm grip on the grenade with my left hand making sure to keep the handle trapped. I reached into my right pants pocket and pulled out one of the paper clips I'd taken from Dad's workbench earlier. It was already unfolded and as I lined it up with the hole in the fuse I realized it was a little too thin. I put it in my teeth and felt around in my pocket until I pulled out a slightly thicker paper clip that I'd also prestraightened. This one looked like a better fit so I carefully threaded it into the fuse hole. When the long end poked out the other side I bent both sides around the fuse to hold it in place. For insurance I took the roll of black electrical tape I'd also swiped and wrapped it first around the makeshift pin and then taped the handle to the grenade body with most of the rest of the roll. Now for the moment of truth: I let go of the handle. Nothing happened and I let out my breath and relaxed for the first time in two days.

I didn't want to leave the grenade for some other kid to find so I put it in my pocket. I'd figure out a way to get rid of it safely later. I picked up the sword and headed home. I didn't plan to tell my dad how I got it back and I had the feeling Billy Thompson wasn't going to talk about it either.

01 September 1990

"Do you know what I learned from that experience?" Erik Montero asked, after he finished his story.

"Once you pull the pin Mr. Grenade is no longer your friend?" Andy said, trying to make a joke in response to what was obviously a tall tale. A ten- or eleven-year-old kid doesn't threaten another kid with a hand grenade and get away with it, even back in the 1950s.

"No," Erik responded, looking at his son with a mixture of exasperation and disappointment. "I learned to commit. Once you are willing to do whatever needs to be done, no matter what the potential cost, you can't lose. That's how I got through 'Nam. That's how I got my men through 'Nam."

Andy looked at him, more seriously now. "This was all true?"

His father nodded.

"So, was the grenade real or a dummy?" Andy asked.

"I don't know, and neither did he. You don't know what you are capable of until faced with the choice."

He handed Andy the sword. "This is yours now. Your grandfather earned it in battle. I learned a lesson from it that stayed with me the rest of my life. Maybe you'll have a story to tell about it one day."

25 February 1991

Erik Montero watched CNN as he ate dinner. The long-expected ground offensive into Iraq had been an overwhelming success. Images of destroyed Iraqi vehicles and hordes of ragged prisoners filled the screen. The president had stopped the thrust into Iraq once the main objectives had been achieved. The press was now calling it "The Hundred-Hour War."

He'd gotten a brief call from Andy a few days before the balloon went up. They passed the time with talk of inconsequential things. It was good to hear his son's voice, if only for a few minutes, and he made it a point to tell him how proud he was.

Andy had jokingly asked him if he was taking good care of the sword. He'd left it in his dad's care rather than risk having it confiscated under the "No personal weapons" policy. The sword was proudly displayed on Erik's mantle next to a photo of Andy with his Bradley Scout Vehicle crew.

He'd thought of that conversation as he scanned for news of Andy's unit, the 2nd (Blackjack) Brigade of the 1st Cavalry Division. His patience was finally rewarded with a report on the diversionary attack the brigade made into southern Iraq at the start of the ground war. The raid kept the enemy's attention from the wide Hail Mary thrust from the west.

Erik finished eating and was cleaning his dinner dishes when the doorbell rang. He wasn't expecting visitors so he glanced through the window before answering. His heart went cold at the sight of an Army sergeant first class in a class A uniform standing with a captain from the Chaplain Corps.

Reluctantly, he opened the door.

"Sir, are you Mr. Montero?"

"Yes." He was icy calm, but he knew exactly what this was.

"Mr. Erik Montero, father of Staff Sergeant Andrew Montero?"

Erik nodded, unable to speak.

"I'm Sergeant First Class Griffith from the First Cavalry Division at Fort Hood, and this is Father Samuel. May we come in?"

Erik gestured them into the living room, went to his favorite chair and sat down. They ignored his wave at the couch and remained standing.

"You are the father of Staff Sergeant Andrew Montero, assigned to the Second Brigade of the First Cavalry Division?"

At Erik's nod he continued.

"Sir, the Secretary of the Army has asked to me express his deep regret that your son, Staff Sergeant Andrew Montero, was killed in action in southern Iraq. The Secretary of the Army extends his deepest condolences to you and your family in your tragic loss."

The soldier continued talking. He said something about how Andy would be returned to the U.S., and the assistance the Army would provide. The words droned on. He placed a packet of information on the coffee table.

Erik looked up, past him, to the photo of his son on the mantle. The last photo of his son he'd ever have. Next to it was the sword. The blade, hidden from view in its scabbard, was no less sharp and deadly for the fact it couldn't be seen. The pain he felt was as pure and true as a thrust from that ancient steel.

"This is it. Montero," Pat Luby said as he pulled up with his crew.

The state made out pretty good, he thought, from people who died without wills or relatives. He and the crew were going to clean out the house so it could be auctioned, any valuables auctioned, and personal stuff either trashed or kept for a few months against claims, then trashed.

Usually it was a bunch of crap, but this time it looked like there might be some good stuff.

The Salvation Army truck was already there to get the furniture, and someone had mowed the lawn. They probably billed the estate two hundred bucks for that, too.

"Let's get to it," he said. He meant they were going to get to it, and he was going to supervise. He'd done enough grunt labor over the years. He was foreman.

"Milford, start in the garage. Tools go for auction, toss any junk."

"Yup."

"Jackson and Taylor, start in the kitchen."

The place had some artwork up, musty furniture, photos, kitchen crap. It was a bit above average for some of the dumps they got. The photos and most of the kitchen stuff were going straight into trash. The bedding and clothes, too. There were a couple of boxes of tools and a bench grinder for the auction house.

The crew pulled and tossed, lugged and carried, bumping doorframes and not caring. It was just one more dump to vacate. Most of the furniture went straight to trash. Months sitting while the courts ruled on the estate meant it usually wasn't any good.

He kept an eye out. The younger morons would snag change and other stuff, and sometimes try for jewelry. After a few months, they got jaded and would just toss everything. He'd rescued silver coins and stuff sometimes.

There was a long footlocker in a closet. He said, "Stop," and opened it up.

"I'll hand you things," he said.

He shooed them out of the room and started pulling stuff.

Huh. Old Army uniform. Looked like Vietnam. The local museum might be interested. Some personal letters. Those should go straight into trash. Some old magazines, including classic *Playboys*. Salvation Army wouldn't take those, and the state regarded them as trash.

"Hey, Milford, here's some stroke material for you."

Milford took the stack carefully and said, "Yeah, joke away, but these are collectible."

"Sure they are. Enjoy."

"Thanks."

More clothes, random documents, and...

That was a pretty cool sword. It was cool enough a museum might want it, but they might just sell it anyway.

Pat was just going to keep that. He rolled it in a blanket on the floor, and kicked the empty locker closed and out the door to the landing.

"That's it for this room," he said. "Load up what got tagged and the stuff we put aside." It was getting late.

Back at the shop, he parked the truck, then walked over to his car, carrying the wrapped bundle. He stuck it out of sight behind the seats and locked it again. Then he went to clock out.

It being Friday, he grabbed a six-pack of Coors. He didn't have any dates for the weekend, so he may as well drink and have the guys over for poker and bullshit. He called around and left messages, and ordered his usual pizza.

Once Rod, Stumpf and Max were at the table, he brought out the sword.

"Keep your greasy fingers off it," he said.

Stumpf said, "Huh. World War Two."

"Yeah. A real samurai sword."

Stumpf said, "Nah, most of them were mass issue by then. Not worth much."

"Oh, fuck you." Stumpf always thought he knew things.

Rod and Max liked it. Max used his thumb to check the edge and said, "A lot of nicks. I bet it has four or five kills. Probably belonged to an officer."

"Yeah. And taken from him when he died."

Stumpf said, "Probably bought in Tokyo, after the war, and beat up by some kid playing Marines and Japs."

Max's story was better.

Pat stuck to poker and beer. When the beer ran out, he switched to Jack on ice. He was actually fifteen bucks ahead at nickel ante by midnight, and still a couple of bucks up by two.

"Alright, I gotta sleep," he said.

The guys left.

What he wanted was to drink some Jack and handle the sword more. Yeah, it was World War II. That was a real sword, no matter what Stumpf said. They'd used these things in the Island Campaign.

He drew it out, balanced it across his finger, then gripped it.

"These things will cut machine-gun barrels." He swung it overhead and down, and hit the arm of the couch at an oblique angle. It suddenly got lighter and he heard a clattering sound.

The blade was on the floor, and he held a hilt and fittings.

He started to throw that, realized it was a bad idea, and dropped it on the couch.

"Goddamn, what a piece of shit. Fucking Stumpf. I guess I should have known it was a fake."

Looking down, he realized the sword had gashed his arm and he was bleeding at a steady seep.

He muttered, wrapped a towel around his arm, and sat down to rest his eyes for a few minutes.

When he opened them, it was dawn.

"Goddamn," he rasped. His throat was raw and his head pounded. His arm hurt like hell.

Oh, right. That POS sword. Maybe he could get a few bucks for it at the flea market.

The goddamned handle was unraveling, too. He wrapped some tape around it and decided to lie down until he was well enough to drive.

This culture had abandoned swords. They thought of her as just an oversized knife, to be flung and broken.

She had lived so well, but there was nothing now but to wait for the slow decay of death, or the butchery of some peasant who would make chisels of bits of her. Or worse. From other metal she felt nearby, she deduced she was in some sort of workshop, but it was a shop of demon horrors, not craftsmanship.

Broken Spirit

Michael Z. Williamson and Dale C. Flowers

Frank studied the broken blade of the sword. The dealer had called it a "Genuine Ninja Sumaria Sword blade." He knew that was ridiculous. The ninja weren't samurai, and that wasn't how you spelled it. It was a World War II officers' samurai sword.

"Where's the rest?" he'd asked.

"It was broke. I sold the metal bits to a coin shop."

"Damn. Those could have been cool." Though he didn't know how they were put together anyway.

Back home in the garage, he decided that elephant tusk with the carved dragons would fit on the butt end. He'd gotten that at an estate sale last year, and it must have been preordained. Narwhal or bull elephant seal ivory would have been nicer but laminated fake "ivory" plastic had killed that market like punt guns had the passenger pigeon. Besides, an Oriental sword needed Oriental ivory. The curve was almost double this curve, so it worked into an arithmetical aesthete. But he didn't want to shorten the blade to mount it. Wouldn't be enough for a letter opener with the

145

cut off piece. Besides, it would look funny. And the ivory was skinny.

He found a piece of all-thread, one he'd pulled from his tire the week before. He figured it was a seventy-eight-dollar piece of metal because of that. He burned off the zinc plating with the oxyacetylene torch, grabbed the stick welder, and figured a thick bead would hold it.

He dug through the brass bin and found bus bars salvaged from an REA transformer station under construction. One of those pieces would make a good stuba, or whatever the guard thingy was called. He called it a handguard, in the American way. Mouthing French words for sword parts seemed kind of gay for a slicing and skewering instrument of death. The brass was a bit scratched, but he could antique it out with the Dremel tool and a worn rasp. And damn, was he sweating up a river in the heat. He took a break to grab a PBR.

He came back sipping the brew and looked at his work so far. Dammit, the hole wasn't quite centered, but nothing some judicious wallowing with a drill bit wouldn't fix. So the larger side would be a knuckle guard. He wondered why the Japanese had never done that. Probably too stuck on tradition. Didn't they cut off fingertips in matters of honor? That reminded him of some of the Japanese TV shows he saw bits of on cable. They were seriously fucked up. Maybe those two bombs had done more damage than people thought, and "maybe they should have done a bit more," he muttered.

Before assembly, he'd have to clean that blade up. He spun up the buffer and loaded the wheel with emery buffing compound. A flapwheel wouldn't do for this old piece. It needed a precision buff with a light touch. He grasped the blade firmly in his gloved mitts and leaned one side into it for just a second.

Wow! That was actually pretty damned shiny even with the slight texture imparted by the emery. He'd thought it would be harder than that. The steel that is. This polishing was easy. Didn't the Japanese use stones and linen strops with natural salt crystals or something? And here was Frank with a modern buffing wheel getting the same job done.

He gripped it at each end and got to work. Not too fast but with a tender touch and enough speed to gain the desired result. Things like this you just had to let come natural and not force the issue as it were. Once again he thought, *That's what she said*. It applied to everything in the shop. It was a man thing.

He knew the Japs had some wiffly looking edge on the blade, something about heat treating. He'd heard the phrase, "Heat it hot and quench it quick." *That's what she said*. But the idea was to harden the steel by quick immersion after heating it to a cherry-red glow. First the heat then the knap. Kind of made sense.

He called, "Hey, Josh."

"Yeah, Dad?"

"Bring a big, wet cloth out. Look at the tag and make sure it isn't Rayon or such. At least sixty-five percent cotton. Not one of Mom's dish towels, she'll flip her shit and have a cow. That old purple one with the hole will do it. Soak it."

"Okay."

Josh came out with a dripping towel, and some of the drips on the front of his pants and new shoes.

"Goddammit, put on your boots. This could get messy. Shop means boots."

Josh went and did it, and hadn't he told the boy that five times this month? Where did the boy get those smarts, or the lack of them?

"Okay, I'm going to heat the edge a bit at a time, then you slap the cloth on it to cool it, okay? Use a big wad of it. It's going to steam. You don't want to get burned."

"Got it, Dad."

He turned the torch down to a pencil point, waved it toward the edge, and had a blue spot in a second.

"Damn, quench it now, Josh."

Josh wrapped the cloth around it, and it sizzled, more like that turkey bacon than the real thing but polyunsaturated origamic fats or something. But it sizzled. When he skinned it back... yup, still blue. Very pretty color, veiny even. Blue was what old gun springs were. This should work. He went along the edge bit by bit, varying the depth, making sure not to go past blue. He didn't want to distemper it.

When done, he liked what he saw in the mirror finish. The blue edge faded through purple and straw to the polished steel. That was sexy looking. Purple helmeted soldier of love... blue-veiner... so many great lines.

Then he turned to the ivory. He couldn't remember where he got that. Some little Chinese guy in San Fran. It was a coat hanger or something. You didn't really want to buff out scratches in ivory like you would metal. Totally different medium. Anyone ever sat in a dentist chair and had an old filling replaced knew that. When that enamel heated up in whatever gummy friction that happens at high RPMs while you were leaning into your work, the smell was so off-putting that you couldn't hold down breakfast. A whiff of burnt tooth enamel and a hint of bile gurgled up your esophagus circulating in that nether area between the septum and upper palate...you didn't ever want to go there. No, you wanted to fill in scratches on ivory and mother of pearl like they do when they rub in white crayon on a gun's proof marks, stampings and warning labels like when a seller wants to highlight them. Only for the opposite reason, to hide the flaws. Kind of like when you putty in some Bisquick dough in the sheet rock of the kitchen ceiling if you had your Glock go off when you were cleaning it. It was best to prevent the scratches in the first place unless you were deliberately ageing a piece to make it appear period authentic. Kind of a stonewashed jeans thing.

He had a whole afternoon in it, but damned if it didn't look a lot better than the burned trash it had been. More of a proper sword now than a used lawn-mower blade.

Maybe he could find a few more broken swords and dress them up, like those old Turk Mausers he'd Varathaned and chrome plated.

He'd hit the gun show and see what he could get for it. It ought to get snapped up. Just be sure to get a booth next to that *Baywatch*-looking lady that sold ProMag and MAC gadgets. Several vendors would let you share a corner of their table for a percentage of your sale, especially the guy with the Hi-Points or the old gun mags and survival books. He got a lot of traffic, with Clinton trying to turn the country into Europe.

—⁓—

She cursed him, for his *soyana* idiocy. He had no concept of the rape he committed, expecting her to appreciate it and thank him.

He added nothing to the art, nothing to the craft, and was a blight on the world. He was no smith, no warrior and a man only barely in the sense of his anatomy. He had violated her beyond the abuse she'd already suffered.

She wished him a meaningless, ignominious and spectacularly public death.

—⁓—

He arrived early on Saturday for the show. You had to get there early or all those posers with the phony handicap stickers got all the good spots. A lot of them were in better condition than he was, with his knee. Social Security didn't believe it was work-related, even with the circular saw scar across it.

The fairgrounds were packed so he had to park across the street. Goddamn horse trailers took six spaces each.

Still, there was a decent line to get in, and the dealers would like that. He liked that. He wasn't a dealer per se, but he was showing and selling. Yeah, you consider the stuff that walked in and it was almost like show-and-tell.

He had the sword wrapped in a quality silicon impregnated cotton towel with a stitched up hem Chivas Regal style but without the knotted cords. He didn't want to scratch up the ivory or his work.

He had a poster board sign over his shoulders with cable ties, reading JAPANESE WAR RELIC SWORD W/ GENUINE IVORY HILT. $350.

Once inside, he checked his Glock and let the cops run a cable tie through it. He guessed he saw the sense in that. If he could put a hole in the kitchen ceiling while cleaning it, what would some idiot do here? The damned lawyers would own the show, the promoter, the fairgrounds and probably every gun in the place.

He was on foot, walking the aisles. Like they say in real estate, "Location, location, location." There's truth to it. Grocers know it. Best place to sell a weekly news magazine, aspirin or breath freshener is near the checkout counter. Best place to sell a sword is near the grill where they were dicing up onions and bell peppers for the sausage dogs. But knife sellers usually had those tables sewed up. You could pay premium rates and get a table at the entrance and catch people coming and going but the smart money—and this was counterintuitive—was to rent a table near the bathrooms. Sausage dogs, you know. Those were high-traffic tables and mostly at a lower rate. Josh knew, he'd sent a few that way. Slim Jims and beef jerky were about as popular as loose 8mm, .303 and Nagant ammo for five cents apiece. A little green tinge on either never hurt nothing.

He tried the Japanese sword and WWII dealers first, just in case. One of them shook his head and said, "Not interested, it's been modified." The second literally sneered and turned away. The third said, "I'll give you fifty bucks for the ivory. The rest is junk."

He moved on, trying not to be pissed. He'd expected

that. Snobs. They wanted stuff that looked like it was in picture books. The sword dealer's stuff started at fourteen hundred bucks. Who could afford that? His wasn't anywhere near that pretty, but it was a real blade, not those stamped junk ones everyone got from Taiwan and India.

All of the blade dealers turned him down, most of them politely. The best offer was one hundred dollars, and he knew those fuckers would turn around and sell it for four hundred.

He had nachos for lunch, and those were four and a half bucks. Add in parking at three, and the admission, even discounted, at three, and he had to figure the gas, too. He considered trying to sublet or consign it on someone's table, but they'd want twenty percent just for a few square inches of space, and wouldn't try to sell it. He rested his feet and knee a bit and kept walking.

He kept an eye out for other projects while walking. Spotting gems in the rough was a talent he had. Take some Arab gun like a Persian Mauser, a Hakim, Helwan or a Martini Henry. With some light sanding, the application of tinted shellac, some brass upholstery tacks and maybe a thumbhole, tastefully done of course, you could turn a piece of junk into a C&R treasure. Upgrades were Frank's forte, and hadn't it been said by that famous nineteenth-century dualist philosopher, Oscar-something, "Nowadays people know the price of everything and the value of nothing." Now there a was a man who knew what he was about. And hadn't Frank done justice to that sword? Life was all about upgrades. Some people never got it.

But it was afternoon and no one was biting. Frank took off his sandwich board and with a bold stroke of his Sharpie penned in OBO next to the $350 on the sword tag.

He'd just done that when an older guy came up. Fiftyish, but in good shape.

"Can I see it?"

"Sure!" he stepped back against the wall and unwrapped it. He didn't want to poke anyone.

The guy took it and looked it over, tip to tail, and screwed his face up a bit.

"Well, it is antique," he said. "A hundred years, maybe more, from the shape. But it's in rough shape."

"It was cleaned up not long ago," Frank said, not wanting to jinx anything.

"Yeah, and it shouldn't have been. And this torching is completely wrong. That looks like something out of an anime and was bad for it. And it looks like it had fire damage and was broken before that."

"Yeah, it was out of an estate," he said. At least this guy was looking. Wasn't anime those kinky Japanese cartoons? This looked like one of the swords in those things, that probably got used as a dildo in a cartoon?

He was about to lecture the guy on decency, but the man started talking again.

"So someone put a decent piece of ivory on a sword, but they don't really match."

That was a matter of opinion. Frank thought they worked very well together.

He said, "I got offered a hundred for the ivory. Alone." Crap. He should have said two hundred.

"I'll go one fifty," the guy said. "As rough as the blade is, it's hard to go more."

If all these guys thought there was something wrong with the blade, there must be, but he couldn't figure out what it was. It seemed sound.

He said, "I mean, ivory, and the blade, three and a quarter, even if they're parts."

The guy shook his head. "Two hundred. As high as I can go."

"Well..." He did need the money. He felt like a whore for thinking that, but he did need the money. He'd done what he could for the thing, but the purists were too snobbish to look at him.

"Deal, but two oh one...you gotta throw me a bone here. I got a little Jew in me. Ha-ha," he said.

"Yeah, must be a small fella to fit under your coat!" the buyer smirked. "All I got is fifties and no change. Two hundred even."

The fifties were crisp and new. He shrugged and took them. That would take care of the balance on the tires for the Camaro. Kinda ironic he'd used the all-thread that punctured one of the old tires. Then he'd work on glasspacks and shackles.

He took the money, handed over the sword and shook hands. Once the guy turned away, he hit the bathroom. He needed to take a leak, and he didn't want to be where the guy could see Frank if he changed his mind.

So he walked around the outside ring of tables, and went to the exit that way. He had no packages to inspect, and went out the fast door.

He stepped out into the sun, lighter in metal and heavier in cash. He could even grab a couple of Miller quarts on the way home. And he'd better hurry. It was five already. There was some sort of nerd thing at the convention center, too. He'd need to avoid downtown and take the freeway around.

The show had been packed. He walked to the pedestrian gate and across the street to overflow parking where the Camaro was. It was a sunny day and he had four fresh fifties in his hand.

A crashing blow slammed him to the ground and everything went black.

Steven wandered through the back of the hall, hoping to find some other deal. There were a couple of Max's Mausers he wasn't going to waste time with. That was an entire industry set up to butcher artifacts. The accessories they "included" weren't even Mauser—they were Enfield.

Nothing else jumped out at him. Either they were real antiques priced accordingly, or complete crap only fit for spare parts, but some guys obsessed over those.

He wasn't sure the sword wasn't in that category, but he had to save it from a fate worse than death. Call it a sensitive streak. Or maybe he was obsessive over junk.

He sighed as he ran fingers along the abused blade. You'd never do that with a properly maintained sword. Fingerprints would rapidly lead to rust. But this poor thing couldn't have been abused worse if that stupid bubba had consciously tried. And try he had, even if he claimed it was an "estate." What a soulless man that creep had been. Clueless too.

Something flickered, and he looked up to see a vague hint of a flash. There were emergency vehicles outside.

"What's going on?" he called over to the guy at the exit.

The staff man on security detail there said, "Oh, hey. Yeah, that guy you bought the sword from earlier? He was crossing Thirty-Eighth in a hurry and got smeared by a bus. Dumbass looked like he was counting cash."

"Oh, Jesus." He rolled his eyes. The assclown really was that stupid.

—⟁—

The new bearer wasn't a warrior. He had been once, but warriors now were different. Swords were less and less regarded, she'd noticed.

The first thing he did was lave her in oil. It wasn't good oil, but it soothed and nourished her skin. At least he knew something.

Then she was put on a shelf, and the oil soaked up dust from the air. She was again inside a place where tools were used, tools that cut horrifyingly fast. She envisioned her demise, being sliced or bent into something not at all a sword, some piece of "art" that lesser beings idolized.

The hideous tang that deformed her was removed, along with a thin slice of her body from next to it. She was nothing here, it seemed. Her death would lack dignity.

She despaired. Her life was to end in an unmarked grave, in a room full of metal bars, amongst people who'd not know the difference between raw stock, a carpenter's tool, and her.

When after a long time, hands took her from the shelf, she gave up and withdrew.

Fire.

There was warmth, and there was gentle scraping. Her butchered end shivered under a hammer, and was drawn out.

Was that flux? It was. Not like other fluxes, but it held the heat and cleansed her surface. Then new metal was laid against her.

She welcomed the new metal as the hammer mated it to her. It was good steel, remarkably clean and even. It lacked soul, but it had strength.

It was shaped into a new tang, drawn, tapered, beveled. Part of her was drawn with it, then came that moment that all the metal was one.

She felt a thrill of new life. This smith wasn't any kind of master, but he did care.

She would be at least a gentleman's blade. She would not be the queen she had been, but she would be a dowager lady.

She ached as she was beaten back into shape, but it felt wonderful when done. Once again, she was true and aligned. Her beautiful curves were forced out, but that was part of a process. She maintained hope.

The bearer took her again, and commenced gentle scraping of her bevels. He was a craftsman, though not a swordsmith. Still, draw by draw, day by day, with gaps in between, he shaped her sides.

The smith took her back, and wrapped her in a gown of clay. She was worried. It wasn't the clay she knew. It was harder, coarser.

But the smith knew his craft, and the fire warmed her to the core. She braced as the water struck her and chilled her back down, and the clay fell free in places. She was curvy and pretty once more.

The rest of the clay fell off to a hammer.

Then the bearer used fine stones and paper to polish her skin, bring out her color, and show her proud temper line. They weren't proper water stones, but they did an adequate job. If not a warrior, she was at least a guardian, and had her long life to show.

The fittings were a mix of old, of a style she remembered from two centuries past, and a new, handcrafted fuchi in silver and copper. It didn't quite match the other mounts, but it was handmade for her and she appreciated the intent.

The scabbard she was fitted to looked plain and elegant outside, but was a bit irregular inside. Still, given the shameful death she'd almost suffered, it was a small thing. And when would she be called to serve?

The bearer, not being a smith or polisher, had done an impressive job of keening her edge. He held her professionally enough, if a little close to her guard.

No, he was no swordsman. An apprentice at best.

But he'd given her back her life. She owed him and would wait, hoping to repay his respect in kind.

She waited, cloistered in his home. She had a padded rack of fine wood to rest on. She was admired by guests, and handled delicately and with deference. No fingerprints marred her here.

But she did not fight. The bearer had retired as a warrior. Nor had he seen blood up close. There were strange warriors these days, who fought things at a distance, or acted upon tools.

She could feel his disappointment. He'd hoped battle would come to him, but it never had.

He was not without means. She tried to plead with him to use those means to seek out adventure and battle, but the thought was too fine to transfer through their touch.

Then her bearer died, after so much attention. She was sad for him. Such dedication and devotion, never rewarded with battle.

She was wrapped carefully and placed into a crate with so many of his other possessions—pistols, bayonets, silver coins, books and small items.

When she was unwrapped, dozens of people stared at her, most of them decadent and soft. She changed hands and wound up on a rack with other charitably-called "swords" that were mere copies in dull, mindless metal.

All she could do was hope.

—⁂—

Okoyyūki

Tom Kratman

December 2002

They say that when a sword wants you to know her name, she'll tell you. By the time this one had told Captain Reilly her name, he'd already begun to call her "Audrey." She didn't like it, insisting then that her proper name was, translated from old, old Japanese, "Luminous and Dainty Blood Sipper."

"Right," Reilly agreed, "Audrey, it is."

It wasn't until he put on the movie, then unsheathed the sword and laid it across his bare thighs that she'd understood. "But I'm not a plant," she insisted, when the movie was done.

"There is carbon in you, and that came from charcoal that came from plants," he countered.

"Good point," she agreed. "But you drew me so you owe me now. And besides, that movie? Who knew swords could approach Nirvana outside of in battle? And I'm always hungry afterwards; you know that."

"Right," Reilly answered again, before nicking his

left thumb on the point. He made a mental note: *Put sword away before watching any Clint Eastwood movies.*

"Clint Eastwood movies?" the sword asked, expectantly.

"Not on your life; I only have so much blood to give."

Her style indicated Bizen Province, as did the metal of her skin, though there was no signature on the tang to claim such. She, herself, insisted, "I'm from Ise. I used to have a signature. And I am a *lot* older than I look." Beyond that she would not say.

She did, however, say, "Domo arigato. And 'Audrey' will work well enough. It's not like I haven't had many names over the centuries, after all. More than a few have called me, 'Mad Courage.'"

Three months earlier

Farmers' fields and pastures ripped by in a blur. There was a song in Reilly's heart as he drove at near suicidal speed along Interstate 75, southeast of Fort Knox, Kentucky. The post was hours behind him now as he made a mad dash for freedom at Fort Bragg, and far, far from the clutches of Army Recruiting Command.

Once I get to Bragg and settled in and assigned, he exulted, *they'll never be able to drag me back and chain me to a computer. HAHAHAHAHA; no more churning out useless stats that nobody reads! No more assembling reports that could be done as well by a moderately bright Private First Class. HAHA-HAHAHAHAHA!* "You'll never take me alive, coppers!" *HAHAHAHAHAHAHAHAHA! I'm going to* war, *motherfuckers!*

Actually, the song wasn't just in his heart; out the

open windows the speakers blared a medley of Scottish bagpipe tunes, at the moment, "The Duck."

"What?" he asked aloud, though nobody was there to have caused the question. At the volume the pipes were blaring, it's unlikely he'd have heard anything even if there *had* been someone in the car with him. Still, he'd heard something; he knew he had. It had sounded almost like a command, though soft and weak and from far off in the distance. Or maybe it was a plea, begged for with a degree of desperation that gave it some of the force of a command. *Whatever*, Reilly mentally shrugged, then glanced at the fuel gauge. It was a long way from empty, but, *may as well fill up while I have the chance.*

A sign advertised fuel at the next exit. He eased over, tires thump-thump-thumping on the raised pavement markers before thrumming over the rumble strips. He corrected slightly left for a moment, to stop the thrumming, and then pulled right again and turned off. There followed another sign, indicating fuel, and another turn to the right. The gas station was on the right but he passed it, continuing on to a largish pawn shop—Crazy Mike's Pawn and Guns—that had caught his attention, sandwiched in between the gas station and an adult store with a morally worrisome number of cars parked all around. The pawn shop looked even seedier than the store catering to adult tastes, if "tastes" was quite the word. Seedy or not, he turned the ignition key to off, killing both engine and pipes. Reilly half leapt from the car, slammed the door behind him, and walked briskly into the pawn shop. From a speaker hidden somewhere in the shop Pat Benatar belted out "We Belong."

"May I help you?" asked a withered old man behind a long line of glass display counters. The counters encased a mix of cheap shotguns, watches, the odd bit of lead crystal, some tarnished silver flatware, quite a bit of mostly tacky jewelry, and various other items someone had never managed to redeem. The old man reached under the counter, reducing the volume but not quite killing the music.

"I'm not quite . . . just nosing around," Reilly replied.

Behind the counters, fanning out to both sides, ran racks of rifles and shotguns. These framed a display of modern manufacture Japanese-style swords, which Reilly instantly dismissed as junk.

But then, "Did you hear that?" Reilly asked of the old counter-jumper.

"Hear what, son?"

"I'm not sure . . . it was faint . . . less than a whisper."

"Nope, didn't hear a thing." The old man shrugged, before sticking a little finger in his ear and twisting it. "But then, my hearing ain't been so good since fifty-two . . ."

Reilly shook his head, then turned his attention back to the rack of horizontal swords. He still felt confident in dismissing most of them, but one seemed to have a little more character, and possibly some age to it.

"May I see that?" he asked, pointing.

Wordlessly, the old man took the sword from the rack and passed it over. As soon as Reilly wrapped his hand around the tsuka, or hilt, palm and fingers coming to rest on the bronze menukis, small ornaments that covered the pegs that held the tsuka to the sword, he heard it very clearly: *Buy me. I heard your exultation at going to war. That's why I called*

*out to you. Buymebuymebuyme. Whatever they ask
for me I am worth it. Buybuybuybuybuy*. A touch
of anguished despair crept into the feminine voice.
*Please buy me; I have been so alone and so lonely
for so long.*

Keeping his face carefully blank and his grip firmly
on the menukis, Reilly looked over the mountings,
from bronze endcap, to the gold-colored silk wrap-
pings over the ray-skin covered hilt, to the tsuba, or
handguard, and then along the black lacquerwork of
the scabbard. He drew the blade partly out of the
scabbard . . .

Yesyesyesyesyes!

That was no nonsensical acid-etched pattern on
the blade, but an extremely active genuine hamon
that evoked the mountains of Chinese and Japanese
paintings, the height and slope terribly exaggerated,
but graceful and beautiful for all that. It was the
peculiar charm of such mountain paintings that the
viewer always knew that there were no such mountains,
anywhere on Earth, but deeply wished there might be.

"Ummm . . . how much for this?" Reilly asked the
shopkeeper.

"It's on the tag."

*Two things really must be understood at this point.
The lesser was that no words were actually exchanged
between steel and soldier. On Reilly's part, the message simply formed in his mind as if he had heard it
through his ears. Audrey, AKA "Luminous and Dainty
Blood Sipper," never really explained how it worked
out on her end.*

The other was that Reilly, though outwardly sane,

was mad as a hatter, always had been, and—especially since he hid it well—always would be. Though well, he also hid it unconsciously; indeed, he wasn't even remotely aware of his condition, never having quite made the leap from "everyone else strikes me as a little odd" to "maybe it isn't everyone else." Every man seems normal to himself, after all. But a man conscious that he was sane or going insane would probably have panicked when the sword spoke to him. Reilly just thought, Neat, *as he looked at the price tag and answered,* "Okay."

From the first it was a match made in...well... in Ise, either the province or the town, actually, and just possibly both, though not consummated until much later, and far, far from any of the domains of the emperor's august self.

Four months later

Reilly awakened from a sleep with every muscle but the one hanging between his legs shrieking with pain. He had some idea as to why, though the memories were faint, dim, and spotty with holes.

"What the fuck was bothering you, last night?" asked one of the captains with whom he shared a room in the villa of the supposedly Bedouin-oriented housing area of Eskan. The village was a temporary transit point for some soldiers on their way to the assembly areas in Kuwait, prior to the anticipated invasion of Iraq.

"*Watashi no hobākurafuto was unagi do ippai desu,*" Reilly answered, speaking straight upward, toward the ceiling. His face immediately acquired a horrified look, eyes crossing downward as he attempted to see what was speaking from his own mouth. The problem wasn't that he didn't understand what he'd said. Rather, the problem was that he did, that he'd never taken a Japanese lesson in his life, and that what he'd just said made no sense in either Japanese or English.

The roommate just shook his head. Speaking Japanese was not the weirdest thing any of them had seen from Reilly, even lately.

Reilly lay flat on his back, inside a bedroom of a fairly plush villa, on a standard US Government Issue folding field cot. He didn't have a clue about how he'd acquired the language but he knew why every muscle ached. It was a result of Audrey putting him through dream training, which still caused his muscles to tighten and twitch to exhaustion. The training itself was a blur of slashed throats, spilled intestines, disconnected arms, legs, and heads, and a sea of flowing blood.

His left hand cradled his head while his right curled around Audrey's tsuka, "Eskan," he muttered aloud, "shit, still in Eskan."

"Well," answered Audrey, "you could always go fuck the Air Force girl who runs the rec center. Tanya, right? It's not like she hasn't made it pretty plain you can have her on command." She then added, hopefully, "That, or kill the queer-as-a-five-gram-*wadokaichin* first sergeant."

As to the latter, don't tempt me. For the former . . . nobody else's wife, Reilly began, before the sword cut him off with, "Nobody else's girlfriend, none of the hired help. Yes, yes, I know that, but she's not in your service so she's not *your* hired help now, is she?"

I suppose not, Reilly agreed, adding, *I'm a little surprised you're not jealous.*

"Jealous of what? I've got the part of you I want; what do I care in whom you stick the part of you in which I have no interest because I cannot use it? And it distresses me when you're bored."

Tanya is rather pretty, Reilly said, sitting up, *if not so pretty as the blonde Air Force cook in the mess tent. And she's very sweet, too.*

"She'll be a better lay than the spoon," Audrey insisted, adding, "and before you ask, you'll just have to take my word; we girls know these things."

Three weeks later

Cold as it was, Reilly still dripped sweat from his practice session in the otherwise useless volleyball sand pits behind the villa. He leaned against a steel upright, intended to hold a volleyball net. If it had ever held one, there was no sign. He was inclined to doubt it, anyway. Eskan was something of a Potemkin village, after all, claimed to be able to hold about ten thousand Bedouin, but with a mosque that would have been tight for a corporal's guard. It had always been intended to house Americans, was his guess.

"You never told me," Audrey said, "just how it came to pass that you learned to use a katana. And I haven't seen a style quite that complex since . . . oh, it must be about four hundred and fifty years, give or take."

Oh, he replied with a smile, she might have sensed but couldn't possibly have seen, *it was a theory I had once upon a time, that the next big war would bog down into a stalemate, a lot like the First World War—*

"I was there for that one," the sword interrupted, brightly. "Wasn't much of a war out east. The one before that was much, much better; bodies every-where . . . massive sacrifice . . . I was never so proud of my people."

Reilly mentally harrumphed. *I thought I was your people, now.*

"You are now; they were then. I hope someday you will make me as proud."

Fair enough. Anyway, when things bog down one of the activities infantrymen undertake is the trench raid. You don't carry firearms. Instead, you creep across no-man'-land with grenades, entrenching tools, knives, axes, clubs, bicycle chains, things that that.

"Ah," sighed the sword, "that's the way for *real* men. None of this standing off half a mile and blast-ing away. Up close and personal, that's what war's supposed to be about."

They didn't actually do it for that reason.

"No matter the reason; what's important is that they did it."

If you say so, the human agreed, amiably. *But if you'll let me continue? Ah, good. Anyway, I asked myself what was better than all those things and came up with the answer, "sword, good for both stabbing and chopping," and that led me to katana. Unfortunately, there wasn't a katana school within two hundred miles. There was, however, a Korean school that taught the same basic things, though arguably better.*

"I don't like Koreans," sniffed Audrey.

You would have liked this one, Reilly replied. *Tough as nails and a true lover of people like yourself and your sisters.*

"My nieces, my cousins, and my daughters," Audrey said. "I have no sisters, no peers."

Yeah... whatever. So, I only had about seven or eight months before I had to go back to the Army, and the master said, "Not 'nuff time. Take minimum two year get even faggot last class first dan blackbelt."

"Private lessons?" *I asked.*

He told me, "Seventy-five dorrah an hour."

I found that a bit steep. So I asked him, "Were you ever in the Korean Army?"

He answered, very proudly, "Yes, Capital Division!"

So I said, "I will use the knowledge to kill communists."

He smiled and sneered, somehow both at the same time, and both with his whole being and presence and said, "Ten dorrah an hour."

The sword seemed to vibrate in his hand, almost as if it were laughing. "Say, you're right; I *would* have liked him. And, I have to admit, he did a pretty good job with you. Not that you know as much as I do, but you're only human, after all."

Thanks... I think.

Two weeks later

The border town had never been much. Now it was a series of ruins, buildings scorched and smoking, flames licking up from the odd piece of wood in their construction, and towers that looked to have been chewed by oversized dinosaurs. Shattered mud brick lay in random piles on the ground, some small but others quite large. Occasionally another wall would crumble into the street. There was a fairly solid-seeming set of stairs, also mud brick, that led upward but to nothing still standing.

There were bodies everywhere, though most seemed to be face down with their heads to the north. Climbing the stairs, Reilly looked north. The desert was littered with still more bodies, possibly as many as two hundred of them.

"We sure liberated the fuck out of this place," said Reilly, aloud. Audrey could hear and transmit to him, mind to mind, soul to soul, much better now, even without his having physical contact with any metal.

"Isn't it beautiful?" asked the sword.

"It has an element of beauty to it, yes," Reilly agreed.

"What happened here?" Audrey asked.

"I suspect the enemy actually tried to make a stand," he answered, "or at least thought about it, before panicking when our column came out of the desert. Then they broke and ran for safety." He swept her across the vista from the northeast to the northwest. "That's how much safety they found. We'd probably have taken prisoners, since they hadn't really put up much of a fight, if, indeed, any fight at all, but their own propaganda ministry convinced them that we tortured prisoners for fun, before cooking and eating them. So they ran rather then turn themselves in. And we weren't about to let them get away."

"What's wrong with torturing prisoners for fun?" she asked. "Soldiers should never surrender; torture reminds them why not. And why not cook and eat them? Why, did you know that Colonel Tsu—"

"Who?"

"Ah, never mind, I just remembered who it was that he ate. Were these the Republican Guard you've mentioned?" she asked, changing the subject.

"No," Reilly replied, "not according to reports. The

RGs probably suck, too, but they'll be better than these rabble." He glanced over to the Arab armored column to which he had been attached, telling the sword, "Sorry we haven't had anything worthwhile to do...worthwhile for you, I mean. Maybe in the city, when we get to it."

"In the city," she agreed, "when we get to it. I have a feeling..."

Three days later

Despite her attempts to cheer him, Reilly was almost suicidally despondent, sitting on the floor of a bombed-out shop with his head on his knees. The armored column to which he'd been attached really neither knew nor cared what he did, as they flushed out and shot enemy stay-behinds. Unlike the previous war, nobody was shooting food hoarders, or collaborators. Reilly and others just commandeered and distributed their food when any was found, giving the owners a receipt to be exchanged for cash later.

Where were the gallant charges he'd hoped for? Where the danger? Oh, he'd get a combat infantryman's badge out of the deal, but, under the circumstances, that was like winning second place in a race with the legless. In short, there had been hardly any of the action of which he'd dreamt since earliest boyhood.

"And being sniped at," he half moaned, "by people whose idea of the eight steady hold factors is shouting 'Allahu Akbar' while jerking the trigger? No, that doesn't really count." Of the Iraqi stay-behinds, he sneered, "Why did they even bother to stay behind if they're too useless and incompetent to actually do anything. You know they can't even hit you, provided they're trying to."

"There may be some better ones," she said. "Let's go hunting, shall we?"

"What would be the point?" Reilly sniffed. "Hunting mice isn't exactly a challenge."

"Maybe if there are enough mice," she said. "Maybe if they're bigger and somewhat tougher than most mice."

"You know something?" Reilly demanded.

"Let's just say I have a feeling. Now, are we going hunting or not?"

Without a word in reply, Reilly slung his rifle across his back, picked up Audrey, and sauntered out to his vehicle. The rifle went into the one rifle rack next to the door, the butt held in a metal oval on the floor.

Three hours later

Slamming his head and back against the concrete wall, around the corner of which he'd just peered, Reilly gave a softly exultant, "Holy fucking shit! Tanks? Four fucking tanks? Just for me? *Domo arigato gozaimasu, Audrey-chan. Aishiteru wa!*"

"*Suki yo, Reilly-chan,*" the sword replied, demurely.

What Reilly has seen were four stay-behind tanks, turrets alternating left and right, one close upon the tail of the other. Someone on the other side had been thinking; the tanks had just recently emerged from the warehouse—the huge garagelike door of it was still open—in which they and their crews had taken cover. Whoever it was had also predicted that there would be, as there was, a not especially small logistics area, completely defenseless from an armored assault, perhaps a kilometer and a half away.

Reilly thought about it for a moment, then felt his exultation drop like the liquid of a leaking bucket. "On the other hand, you, while I am sure the best sword ever made, are not getting through the armor of a T-72. And I have no antitank weapons."

"Don't you have hand grenades?" she asked.

"Yes . . . four of them, and eight more in the Hummer. But those won't . . ."

"They will get through open hatches," she cut him off. "And in just a minute, those hatches will open. We have to time it right, though. Go stash a couple more grenades about your person, just in case. I can watch them through their own tanks."

"Are they intelligent, like you?" he asked, jogging over to the vehicle and taking two more hand grenades from the back, along with a couple of smokes, the handles of which he twisted around his load-bearing harness. The explosive ones, including the four he already had on his person, he used his fingers to straighten the pins of, while leaving the safety clips still attached.

"No, not really," she replied, as he sorted out his armaments. "They're not old enough to have been given souls and become *Tsukumogami*. And they're not nearly beautiful enough to be *Yorishiro* and attract their own *Kami*. Worse . . . well . . . I've listened to your side's tanks. They're stupid but their hearts are in the right place. Sort of like a pack of hunting dogs: 'Letusatem-letusatem! Ahoooowwww!' These tanks? They're all about bribes and buggery and not trusting each other because their humans don't really trust each other. It's not even thought; it's just an aura and some thin instincts. They'll neither help nor hinder anyone. Before you ask, no, I can't control them, but I can listen through them."

Reilly hadn't shown any hesitation about taking on four tanks. He figured, *They're probably on radio silence, but even if not, the gunners won't have access to the radios, only the commanders will. I will need to kill the tank commanders first on each tank. And they're*—he wracked his brain for an old memory—*ah, yes; they're on the right side of a Soviet-built tank, the gunner's on the left.*

"You really are crazy, aren't you?" Audrey said. "Listen, Reilly-chan; I can't control the other weapons, either. You may be killed, so it is your decision whether to attack or not. And I will be sorry to lose you. Still, it's your decision; I can help you, if you do."

"You mean you can control me?" he asked.

"No, not control. I can *help*. It will be like it is in the dream training. I can make your eye sharper, assist in hand-eye coordination, make your strikes truer and maybe even a little stronger. You will think faster. I can help you time your steps and your leaps. I cannot get you atop the rear deck of the last tank, though; that you will have to accomplish yourself."

"Fair enough," he said, laying his back once again against the concrete just his side of the corner. "Tell me when."

Audrey sounded very sincere, saying, "I am very proud of you, more than I have words for. Draw me . . . and we go . . . right about . . . now."

Leaving her saya, her scabbard, propped against the wall, sword in hand, Reilly ducked low and leapt

out from around the corner. He took in the entire
scene in something a higher ranking and much more
famous officer of a couple of centuries earlier would
have called a *coup d'oeil*. Almost all the enemy were
in their tanks, with the engines started and roaring,
but hadn't begun to move. They were all facing front.
At the front of the column, a single officer scampered
up the side of his T-72 with commendable agility. He,
too, however, was looking forward.

I've been looking forward to this all my life, Reilly
thought, racing for the rearmost tank. He was racing, he knew, but suddenly everything slowed down
to about a quarter speed, then became slower still.
His vision also narrowed to a small fraction of his
usual field of view, though he didn't think that was
Audrey's doing. The tank-climbing officer to the front
seemed to become nearly a statue, so slowly did he
move. Even the spots of worst vibration on the tanks
had ceased to be the slight blur one usually saw and,
instead, they could be seen moving up and down, and
not all that briskly.

Reaching the rear of the rear tank, Reilly put his
left foot on the downward curve of the steel towing
cable, while grasping the upper part of it with his
free hand. Pushing with the foot and pulling with the
hand, he began to rise. His right foot kicked down at
the sharp pintle that held the cable's end, adding to
the force of the move. He rose over the back of the
tank almost as if levitating, then began what seemed
to be a slow descent. When he landed, the rear deck
felt like a surfboard cutting along the waves.

The enemy tank commander and gunner, both
facing forward, felt nothing of the landing; Reilly's

little bit of kinetic energy counted as minor against
the power of the tank's V-12. He held Audrey in his
right hand, parallel to the left side of his body, and
perpendicular to the ground, Reilly crouched, right
foot forward and left behind that and at a right angle.
He shuffled forward one step, two steps, three. He
twisted right slightly, on the ball of his right foot,
such that he was facing the tank commander who, still
oblivious, faced front, his hand resting on the 12.7mm
machine gun that served for both antipersonnel work
and air defense.

The sword lashed out, though to Reilly's eye and
mind it seemed to move as if through a thick liquid
medium. He saw it pass through the spiraling cable
that connected the commander's helmet and the
communication system. The cable parted, the ends
separating as the sword first touched, then began to
slice through the tank commander's neck, under the
padded mesh helmet. It didn't even pause or slow
for the vertebrae, but went through as if through
softened lard. The sword was all the way through, the
last thread of flesh parted and the head beginning to
fly off to the right, before the blood began to gush.
When it came, a brief but intense upward spray of
deep crimson, Reilly didn't even notice. He was already
recovering and reorienting to swing at the gunner.

"Banzai!" shrieked Audrey, in semiorgasmic glee.
"Kill! Kill! Kill!"

The gunner's head parted from his body as easily
as had his chief's. Without looking to see where the
head even landed, Reilly ran between the two now-
headless corpses sticking above the turret, right foot
slamming off the rear small-arms ammunition can,

using his left hand to slap the gunner's hatch, in front
of the late gunner's still-shuddering chest, in order to
add speed in his passage. Over the turret he went,
then down to the deck behind the driver. The driver
was already reaching up to swing closed his hatch, not
because he was aware of Reilly's already murderous
spree but because the tank commander had told him
to moments before. Reilly raised the sword halfway
to the vertical, then slashed downward, splitting the
driver's brain neatly in two, Audrey passing very precisely through the nose and between the eyes.

"Oooo, that felt good. More!"

He leapt then, leapt from the glacis of the last
tank in the column and onto the rear deck of the
next to last. His sword was not fully recovered from
slaughtering the previous driver. Indeed, it was pointed
nearly straight forward. He drove it, therefore, into and
through the neck of the right-hand man on this tank,
then twisted it and pulled it out with a slash to the
left; Audrey's peerless edge didn't need any built-up
momentum to slice her way free. The momentum of
that, however, carried the sword out of line to kill the
gunner. No matter, Reilly did a full three-hundred-
and-sixty-degree pivot, then took the gunner's head
off as neatly as the last gunner's. Once again, he ran
forward and, once again, he slapped the left-hand
hatch to propel himself.

This driver, still unaware of Reilly's assault, had his
hatch almost half closed, his head below hatch level.
Another head-bisecting slash was right out. Reilly
twisted the sword until the point was down and the
handle, the tsuka, toward heaven, then knelt forcefully as his arm drove the sword's point downward,

down into the juncture of the driver's neck and right shoulder, down into the spine. The driver shuddered, reaching to grasp the unseen source of his anguish. Slashing forward to free the sword, even as he pulled it upward, he severed the fingers of both the driver's frantically grasping hands, then the right carotid, setting the writhing wretch to spraying his life's blood all over the right side of the compartment. The driver, perhaps not quite dead yet, slumped forward against the ring inside his hatch.

Before arising from his kneel, Reilly took a fraction of a split moment to glance forward at the next tank. Still not a clue but...

"The driver of that one has closed his hatch," Audrey informed him. "You will need to use a grenade or, better, two of them, after we dispose of the turret crew."

Only distantly aware that the sword couldn't actually see him, Reilly nodded. *Risky*, he thought at the sword. *If the ammunition goes it will be most unpleasant to be anywhere near the tank.*

"Survivable?" she asked. "I don't know anything about things like that; my time was before. It was a more civilized time."

Maybe survivable. If the propellant of only one or two rounds go, and they're kinetic, no problem, except for anyone in the tank. If a high-explosive round goes, maybe a big problem because it will set off all the rest. The concussion will be a bitch, but a turret falling from a height of several hundred meters would be worse.

No matter; let's go. I think the tank's beginning to move.

It had begun to move, but in the fraction of a second that took up their "conversation" it hadn't moved more than a few inches. He was still able to make the leap from the glacis on which he'd knelt to the next tank's rear deck without any serious effort. He wasn't sure it would have been so easy without what he felt was Audrey's coaxing of his muscles and aid with his timing. In any case, he landed on the deck of the moving tank, spending a half a second of real time adjusting himself to its movement. Slash, turn, slash, and commander and gunner both died in great sprays of blood, which arose and then gracefully fell, baptizing the tank's turret in red. He put Audrey down for a moment on the empty spot on the turret between the hatches, then took two grenades from the forward positions on his ammunition pouches. He flicked each safety clip off with his thumbs, then locked index fingers through the rings. Pulling his arms apart, he withdrew the rings. Then he simultaneously released the spoons, which flew off in surreal slow motion.

No sense in counting, my sense of time is gone. No matter, either, since I'm not going to cook these off.

Having released the spoons, he immediately pushed more than dropped the grenades, one down each hatch of the turret, each in a space left by the body in the hatch. Then, grabbing Audrey, he held her high to avoid slashing himself, jumped off the tank, fell and rolled. Only then, and only somewhat distantly, did he become aware of the buildings to either side, buildings his narrowed vision hadn't allowed him to see.

He turned to look at the tank. Both headless occupants of the turret were rising on pillars of flame.

Oh, shit. Reilly turned back and ran for the shelter

of the nearest alleyway, reaching it moments before a massive blast knocked him face first to the ground. He rolled over onto his back to be greeted with the sight of a nearly fifteen-ton turret flying end over end through the air, as if under the control of some mad frying-pan juggler. Mesmerized, stunned, his vision still effectively slowed by Audrey, the turret seemed to take forever to reach apogee, before beginning to fall... directly onto the spot where he lay.

"Fuuuuck!" Reilly used anything that would touch the ground to propel himself forward, feet, hands, earlobes, lips... anything. He even used Audrey's tsuka, once, eliciting a deeply offended "ouch."

Sorry.

"Never mind; just get that last tank."

Right. Confident that he'd gotten out from under the falling turret's footprint, Reilly asked, *What's going on in the lead tank, if you can say?*

The sword didn't answer immediately. Then she said, "The commander of the tank and the unit knows that the one behind him blew up. Hard to miss that, right? He doesn't seem to know why. He's stopped and taken cover, as best he can. He's trying frantically to get communication with the first two we took out, and doesn't understand why they're not answering. There's a dense cloud of smoke from the last one that he can't see through, either."

While Reilly was digesting that, the turret slammed into the ground, at the mouth of the alley, raising a cloud of dust and causing a minor tremor.

"Neat," he observed.

"Yes," said Audrey, "you're insane. Did I ever mention that I like insane?"

Never mind, let's go get that tank.

"That just became easier," she said. "The commander left his tank and is walking this way. Shall this be sporting or otherwise?"

With a gunner and driver still in a functioning tank? Don't be silly.

"Right, unsporting it is."

Reilly left the alley in which he'd taken shelter. He stepped over the still-smoking turret, and took a position behind the burning tank, more or less enveloped in its smoke. The desert day had been hot, but with the heat from the flames and radiating from the superheated metal, it was nigh unto unbearable. He bore it anyway and crouched down, waiting for his next victim to make an appearance. A strange odor assailed his nostrils, something like pork ribs left too long on the barbecue. He assumed it was the remains of the driver, since he knew that the other two members of the crew hadn't stayed in the tank.

Nothing personal, he directed at the driver's spirit. *And I hope it was quick and as clean as possible.*

"And that's another reason why I love you," said Audrey. "Oh . . . look left."

Reilly looked, and saw the strangest damned thing, a pistol, grasped in a hand, slowly emerging from the smoke. He flicked the sword into an upward arc, severing the hand and raising a horrifying shriek. A body, still very much alive, fell out of the smoke, remaining hand reaching for the gushing stump. Before the body reached the ground it was missing a head from the return stroke. Before the head hit the ground, Reilly felt and then heard the passage of heavy machine gun fire, all around him, spattering the street and ricocheting off the moribund tank's hot armor. One bullet passed between his legs, dangerously close to some important matters.

"You have a use for those," said Audrey, "even if I don't. I think you had best move."

Reilly's answer was to take the two smoke grenades he'd brought along hooked to his harness, pull the rings, face in the direction of the hand and headless body on the ground, and toss them into street. Smoke began to billow, adding to the screen from the burning hulk of the tank. A massive burst of fire tore through the screen even as he turned the other way and ran for all he was worth for the alley. He made it and entered just moments before there came a distant blast, followed too quickly even for him to distinguish, had he been looking, by a second much-closer blast and the disintegration of a corner of a building framing the mouth of the alley. The spall of mud bricks from the corner barely missed him. Even so, the blast stunned him once again, even as it sent him and the sword flying.

Arising from the dirt and gravel, Reilly thought, *Fucking Russki tanks and the people who use them generally have high-explosive up the spout. I guess the gunner's figured out what happened to the other tanks and his boss.*

"Seems likely," agreed the sword, "but probably not in any accurate detail. I mean, who would suspect that *I* or anyone like me could be a part of it? The gunner ordered the driver to move the tank, by the way. Is *lif yameen* turn left or turn right?"

Not a clue. Sorry.

"No matter, really," she said, in his mind, "because the tank's turned completely around and is coming here."

And now is when I really need an AT-4, Reilly said.

"Oh, ye of little faith. Climb to the roof of this building and keep low when you get there."

Reilly saw a set of steps that led upward. He followed them up until they came to a roof above the second floor. Crouching low, he moved toward the end of the roof. Below him, he could hear the roar of a powerful diesel, growing louder as it drew closer. Since he couldn't see the tank, even when he was only a dozen feet from the edge of the roof, he assumed it was below. A sudden increase in the diesel's roar confirmed this.

Death from above? he asked the sword.

"You have a better idea?"

Yes, a slightly better one. He pulled another grenade from the side of an ammo pouch, then unsnapped the retaining strap on the last one held there. Again he flicked off the safety clip. He didn't let go of the sword this time, but pulled the pin with a finger from his sword hand. He slid forward carefully, stopping when his eye caught the edge of the tank's rear deck. *Take me off the time-dilation trick you've been using.* He felt a moment of disorientation then realized, once he saw smoke rising normally, that he could count again and be sure of the count. He almost giggled, remembering, *"Three shall be the number thou shalt count, and the number of the counting shall be three. Four shalt thou not count, neither count thou two, excepting that thou then proceed to three. Five is right out."*

He released the spoon on the grenade, heard the crack as the spring-loaded striker found the primer, and counted off, aloud, "One thousand . . . two thousand . . . three thousand." On "three thousand" he flipped the grenade over the roof's edge. It went off almost immediately.

Time dilation back on! Almost instantly, the rising smoke slowed to where it was barely moving. Reilly stepped briskly to the edge of the roof, looked down, took Audrey in both hands, and jumped for the turret of the tank below.

The last enemy gunner was hurt by the grenade, bleeding—though not badly—from perhaps a dozen small holes and a couple of larger ones. He was a bit stunned, but not to the point of insensibility. His left hand was still on the machine gun. The grenade—he thought it had to have been a grenade—had come from somewhere above him. Whoever threw it was going to follow. The machine gun, the lighter of the two carried atop the tank, couldn't elevate enough, he knew. With his right hand he drew his pistol and, looking up as he pointed it up, he saw a demon wielding a sword falling down upon him. Screaming with terror, the gunner still managed to point the pistol in the generally right direction, getting off two shots. He didn't know it—indeed, he would never know it—but one connected, passing through Reilly's lower abdomen and exiting his upper back.

Reilly, for his part, felt the bullet strike, then felt—worse than he'd ever imagined it would be—the internal shock wave and rippling of his inner organs as the lump of lead and bronze made its way through him and out of him. The rippling continued for some time, and it seemed a very long time, after the bullet had passed. It was sickening, which made him grasp Audrey more tightly in his hands. She cried out, a cry which almost made him loosen the grip. Then he realized she was upset at his injury and that there was no way any grip of his could cause her body any pain.

He continued to fall for a long fraction of a second. At the moment his feet hit the turret he slashed down, splitting the unfortunate gunner from crown to about midchest. Reilly continued to fall though, his legs unable to hold him upright. First his ankles buckled. Then his knees slammed painfully into the turret's unyielding steel. He began to fall over to one side, but the sword, still firmly gripped and firmly lodged in the dead gunner, held him upright. The gunner's body gave before the grip did. Reilly fell over to his side, then rolled onto his back. He thought he felt, rather than heard, the driver's hatch swing open, then heard a screaming man running off into the town on foot.

"Am I dying, Audrey?" he asked.

"I think so." She effectively wept. "I do not sense help is near, and your wound . . . it is bad. But, oh, you were marvelous. This was pure beauty. You will live in the legends of your army forever for this."

"No," he said, firmly, "no, I won't. The Army will sweep this under a rug, bury it in red tape, and do anything rather than admit that it has people like me in it. I am quite sure that all these tanks will turn out to have been destroyed by a combination of aerial attack and the latest in high-tech wizardry. All on the orders of a general in need of a medal to make another star. Surely that will be it."

"Is that so? Then you will live forever in me," she said. "Grab hold of my tsuka. Yes, use both hands. Lay the blade along your cheek. Now close your eyes and sleep, yes, sleep and dream."

❖   ❖   ❖

Reilly dreamt of a scene of impossibly steep and beautiful mountains, real looking, yet with a touch that said an artist had designed them. They looked familiar, even if impossible, but he could not quite remember where he had seen them before. The grass under his sandaled feet was greener than any he could recall ever having seen. The sun . . . he couldn't see it . . . and yet there was a sun's warmth on his face.

Ahead of him, on a blanket spread upon the grass, knelt a beautiful Asian girl, her age impossible to guess. She sorted various bowls, containing what he sensed were sauces and delicacies. He didn't need to know her costume to know she was Japanese.

"Hello, Audrey," he said.

"Hello, Reilly-chan," she replied, looking up. "Welcome home."

Five weeks later

> Posthumous Citation to Accompany the award
> of the Medal of Honor . . .

Deep in the bowels of the five-sided puzzle palace in Arlington, Virginia, the general read aloud: ". . . his extraordinary heroism and determination, against the most fearsome odds, are in the highest traditions of the military and reflect great credit upon himself and the United States . . ."

He shook his head and looked up, asking his aide-de-camp, "What idiot wrote this shit?"

Without batting an eye the aide responded, "Colonel Tomlinson, commanding the brigade to which he was attached."

Pursing his lips and putting the citation aside, the general drafted a quick note on Army stationery, to the effect that the unfortunate Tomlinson had demonstrated a lack of political insight rendering him completely unfit for promotion or any measure of increased responsibility, and suggesting that it might be best if he retired from the service forthwith. Handing it to the aide, the general said, "Make sure this gets into Tomlinson's file before the next promotion board. And file-thirteen this citation."

The aide looked puzzled. "Why trash it, sir? Shouldn't we just downgrade it to a Silver Star or, at worst, a Bronze Star with V device?"

"No," the general said. "I won't hold this against you, this once, but let me explain. If we award anything then the incident will have officially happened and the award certificate will be out there somewhere. Given those two things, it might be noticed. If noticed, someone might wonder why not a Medal of Honor, as in a more militaristic, less sensitive, and less aesthetic age, the late captain clearly would deserve. In that case, it might be upgraded, in which case—rather, in the first place of which case—the media will start screaming "Atrocity!" and "War crime!" even though it wasn't, and, in the second place, we, the Army, will come under close and unfortunate scrutiny to determine why we failed to rid ourselves of people like the late captain, long ere now.

"Note well: Had he managed to save even one life by taking out those tanks I could probably have let it go through, had we finessed the citation and made 'ancient sword' into 'modern antitank weapon.' But it wasn't about saving life. It was about attacking and taking life. That, our ever-so-sensitive and caring political masters cannot tolerate."

"I see," said the aide. "Thank you, sir, for the lesson." *Though the upshot of that lesson is that I will not shred and trash this recommendation. Rather, I will bring it home and keep it very secure and leave it to my heirs, if it takes that long. The day may come when we're not a cabal of political whores and can recognize the realities of the world again. When ... if, that day ever comes, our grandchildren may need the example of Reilly.*

That bearer had been thoroughly mad, but she appreciated and respected him. He had felt her presence, and taken her back to battle. He craved war, and his culture denied it to him. It was tragic, but with her help he had succeeded.

She really had no idea what all those things he'd said to her meant. Even if she could grasp more than emotion, a gulf separated her from these weapons that flung metal in every way possible. There was also something rather disturbing in how he saw her personified. She understood it was what he had needed, but it was not who she was.

But how he had fought! Such ferocity, dedication and purpose.

She returned with his other, lesser possessions in a box, and made her way through Reilly's sister to a cousin's wife's brother. She thought. It was very confusing. However, the new bearer had been a warrior in that same conflict, and he knew how to care for a sword. He had her professionally cleaned and sharpened. She retained hope.

She could still hear Reilly's voice, wishing her comfort and battle.

—∿—

The Day the Tide Rolled In

Michael Z. Williamson and Leo Champion

James Chesterson scanned the horizon from the deck of the *Verboom Astrid* dockside at the end of the pier, just before the floating extension at Sulawan. He was *Verboom Astrid*'s electrical engineer, in charge of everything from radar to navigation equipment to network security. Anything that flowed electrons was his job.

It's changed, he thought, from when he'd first seen the place. Ten years ago Sulawan had been just another large, barely inhabited island in the Indonesian archipelago. Larger than most, but still one of thousands like it. Then Marcus Tani, the billionaire founder and executive of the Tancorp conglomerate, had bought the place, at first apparently just as a personal vacation spot.

At first Tancorp had been one more restaurant chain, just with some unusual ethnic choices. The conglomerate now had pieces in just about every industry, operated globally, had its shares listed on three stock exchanges.

Sulawan, for its part, had grown as well. Tani had moved some company management operations to the island along and built a residence, and found that other Western companies were interested in the same thing; a secure island base in a chaotic region. He'd happily leased space for them, and support industries—hotels, restaurants, the first of several casinos—had followed.

A private tropical island big enough for hotels and casinos became a cash cow once the corporate world had been clued in on being able to hold secure business meetings and functions, private shindigs, and take the tax losses. It wasn't as wild as occasional articles made it out to be, but it did offer discretion for the occasional drunken faux pas, and the press were not welcome, which was why they claimed it was everything it wasn't. They claimed hookers, drugs, ganglords and every depravity imaginable. Chesterson figured that was ten percent fact, twenty percent exaggeration, and the rest pure BS to sell headlines.

When Indonesia started to collapse in the late 2030s, Sulawan had already been on its way to becoming another Hong Kong or Singapore, a thriving capitalist city-state. Floods of refugees had followed; Chesterson had seen busy boat cities on either side of the ship as they nosed through the channel.

Chesterson was a practical sailor. He had been a practical Marine. Sulawan was a viable port with a well-built new harbor. It had good security, and offered reasonably priced on-shore entertainment for sailors, with decent cops and treatment. It was one of the ship's regular stops, and he enjoyed it.

Now, though, the entire archipelago was a war zone. Java and Aceh had a major conflict between them, and stops at either Banda or Jakarta had become sketchy. One stayed aboard, and the ship sometimes had an element of Gurkhas to prevent boarders and occasional pirates.

This might be the last port call by Verboom shipping; the markets on Sulawan were booming but supply through Indonesia was drying up, and he'd been fairly certain that their last pickup, metal stock for a ship builder here, was going to be the last that that mill was likely to produce, at least for a while. The entire nation—former nation—was a shambles, and until there was a working economy and secure sea lanes, he wasn't sure anyone was going to risk ships or transfer. For that matter, he wasn't sure how long the production facilities were going to remain intact.

In the news, though, the Javanese were turning what remained of their navy onto this tiny island. He'd just seen the advisory to all ships and crew to remain aboard, and guaranteed their safety if they did so. Java intended to "secure the rogue province" and then take over port operations. On another feed, someone's drone footage showed a frigate and a large ferry that was being used as an ersatz troop transport. They were west of here, not far offshore.

He liked Sulawan's people. There was a spirit, here, of constructive hustling you just didn't see many places these days. The inhabitants had come here to make something for themselves, and by God they were going to. Everyone had a side project they were working on. People were *building* things here.

Besides, there were families here, and children, and he had no doubt the invading force was going to rape and slaughter most of them.

It wasn't his island, but there were some things a man couldn't sit back and watch.

He reviewed an earlier video again. It showed Javanese troops "liberating" one of the other small islands. Unlike Sulawan, it was mostly native villages with some small local factories churning out cheap parts for assembly elsewhere. The smuggled video carried a "sensitive content" warning. Even to his old eye, it was rough.

Given the money and industry tied up here, he figured the Javanese would fuel jealous rage with stolen booze and violate every decency known to man. And that was assuming their dictator Jalan Jaksa hadn't ordered them to. The man was as bad or worse as several of the previous century's nutjobs.

James had drunk beer here, played with the local kids here, smiled at the casino girls as they dealt honest cards. There was no way he could stay afloat, or sail away, and leave them to that fate.

It was going to be his war, too.

He returned to his cabin and changed from his coveralls to a tan pocketed shirt and cargo pants, and his favorite old pair of walking boots. Then he took a case from under the bunk, gripped it comfortingly, and headed up to the cabin marked CAPTAIN—M. OLESEN. He knocked and waited for an answer.

Captain Olesen called, "Enter."

He stepped inside and said, "Sir, I need to go ashore for a few hours."

"Where are you off to, James?" Olesen asked. It sounded casual, but Olesen was quite serious. He was former Royal Danish Navy, very professional, and had been in these waters quite a bit.

Chesterson said, "Sir, I'd really rather not answer that question this morning."

Olesen looked at him, looked across the pier, and back.

"You're on your own, you understand."

He replied, "Yes, sir. See you in a bit."

"If we have to leave..." Olesen hinted.

"I guess I beg the company to consider the circumstances."

Olesen said, "If so, I can put in a word for you."

"Thank you, sir."

He strode briskly along the pier, watching swell lap gently at the shore, wondering what the hell he was doing, and in fact, what he was going to do. At fifty and nevermind years old, he wasn't as tough as he used to be, or as spry as the youngsters galloping past in front of him. But he was old and determined, and that was better in the long run than wind that was usually wasted in boasting.

At the pier gate, he slowed and waved to the security guard, who probably would speak English. The man already had body armor and his rifle was on a rack next to him, loaded. He looked rather nervous all by himself.

James inquired, "Excuse me, but where would I find one of your military units or the armory?"

"Why do you ask?" the man replied. He sounded Malay, but his English was excellent.

"I wish to volunteer."

With a wide-eyed stare that said Chesterson was crazy, the man pointed.

"A block that way is HQ. Supply and the armory are on the far side."

"Thank you, sir."

Well, that part had been easy.

There were lots of people running to that building, and running from it, and at least the ones running from it had weapons. They were in small elements that meant some sort of organization. He just wasn't sure what training they had.

They were multicultural to an extreme—Malays, Indonesians, Chinese, Europeans and Americans, some looked South American, African, Indian and Southeast Asian. They did seem to know how to carry rifles, at least.

He reached the corner and turned along the building. There was an open bay door, and he joined the line of arriving men and some women. He took a deep breath. This was a turning point.

He was going to need lots of attitude. Supply clerks everywhere tended to be officious and wrapped up in red tape. He reached the door and ducked inside between two young, serious-looking troops who were clutching at rifles and helmets. They were panting as hard as he was as they headed out. At least he had exertion as an excuse. It had been a long walk.

That uniform seemed to indicate a senior NCO.

"Sergeant, I'm James Chesterson, Gunnery Sergeant Retired, US Marines." He held out his retired ID card and his crew card. "I'm volunteering to assist your forces. Please issue me a weapon and tell me where I can be of assistance."

The sergeant looked at his ID three ways, and almost smirked. Chesterson didn't appreciate that at all.

The man said, "I don't think so, sir." He spoke perfect British English.

James put on his gunny persona and said, "Son,

you don't have time to quibble. This is a war, I've got experience, and I bet five drinks and a bar girl of your choice most of these kids don't."

The sergeant shook his head. "Sorry."

"Then let me talk to whoever's in charge, please."

Right then, a middle-aged American stepped through from the rear. US insignia, a first lieutenant, but that hopefully meant he had military experience.

The LT said, "What the hell's the problem, Faris?"

He gave the sergeant this, the man had good bearing.

The sergeant braced up, turned to the LT and said, "Sir, there's an American ex-Marine here who's now a merchant sailor. He wants to help. He wants a weapon." He looked put upon, confused, and slightly amused.

"Yes, I'm an American merchant seaman," Chesterson said. He held his card out for the LT to look at. "But I'm a *retired* US Marine. The only *ex*-Marine is a *dead* Marine. You've got civilians in trouble, you've got a shortage of manpower, and I'm here. Now please issue me a fucking rifle! Sir."

The lieutenant reached out and took the ID card. He glanced it over, his head swiveled to Chesterson, to the card, and back to the NCO.

"Sergeant," the LT said with a toss of his head, looking tired and amused.

"Yes, sir?"

The lieutenant smiled faintly and said, "Issue the Marine a fucking rifle."

"Yes, sir!" the sergeant replied with no hesitation.

The sergeant grabbed a G36 very smartly, locked the bolt open, checked it, and passed it through the cage. James took it. The sergeant followed that with a pack of four magazines and a satchel with boxes of ammo.

The lieutenant turned back to Chesterson. "They need someone to help some augmentees dig a position. I'm sending you to see a Sergeant Ibson. He'll get you placed, you show his augies what they need to know about digging in. You can dig in, right?"

"Yeah, I have some experience." Chesterson smiled back. It was a thin smile. But the officers here knew how to take responsibility and make decisions. That was one very bright sign. His smile was genuine.

He checked the weapon and satchel, which was a random commercial day pack, slung it over his shoulder so he could load as he moved, and turned for the door.

"Go west along the Shore Road," the LT said as he walked out the door. He had a slight limp. "Sergeant Ibson will be about two klicks down, where the harbor ends and the beach starts."

"Ibson. Will do, sir. I didn't catch your name."

"Griffiths, late of the US Army Artillery."

"Good to meet you, sir." He saluted.

The return salute was crisp and professional.

"And you, Gunny. Thank you."

The Sulawan troops were western or western trained, decisive and disciplined. If for no other reasons, they deserved to beat the rabble trying to invade them.

He had a rifle and a sword, comfy boots and a water bottle, and a name of a contact. He didn't have body armor, commo, or anything else twenty-first century.

He realized now that being American wasn't going to cut any knots if he was captured. There were quite a few Americans resident here, and he was arguably a mercenary. He couldn't imagine how this little island was going to fight off Java, and even if they did today, there'd be more Javanese tomorrow. A million or so.

Hopefully someone would intercede before the next wave. India. China. Australia. The Philippines had an interest in keeping it stable. It was possible the UN or the US might even bother. Maybe. In the meantime, they had guts, some western veteran leadership, and James Chesterson.

It would have been a fine tropical day if he wasn't hiking all over. He walked along the road, and the port rapidly curved back toward the shore. That taillike spit from the island was entirely covered in concrete. Here, though, the shore was built, then beyond the road was raw jungle that hadn't yet been exploited. It screened the industrial sector from the wealthy cottages up the hill, and the hotels and resorts around the coast.

Yes, there was a unit where the beach started. They weren't exactly "digging in." There were concrete bollards and walls to use as cover. Very conveniently placed bollards and walls.

Someone was thinking ahead, he thought approvingly. That was a plus.

"Sergeant Ibson!" he shouted.

"Yes?" one of the party asked, turning. He was an English speaker.

"Gunnery Sergeant Chesterson, US Marines, now a volunteer. Lieutenant Griffiths at Supply said I should report to you." He held out his card again.

Ibson glanced at the card. "Very well. Did he send you for something specific?"

"No, Sergeant, but I'm experienced if you want to assign me to anything."

Ibson turned. "Banbang, get Sergeant Chesterson some armor and a helmet. At least a hard hat. Stripe it so we know who he is." Ibson's accent had a cant to it. Dakotas or Canada possibly?

One of the troops replied, "Yes, Sergeant!" sounding very British, and ran off.

Ibson turned back and said, "We're using phones because we don't have enough radios. We do have a pretty solid, reliable network and an encryption app."

"Gotcha." Chesterson pulled his out, and tapped with Ibson to swap numbers and load the app. Ibson then took James's phone and did something to authorize the app.

"So they issued you a rifle. What's in the case?"

"A sword I inherited from a crazy uncle." Actually, it came from his sister from her husband's cousin, he thought, but what did the details matter? He opened the case, unzipped the fleece bag, and held up the sword.

Ibson glanced it over and nodded. He had a large bowie, damned near a short sword itself, hung off the left side of his armor. The others had knives, too. It was Indonesia. Everyone had a bolo or equivalent.

"We're holding here, because we don't know where an attack is going to be. If they're avoiding the harbor, it's probably not going to be right here but further west. That makes us reserve. But we won't know. We're using the hard cover here, but I would like to detach a handful across the street into the trees for possible crossfire. Can you do that?"

"Absolutely." The trees would offer more concealment, some cover, and plenty of mask over how many troops were actually there.

"I'll send three...two with you. Skelton! Malik! Go with Sergeant Chesterson. You're across the road."

Banbang came back with an old Kevlar helmet and a police ballistic vest with some sort of plate on the chest. Chesterson tried not to grimace. That wasn't much protection, and was a lot of overhead weight, but it was better than nothing, and they'd dug it up for him.

"Thank you," he said. He threw on the vest, donned the helmet, and snugged the strap. Good enough for now, he could adjust it later. There were convenient velcro straps to stick his sword up the side, like the machete mount on a ruck. Thank God it was a short sword or that wouldn't work.

The shoulder and chest of the tan vest had three chevrons hand markered in black. He was a sergeant.

The troops had a variety of G36s, Sigs, FNs and AR patterns. They had common mags and ammo at least.

Skelton was American, short, round and female, but looked sturdy. "Jacqueline," she said. Malik looked Indian, shorter but fit. "Mohammed." So he was probably Pakistani. They nodded and followed him.

There was a surprising amount of traffic on the road, lots of it crew returning to ships. Quite a bit went the other way, both cars and bicycles. The second wave of high school kids on bikes with target rifles didn't surprise him. It wasn't as if they weren't going to suffer if they didn't fight.

What the fuck did I just get myself into?

He hopped across a ditch and waded through thick tropical undergrowth up into the trees. They were mostly in scrub, really, with an ugly mix of palm and mangrove with lanias all over.

He expected nothing to happen for a while, and he was right. They sat and waited, knee deep in undergrowth that was crawling with bugs. He sweated and got clammy under the armor and his scalp itched even with short hair. After several minutes, his phone chimed. He switched it to vibrate as he flashed the message.

Ibson: *see movement on map.*

The attached image was an aerial shot. There was that ersatz amphibious craft at about nine o'clock to their seven o'clock. There were some smaller craft along the beach—an actual beach, near the Hilton Resort Sulawan. Fuzzy patches were probably troops reaching the shore.

He tried to estimate how many it might be. Hundreds possibly. Dozens certainly. At least a couple of hundred. Assume small arms with some organic support weapons, and could they get supporting gunfire or CAS?

That latter was answered when a howling whistle and a series of five explosions sounded further west. He didn't feel any tremors, so they were small shells, likely not larger than an old five-inch. That had to be the frigate. Oto Melara 76mm or a similar deck gun?

Why shell over here? he wondered.

Another text buzzed through.

Arty fire to cut us off from supporting. Have to advance through it. Approaching treeline with squad. Acknlg.

He texted back, *OK*. It made sense to text when time allowed. Silent, more lucid, kept a record for AAR or even to refresh events.

There was movement at the ditch, and the rest of

the squad came silently into the trees. Ibson appeared ahead of him, shifting fronds quietly.

"We're going to use the ditch to advance. We may use the road if it's—"

Another shell interrupted them.

"—clear, but I'd prefer not to be seen so they don't escalate fire. They're alternating both sides of their assault."

"Got it. Wade and cover as needed. What's their objective?"

"They're probably trying to go up the hill to Government House, and this way toward the port control."

James said, "Makes sense. I'll follow. Any instructions?" He only had vague notions of the local map.

Ibson asked, "Have you been in combat?"

"Briefly." It had been the tail end of Iraq, but yes.

Ibson nodded and frowned sheepishly. "Then I need your input to make sure I'm acting straight. Text or yell depending on urgency. You bring the second fire team, I'll lead."

"Got it."

"This is Lawrie and Katirci." An American and a Turk. Skinny and broad.

"Hi." "Hello."

"Hi. Chesterson. Follow me then," he said.

Ibson disappeared and the others moved out one at a time. He followed as the last of the first team slipped away. His element followed. They moved in good order, spaced out, using the tree line for disruption. They were definitely professionally trained. Some might be green, but they were trained green and expecting to fight.

The ditch varied from knee-deep to shallow, mowed

grass. Every thirty seconds or so, a random shell dropped down on the gravel of the beach, or once onto the road, and they'd drop. Twice he heard fragments whiz into the trees. It was harassing fire, but they didn't want to lose effectives if it was avoidable.

Ahead was another divider between this gravel area, which was marked off with survey sticks—Chesterson had seen a sign by the road announcing INDUSTRIAL DEVELOPMENT COMING SOON—and the beginning of the commercial zone.

Again there were heavy bollards and walls. It was almost as if the entire coast had been designed with defense in mind. He wanted to shake the engineer's hand.

Buzz. Ibson: *Another element will be crossing in front of us.*

He texted: *R*. Then he realized they might not get the abbreviation and sent *Rgr*.

The element sounded like six to eight men, and ran along the road, then to the far side.

A couple of minutes later there was a rifle shot.

His phone buzzed, and he pulled it out, almost dropping it in the muck, then getting hold of it again.

Ibson: *Contact ahead, apparently a forward patrol. May be splitting along the coast.*

"Here we go," he muttered to himself. He gripped the rifle and hunched a bit more.

More shots sounded, interspersed, then some automatic fire.

The slow punctuation told him the Javanese were also well trained. No one was shooting without a clear target.

Another shell dropped on the road to their rear.

Hopefully, that naval gun wouldn't shell too closely to their own troops.

Ibson: *Cross and engage. NME should be back to us, coffee, boat, rstrnt.*

He spoke clearly without shouting as he read. "Element, we're crossing the street and engaging the enemy from the rear. With me."

He hoped at least the nearest had heard him as he squeezed between two trees and zigged across, helmet bouncing on his head.

He dove down behind a bollard and saw movement as others did the same. Good.

The fighting wasn't clear cut. That was an Indonesian uniform, though, on that guy, and he lined up a shot. And was he actually going to try to kill this guy before he'd even had a chance to commit any war crimes, over James's assumption of the conflict?

Yeah, he better.

He wasn't the only one. Four or five people shot in close succession, and the guy flopped, twitched and stopped.

There were shouts in Bahasa, and he recognized some cuss words and *"Lho!"* indicating surprise. Then sand and rocks started flying as a squad weapon opened up. He flinched behind his iron bollard and tried to pull himself in tighter.

Now what do I do? he wondered. *I can't wait here to die, I can't charge a weapon in use.*

But the bursts moved over.

Fuck it.

"Let's move!" he shouted as he rose to his knees and dove. He fired off a couple of bursts for suppression, took three driving steps and dropped back down at the edge of a boardwalk. The helmet whacked his spine painfully and he wished he had something more modern.

Now he understood the last text. There was a coffee shop, restaurant, and boat rental along here, and some little kiosks. There was also a Jav shooting at him from behind a decorative boulder between the boat rental and the restaurant.

A moment later he heard a shotgun blast, and the rifle fire stopped.

From the top window of the restaurant, someone shouted, "Got him!"

Well, shit.

He moved again, and a glance showed yes, most of the team were with him, one unaccounted for.

"Who's missing?" he called as he reached the building corner and slid flat to it with his rifle at high ready. He glanced at the windows, looking for reflections of anything.

Someone called, "Lawrie stayed in the trees. Says he's covering us."

He had no idea if Lawrie had any task beyond rifleman, or if he was covering or cowering. He shrugged to himself.

He realized he was grinning like an idiot. He'd had this rush before, and he missed it.

A bullet damned near took his head off, and he swung and snapped the trigger. His first round cracked against the Indo's body armor, his second ripped the guy's throat out. Then another round cracked close enough to make his right ear ring.

He threw himself against the restaurant door and tumbled in, ripping his shirt and grazing his left arm on the edge. It hadn't been latched. He shot out into the walk.

Someone came into the doorway, silhouetted, and he tightened on the trigger, realized it was Skelton, jerked the rifle to the side and shot just past her. The round made someone else duck, and Skelton turned and shot whoever it was point-blank.

Another Indo across the walk suddenly convulsed and dropped dead, his face half blown away.

"Who the fuck did that?" James asked. He rolled and carefully stood.

"Not us," Skelton said. She reached down and helped him to his feet with a heave.

Ibson appeared.

"Apparently one of our police staff. From their HQ," he said, pointing at a building half a klick away. James could barely see it through gaps in the awnings.

"Tell him thanks."

"Her. I did."

James asked, "What now?"

"We keep advancing. They were moving uphill toward Government House, and this way along the shore. Apparently, they expected the casinos and hotels to be safe."

"Oh?"

"Well, there aren't many guests, but we deputized hotel security if they wanted to be, and there's a platoon of ours there, and some of the boat people."

"What the heck are they armed with? The boat people?"

"Home-built pistols and shotguns, some ancient civilian stuff, and a bunch of barongs and clubs."

That would do it.

"This is one fucked up way to fight a war."

Ibson shrugged. "It's the only way we have. Are you fit to move?" He handed over a loaded STANAG magazine that would fit James's weapon. Looted, James assumed.

He took the mag and pocketed it.

"I am. I seem to have lost track of my team."

Skelton helped him out the door. He shook the woman off and strode alongside Ibson as the others fell into loose march. Katirci had an Ultimax squad weapon, looted from the Javanese.

Ibson said, "Malik is wounded but stable. The owner next door has him secure. They're both armed if anything else gets this far. Lawrie seems to have bailed on us. We'll deal with that later."

"Yeah." Deserting wasn't cool. If you couldn't serve, you shouldn't pretend.

They moved as one element, dispersed, along the tree line for some concealment, but not inside it. His boots were soaked and sand filled; he was scratched, bruised and exhausted; and he felt more alive than he did in any storm aboard ship.

You're too old to be an adrenaline junkie, he told himself.

Two loud, distant explosions rumbled over them.

"Outgoing," Ibson said.

James jogged forward and asked, "What do you have?"

"A couple of one-twenty-millimeter mortars, an old one-oh-five howitzer, some US Navy prototype thing they were trying to get working, and some homemade rockets."

That wasn't much, but it was better than nothing.

Barely. This place had an army with artillery, and a navy. Not bad for sixty-five square kilometers of resort and beach. Did they have an air wing?

They ducked in and out of the tree line and ditch. He looked back to make sure they weren't forming a snake of people who could be identified. Nope. They did know how to move.

He asked, "What happened to the other weapons from our engagement?"

Ibson said, "The Javanese gear? That was all taken by locals. They figure they're going to need it."

"I saw teenagers, too."

Ibson frowned. "You'll see preteens if this goes on. What choice do we have? The UN wants to 'reunite' Indonesia, Jaksa only wants to do that as dictator. The UN won't recognize Aceh. We don't have anywhere to go."

James said, "I understood Malaysia said they'd repatriate people to their home nations."

"If we were desperate and could get there. Most of the Asians can't risk that. And you're still here."

"I'm still here," he agreed.

Ibson said, "We made this our home. I could leave, but I can't leave my friends to die."

"Yeah, that was my thinking." What man could?

Then he was diving for cover. Someone had ranged them with a machine gun.

They were in another industrial section, though it was mostly pole barns and shacks rather than heavier buildings. On the other hand, the climate here really didn't require more.

In the growth next to him, Ibson said, "Looks like the battle came to us."

There were a lot of invading troops there, but it was clear they'd been hurt. Many were light on gear and ammo. There were obvious holes in squads. On the other hand, part of why it was apparent was the number of them with Ultimaxes, Minimis and FN MAG machine guns instead of, or as well as, rifles. There were grenade launchers, too.

James snuggled up to a low, concrete wall, then flinched as automatic fire started chewing into it. He rolled around until he was fully in the shadow of it. Damn that helmet. He found a drainage break, reached his rifle around and made a tiny profile as he took some careful shots. He got off three before a burst of incoming showered him with sand. He jerked back.

The others were shimmying into the nearest building. Really, staying dug in was the best choice. Between ditches and bollards, they had excellent cover, and the Javanese had to come to them. Without any fire support, the attacking infantry only had the machine guns, and hopefully limited ammo.

An explosion blew dirt and concrete from in front of the building.

Right, and some grenade launchers.

He made it to the edge of the wall, then sprinted for a bollard as more fire stirred the ground around him. They hadn't run out of ammo yet.

He dove, tucked and leaned around the bollard and waited. There. That one looked like a senior NCO, and he was low and moving, but pretty much straight at James. He aligned the sights and shot, missed. He tried slightly left and missed, slightly right and hit the man in the right collarbone.

Guessing the range, he moved the rear sight three

clicks right and figured it was good enough for now. He was finally battle sighted.

The others around him had started shooting when he had, and they weren't bad. That platoon was quickly losing capables to rifle fire and sand. They kept advancing, though. They might be afraid of something, but they weren't afraid of rifle fire.

In short order, everyone got inside the machine shop. If the staff were around, they were in hiding, and hopefully they'd be good for a few shots themselves, like the restaurateur. Untrained rabble might suck, but they could still be deadly, and every troop they took down was one you didn't have to fight.

James realized he was on his fourth magazine, and had a fifth looted from the previous fight. That was it. Where had it all gone?

On the other hand, he saw the FN MAG from the nearest attacking element, abandoned in the sand.

The Javanese fired bursts, his unit shot back, from windows, ground vents, doorways. The plastic walls of this place were turning into a sieve, and the machines were probably nonfunctional, their motors and controls taking occasional hits.

Skelton shouted, "Hit, leg! AarrrgggH!" She suddenly did sound female, and hurt.

Banbang darted over, fumbled a tourniquet onto the limb, then helped Skelton crawl to a harder position she could still shoot from.

Skelton said, "They are getting low. Shorter bursts." She sounded hurt, but coherent.

"So are we," James replied. He had maybe fifteen rounds left.

Something moved right outside from him, visible

under the cracked open bay door. He rolled his rifle sideways and capped off two bursts. He might have hit the guy in the foot.

Then the invaders came through the side door "dynamically." A flurry of motion resolved as six troops in a stack, fanning out and clearing the building. The dust and shadows helped hide James and the rest for a few moments.

The Javanese shot, Ibson shot, Banbang shot, Skelton shot, someone else shot, Katirci fired a burst, he shot. His rifle clicked empty. Three of the intruders were down.

No one had any ammo.

That's why he'd brought a sword. Banbang had a large golok. Skelton had a machete. James rolled to his feet and reached around for his sword.

He felt a punch as a bullet hit the plate on his body armor. It knocked the breath out of him, and stung, but he didn't think it penetrated. He stuck his hand under the vest. There were plate fragments there, and it seemed the round had broken through it, and apparently flattened out inside the vest.

Banbang reached the guy and split his skull laterally through the ear. The scream gurgled and whistled oddly through all those open passages. Revolting.

Then a Javanese popped up in front of James. He managed to deflect the man's rifle with his sword just as the guy fired, and heard the report slap against his right ear. He wouldn't be hearing much for a while. He tangled with the man and fell, but kept the blade oriented edge away.

As they hit the ground, he heard the Jav shriek in pain and panic as the razor edge cut into his collar.

James rolled off and pulled the sword as he did. It cut deeply and the man screamed more, blood soaking his uniform. He wasn't dead though.

There was gunfire overhead and he was amazed he was still alive. He stood up right in the face of someone else. He and that man paused and stared at each other for a moment, before he jabbed the sword into the guy, under his armor, near his groin and lower guts. He saw the man's eyes bug and his mouth grimace, and he yanked back.

The first one was now on his feet. The sword had cut his armor straps, and his plate and inserts had slipped down around his ass. He didn't seem aware of it, and James's thrust caught him right under the solar plexus. He almost overbalanced and fell. He pulled the sword free and the man bent over his guts, with the most amazing rictus on his face.

Steady, he cautioned himself. He was still alive, and his unit was still together. Mostly.

His unit. Yeah, he'd assimilated, for now. They were his, he was theirs. He advanced on the door. If they had to fight...

Two others came through the door, and he grabbed a hot rifle barrel and shoved it away. He felt his left hand sizzle, and grunted into a keen. He managed to twist his right arm to get the sword tip in position, and drove it through the guy's eye.

The man screamed, twitched and thrashed, dropping his rifle and grabbing for the sword. He sliced his thumb half off doing that.

James dropped the barrel of the falling weapon, the skin of his hand leathery and crackling from being cooked.

The noise outside increased, but it sounded odd. Then his brain processed. There were dozens of different weapons. Those weren't Javs; they had to be locals.

One more guy ran through the doorway and James stuck him right through the throat. It was a sergeant, who gurgled and pivoted, his neck stopped while his feet ran. He died before he landed flat on his back.

James cautiously moved to get a viewing angle to the outside. Once he had a glance, he moved for a better one.

There were locals out there, armed with everything from rifles to shotguns to revolvers and goloks and parangs. He actually felt sorry for the poor Javanese bastards. They were being butchered and the bodies stripped of everything useful or valuable as it went. He watched a tall African woman in what looked like a police uniform flying-kick an injured Javanese to the ground, stomp his head and grab his rifle with barely a pause. As she left, she made a parting whack with a huge bolo. The woman sheathed the machete, checked the rifle's mag and the bolt, and brought the weapon into low carry.

Inside, Banbang had apparently already looted the bodies, and handed James four more magazines.

"Just in case," he said.

"Thanks."

He pocketed three, found his rifle on the ground, secured it and reloaded slowly with the last. His left hand hurt like a sonofabitch.

James was pretty sure the island now had more small arms than the Javanese could afford to send. They'd need what they had to fight Aceh.

This area was pacified. He was certain any further

incursion would just be slaughtered on landing, if they even made it that far.

Gasping for breath, his hand on fire, bruised and buzzed on adrenalin, he looked over at Ibson.

Also straining for air, Ibson said, "One of our patrol boats sank their troop carrier, and their second frigate is down, too."

"Well done." As he understood it, the Sulawan "Navy" was four patrol boats, an old Coastie cutter, a couple of refurbed gunboats and a cargo catamaran as both amphibious craft and support. If they'd sunk a transport and a frigate with that, yes, very well done indeed.

Ibson raised his eyebrows and added, "And a US Navy destroyer is ordering the Javanese to stand down."

James said, "We did it."

Ibson grinned, "Yes, we did. Let's hope we don't have to do it again."

If they did, James would fight at their side. Any time. It wasn't how he intended to find a home, but here he was.

> With the thanks of a grateful new nation, the Office of the First Citizen awards the Valor Medal, and is pleased to extend the offer of citizenship...

This nation was closer to her birthplace, and there were people from there. More importantly, there was spirit. There was art and culture and respect, and far less decadence. They had fought for their existence and appreciated it.

It was good to be home.

Once again, there was dormancy. Conflict happened all around, but it was done with money and subterfuge. It seemed to be necessary, but it wasn't honorable. Her bearer adopted a family, and all of them understood the value of the sword.

It was years, and generations came and went. She moved around, changing homes but never fighting. Until one day she boarded a most unusual ship.

Ripper

Peter Grant

"All right, pay attention this way!" The order was accompanied by the sharp rap of knuckles on the head table. The technicians looked up from their breakfast ration trays, and murmured conversations trailed off.

The landing coordinator looked harassed as he began, "Visuals from the satellites confirm that the robotic constructors left on Grainne by the Recon mission ten years ago have done their job. The spaceport and initial settlement site have been cleared and are ready for our Pioneer mission to begin installing basic infrastructure. We've got to have everything ready for the Settlement mission when it arrives in five years."

"The spaceport'll keep us busy for the next few weeks," the redheaded woman sitting next to Tom murmured *sotto voce*.

"What'll you be doing?" he whispered back as the speaker began to list the teams going planetside in the initial landing party. It didn't serve any useful purpose—everyone already knew the schedule—but most of those on this mission had served in the military, and they'd all grown accustomed to such constant repetition. Tom could still remember the class on instruction he'd taken in NCO School. *Tell them what you're going to tell them; then tell them; then tell them what you've just told them.* The sardonic military motto, "Hurry up and wait!" hadn't been coined by accident.

"The team will set up prefab buildings for the control tower, landing beacons, warehouses and administration offices. I'll be supervising the installation of the electronics—beacons, computers, radar and navigation systems. We put the whole system together on Earth and tested it, so it should be just a matter of installing a network, connecting everything and double-checking it all."

"Unless Murphy's Law applies, of course."

"Murphy was an optimist!"

Tom chuckled. "Work fast, sweetheart. I won't be able to see you again until you finish there and your team joins ours."

"That's a heck of an incentive," Sue admitted, grinning as she slipped a hand beneath the table and squeezed his muscular thigh. "I'll do my best. We have to work fast, anyway. They can't bring down most of the equipment and supplies until the warehouses and inventory system are ready."

The coordinator concluded, "Teams One through Five will embark in Shuttle One. Teams Six through Eight will be in Shuttle Two, and Teams Nine and Ten in Shuttle Three. Your preliminary cargoes are already loaded. Boarding time is zero-nine-hundred. Departure is at zero-nine-thirty."

Tom glanced at the bulkhead clock as the man

finished speaking and turned to leave. "It's already zero-eight-ten. We'd better get moving."

"Uh-huh." She pouted slightly. "Dammit, I know we said our goodbyes last night, but now I want to do it all over again!"

He suppressed a *frisson* of excitement at the thought. "Me too, honey, but there's no time now. When we're together again at the dam site, you and I need to have a long talk."

Her green eyes flashed as she looked up at him. "About?"

"Us."

"Hmmm. Anything I need to worry about?"

"Only if the prospect of years in my company is too much to bear."

A slow smile came to her lips. "I can think of worse things."

Tom grunted as he walked down the shuttle ramp, heaving his pack higher on his shoulders. It, and he, weighed almost a fifth more in this planet's gravity than they had on Earth. He sniffed the air, feeling his sinuses protest at its unaccustomed dryness, but savoring the scents it bore. They were very welcome after weeks in the canned, recycled atmosphere aboard the spaceship. His nose, at least, promised that he was going to like Grainne. *I'd better,* he thought to himself with a grin. *I signed a five-year Pioneer contract. I can't leave even if I want to!* On the other hand, he reminded himself, successful completion of the contract meant he'd be awarded a large farm site of his choice as a bonus, complete with a basic outfit of equipment and supplies so he could help the colony become self-supporting in food production as quickly as possible. For years he'd longed for a country life, far from the congested, overcrowded cities of Earth. Grainne had offered him his chance at the brass ring, and he'd grabbed it.

He looked around with interest. The local star, Iota Persei, was much brighter than the Sun he was accustomed to on Earth, its light mitigated only a little by Grainne's greater distance from it. This close to midday, the glare was impressive. *We'll have to wear sunglasses all day, every day until our eyes get used to it. We'll need sunblock, and eye drops, and skin moisturizer—and water. Lots of water!*

To one side, the long runway the robot constructors had carved out of the brush stretched into the distance. It was still bare dirt, not yet fused into a hard surface, but their first-wave shuttles were built to handle such primitive conditions. He waited until the last of the passengers had disembarked and everyone had moved away from the loading ramp, then called, "Security detachment for Team Six, to me!"

Twelve men and women walked toward him, enough to form a full squad of three fire teams. He led them to one side and lowered his pack to the ground. They followed his example as he released a short, stubby carbine from his chest harness and checked—for the umpteenth time—that the magazine inserted in its well was loaded. He cycled the action to chamber a round, and watched the rest of his team follow suit.

"Keep your weapons loaded, locked and ready at all times from now on," he warned them as he leaned the carbine against his pack and pulled out another long, thin object. "We know this planet's food supply is big enough to support a whole bunch of predators, large and small. They don't know anything about us yet. They'll see us as lower than they are on the food chain until experience teaches them otherwise. Don't take chances."

"What's that, Boss?" David, the youngest of the squad, asked as Tom slid the object into his web belt, making sure a stud on its side engaged an eyelet that had been placed to hold it.

Tom had to raise his voice as an earthmover drove down the shuttle's ramp, the loud whine of the electric motors powering each wheel making it difficult to hear. "It's what the Japanese call a *wakizashi*, a short samurai sword. This one's longer than most of its kind, almost a katana. I like its balance."

"He can use it, too," Mika, his second in command, assured David. "Tom was my platoon sergeant with the UNPF on the Tsarnoff mission." He took a similar weapon from his pack and attached its worn sheath to the left side of his belt as he spoke. "He used his to save my ass once, when I was wounded and couldn't defend myself. I watched him take out three rebels with it." He patted the blade at his side. "While I recovered, I paid a fabber operator to make this for me, modeled after Tom's, and had him teach me how to use it. It's come in handy a time or two."

David nodded seriously. "Maybe I should get one too."

"I'll teach you, too, if you do," Tom offered. He looked around at his detachment. "You've all seen the images of known predators. Well, there's another one to worry about. I got the updated report on the way down. The Recon mission left planetary sensors that have been recording during the ten years since they left. They've found a really big predator—one the mission didn't notice. Stand by." He triggered his comm unit to transmit the series of images to every member of his team. "It's only been spotted in forested or hilly terrain where there's more cover, not in open country like this. The dam site might be prime territory for it."

"It's as big or bigger than an Earth lion or tiger, if these estimates are right," Mika observed as he viewed the pictures. "If its temperament is anything like the other predators here, it'll be real unhappy to have us intrude into its territory."

"Does it hunt by day, or by night?" another guard asked.

Tom nodded approvingly at his question. "All the sensor images we have were captured at night, but that doesn't mean it won't prowl during the day, particularly if it's disturbed by a construction crew."

He looked at each member of his team to emphasize his final instructions. "Each of you was a combat engineer in the UNPF. That's why I hired you to join my security team. We all know from experience how easy it is for techs to become too focused on the task at hand, and lose situational awareness. We can't make that mistake. It's up to us to stay alert and keep everyone alive."

The next three weeks were filled with nonstop activity from dawn until after dusk far into the evening. Daily, one fire team rode with the techs aboard the heavy machinery, keeping a wary eye out for predators they might disturb while uprooting trees, clearing brush and leveling the ground. A second fire team stood overwatch, and the third guarded the base camp and escorted vehicles running between it and the work site.

Their efforts to maintain security were hampered when most of them developed upper respiratory-tract infections, caused by a virus and aggravated by the very dry air. Aching muscles and joints due to the heavier-than-Earth-normal gravity added to their woes. Everyone found it hard to stay alert under the triple whammy of illness, soreness and medication, but they soon learned that they couldn't afford to be distracted.

On one of the first mornings, carving a road from the future spaceport toward the site for the dam, an earthmover uncovered the entrance to the den of a small, stocky, muscular predator resembling a cross between Earth's wolverine and honey badger. It came barreling out of its burrow, eyes blazing, chattering furiously, and hurled itself at the machine, undeterred by the disparity in size. Unable to make any impression on the metal, it clawed its way up one of the huge tires, spotted the operator and his escort, and launched itself at them in a full-on homicidal leap. The security guard shot it in midair, but its teeth and claws still caused superficial injuries as its dead body slammed into them. The crew had to be relieved briefly so their wounds could be treated.

"Damn thing nearly got us!" the security guard muttered, shaken, as he climbed down. The name stuck. Before long everyone referred to the small predators as "damns," or for those of a more secular bent, "goddamns."

Its demise soon revealed another predator. As the

construction equipment moved on, leaving the animal's
body by the side of the cleared strip behind them,
Tom happened to look back at the right moment.
A bush rustled and a big, stocky beast with rough,
brindled fur appeared, looking warily at the receding
machines. Satisfied that they posed no immediate
threat, the new arrival seized the dead animal in its
powerful jaws, lifted it effortlessly and disappeared
back into the brush. It was about the same size as
an Earth hyena.

That night Tom described the animal to the team
and passed around sensor images of others like it. "It
wasn't scared of us or our machines. If it's as aggressive
as the other one, it's big enough to be a real danger.
Sentries, keep your eyes open." His squad muttered
assent as they studied the pictures.

After supper they watched with interest as he cleaned
his sword, the first opportunity he'd had to do so since
his field gear had been released from the secure bag-
gage compartment before they disembarked. He drew a
small wooden box from his pack and from it took three
squares of paper, a little cloth ball on a short stick, and
a bottle of oil. He wiped the sword with a sheet of
paper, then dabbed it with the cloth ball up and down
both sides of the patterned blade, leaving a faint trace
of powder at each spot. This he spread carefully across
the blade using a second sheet of paper.

"What's that?" David asked.

"The paper's called *nuguigami*. It's soft, made of
rice pulp for cleaning traditional Japanese swords with
their folded-steel blades. In the old days, the powder
in the silk ball would have been the residue from
sharpening stones. Nowadays it's a synthetic equivalent.

It cleans and polishes the blade. This"—he nodded to the small bottle—"is *choji* oil—also synthetic; you can't get the real stuff anymore. It keeps the steel in perfect condition."

"Seems like you have to go to an awful lot of trouble. Wouldn't a modern battle steel blade like Mika's be easier to maintain?"

"Yes, but it wouldn't have the history this one has." Tom brushed off the last of the powder, placed a few drops of oil up and down the blade, then took the third sheet of paper and began to spread them. "My father asked an expert about it. He said it's similar to museum specimens that are over five hundred years old. My grandfather came by it back on Sulawan."

"I guess that makes it pretty special," David said wistfully.

"It does to me. I hope I have a kid one day who'll join the Army and inherit it from me."

"And if none of your kids do?"

He shrugged. "Then I guess I'll have to find a soldier worthy of it, who'll agree to carry on the tradition in his own family when the time comes. This is a piece of history. It's too important to be given to just anybody."

At 0320 the next morning, Tom was jolted out of a sound sleep by a yell of alarm and a coughing, rasping snarl, seeming to come from right next to his shelter. Three shots sounded, rapid fire, and the snarl changed to a scream as something big and heavy slammed into the thin plasfiber wall, buckling it. As Tom and Mika frantically tried to get out of their sleeping bags, four razor-sharp claws slashed at the wall, tearing it open. A brindled head thrust through the gap.

Only halfway out of his sleeping bag, adrenaline coursing through his body, Tom grabbed the sword from next to his field cot. His left hand pulled the scabbard as his right tugged at the hilt. Flinging the scabbard away, he slashed one-handed at the head as it lunged toward him, jaws open to display a vicious set of teeth, its rank breath like a slap in the face. His blade cut right into the open mouth, severing part of the tongue and carving into the back of the jaw as he sliced across. The creature yowled in pain and tried to bite down on the blade as its mouth spouted blood, but the muscles and tendons that opened and closed its jaws were no longer working properly. More shots sounded from outside. Its body jerked and twitched as they struck home. It tried to back out through the tear in the wall, but Tom rolled onto his knees and thrust his sword two-handed up through the roof of its still-open mouth. With a final shudder, the beast collapsed.

Releasing his sword, Tom kicked off the sleeping bag and grabbed his carbine, lining it as he flicked off the safety; but the weapon wasn't needed. The animal lay unmoving.

A shout came from outside. "*Boss!* You okay?" The voice was shrill, almost fearful.

Still shaken, Tom had to concentrate to keep his voice controlled and steady. "I'm all right. I'm coming out."

He emerged to find his entire security detachment converging on the scene, carrying their weapons. One of the sentries on duty was waiting for him.

"I didn't see it at all until it peered out from between your shelter and the next one, Boss. I reckon it musta snuck into camp behind the charging station, moving real quiet." The guard nodded toward the serried ranks of capacitors from the construction vehicles' power packs, being charged overnight by the camp's mobile fusion microreactor. "I fired at it, but instead of running it turned and attacked your shelter."

Tom nodded slowly, looking down at the dead animal in the beams of his team's flashlights. He could see it was the same breed as the one that had snatched the body of the smaller predator that morning. "It nearly got me. Good shooting. I finished it with my sword."

He looked around at his people. "We can't afford to be caught in our sleeping bags by something this dangerous, especially if it can sneak up on us like that and go through our shelter walls as if they didn't exist. From now on we sleep with bags unzipped, even if we have to wear heavier clothing against the night cold. Everybody got that?"

A chorus of emphatic assent answered him.

"Next, from sunset to sunrise the perimeter guards will wear night-vision visors, and the sentry in the duty vehicle will put up a sensor mast and use it to scan all around outside the perimeter. These things may be able to hide in shadows, but their body heat will show up. We'll light the interior of the camp better, too, so we can spot any that get inside."

"We've only got four NV visors," Mika pointed out, his voice worried. "Will they and their capacitors hold up under that sort of heavy, constant use?"

"They'll have to, won't they? They're all we were issued. I'll send back to the spaceport for more of them as soon as they start bringing the expedition's main supplies down."

He pointed at the ruined wall of his shelter. "I'm sure the scientists have some fancy name for this thing, but given the damage its claws can do, let's call it a 'slasher' among ourselves. It's a short, easy name to remember." There was a rumble of agreement. "I'll recommend to Mr. Enquist that we improve our perimeter defenses, to stop it and other beasties like it getting inside. That'll mean building an earth berm, maybe topped with some of the thorn bushes we saw today—the ones that look like Earth brambles. We'll also clear away all the brush inside the berm. We'll probably have to move the camp less often in order to make it more secure, and accept the penalty of a longer ride to and from the work site each day."

After examining the body of the intruder the next morning, and realizing the damage its teeth and claws could inflict, the chief engineer was all in favor of Tom's recommendations. The techs carved out a ditch around the camp, piling the excavated dirt into a berm. However, they didn't cap it with the thorns, which proved to sting very painfully and tangled themselves inextricably around anything and anyone trying to handle them. Instead, the operators piled a tangled mass of uprooted bushes on top of the berm.

"That should keep out all but the most determined intruders," Enquist assured Tom.

"That's what worries me," he retorted unhappily. "Those slashers *are* determined—at least, that one was. And what other threats are out there that we haven't run into yet?"

As it turned out, there were more than a few. Every predator they encountered seemed determined to find out for themselves whether humans were edible or not. Even the small ones were brazenly unafraid in trying their luck.

Tom was able to illustrate this to Enquist the first time they crossed a river. The construction crew spent a day carving out an approach road to an accessible part of the bank, then brought up a military-style mobile bridge. In response to Tom's radioed alert, Enquist came forward with the bridge parts and joined him on a transporter.

"What is it?" the engineer demanded.

"See that critter?" Tom pointed to a small animal, looking like a cross between an Earth otter and a beaver, peering at them from beneath a bush near the river. It seemed quite unperturbed by the noise and bustle of the construction site.

"Yes, I see it. So what?"

"Would you believe that little bugger's one of the most dangerous animals on this planet?"

"Oh, come *on*!"

"I'm not joking. I sent up a drone after watching it try to bite our tires earlier this morning. Let's get in the cab. I want to show you what it saw a couple of clicks upstream."

The vid recording showed a ford across the river. A large ungulate-type animal started to cross, then kicked its right hind leg irritably. The vid clearly showed the figure of another of the small predators diving into the river as the former was shaken loose. It had apparently swum up and bitten the creature's leg. Within a few seconds the larger animal began to shake and quiver. It turned back to the bank, took a few steps out of the water, then fell to its knees. As it did so, more of the little animals emerged from the cover of the bushes, several of them biting it as well. A short while later it was on its side, apparently dead or unconscious, and the creatures began to rip chunks of flesh from its body.

"I checked the records of the Recon mission," Tom informed the engineer. "They called that thing a 'poisontooth.' Its bite injects a neurotoxin. Several of them live and work together as a pod. When their prey goes down, they can strip the meat off the bones in only an hour or two."

"Nasty," Enquist muttered, clearly shaken by what he was seeing. "Is that why you ordered everyone to stay on the vehicles unless they have an armed escort watching their every movement?"

"It sure is. We've seen several of those critters around here, and two have already tried to bite us. I'd as soon shoot all of them on sight, but that's not allowed."

"So what do we do about them?"

"I've talked to the fabber operators. They can make gaiters out of woven synthetic silk that'll be proof against a poisontooth's bite. They'll have enough for the whole crew by the day after tomorrow. We'll wear them over our boots. That'll protect our legs up to the knee. I've also asked the earthmovers to cut back the brush even further around the work site, so the poisonteeth won't have enough cover to sneak up on us."

"What about after we've moved on? How will we warn others using the road?"

"We'll have to put up signs on both sides of the bridge, about a kilometer out, to tell drivers and passengers what to look for, and warn them not to dismount until they're through the danger zone."

"Fair enough. I hate to admit it, but I hadn't even considered such risks. I've been focused on the technical, geographic and geological challenges in getting to the dam site."

"That's why you have a security team. We carry that load for you. Please see what you can do to expedite the extra night-vision visors. Also, if we run into any of the big predators the sensor network told us about when we landed, we'll need something more powerful than carbines to deal with them. I want them to issue us some of the heavier rifles from the armory. Oh—and what's happening with the insect repellent they said they were working on?"

"They're trying to develop a pheromone-based lotion. The scientists and chemists say they may have something for us in a few weeks. Until then, I'm afraid our only defenses are long clothing, face veils, and nets over our beds. As for the weapons and equipment, they're in the main bulk of the cargo toward the rear of the holds. That can't come down from orbit until the warehouses and logistics computer have been set up at the spaceport. It'll be at least a month, probably longer, before we get them."

"We'll do our best with what we've got until then... but I don't like it."

Enquist grinned at him and punched his shoulder lightly. "Hey, you're our security chief. It's your job to be paranoid!"

As the engineer climbed down, still chuckling, Tom thought to himself grimly, *That's all very well, but it's not paranoia if they really are out to get you—and as far as these critters are concerned, we're food!*

Three weeks to the day after their departure from the spaceport site, the dam crew reached the river separating the plains from the foothills of the mountain range ahead of them. The dam site was only five kilometers ahead in a straight line, but to reach it they'd have to cut a winding, laboriously climbing switchback road up seventeen kilometers of undulating, heavily forested slopes.

The crew spent the afternoon preparing abutments for the military scissor bridge they'd erect across the river. As Tom watched, standing with Enquist on the bank, he asked, "Where will our next base camp be?"

"There's no room for one near the dam. The road will be cut up steep hillsides with no level areas nearby, and the work site will be crowded with equipment, supplies, and a plascrete plant to supply the raw material for the dam. We'll build a long-term accommodation site on that flat hilltop across the river." The chief engineer pointed. "We'll put up a bigger perimeter berm than usual, and fuse the earth, and erect proper lighting and sensor masts around and inside the camp."

"Sounds good. I'd like razor wire on top and in front of the berm, and sentry towers at the corners, too. We should probably do the same thing at the dam construction site. I hope we won't need the extra precautions, but it's better to be safe than sorry."

"We'll have to ask the spaceport for whatever razor wire they can spare. We hadn't considered it as a defense against predators. The asteroid mining project will start production next month. I'll ask the refinery ship's manufacturing plant to give razor wire a higher priority, but it may have to wait its turn behind a huge order of rebar for the dam and our other big projects."

"Thanks. I'll improvise something until it's available."
Tom glanced up at the mountains ahead of them. "What
made them choose this site for the dam, anyway?"

"There's already a landslide dam up there. It was
formed by material that came down a hillside, blocking a valley. It happened between the Discovery and
Recon missions, so it's been there for at least a decade.
The Recon team noticed the lake from orbit, realized
it wasn't shown on the Discovery mission's planetary
scan, and took a closer look. A few kilometers further
down the valley they found a perfect dam site, with
good solid bedrock to anchor and underpin the wall.
We'll build the dam and powerhouse there, then carve
a sluice into the landslide dam upstream to allow the
water to flow down and fill the intervening valleys.
The dam'll be big enough to supply the colony's needs
for at least half a century, both water and hydroelec-
tric power. The turbines will come in with the first
Settlement mission, five years from now."

"And by then our Pioneer contracts will be almost
over, and we'll all have selected our land grants ahead
of the rush." The two men smiled at each other.

A radio call from the base camp interrupted them.
"The spaceport crew's transporters have just pulled in.
Their fusers are on the way to your position."

The engineer keyed his microphone. "That's great
news! Get the crew settled in. I'll head back to meet
the fusers."

Tom couldn't help a shiver of excitement. The
spaceport crew, having finished erecting the facilities
there, would spend the next few weeks helping to
complete the road, including the installation of navigation beacons and a traffic control system. That would

allow autopiloted transporters to ply the route without needing drivers. Sue would be in charge of that task, so they'd share the same camp for several weeks.

He escorted Enquist to meet the fusers, which were still about eight kilometers from the river. The big machines had taken up echelon formation along the bare roadbed prepared by the dam crew. They were fusing its surface into a hard-topped two-lane highway, with shoulders broad enough for vehicles to pull over and park if necessary. The fusers drew up as they saw Enquist's utility vehicle approaching, and the operators climbed down to exchange greetings.

"What the hell happened to you?" Tom exclaimed as one of the drivers came up. His face was scarred by several slashes running across his forehead. Another ran diagonally across his nose and down his left cheek. They were obviously recent injuries, as they were still heavily scabbed.

"Stoopers," the man said, scowling. "They're a lot like Earth falcons or eagles, but much more aggressive. A breeding pair had their nest in a clump of trees off the end of the runway. The boss decided the trees were too close to the approach path, and sent me out to cut them down with a tree-feller. The birds didn't like the idea, and my size didn't faze 'em. They dove at me, then banked sharply past my head with their claws extended. I didn't even see them coming. I was concentrating on cutting a path to the trees. They cut my forehead to ribbons—almost took my eyes out!" He added a few choice obscenities.

Enquist was listening, his face growing longer and more concerned. "Did you call for help?"

"*Call?* I was screaming blue murder on every frequency! I was blinded by blood, so I just backed right out of there even though I couldn't see where I was going. The medics met me at the runway. Turns out stoopers' claws are contaminated with rotting meat from the carrion they eat. My wounds got infected. Took some pretty strong nanobiotics to deal with it. They kept the bandages on for two weeks, then took 'em off two days ago to let the cuts breathe while they heal. I'll need surgery to remove the scars as soon as they build a proper hospital."

"Add stoopers to the list of Grainne critters that think we're easy meat," Tom grumbled. "I'm beginning to think they're *all* out to get us!"

Enquist took pity on Tom's obvious, barely suppressed anticipation, and drove back to the base for lunch. "That'll give you a chance to see your lady again," he said with a grin.

Leaving the engineer at the mess hall, Tom hurried over to the previously empty part of the encampment where the spaceport team had parked their vehicles and erected their shelters. He asked for Sue, and was directed to a shiny new trailer parked behind a transporter. He knocked at the door, and heard her familiar, beloved voice call, "Come in!" A moment later he was in her arms.

A timeless interval later, they pulled apart just far enough to breathe. She looked up at him, her eyes misty with joy. "*Damn,* I've missed you, lover!"

"Not half as much as I've missed you."

She laughed shakily. "I'm not going to argue about that now. How do you like our new quarters?"

"Ours?"

"Yes. I'm the chief electronics tech, after all. I have to make board- and chip-level repairs to components. I told the boss I couldn't do that in a fold-up shelter: I had to have a secure, clean, dust-free workshop, one I can take with me to my assignments. He finagled this big trailer for me. I've set up a clean-room workshop at one end, a small office and storeroom here in the middle, and my living quarters at the other end. I made sure the bed folds out to be big enough for two. When you and I get busy, I want us to have some privacy, thank you very much! I don't want the entire camp listening and laughing, like they would if we were in a shelter right next door to everyone else!"

Tom grinned. "I'll put a sign on the door: 'If this trailer's rocking, don't bother knocking'!"

She snorted with laughter. "Speaking of that, have you eaten yet?"

"No. Seeing you is far more important than food. I'll snack on a couple of emergency ration bars on the way back to the work site."

"I can do the same—which means we have about fifteen minutes to spare. Brace yourself!"

She tugged him toward her living quarters. He offered no resistance whatsoever.

The crew took several days to build the semipermanent construction camp on top of the hill beyond the river. They cleared a space about a kilometer square, removing all the trees and brush, leveling the surface, piling up the dirt into extra-tall berms and fusing them, digging drainage channels and laying sewage and power lines. A vehicle park was set up next to the camp, enclosed by its own berm.

Tom had the crew collect truckload after truckload of reasonably straight branches while cutting the road up the hill and clearing the camp site. The construction machines stripped the branches and cut them into three-meter stakes. The fabber fashioned short, heavy machetes out of steel from broken equipment and parts. The crew used them to sharpen each end of the stakes, then took the tough vines hanging from the trees and bound the stakes into bundles, points sticking out in all directions in a Czech hedgehog. Some of the bundles were lashed together in a continuous row around the outer base of the berm in an abatis. More were hoisted by construction cranes and secured to posts sunk into the top of the berm as a palisade, making it almost impossible for anything or anyone to get through or over the perimeter. Tom reserved their limited supply of razor wire to protect the sentry towers at each corner of the berm.

There weren't yet enough of the bundles to completely enclose the camp, and the vehicle park was as yet unprotected. However, Enquist assured him that after a few more kilometers of road had been cleared, that would no longer be a problem. "We'll send back a couple of transporter loads of branches every day. You'll soon have enough stakes to make all the obstacles you need."

"Thanks. The sooner we can ring the entire place with them, the easier I'll sleep."

The following morning a trio of felling machines were at work no more than a kilometer above the camp, cutting down trees and piling them on transporters, making room for bulldozers and graders to level the newly cleared road bed. Tom, supervising the installation of more stakes on the berm around the camp, heard a sudden eruption of radio traffic. Several voices tried to yell over each other on the common channel, making it impossible to understand what was being said in the hubbub. The distant sound of shots, first one or two, then a rapid staccato burst of them from multiple weapons, confirmed that something was badly wrong at the work site.

Yelling at the others to shelter in place, Tom ran down the berm toward his utility light truck. He cursed as he slapped at the empty space on his left side. He hadn't been assigned to outside duty that morning, so he'd left his sword in Sue's trailer. There was no time to get it now.

It took him less than three minutes to reach the work site. As he braked to a skidding, sliding halt and jumped out of the cab, carbine in hand, he saw the techs huddled on two transporters at the rear of the line of machines. One of the guards was standing on top of a transporter cab, scanning the trees intently. A second knelt by the side of an unmoving body behind the tree-fellers. There was no sign of the other two guards.

"What happened?" Tom called.

The guard on the transporter answered without interrupting his scan of the forest. His voice quivered with shock. "Big critter—bigger than anything we've seen before—came out of the trees, jumped clean over a tree-feller and got Rafe as he stood behind them. We shot at it. It let go of Rafe, but made it back into the trees. Simon and Carl went after it."

"The bloody *fools!* Didn't they listen to a single thing I told them? You *never*—"

Tom's words were cut short by a hideous gurgling

scream of agony, followed by a burst of firing, then another yell, this one sounding more like panic than pain. He ran forward to the other security guard as they heard a thrashing in the trees ahead of them. Carl staggered out, his ashen face bloody where branches, vines and thorns had lashed it as he ran.

"Where's Simon?" Tom called, eyes scanning the forest frantically.

"I—I dunno! I think he—he's dead!"

Tom fought down the sick lurch in the pit of his stomach. "*How?* What happened?"

Carl sucked air into his lungs, panting, trembling. His awkward walk, the damp stain on his trousers and the fecal smell as he drew nearer told Tom that he'd voided his bowels in panic. "W-we went in to find the body of that...that *thing* we shot. It's hard to s-see anything in there—the trees and brush are real thick. We'd gone about ten, fifteen meters when a big critter—maybe the same one, maybe not, I dunno—jumped out from behind a tree. It grabbed Simon's neck and shoulder in its mouth and jerked him right off his feet. He—he screamed and tried to fight it off, but it bit down harder and he...he just went limp, like a rag doll. He dropped his carbine. I fired, but I was shaking so hard I missed. Even holding Simon in its mouth, it growled at me. I—I turned and ran. I couldn't do anything for Simon. I *couldn't!*"

"*Goddammit, Carl!*" Tom raged. "You should *never* have gone into the forest. That's where these things live. They're at home in it. We're not. You handed them the initiative."

"But—but it killed Rafe! We couldn't let it get away after that!"

"You damned *fool!* Didn't I tell you to *always* make sure you can see a threat coming before it reaches you?"

Carl sucked in a trembling, shaky breath, and nodded brokenly. "Y-yeah."

"This is what happens when you don't listen. Now Simon's dead as well as Rafe."

Tom knelt and examined the body in front of him. The feller operator's torso had been ripped open from chest to groin. He'd fallen forward onto his internal organs as they spilled out of his abdominal cavity. His head showed deep bite marks, penetrating the skull. The stench of blood and intestinal matter was overpowering.

"How the hell did that thing do so much damage?" he demanded thickly, swallowing hard to contain his nausea at the sight and smell.

Gil replied grimly, "It jumped up, bit his head, put its front paws on his shoulders, brought up its hind legs and ripped down with its rear claws. It all happened in a split second. I saw the whole thing. I was standing not five meters from him. I shot at it, but too late to save Rafe."

Tom shuddered involuntarily. "Hell of a way to die. It tore him up real bad." He took a deep breath as he stood. "All right, let's wrap Rafe in a tarp, load his body on a transporter, then get everyone back to camp. We'll come back later for the rest of the equipment."

"But—but Simon..." Carl began to object.

Tom shook his head emphatically. "We can't do anything for Simon. We can't see those things coming in forest this thick. If we went in, all we'd do is give them a chance to up their body count."

As they lifted Rafe's corpse onto the tarpaulin, Tom said, "Tell me more about that animal. Did it look like the images of that big critter I showed you—the ones from the Recon mission's sensor network?"

"Y-yeah," Carl replied. "It was dark-skinned—blended in real well with the trees. It had two fangs protruding from its upper lip. It was *big*, much bigger than a slasher. I'd say it's gotta be at least a hundred and fifty, maybe as much as two hundred kilos, with big bones and muscles."

Tom frowned. "That's big, all right. If this ripper thing's got strength and speed to match its size—and judging from this, it has—then our carbines are going to have problems stopping it."

"Ripper's a good name for it," Gil observed.

They loaded Rafe's body onto the transporter, then Tom allocated the guards. "Ken, front transporter load bed, look over the cab, watch front and right side. Carl, front transporter, left side and rear. Gil, second transporter, front and right side. I'll take left side and rear. Drivers, be careful! The road surface is still loose and unstable. Stay in all-wheel drive and shift to low gear. Listen for orders from the guards."

As if to echo his last words, a low, savage growl came from the forest behind them, rising to a roar of pure fury. All four lined their carbines at the place where the sound came from, but could see nothing.

"I reckon that ripper wants Rafe's body back. Let's go! *Now!*" Tom commanded.

The others needed no urging. They scrambled aboard the transporters, which lurched into motion down the steep, unfinished grade. At the rear of the second vehicle's load bed, nearest to any pursuit, Tom kept his carbine in a low ready position at his shoulder, eyes scanning from the left side to the rear and back again, first close in, then further out. As he scanned, he pondered the weapon in his hands. Their military-standard carbines didn't fire a very powerful round. Like all UNPF personal weapons, they were intended for use against humans rather than large animals. On the other hand, they were relatively easy to control and keep on target. Their projectiles didn't impart much shock power. Several of them in the right place should do the job . . . but only if they could penetrate deep enough to reach vital organs. He made a mental note to ask Enquist to hurry the unloading of larger, more powerful weapons from the spaceship.

They'd traveled no more than a hundred meters when Tom saw a big, dark shape emerge from the bushes at the work site. It padded over to where Rafe's body had lain, sniffed the earth, raised its head and let out an eldritch scream; then it broke into a loping run, chasing the transporter. He realized with a chill that it didn't see humans as anything except prey. If it was the same animal the guards had shot at, they hadn't struck anything vital, because it was closing in smoothly and purposefully, showing neither fear nor hesitation.

"Heads up!" he shouted over his shoulder. "It's coming!" Behind him he heard scuffles from the techs as they crowded away from the tailgate.

He tried to line his carbine, but found it impossible to draw a bead on the animal because of the lurching and bouncing of the transporter. He realized instantly that it would be more dangerous to stay in the vehicle than to get out. *I can't hit it from here, but it can jump into the load bed and kill me in a heartbeat. I've got to have a more stable shooting platform—and there's no time to wait for the driver to stop this thing.*

He bellowed, "Keep moving!" As he placed a hand on the tailgate and vaulted over it, he heard Gil echo his command to the driver.

Tom landed on his feet, staggered as he regained his balance, then dropped to one knee, lining his carbine at the animal. It was coming straight for him, eyes seeming to bore right through him, charging in faster than he'd have believed possible. He gulped, settled the carbine against his shoulder and began to squeeze off single shots, blessing the scientists on the Recon mission who'd determined that Grainne animals mostly followed the Earth pattern of brain placement. He put the tip of his sight chevron right on the ripper's nostrils, trying to slip his rounds up its nasal passages into its skull rather than have them bounce off the heavy bone above its eyes.

His first shot produced no visible result; likewise, his second. *Steady! Settle down!* he told himself, and took an extra split second to be sure of his aim before squeezing the firing button again. The animal stumbled, roaring in pain, tossing its head, revealing its throat, which he instantly hit with another round; then, as it dropped its head, he fired again at its nose. The creature collapsed onto its belly, sliding, raising a small cloud of dust and dirt, stopping less than five meters from him. Its eyes glowed with hatred and anger as it tried to snarl again, a strangled, agonized sound. Its limbs jerked and twitched in nerve-wracked spasms, evidence that his rounds had disrupted its motor nervous system. He surged to his feet, aimed down between its eyes, flicked his carbine's safety to full-auto, and sent a burst of fire into its head at point-blank range. The top of its skull shattered under the impact of his rounds, spattering blood, brain matter and chips of bone.

Tom could feel his heart pounding in his chest, as though he'd just sprinted a hundred yards at full speed under fire. His breath rasped in his throat and lungs, and his limbs trembled involuntarily. *All right,* he told himself shakily. *It's not getting up from that.*

He reached for a fresh, fully loaded magazine as he turned back to the transporter, which was still moving away slowly. He beckoned urgently, and saw Gil bend to relay his order to the driver. The vehicle braked to a skidding stop, then began to reverse up the road. Gil looked back. His eyes widened, then he waved urgently and pointed toward the work site they'd just left. Tom spun around again as he dropped the used magazine and locked the new one into his carbine. Two more of the big beasts were crouched beside the silent tree-fellers, looking at him. *They must be trying to figure out what just happened,* he realized. *They don't know why the other one's not moving. They probably haven't connected the sound of my shots with it going down.*

The transporter ground to a halt behind him. He heard Gil call, "What now, boss?"

He dared not take his eyes off the two animals. "Have some of the techs load this damn thing into the transporter. The scientists will want to see it. Make it fast! We've got to get out of here before those two decide to join in."

He watched the critters as Gil tried to get some of the passengers off the transporter. From the thuds and curses he could hear, it sounded as if the guard was using his boots as encouragement. Several techs scurried forward, panting heavily with stress and fear, grabbed the limp body of the animal and dragged it past him. A few seconds later he heard Gil call, "It's aboard!"

"Cover me!"

"Yo!"

He clambered back into the transporter's load bed, then called to the driver, "Let's go!"

As they headed down the road once more the two animals started after them, moving slowly, not trying to catch up or overtake, just keeping pace, padding silently along the trail. Their heads and eyes followed the transporter's every move, seeming to exude menace and implacable determination.

The vehicle turned into the main entrance to the camp, flanked by berms already topped with stakes, to find the other transporter waiting inside. People had gathered to listen to the excited, panicked reports of the road techs aboard it. They thronged around Tom's transporter as the techs in the load bed tossed the ripper's body to the ground, then lowered Rafe's tarpaulin-wrapped corpse more gently. Exclamations of astonishment and fear rose on all sides.

"*Quiet!*" Tom called from the load bed without taking his eyes from the road. "There are two more of them out there." He pointed. The predators had paused a couple of hundred meters away, and were watching everything with unblinking eyes. More gasps and shouts rose from the onlookers.

"I said *QUIET!*" Tom bellowed as the beasts padded off the road and vanished into the thick forest. "Driver, pull this transporter across the entrance to block it. Tower guards, stay put; Rob and Janice, guard the gate; all other guards, get to the west berm. It's nearest to them, and it's still got a big gap in the stakes. The rest of you, get out of the way! *MOVE!*"

The crowd scattered as the guards charged through them toward the western side of the camp. As Tom jumped down, Sue hurried forward, holding his sword in her hands.

"*Bless* you!" he said in heartfelt gratitude as he hit the ground. "I felt naked without it." He took it from her and started running toward the west berm, holding it in his left hand while his right gripped his carbine. She jogged alongside him.

"I figured you would. What next?"

"We wait to see whether they're going to try for another kill. They're not afraid of us at all."

"What happened up there?"

"They killed the tree-feller operator and one of my guards. He was a damned fool—went into the forest after them. I killed that one as it charged after us. Two more followed us all the way down."

As they came abreast of a pile of stakes, waiting to be tied together to form more barricades, a shadowy dark shape leapt over the west berm. The foremost guards skidded to a stop as they saw it, raising their carbines and shouting the alarm. It raced into their midst, seeming to flow like water over the ground, its movements were so fluid. The first shots sounded as a guard yelled in pain, the creature's claws ripping at him in passing, laying his leg open to the bone. He collapsed

to the ground. The others opened up, sending dozens
of rounds in their assailant's direction as it screeched its
defiance... but in their focus on the immediate danger,
none of them saw the second ripper as it swarmed over
the berm and dropped to the ground.

Tom, further back, didn't miss it. He tossed his sword
to one side and swept his carbine to his shoulder as he
slammed to a halt, bellowing at the top of his lungs to
warn the others. The new attacker heard and saw him
as it sped toward the fight. It swerved in his direction,
jaws open, lips drawn back in a screaming snarl of fury.
Sue, beside him, caught his *wakizashi* in midair and
dragged it from its scabbard, poised to support him in
any way she could.

Tom flicked the safety catch to the full-auto position.
There was no time at such close range for careful aim
or precision shots, particularly with an underpowered
weapon. He emptied the magazine in a single roaring,
rocking burst of fire as the big predator streaked toward
him. He could see his rounds impacting on its upper
forelegs and chest, rising to encompass its jaws and
head, tearing fur and bits of flesh from its body, blood
spattering; but the projectiles were too light to stop its
headlong charge. The carbine clicked as its magazine
ran dry. The ripper sprang, roaring in pain and fury,
aiming its entire body at Tom's head and shoulders.

He dropped to one knee, ducking low as the creature flew over his head. Its outstretched forepaw
struck his raised carbine and knocked the weapon
out of his hands, sending it bouncing end over end
across the dirt. The paw scraped across his shoulder,
drawing a spray of blood as its claws cut into his
skin; but because he was already so low, they couldn't

sink deep enough into his flesh to drag him over and pull him down. Beside him, Sue slashed at the ripper with the sword as it passed over his head. Her blow caught its rear leg, cutting it to the bone just above the ankle, drawing an enraged snarl from the animal as it landed and stumbled.

Tom knew his carbine had been knocked too far away for him to reach it in time. He grabbed a sharpened pole from the pile next to him as he whirled around to face his enemy. The ripper spun around, slowed by its injuries, and launched itself toward him once more. Tom slammed the base of the pole into the ground, stamped his boot down on it to provide extra purchase, and braced himself, grasping the stake with both hands as he aimed it at the beast's chest. The ripper ran right onto it, the sharpened point spearing deep into its flesh under the impetus of its own momentum. It screamed in pain as it impaled itself, struggling to reach him, half rising onto its only sound hind leg, lashing out with its front paws, jerking the stake to and fro, almost wrenching it from Tom's grasp. He knew that if it hadn't already been weakened by its wounds, it would have been far too strong for him. He clung to the stake for dear life.

A burst of fire sounded from the guards behind him, joined almost immediately by a second. The animal rocked under the impact of the dual spray of bullets. It sank to the ground, yowling in pain, still struggling weakly as the weapons fell silent. Tom held onto the pole, not daring to take his eyes off the ripper. As the clatter of magazine changes sounded behind him, Sue charged in from the side, holding his sword. He opened his mouth to yell at her to stay clear, but she was moving too fast. The ripper turned its head, snarling at her, trying to tense its tormented body to leap. She stabbed it through the eye, driving the blade so deep that its point went right through the brain and stuck in the back of the creature's skull. Its head dropped at once as its body went limp, motionless.

Sue stumbled back, releasing the sword, which stuck out of the ripper's head at an angle. *"Tom!* You're bleeding!" She pointed to his slashed shoulder.

"I'll be okay," he gasped, staggering as the pressure on the pole was suddenly released. He dropped it, feeling the fear and tension still vibrating through him. "Why the hell didn't you let the others take care of it? It could have killed you!"

"It could have killed you too!" she flared. "I'll be damned if I let some critter murder my man while I just stand there and watch!"

"Your man?" Tom suddenly grinned. "If that's a proposal, I accept."

"You—oh, *Tom!"* Tears came to her eyes, and she fell into his arms. They ignored the sound of the just-in-case shots that delivered the *coup de grace* to the ripper as they embraced.

At last he pushed her back. "You've got blood all over your shirt." It had trickled down from his shoulder onto her chest.

"It's your blood, not mine, so I guess I get to blame you for that." She smiled at him shakily.

"You realize that by using my sword against my enemy, you've made yourself my sword brother?"

"Huh! I'd rather be your sword *wife,* thank you very much!"

He laughed. "Me too!"

He staggered as a wave of dizziness hit him. He knew it was a combination of delayed shock at his wound, accumulated tension from the past half hour of intense concentration and combat focus, and sheer relief that the fight was over and he'd survived. He leaned on Sue for a moment to steady himself.

As the feeling subsided, he looked around. The other ripper was also down, some of his guards standing over it. Two of them were kneeling by the injured man, cutting his trousers off to get at his wounds. Three more surrounded his and Sue's victim. He nodded to them. "Thanks, guys. That was just a little bit hairy for a while."

Mika snorted. "You can say that again!" He bent, tugged the sword out of the ripper's eye, wiped the blood from its blade on the creature's fur, then snapped it up vertically in a formal salute to Sue. "You did real good. With only one rear paw working, it couldn't get full leverage against Tom." He reversed the weapon and held it out to Tom hilt first.

"Thanks." Tom accepted the *wakizashi*, wiped it on the hem of his shirt, then walked over to where Sue had dropped the scabbard. Picking it up, he sheathed the sword, then slipped it into his belt.

Enquist ran up, his eyes wide with shock. "Wh-what do we do now? We can't go on cutting the road if those things are lurking in the forest."

"The hell we can't! We'll just change our approach. We won't have anyone standing in the open where they can get at him. We'll weld steel cages around the operator positions on all the machines. Those who'd normally walk behind their machines will be in utility trucks, also with steel cages around their cabs. If the rippers can't get at our people, they aren't so great a threat; and if they show themselves, we'll kill them.

"I want you to get on the radio to the spaceport and give them a nudge about those heavier weapons and extra sensors. I don't care if it disrupts the unloading schedule or not—I want them here in two days! Tell the spaceport our carbines are too light to reliably stop these things, and we need more sensors to detect them in the thick forest. To prove our point, we'll fly one of these carcasses over there aboard a shuttle. That'll show them we're not kidding. While we wait for the gear, we'll weld protective cages onto the equipment and cut more stakes to make abatis. I want them around and on top of the entire berm, and the vehicle park too—yesterday, if not sooner! Until that's done, we'll double the guards over the unprotected area."

"I—yes, of course. I'll get onto that right away, and call a shuttle to pick up one of the bodies."

"Not this one." Tom gestured to the ripper in front of him. "I'm going to skin it and cure the pelt; maybe mount the skull, too. Sue and I fought it together, so it'll be a shared trophy in our home. It'll make quite a story for our kids." He bent to examine the animal's body more closely. "I guess these things are Grainne's version of the Tsavo man-eaters."

Enquist looked puzzled. "Tsavo?"

"I read about them as part of my preparations for this mission, studying how other places had been settled. Almost a century before the Space Age began, the British built a railway in Africa. They came to call it the Lunatic Express. Two lions decided to treat the labor force as a buffet line. They killed and ate a bunch of them. The entire project ground to a halt until they were hunted down."

"Are you sure these critters won't do the same to us?"

"Not a chance! Once we've got protective cages on the construction equipment, and brought in heavier weapons and more and better sensors, we'll be able to deal with them. We've got a road to cut and a dam to build, then Sue and I will have a family to raise together. These things won't stop us. This is our planet now—no, more than that; it's our *home.*"

His bride-to-be grinned up at him. "It sure is! Now, come down to the sick bay and let them clean up that shoulder. Heaven knows what infections those critters may carry in the muck under their claws."

Smiling, Tom settled the sword at his side, picked up his carbine and slung it, and allowed Sue to lead him away. Behind them, the bodies of the rippers lay lifeless in the sun.

From the Office of the First Citizen: Thomas McLaren is recognized for bravery at the risk of his own life during an incident...

She had never thought to fight mere beasts. Those beasts, though, had wits, intent and great prowess. That had been a worthy fight.

The family, too, respected her. In this strange frontier, they kept her proudly on display.

There was no fighting. This place was remote beyond imagining, and there were no battles. She did not fathom it, only the innate wrongness of it. Without battle, how could people and cultures be tested and improved?

There were battles elsewhere, though, and after an aching eternity of waiting, she was brought forth once again.

Case Hardened

Christopher L. Smith

The antiarmor rocket outright killed Corporal Opalenik, the explosion tearing his left side to bloody scraps. It all happened in slow motion, fire and death erupting out of a quiet night. PFC Kai Shield hadn't fared any better, barely clinging to life before the second shot blew the vehicle off its wheels.

Mercifully, training kicked in when intellect took leave. Cook had been fortunate—on the driver's side but far enough away from the blast to avoid major damage—allowing him to exit through the roof. It kept the Grumbly between him and the ambushers, blocking him from view as he turned to look back inside. Sergeant Ward struggled to rise, pinned under what was left of Shield and the various unsecured and formerly secured supplies.

"Give me a hand, Cook!" Ward said, gasping. "LT's still breathing! We gotta get him out of here." A quick look at Lieutenant Broshear confirmed it. Opalenik's body and the heavily armored door had taken the brunt of the first blast, Shield and the crates most of the second. Ward struggled against the dead man's weight. "Hurry up and get him offa me."

Cook reached, hesitated, withdrew his hand. Voices, calling out in the local pidgin dialect, were fast approaching.

"C'mon, man, give me a hand!"

Cook reached in again, grabbing the carbine as the voices came closer. He pulled, stopping as something hung up on the rifle's muzzle, keeping it wedged inside the truck. Shield's sword scabbard sling twisted around the barrel, caught and held fast. Cook heaved, yanking the sword free, leaving the rifle behind.

"What are you doing, Private?" Ward looked desperate. "Help me!"

"I'm sorry, Sergeant," Cook said, backing away. The skinnies were coming. "I'm sorry."

He turned, running full speed away from the smoking Grumbly, Ward's voice trailing after him.

"Cook! Cook!" He plunged headlong into the low scrub along the dirt road, the sergeant's voice barely audible over the sound of his own breathing in the thin atmosphere. "Fucking bastard!"

Bullets whipcracked around him as he ran through the underbrush, driving him forward. His pounding heart, coupled with the helmet over his ears, almost kept him from hearing the shouts of the skinnies.

Nothing could drown out the curses of his squadmate.

He bounded in the low G, putting as much distance as he could between himself and any pursuit, angling toward the thicker vegetation to his left. The trees, small but relatively thick, would provide more cover in what was left of the Boblight.

He pitched forward suddenly, his foot landing on empty space. A turned ankle and short tumble later, he hit the water in the bottom of the ditch hard, searing pain erupting in his left thigh. Clenched lips held the scream in, and the muck out, as he raised his head, only to duck it back down again at the sound of an approaching engine. He crawled forward a little, taking advantage of the fallen branch he'd landed near.

Cook didn't want to think hard about what he was covered in. Putrid water soaked into his uniform, providing some relief from the heat—small comfort in light of his current situation. Best he could tell, he'd fallen into one of the small streams that fed the nearby swamp.

Skinny voices, no more than three meters away, carried disgust as they floated through the deepening twilight. He watched them through the leaves of his cover, grateful for the dark skin he'd gotten from his dad.

Concealment. He corrected himself.

"Hoowee—sho he gon thisaway?"

"Ya, saw'm mine self. Runoff inna trees."

"Hmph. Don' see'm. Mebbe he fudder up dah."

Cook held still, not daring to breathe. The two men continued to stand near the edge of the stream bank, one fumbling at his crotch. The sound of one stream of water striking the surface was joined by second.

"Betchoo can' hit far side."

"Ya? Bechoo I can hit tha' branch."

Cook closed his eyes against the patter of droplets, thankful his helmet deflected most of what came his way. *This is definitely something they didn't cover in boot.*

It seemed long ago, now, though it had only been eight months since graduation. Mom had looked proud, and scared, watching him march on the parade field with the rest of his class. Dad...well, Dad was less than thrilled.

"Congratulations, *Private*." The old man had worn his dress greens, medals and ribbons thrust forward as he approached his son. Still, he had shown up. That had to count for something. "I didn't pull those strings on Earth to see you blow them off and enlist."

Sorry I'm not the soldier you were, Dad. Hell, he'd only enlisted because the thought of four years of Academy made him cringe. That, coupled with the service requirements after graduation, would put him on the Army's hook for more than ten years. This way got him out in six, with no obligation after. It was a small bit of rebellion on his part. Petty, but satisfying at the time.

On an alien planet, eyeball deep in filth, and being used as a urinal cake by the locals, he seriously reconsidered the wisdom behind that decision.

No real man would let some skinny piss on him. He could actually hear him in his head. *Just as worthless as a soldier as you are a son.*

The men walked off, followed by the cough of an engine and gravel crunching. Cook waited, tense, as the sound faded into the distance, counting slowly to one hundred.

You could've taken them. A real soldier would've at least tried.

He ignored Dad's voice as he worked his way up the wall of the stream, the loose-packed dirt and rock crumbling beneath his fingers and boots. The meter-and-a-half climb taking more time, and more out of him, than it should have. It wasn't the body armor in this gravity. He was just a pathetic mess from shock.

He made his way toward the trees, staying on the drier ground as much as possible. More concealment was never a bad thing. Scraping at the slime and filth, he did what he could to get as much of that crap off as he could. After several minutes, his face and hands were at least cleaner, if still disgusting.

His uniform was a lost cause, needing a few heavy cycles in the base laundry to get everything out of them. If that. Most likely solution was a gallon of fuel and a match. Probably the body armor, too.

A quick drag on his water bladder's straw told him all he needed to know about its contents, or lack thereof. The few drops of water that hit his tongue did little more than tease him.

He was lost, several klicks away from the closest FOB or checkpoint. He knew they had been heading north before the attack, but hadn't been paying close attention to landmarks on the way out. How far he needed to go was a question mark.

And which way is north? He struggled to remember if the local star, Bob, set in the East or West. Didn't matter either way. Dusk meant Bob was below the horizon, and no help.

His thigh began to throb as the adrenaline wore off, reminding him of the wound. He pulled open the torn cloth and inspected the gash. A bit deeper than what could be considered shallow, but not deep enough to be immediately life threatening, the torn edges of the wound red and swollen. He struggled to remember the brief they were given during the flight to this backwater shithole. Something about local fauna not registering humans as food and therefore being basically harmless. Did that extend down to the microbial level? He couldn't recall.

No matter, really. The lack of rain recently meant the water in the stream had been sitting there a while, getting some cross contamination with the swamp. If the smell were any indication, on top of the rotting vegetation, the local animals were using it as their own personal slit trench. That meant infection. He needed to find a first-aid kit and water, quick like.

Weapons were another matter. He emptied his mag pouches. Two for the sidearm, two for the carbine he didn't have. Total of ninety rounds, only thirty he could use. One field knife. One katana.

Shield had considered the sword his good luck charm. Old family heirloom, he'd said, from his mother's side. He'd been able to convince Ward and the LT to let him bring it on patrol.

It didn't seem too special, at least not in the deepening shadows. He turned the sheathed sword over in his hands, trying to make out the faded patterning. It looked old—the hilt's wrapping was almost smooth to the touch and frayed in places. Cook resisted the urge to draw the blade and examine it—there were more important things to worry about right now, like shelter.

But which way? Cook scanned the horizon. There—in the distance a plume of smoke caught the last bit of fading light. A house, maybe, or what was left of the Grumbly. Either way, a chance that he might find something he could use. Water, first-aid kit, radio—something.

Hope you're better luck for me than Shield, he

thought, lurching to his feet. After one last look at the katana, he slung it and limped off.

Cook watched as the boy walked out of the shack, a small bucket of feed swinging with each step. The scrawny chickens clucked and jostled for attention at the fence, fighting amongst themselves for food not yet scattered. The kid, with typical mild cruelty for his age group, grinned and watched the stupid birds swing their heads back and forth as he moved the bucket. He'd occasionally toss a few kernels into the mass, enjoying the resulting scuffle. A man's shout from inside got the boy moving again.

The knothole in the wall of the cramped tool shed didn't offer much in the way of surveillance. Cook lost sight of the kid as he entered the coop, the occasional surprised *bawk* of an overeager bird carrying across the small yard.

"Farm" was generous. One crappy shack, one small fenced-in chicken coop, and a tool shed with not much more than a scant handful of items wasn't what he'd consider a farm, especially compared to the sprawling acres back home. He supposed the man and his son scraped by on eggs and pure luck. They did have water—the boy used the pump between the house and shed to fill the empty feed bucket before dumping it into a small trough in the coop.

Cook shifted slightly, trying to get as much weight off his bad leg as possible. It was hard to tell if the pain had lessened, or if he'd just gotten used to it, but it wasn't quite as bad as it had been earlier. Too dark to see clearly, he prodded at the gash with his fingers, the area around it hot to the touch.

The sound of the door closing brought his attention back to the yard. The boy, finished with his chores, had gone back inside. Cook gave them a few moments to get settled in and focused on something else before he made his way out of the shed and toward the pump.

He resisted the urge to revel in the fresh water. Instead, he filled his "camel," wincing at every squeak of the handle. He drank deeply, the iron-laden water making him gag slightly as it hit his parched tongue. He ignored the taste and forced it down, emptying the canteen in one long draft. He refilled it before taking off his helmet and filling it too.

Back in the tool shed, he used the knife to cut a strip from his shirt, rinsing it with water from the helmet before cleaning his leg. He grimaced at every touch—even the slightest pressure sent flares through his thigh.

Short streams from the drinking tube cleaned another strip of shirt. Cook took two deep breaths, set his jaw, and packed the wet cloth into the wound.

It took everything he had to keep the scream from erupting through his clenched teeth.

Fighting the darkness threatening to overtake him, he tied another strip around the bloody mess to hold everything together.

Not going to do much, he thought after the pain subsided, *but better than nothing until I can find a real kit.*

Next task—food. Chicken was off the menu—not only would the noise bring unwanted attention, cooking it wasn't possible. Trying to gather eggs in the dark was just stupid. However, there was a bag of grain just outside the front door . . .

If he could get a scoop of feed and soak it for a

while, it might be possible to eat it without breaking a tooth. His stomach growled, adding its two cents. He drank the last of what was in the helmet and lurched to his feet.

A few of the chickens roused themselves, clucking softly as they watched as he scooped feed into his helmet. A quick pump and the mix of barley, corn, and something unidentifiable was swimming. It wouldn't help right away, he was sure, but he didn't know how long it would take to soften the feed up to the point it was edible. He limped back to the shed, cradling his treasure.

An hour? More? He put the full helmet off to the side and leaned up against the wall of the shed, closing his eyes.

Cook snapped awake. An old-style diesel engine desperately needing a tune-up was approaching the farm.

At the door of the shack, he could just make out two silhouettes, the taller pointing at the shed and pushing the smaller toward it.

Shit! Nowhere to go, at least not without being discovered. He prepared himself to grab the kid as soon as he hit the door.

It was seconds only when the hinges squeaked.

It didn't take long. Cook moved quickly, pain flaring in his thigh as he took the boy by the arm. His other hand went over the kid's mouth, clamping down hard to prevent any noise. An elbow to the gut made him grunt—the boy was much stronger than he looked. Cook had mass on his side, however, and quickly subdued his prisoner. He leaned in, lips grazing an ear.

"Not a sound. I'm not going to hurt you, but you

need to stay quiet. Nod if you understand." The boy's head moved, breath whistling through his nose in forceful gasps. "Good."

He moved over to the knothole as the engine sound grew louder. An old truck pulled into the yard, the light from the shack washed out by the headlights. Four men jumped out of the bed, raising their rifles to cover the man at the door, as the driver got out. After a quick look around, he pointed to two of the gunmen, then to the coop, rattling off what sounded like an order in the local dialect. The two men nodded and jogged to the gate.

As they left Cook's line of sight, the old man yelled, waving his hands while stepping forward. He was met by the barrels of the other two, the threat of violence doing nothing to stop his protestations.

Cook shivered, a cold sweat breaking out on his forehead. The throbbing in his leg grew worse, the sudden activity agitating the wound.

The leader smiled as he walked forward, wrapping one arm casually around the old man's shoulders. Cook couldn't catch much of what he said, just a few words in broken English—"food," "cause," "soldiers." The last was followed by a sweeping gesture, taking in the other men. The first two came back to the truck, a chicken under each arm.

"No!" The old man shook the leader off as he moved to intercept the thieves, only to be doubled over by the butt of a rifle to the stomach. A strike to the temple put him on the ground, groaning.

Cook tightened his grip as the boy began to struggle, a few frantic kicks making contact with his shins.

"Stop," he whispered, "If they find us, it'll be worse."

Skinny arms flew wildly, causing Cook to shift his hold on the boy. Agony lanced through him as one elbow landed squarely on his wounded thigh, followed by a wave of nausea. Shock and pain allowed the kid to make a break for it, reaching the door just ahead of Cook's grasping hand.

"Papa! Papa!" The kid ran to his dad, squeezing between the men. The leader grinned, twitching his rifle toward the dad's face. The kid dropped to his knees, cradling his father's head. His back was to the skinny aiming at him.

Cook jumped at the pair of shots, tools rattling as his back made contact with them. Six pairs of eyes whipped around, focusing on his hiding spot. The leader motioned again, this time in his direction. Two of the others sprinted toward him.

Cook moved, busting through the shed's door. *If I can just get to... Shit! Where? There!* Not far away, less than twenty yards, the scrub—

He hit the ground hard, betrayed by the sword. White fire lanced through his thigh, blinding him with its intensity. A scream ripped through him, momentarily covering the sound of the footsteps closing on him. He rolled, trying to disentangle himself as he drew his sidearm. The pistol caught on the holster, falling from his weak fingers as the two men approached.

The first kick caught him in the torso armor, the man's curses filling the night at his broken toe. Cook didn't have time to do more than smile, however, as the butt of the other man's rifle came down hard on his forehead.

Stars erupted in front of his eyes. He didn't feel the second strike.

❖   ❖   ❖

The vision of a woman with Asian features scowled at him. He started slightly, the edges of his vision fading to black, until all he could see was her face. Her eyes bored into him, projecting anger.

"Why do you hate me? What did I do?"

A rough voice came from the darkness. "You asking me that? Damn, but you got some nerve, nigga." It was Ward.

The Japanese woman's image remained for another second, fading quickly as he became fully aware of his surroundings. Sergeant Ward sat across from him, one eye swollen shut, the good one filled with hatred.

"You left us there to die, Cook. I barely got the LT out before the skinnies showed." He shifted, trying to find a comfortable way to sit with bound wrists and ankles. His grimace told Cook he'd failed. "Fuckers caught us with our pants down, because of you."

"Wha—" Cook's head pounded, pain cutting off his words. He ignored it and continued. "Where are we?"

"Hell if I know," Ward said. "Some shithole hut in the middle of nowhere. Couldn't see much when they dragged us in."

"Where's the LT?"

Ward chuckled. "Like you give a shit, coward. Ain't like any of us in any shape to help each other, neither." At Cook's silence, he sighed. "Smoke and shit did us pretty good. They did the rest. LT is breathin', but he caught the worst of it."

Ward stopped as voices approached. The door to the small hut opened, closing immediately after Lieutenant Broshear was thrown inside.

He looked half dead. Several abrasions and burns on his face oozed blood, mixing with sweat from his forehead and tears from his red-rimmed eyes. Several raspy coughs tore through him, dust from the ground billowing about his head, only to be inhaled in a repeating cycle of agony. Cook inched forward, carefully using his bound hands to turn Broshear's head upward.

"Oh, so now you want to help?" Ward shook his head in disgust. "There were six of them, Cook. Six. The three of us would've made it. Hell, just the two of us could've held them until the LT came to. Alone? I didn't have a chance, not after getting out of the Grumbly. All you had to do was give me your hand."

Cook shivered, despite the heat and stuffiness of the hut. Roughly two meters square, it appeared to be a leftover prefab unit from the early days of colonization. Cheap but sturdy, the smooth composite plastic walls were windowless. The only seams were in the corners, a sloppy bead of epoxy bonding agent holding everything together. It appeared as though whoever had assembled the unit chose quantity of material over quality of application, but in his experience, it didn't matter with these structures. No amount of huffing and puffing would bring this thing down.

Tunneling was an option, if they had something other than fingernails to dig with, so moot point. The only way they would get out would be through the door. Whether it would be under their own power or carried remained to be seen. He turned back to Sergeant Ward.

"What's the plan, Sergeant?"

"I don't know." Ward hung his head. "I can't think straight right now. I figure they want us for something, not sure what."

"We're a message," Broshear said weakly. "And maybe a payday. Best I can tell, they're holding us for ransom from the UN."

Ward chuckled. "Like the UN will give a pot of shit for colonial augmentees."

Broshear's eyes squeezed shut as another coughing fit came on. A small trickle of blood made its way from his nose to the corner of his mouth. He turned his head, the only warning Cook had. Blood and phlegm struck the wall where his head had been.

"LT, Sergeant, I think I can get us out of this. My dad, he's retired now, but if I can talk to him—" He paused at Ward's snort, unable to tell if he was laughing or just disgusted. *Probably both.* He ignored it and kept going. "He has friends, strings he can pull, people he can talk to. All we have to do is hold out."

"Figures," Ward said. "Too scared to hold your own, so crawl behind the general's legs and hope Daddy makes it all okay." Cracked lips formed a hideous smile, devoid of any warmth. "Yeah, I know who your father is. Reputation for politics to get ahead. You think he can save your ass this time? No chance."

Ward closed his eye and sat back, presumably finished with the conversation.

"LT, I think—"

Broshear turned away, cutting him off without a sound.

They're right to hate you. You know they're right. His dad's voice cut through his mind like a dull knife. *It's not enough to make me look bad—no, you have to use me to bail you out. As usual.*

Fatigue washed through him, followed by nausea. He wobbled slightly, trying to get his balance and failing, then landed on his side in the dirt. Blinking away unwanted tears, the image of the Asian girl came to him, her expression adding to his depression.

Weak. Unworthy. Failure. No words were needed, her eyes held the accusations. *Worthless.*

"Guard! Hey, guard!"

Ward's eye snapped open. "What the hell you doin', Cook?"

He ignored the NCO, rolling over and bringing his knees to his chest. Another wave of nausea as the pain in his leg started anew. He struggled into an upright position. Through the onslaught of dizziness, he shouted again.

"Guard! I need to talk to someone!"

Two men came in, holding rifles at the ready.

"'Choo wan?"

"I need to talk to your boss," Cook said, fighting to stay upright. "I can help him."

The first guard grunted before rattling off something to the man beside him.

"No really, I can get things. Hurk!" The barrel of the rifle caught him in the pit of his stomach, doubling him over. Forehead to the ground, he heaved, thankful he'd not eaten earlier. Drowning in his own vomit would only add more insult to the list of injuries. Gagging, he forced his torso up. "Please, let me just talk to him."

The men left, closing the door behind them. Cook sat back on his haunches, trying to relieve the pressure on his knees. Fortunately, his captors hadn't tied the ropes tight enough to cut off circulation in his hands or feet—there was still some restriction, but he hadn't gone numb yet. There was a little play, but not enough to get his hopes up.

"So that's it, is it? Pitiful." Ward spat toward him. "You're lucky I can't come over there and kick your ass. I hope they slit your damn throat."

"I can fix this," Cook whispered. "Just let me try and fix this. Please."

His head snapped up at the sound of the latch. Two new men came in, rifles slung across their back. One moved around behind him as the other gabbled in some other language.

"I don't understand." More words followed, accompanied with gestures.

At Cook's confusion, the talker motioned to the other man, barking out an order. A sudden blow to his back pitched Cook forward, stars flashing in his eyes as his head made contact with the ground. His feet felt suddenly swollen and tingly as the rope from his ankles was removed, the blood rushing back in full. His wrists remained tied, a fact that became painfully apparent as the first man used them to pull him up. He staggered slightly as he stood, immediately straightening as a muzzle made contact with his spine.

A second, harder nudge made the man's intentions clear. He moved forward, exiting the hut behind the talker.

The original two guards flanked the door, one leaning against the wall of the hut, the other sitting cross-legged next to him. Both rifles were more or less within reach, haphazardly laid on the ground as the men rolled cigarettes.

The compound, for lack of a better term, was made up of several more prefab huts, loosely arranged in a circle surrounding a large tent. Small groups of two to four men lounged around most of them, smoking, drinking and eating. Security seemed to consist of his escort, the two guards outside of his hut, and two rovers at opposite ends of the camp. A quick count gave him roughly twenty-two men visible.

Only five vehicles. Figure six to eight people in each, at most, with the larger truck for gear. Potentially forty people in camp.

Doubtful—it seemed like social hour. This group wasn't exactly up to Army standards on discipline and preparation.

They approached the central tent. Larger than the huts at about three meters square, the dark green aramid flexed lazily in the slight breeze.

Inside, it could best be described as semiorganized chaos. Scattered piles of random gear took up most of the floor space, some of it recognizable from the Grumbly. The portable radio, a few field rats, and a torso clamshell caught his eye, but what really got his attention was the group marked with red crosses. The unit's Individual First-Aid Kits, or IFAKs, had been dumped on top of other gear, along with the larger one from the vehicle. As if in response, his leg sent a twinge, to remind him it was still there. Not to be outdone, another wave of dizziness hit him as he stood, threatening to send him to his knees again.

"My men inform me that you wish to speak." The leader of the group spoke in slightly accented English. He gnawed a leg from the half-eaten roast chicken in front of him, washing it down with a swig from an unlabeled bottle. Cook recognized the man from earlier at the farm. "You have something of value to me. Is this true?"

Cook nodded, mouth watering at the smell of the

meal. Hunger fought nausea, winning by a small margin. His stomach cramped and growled as he searched for words.

Ever since the riot at the capitol a month previous, the locals had gotten more belligerent and restless. The UN and alliance troops had been able to quell most of the violence, getting things back to "normal" levels of harassment, but the outlying communities had been simmering. The scuttlebutt said shit was going to hell soon, based on the rhetoric of the region's tribal leaders. All considered themselves the best candidate to fill the void left by the former President.

"Well?" Annoyance flashed across the man's features. He was about 175 centimeters tall. Like most of the local population, he had dark hair and leathery olive skin. Lean and wiry, either he was low on the tribal pecking order, or actually worked as hard as his men. He leaned forward slightly, giving Cook a brief look at a worn, silk-wrapped hilt. Kai's sword. "What have you to say?"

"My father is rich, and powerful," Cook said. "If I could get a message to him, he could work a deal with you." He glanced at the two men flanking him. "If we could speak in private?"

The man studied him quietly before taking another piece of chicken. Cook's stomach growled again, audible in the relative quiet of the tent. The man smiled at his discomfort, taking in the dirty, injured and obviously hungry soldier.

After a few moments, he waved off the escort, seemingly satisfied that Cook posed no threat.

"You tell me your father has money, yet you are a common soldier," the man said. "If this was true, you would be a general, no?"

"That's not how it works, really," Cook said with a shrug. "Oh, he tried, don't get me wrong. A few suggestions here and there to the right people made sure I got it easy." He forced a tight lipped smile. "I made a few enemies, and their people were more influential than my people."

The man smiled in understanding. The local tribes acted much as their counterparts back on Earth. Old customs die hard. You had to be the big man, or at least be in his good graces, to gain status. Piss off the wrong guy, and you were on the shit list. What Cook was dangling, he hoped, was the means to a quick rise through the ranks.

"That sword? That was my father's." The lie grabbed the man's attention. "He gave it to me before I left. It's an old family heirloom, practically priceless. Would a poor man carry that with him?"

The man reached behind him, bringing the sheathed blade around to study it.

"It doesn't look like much."

"The scabbard is junk, but look at the blade." Cook hoped like hell Shield had kept it up.

The man drew, carefully, examining the steel in the steady light from the camp lanterns. As before, the blade gleamed, almost as though it shone from within. Cook blinked as his vision faded briefly, the image of the Asian girl appearing in front of him. He shook his head to clear it.

"What do you need from me?" the man asked absently, enraptured by the sword.

"I see you have a camera?" Cook jerked his chin toward the corner of the room, occupied by a large cot. Next to it, a video camera—probably stolen from a local news van—sat on a tripod, facing inward. "You can record a message from me, and send it to my father. I assume you have someone you know that can send things off planet? You've done this before, right?"

"Yes, I have a way."

"Good." Cook forced another grin. "I'd keep it quiet as possible, though, I'm sure the . . . fees . . . get more expensive the more people know, am I right?" He made a show of looking around the room. "I mean, you seem like a fair man. You give your men a fair cut of all this, why not keep a little for yourself? You're the one doing all the really hard work."

"And what would you ask for in return?" Suspicion replaced greed on the man's face.

"Not much, really." At the man's raised eyebrow, he continued quickly, "Well, yeah, I'd like one of those first-aid kits, for one. Food, of course. And my own hut. The other two and I don't get along."

His captor chuckled. "Yes, they had quite a bit to say about the coward that left them to die."

Cook couldn't hide his grimace.

"Yeah, well, that's another thing I'll need—those guys get food, water, and first aid." The other man shook his head. Cook said, "It's in your best interest, really. The UN will blow you off, but our colony will be more likely to give in to your demands if you show them you're treating us well. Makes for good press on your side, too: 'Local Leader Helps General's Son Survive after Brutal Attack.'"

"We want you to leave. Showing what we do to those we find is how we will convince your leadership."

"No, you've got that all wrong," Cook said. "What that does is piss guys off. Guys like the other two.

To the point where they want to stick around, just to find you and make you pay."

Something changed in the other man's demeanor, the casual avarice replaced by a fierce anger. He stood, drawing the katana. The scabbard made a hollow sound as it hit the floor, dropped so both hands could be used on the hilt. In less than a second, Cook was looking over the razor-sharp edge, the point less than an inch from his nose. Hunger, nausea, dizziness—all gone, replaced by stomach-clenching fear and adrenaline.

"You think they will 'make us pay,' do you? They can search, but will never find all of us. Any violent action your forces perform, we will use as a weapon against them. We will kill women and children and say it was you." He moved the blade slowly, gently placing the flat on Cook's neck. A sinister laugh rumbled in his chest, bubbling up to escape a cruel smile. "We don't have to beat you, we just need to break your will. Starting with the son of a rich man."

Cook swallowed hard. This was going south, quickly.

"Now, wait—killing me won't do you any good. My father—"

"Your father. Bah. Just like a spoiled coward. Expecting someone else to save you, trying to bribe your way out of any difficult situation. You're weak." The sword tapped him on the shoulder. "On your knees, *boy.*"

The pressure increased, the edge cutting through his shirt and into his skin. Something inside him kept him upright, however.

This is what you deserve. His father's voice. *Dying the way you lived. I wish you hadn't been born.*

The man shouted, calling for the two escorts. They came in, listened to instructions, then moved.

One took the camera, an outdated clunky model from decades past, trying to remove it from the mismatched tripod while keeping his rifle out of the way. After a minute of awkward struggle he got it aimed, giving a thumbs-up as the red light came on.

The other man grabbed Cook's shoulders while kicking his legs out from under him. He hit the ground hard, pitching forward before being roughly hauled upright again. Cook kept his head down as the hands released him.

Not even going to look your executioner in the eye. The voice dripped scorn. *Just going to let them slaughter you—a sheep, too afraid to resist.*

"This is one of your own, intruders. The tribes have no need for your imperialism and intervention in our country." The leader took a sidestep, motioning to the man at Cook's back. Fingers in his hair pulled his head up, forcing him to stare at the camera. "We will fight you, with everything we have. We will win. We are the lion in the savannah, invisible until we strike."

He brought the katana up, brandishing it for his future audience.

"For the crimes committed against the people of this nation, we sentence this man to die. He is not the first, and will not be the last."

Coward! So afraid of dying, you're terrified of living!

You're right, Dad. Happy? I'm finally admitting it. I'm the quitter you always said I was.

No, not a quitter. Just scared. And where did that get you?

It's gotten me killed.

He expected some response, another cutting remark, something. Nothing. The silence was almost jarring, after years of constant berating. In a way, it was a relief, allowing Cook a moment of focus and clarity. Calm washed over him as the sword, drawn back to strike, caught the light.

I'm going to die. The chuckle came unbidden, working its way upward from the giddy feeling in his stomach. *I joined the most technologically superior army in the universe, rode a spaceship to get to a new planet, and I'm going to be killed in a tent by a guy with a SWORD!*

The man in front of him hesitated, confusion apparent on his face. The sudden change of expression made Cook laugh even harder, great heaving guffaws shaking his whole body. To make things even stranger, *she* appeared, a slight smile upon her face.

The smile, a welcome change from the disgust, magnified her exotic beauty beyond measure. It became his only focus, the edges of his vision going dark as he stared, watching her move from behind the table. Time seemed to slow.

She came to him, holding her hands out, beckoning. He lunged, wanting only to touch her—the final, desperate act of a man embracing death.

A sound of contact, followed by a scream brought his attention back to what was happening around him. The fingers in his hair released as a wet warmth spread over his skull, letting his forward motion continue without resistance. Instinctively, he threw his bound hands up and out, trying to catch himself. He clutched desperately as they made contact, pulling hard to avoid slamming into the ground.

The agonized look on his captor's face as Cook practically ripped his balls off almost brought a feeling of guilt.

Almost.

Cook clawed for the pistol on the man's belt as the cameraman dropped his equipment, a life-or-death race for weapons. Cook cleared the pistol from the holster just as the other man brought his rifle around, surprise on his features appearing seconds after the bullets impacted his chest.

He stood, turning the pistol on the leader, emptying the magazine into his chest. The remaining skinny clutched at his wrist, trying to hold his partially severed hand in place. Blood flowed from between his fingers, pooling on the dirt floor.

Cook knelt, picking up the katana awkwardly, his bound wrists making it difficult to get a firm grip as he maneuvered it into position to cut the strap. A little pressure, one quick movement, and it fell to the ground.

He looked up to find the woman. She glanced at the man on the ground, nodding once, pointedly. Cook placed the point at the man's chin, and with a quick thrust, put him out of his misery.

"You died a warrior," he whispered, to the apparent delight of his companion. Her smile reappeared, radiant in the relative gloom of the tent, filling him with warmth and a sense of purpose.

"I'm dead. Aren't I? This is how I earn my way to the next world, isn't it?"

She said nothing—answering only with slight nod and mysterious smile.

He had to move. The gunshots would alert the camp. His only hope was that executions were expected, and no one would come to investigate until later. He quickly wiped the blade on his shirt before retrieving the scabbard. It seemed like the right thing to do.

The woman walked to the back of the tent. Cook nodded his agreement—going out the front would be suicide. Another chuckle escaped his lips.

I'm a dead man, worrying about suicide.

As there was no back door, that meant making his own. He grabbed an IFAK, and approached the rear wall of the tent. It seemed almost heretical to use the katana, but he didn't have time to search the bodies for a knife. It would have to work. A quick slice, and he was outside, following the woman into the darkness.

His eyes adjusted, allowing him to make out the scrub at the edge of the camp in the distance. A quick look around the corner verified what he suspected— most of the men in the camp were looking around, as if they were expecting some sign that things were good. One of the more curious started moving toward the tent. Cook moved to the opposite side, slightly surprised to find no one guarding the vehicles.

If I can get over to that hut, I can work my way to the trucks.

He covered the five-meter gap quickly, realizing that his leg no longer bothered him. While he wasn't willing to trust it at a full sprint, he did notice that the pain had dissipated enough to allow him to move faster than a walking pace. The prefabs gave him enough cover, and shadows, to get within meters of the larger vehicle, a flatbed transport that looked right out of the late twenty-first century. Cook moved around to the front, easing open the driver's-side door. His luck held—the key sat on the seat. A key. Yeah, it was that crude. Yes, they were that careless.

He turned to make sure no one was paying attention,

coming face to face with his companion, anger clearly showing on her porcelain features. Silently, she pointed in the direction of the camp.

"No," he said. "The road is this way. We can get to the base and get reinforcements."

She shook her head while forcefully pointing toward the hut containing Ward and Broshear. He followed her finger, noting that two skinnies had reached the tent, and were talking in front of it. One had his hand on the entrance flap, the other holding him back. It was clear they were arguing about going inside.

Either way, his time was growing short.

"You're right. But there's too many of them, and they'll be on full alert in a second."

This time, he followed her gesture to the ground next to him. A good-sized rock, massing at least six kilos, lay next to his foot, just behind the front wheel. She then pointed to the key.

"A distraction." He nodded in understanding. "Good idea."

Grunting with effort, Cook heaved the rock into the cab before punching the starter. As old as it seemed to be, the engine turned over on the first try. He wedged the rock onto the accelerator and engaged the transmission, jumping back as the truck lurched forward into the night.

He was treated to her smile as he crept along, staying out of sight as shouts erupted from the camp. He made his way to the next hut, sticking to the shadows as roughly half the men ran toward his position, scrambling to get into the other vehicles before his decoy got too far away.

Two stragglers remained behind, a few meters from

his position, their backs to him. Dressed similarly to the others in loose-fitting shirts and cargo pants, they appeared to be armed only with pistols on their hips. It would be so easy to sneak up and skewer one, then the other.

He expected the sword to ring as it cleared the scabbard—too many old movies, he supposed. The reality was that it slid from its sheath with a whisper. But there was something, not audible to the naked ear, that filled his mind. Like the blade was crying in exultation, a hymn that only the bearer could hear. A war cry, a call for blood—it struck a chord deep within him.

He looked up to find his companion beaming, her expression filling him with joy, the radiance of her face echoed in the steel of the blade. His vision wavered slightly at the edges, much like it had in his dreams, giving the woman a softly glowing halo.

I won't let you down.

He held the blade at his side, point in front of him, lined up with his first target. It reminded him of bayonet practice in training—all he had to do was shift his grip some, one hand near the guard, the other at the base. He suppressed a laugh. They had all thought that bayonet drills were useless wastes of time.

Two quick steps and a lunge, the blade slid through the first man's kidney. Cook straightened, extracting the sword as he stood up, turning to face the other man, bringing the hilt upward to connect with his target's jaw. The man's shocked expression remained fixed as Cook brought the edge down on the diagonal, chopping through the base of the neck and clavicle.

The first man moaned in agony, bringing Cook's attention back to him. A quick strike across the neck silenced him for good. He worked fast, laying the sword down, removing and buckling the men's gun belts at his waist, the leather straps forming an X.

Pancho Villa, eat your heart out.

He picked up the sword again. The woman motioned for him to follow, leading him around the perimeter of the camp. The remaining skinnies were alert, gathered around the command tent, with the exception of one guard still on duty at the prisoner's hut.

The distance was just far enough to make pistol accuracy iffy, especially since marksmanship wasn't his strong point. A charge at this distance would give the guard plenty of time to bring his rifle to bear.

With a smile, his guide walked out in the open, once again beckoning him to follow. He obliged, knowing that she'd protect him.

The guard's attention was on the center of the camp, distracted by the commotion. Cook covered about half the distance before he was noticed. The guard glanced in his direction, then turned to focus more intently on the figure coming toward him.

"Hey! Wachoo doon!"

"Boss ne'help," Cook said, pointing toward the tent. He was counting on the general confusion and his sudden appearance to keep the man off balance for a few more seconds as he approached. His guide continued on her path unafraid, not hesitating at the sight of the guard's weapon. Only a few more meters...

The rifle's muzzle, held at hip level, came up as he closed, determination setting in on the man's face. Raising his free hand, Cook kept the katana's blade close to his leg, perpendicular to the ground.

"Go help." Two more steps. "Stole truck!"

He slashed with the sword, an upward strike that took the guard across the chest, but not before the man could pull the trigger. Other than a flinch at the report, the woman showed no reaction. A quick thrust finished the guard as he fell to his knees, the rifle clattering to the ground beside him. Cook picked up the weapon and opened the door.

Broshear and Ward, in the same positions as when he left, looked surprised as he entered. Ward's eye fell on the sword, and widened.

"What the fuck? You sold us out, didn't you?"

"What? No, I'm here to get you out." Cook moved to Broshear, slicing through the ropes around his wrists and ankles before moving to Ward. The woman scowled. "I'm sorry, it's all I have right now."

"I'm not complaining," Ward said. "Just hurry."

"Hm? Oh, right." Cook finished with Ward's bonds and unbuckled the gun belts. "Here, you can have these, LT. Sergeant, this is for you."

Ward took the rifle and checked it, dropping the magazine and working the action.

"What about you?" he asked, reloading.

"I have all I need," Cook said.

"What? The sword? How many are out there?"

"I've killed six, so far. Best I can tell, there's between a dozen and two dozen left."

"That's a pretty wide margin of error, Private."

"We'll be fine." Cook nodded toward the woman. "She'll protect us."

Ward and Broshear looked around the room, then shared a glance.

"Who will?" Broshear asked, rubbing his wrists.

Cook ignored him, walking to the door. Broshear

muttered something about strange women and swords as he joined him.

The remaining men stood near the command tent in a rough half circle, looking agitated.

"We need to wait until their attention is focused in the same direction," Broshear said, "otherwise they'll see us. Any ideas?"

"LT, you and Sergeant Ward make a break for the truck. I'll cover you."

"There's too many, Cook. You won't make it," Broshear said. He drew a pistol. "Here, take one of these back. We'll hit them from cover."

"No, she'll protect me." Before the other men could stop him, he opened the door, striding purposefully toward the knot of men. No one seemed to notice him at first, too wrapped up in the events of the day, he supposed. That, and no one would expect a prisoner to just waltz out into the open. He was somewhat surprised that his companion didn't draw their attention, however. She turned slightly, giving a small nod. Cook checked to make sure Ward and Broshear had gotten to cover; they had. It was time.

He charged, rushing the men with katana held high, the woman keeping slightly ahead and to his right. One of the men, about ten meters away, glanced over his shoulder, doing a double take before facing him with a shout. Several others followed his lead, fumbling with their weapons.

I was afraid of this?

His laugh filled the night air as he watched the men panic, their response worse than a squad of new boots. Rifles held sideways, over their heads, at their hips—bullets whipped through the air around him, none finding their target. Cook focused, time again slowing, using the katana to intercept any bullets that came within reach. Those were sent back at the crowd, dropping a man with each crack of thunder.

A lunge took the lead gunman in the the throat, the blade singing its song in Cook's skull. It became a jubilant roar as he turned, slicing through the neck of the next man. The severed head bounced, rolling away as he continued his bloody work.

Another skinny fell, sliding off the katana, cutting his fingers to ribbons as he tried to remove it from his stomach. His face, eyes wide, froze in an expression of shock and surprise.

A shot, close to Cook's left side, grabbed his attention. The smoking muzzle of the rifle held by the last man trembled in his hands, terror written on his face. Cook lunged, spearing the man's eye.

It was over, the remaining men fleeing from the swordsman. Cook looked down, now noticing the wetness spreading from his chest. No less than five bullet holes in his shirt, all bleeding profusely. He laughed.

"You can't kill a dead man!" Darkness crept in at the edge of his sight as the katana fell from his fingers. He was so tired... The sound of an engine made him turn his head, the dizziness threatening to bring him down. He fell heavily to his knees, trying to make out his surroundings. She appeared in front of him, holding his face in her hands, smiling.

The light from within her blinding him, Cook relaxed into her embrace. Warmth spread throughout him, the knowledge that she was pleased filling him with pride and tranquility. Ward's voice came to him, muffled and distant.

"I covered him as best I could, sir, but he caught a few shots. I'd swear he was trying to hit the bullets back."

"Get him in the bed, and let's get out of here!"

Cook took the woman's proffered hand as she rose in front of him, stepping lightly on air. He felt his body being lifted.

"I'm not leaving you, Cook." Through the light filling his eyes, Ward's face hovered over his. "Stay with me. We're going home."

"Yes I am, Sergeant. She's taking me home. I made her proud."

"You did good, Private."

As he followed the woman into the light, Broshear's voice came to him from miles away.

"The story is he avoided capture and rescued us, Sergeant. That's all that goes in the report. Do I make myself clear?"

"Crystal, sir."

Official Transcript for the Posthumous Award of the Colonial Star...

—⚊—

That bearer had been most unusual. She'd actually felt rapport, communication with him. She had inspired him to abandon his cowardice and fight with honor and ferocity. That was a fine thing, and thrilled her. From shrinking fear to brazen courage, he'd grown and fought.

The family retained her, but the next generation had no martial spirit, and she was sold. Again she waited, held in custodianship by people who respected her in all regards, except to use her in battle.

—⚊—

Magnum Opus

Jason Cordova

In all of life there is a song. A natural rhythm, as it were, to the order of the universe. Every heartbeat, every inhale and exhale, contained a note which ran in perfect harmony with the heart of the galaxy.

For Operative Lieutenant Rowan Moran of the Freehold Military Forces, the music of the universe reached its crescendo whenever he wielded his katana in the embassy's dojo. With each cut a new note was created, with every thrust came a change in pitch and tune. His constant practice in the ancient art of *iaido* could easily be parlayed into a musical score, so quick and precise were his movements.

Even after many years of practice, however, his movements were not yet perfect. The music which was supposed to flow through him in steady rhythm was not present, a clunky thrash piece over the symphonic artistry which he was supposed to feel. The blade felt wrong in his hand, the sword unbalanced. He knew that there was no way the sword was the issue. Neither was it the art. No, he knew that the problem lay within himself. He frowned and made three more quick cuts through the air, the blade of the sword flashing in the bright light with each movement. His frown deepened and his brow furrowed in frustration. *Iaido* was not supposed to be easy, but no matter how hard he tried to lose himself to it, he was unable. This he blamed on his own failings. For as deep into the art as he was, Rowan could never entirely lose himself. An Operative was never fully ignorant of his immediate surroundings.

"Good morning, Ambassador," he called out as he flicked his wrist slightly. The katana whispered through the air and, with movement borne of long practice, the face of the blade was wiped clean on his sleeve. Historically, it was a maneuver to wipe the blood of an enemy off of the face of the blade before the katana was sheathed. To an *iaidoka*, however, it came as naturally as breathing.

"Good morning, Lieutenant," Ambassador Kiem Luc nodded respectfully in reply. He always tried to surprise Moran, and always failed. "Your form looks good today."

"Thank you, sir," Rowan said as he sheathed the blade. He turned and looked at the shorter man. "The answer is still no, sir."

"I could order you to go," the ambassador said with a small smile. There was no heat in his statement, merely fact.

"I still don't understand why you insist on me accompanying you alone to this function," Rowan complained in a low voice. "I told you that I was more than happy to remain as an anonymous member of the protective detail."

"And as part of my protective detail, I want you to accompany me inside the event as my social companion," Kiem said as he took a step closer. Rowan could see that the seasoned politician was doing his best not to let any irritation appear on his face. "Caledonian policy prohibits armed guards within the presence of their royals, which puts the Freehold in a bind. Our ambassadors are not to be unescorted by at least one armed guard anywhere outside the embassy. The Caledonians want us to play their power games and I refuse. I'm irritated, and the Citizen's Council is as well. Caledonia, Novaja Rossia, all of them. They know we want to withdraw from the UN and they're making fun of us for thinking we can. It's time that they learn that their morals are not our own, that our customs and beliefs are not theirs to dictate. We are more than an idea, Rowan. We're an actual nation. It's time for them to quit looking down on us."

Rowan could read the tension in the ambassador's body language and mentally grimaced. "No offense, sir, but you are a bit on the short side."

Kiem smiled. "If I thought I had any chance in hell, Moran, I'd kick your ass."

"Noted, sir."

"Social escort, Rowan," Kiem said, his tone changing ever so slightly. "Please. Just you alone. No one else from the detail. Caledonians should be providing enough security to blanket the entire building, so you alone should be enough on the inside. Outside we'll have a rapid response team ready to move at a moment's notice. That way I get what you want, and you get what you want."

Rowan thought it over. The head of the embassy's

security detail would likely flip out over the idea of the ambassador going in practically unescorted, which made Rowan a bit happy, but they were still following the rules, *per se*. While he respected the woman, a little professional competition never hurt anybody. Plus, there was no reason for him to avoid the "pie with a fork" training he'd received. Still, there was one thing that continued to bother him.

He hated formal functions with a passion.

"I need you, Rowan," the ambassador pleaded. He laid a hand on the Operative's arm. "I won't lie and say that it would be the end of the world if you didn't attend and I had to take someone else, but I can't think of anyone else that I would want on my arm tonight."

"You," Rowan breathed as he bowed his head in acquiescence, "are a slimy politician, sir."

"Not slimy enough for Earth, though," Kiem said with a small smile.

"Thank Goddess." Both men could readily agree upon that sentiment.

The security briefing afterward went about as well as could be expected, given that the usual procedures were being dumped in exchange for making a political statement.

"I'm going in with only one person on my security detail," was met with howls of protest from the security detail, his chief of staff and a few others who were on the need-to-know list. "Let me explain before you all call me crazy, please."

"One," the Freehold's ambassador said as he held up a finger to forestall any further arguments from his protection detail, "and before you begin to protest, I've already decided that the individual accompanying me into the formal ballroom is going to be an Operative."

That revelation worked better than anything else could have. The guards shared looks as they listened to their boss. Their expressions ranged from outrage to wariness to cold, polite acceptance. A few of them were off-kilter, muttering amongst themselves. It was plain that they were not happy with this new development.

While they respected the men and women in the Black Ops element, it galled them when they took plum assignments, such as escorting an ambassador to a formal function hosted by the royal family. They'd follow the orders because they were professional and understood the reasoning. Still, it hurt their pride even more to know that they would only be protecting the exterior and not be allowed inside with the ambassador in the presence of the royal family.

This was precisely what the ambassador had anticipated, Rowan recalled as he watched the men and women in the room. The ambassador did not want the embassy's security detail to protest to the Caledonians behind his back, which was an admittedly low possibility. Going behind the ambassador's back was typically not condoned. Kiem knew that but, should the situation call for it, the head of security could prohibit him from attending by dropping a few choice words about perimeter security and immediate threats to the Caledonians. That, at least, was what Rowan would have done had he truly wanted to screw over his friend. But that could also lead to a diplomatic row between the two nations, and while the Freehold was no longer officially a part of the UN, there were still some within the Council who held some lingering feelings to their former sister states.

Freehold Military Forces Special Warfare teams never rattled. It was just one of the many things which made them so very dangerous.

"Allowing Moran to escort me inside allows different options when it comes to security, the least of which means we can have a human weapon inside protecting me at all times," Kiem reminded them. "It also gives us more than a few options that we won't have otherwise, given the Caledonians prohibiting armed guards in the royal presence."

"Besides," the ambassador continued as a small, predatory smile began to form upon his face, "can you imagine the look on their faces when I show up with a Blazer on my arm? They'll be torn between shock at me bringing a military man and fear because if they say anything which can be perceived as bigoted, it could start an international incident. The horrors! The scandal!"

Everyone in the room laughed at that, hard. Each and every one of them could imagine the faces of the Caledonian security if they knew that Rowan was not merely a Blazer but, in fact, an Operative. If they even knew what Operatives were. That intel was still held close, though had probably leaked to some degree.

Captain Jesyka Washington said, "With all due respect to Operative Moran, sir, I'm in charge of security matters," her features carefully schooled in perfect neutrality. If Rowan hadn't been trained in the art of deception, he would have bought the act. He was nobody's fool, and knew that the embassy's security chief was seething beneath her calm façade.

"Which is why I had you plan for three different exfiltration paths to get me out of there if something goes wrong," Kiem said with a nod. "Moran is very good, but somebody needs to watch his back from afar. You're the only person I trust, Captain."

That seemed to quell any further protests. Or at least, the captain knew enough when she was not going to win a fight. Rowan wasn't certain which, but he guessed she knew it was a lost cause to argue. Kiem was a skilled diplomat who knew how to make contracts and get people to work together without much fuss. Or, in this case, quash any lingering doubts or arguments amongst the parties involved.

Throughout the entire meeting, Rowan remained silent. He had watched the ambassador maneuver everyone in the room into agreeing or accepting his demands with no small sense of awe. Kiem was good at what he did, and Rowan was astute. He knew from the moment he had agreed to go along with the ambassador's plan—another skillful parley orchestrated by the man, Rowan noted wryly—that it would end up this way.

Washington pulled a remote from her pocket and pointed it at the wall. "We have a detailed briefing from the Royal Guards on what they deem to be the primary threats for this event," she said. The room dimmed slightly as the wall showed the base plans of the reception area, as well as the two adjoining ballrooms. The outline of the plans glowed blue, with various entry points marked in red. She briefly laid out the plan and angles, but became repetitive after a few minutes. The layout was a nightmare, though it only took the Operative a few seconds to see what the real issue was. The problem, Rowan noted, was the micromanaging Caledonian security forces.

What they're trying to tell her is simple: let us handle our own security, you third-world pukes, Rowan thought disgustedly as Washington continued.

"Secondary issues are local agitators that we already knew about, a few new groups that the Caledonians did *not* know about before we shared info, and rumblings of a protest, by which I mean riot," she said.

As Captain Washington continued her briefing on security and the arrangements the Freehold had made with the Caledonians, his mind drifted back to his time in the dojo. How ineffectual the blade felt in his hand, and how he did not feel the calming influence of the art. Had he lost the *iaido*, or was it simply more elusive than he anticipated it to be? It was something he needed to work on after the event.

For a bunch of nose-counting stiffs, the Caledonians definitely knew how to throw a party.

Ambassador Kiem had been greeted warmly in the receiving line by the Crown Princess of Caledonia herself, instead of being passed off to a minor functionary as Rowan had anticipated. The Operative—under the guise of Blazer Rowan Jones—had been welcomed with less reserve. As the ambassador had predicted, however, no comment was made due to fear of offending the black man in the perfectly pressed uniform with his katana adorning his side.

Rowan was not surprised that some nations still judged those by the color of their skin. In fact, it was something that Special Warfare oftentimes took advantage of. Playing off of the sensitivities of a host culture was a valuable weapon, so he had attached himself to the arm of the ambassador like a limpet mine, gushing at the dress of the princess and being flamboyantly over the top. Being a black homosexual in a room full of those who were embarrassed by such things but tried to not make it a big deal by declaring they always supported his kind made Rowan's job that much simpler.

He'd been surprised that they allowed him to keep his sword, however. They had not even spared it a second glance after ensuring he did not carry any firearms or explosives on his person. *Assumptions*, he decided after realizing that they believed it to be merely a prop piece, *could get you killed*.

"*Ripper, this is Overwatch. Be advised that your acting skills suck, and the pool is running to see who tries to bed you first tonight,*" Captain Washington's voice came over the comm.

He grunted. The captain was nervous and talkative. The ambassador turned slightly away and redirected the conversation. The movement drew the two functionaries from Novaja Rossia away from Rowan as well without their even realizing it. The move was as practiced as breathing and came just as naturally.

"*Five hundred credits are in right now,*" came the response.

He hated mute comms.

"*Li just dropped in another hundred, but we think he's cheating and using a profile analysis. He picked the Ramadanian chief of staff.*"

Sneaky, Rowan thought. *That's who I'd have picked.* He shifted back around the ambassador's side and squeezed against him affectionately.

Rowan followed the ambassador around as he greeted the various representatives. The Alsaciens merely nodded curtly at the ambassador before politely excusing themselves, something he made a mental note of. He did not harbor grudges, but it was always prudent to watch to see who might be on whose side should the time come. The Alsaciens made it abundantly clear which side they would take.

A server moved past Rowan holding a tray of what looked to be scallops on a puffy white pastry with a caviar garnish. Rowan snagged one and popped it into his mouth, nodding thoughtfully as he chewed. He had guessed correctly, though the caviar was flavored with something he did not immediately recognize. It was delicious nonetheless.

He took a step toward the server with the hors d'oeuvres for a second piece, but the man did not seem to slow down as he milled through the crowd. Rowan stopped and stared hard at the man's retreating back. A strange sense of urgency was in the man's stride. Rowan paused and began to rerun the scene back through his head, his mind looking for something that his eyes had seen but not recognized.

"Something's wrong," Rowan muttered as his eyes scanned the rest of the reception area. He reached for his sleeve phone but stopped. If he raised the alert level and whisked the ambassador out of the room and caused an unnecessary alarm, it could potentially damage political relations between Caledonia and the Freehold. While the Operative found almost all politics distasteful, he was well aware of the harsh realities involved that made it somewhat necessary.

Instead of triggering the alert he adjusted his collar

and stared hard at the server. The man was sweating more than the others, and his eye continued to flick about the room in a nervous manner. The waiter could be two types of men, Rowan decided. One was the nervous individual who tried to do their job for the first time and keep it from turning into a train wreck, and the other was a nervous hostile who considered himself to be in Injun country. He made a choice.

"Hey, Mom, party's great, just updating you," Rowan said into his sleeve phone, which was only transmitting one way to ensure the security could not be easily compromised. "Looking at these hors d'oeuvres and they look scrumptious. I need more."

"Copy that," came the soft reply in his ear. The server was now getting extra attention, to decide if he was a hostile. Alert One was all-in, guns blazing, get everyone of value the hell out of Dodge while eliminating all hostiles with extreme prejudice. It was messy, scary, and would create some lingering bad feelings should it all be for nothing. Not to mention the bill the Freehold would get from repair costs. Rowan had personally designed that plan, much to the chagrin of the Caledonians—and Captain Washington, who had tweaked it enough so that the political fallout would only be devastating instead of something akin to Franz Ferdinand.

Of course, to the Caledonians, Alert One was far different, but they did not need to know that.

The party ebbed and flowed as more dignitaries arrived, including Earth's UN representative. It was not, Rowan noted with disdain, the ambassador but the senior aide to the ambassador, he recalled as he dug through his mental files of all UN personnel assigned to Caledonia. It was a direct slap to the face of the King and Queen, but one that they would endure with their typical stiff upper lip.

Suckling at the teat of the UN still paid better for some nations than being its enemy, Rowan admitted sourly to himself.

"*Ripper, be advised that the party outside appears to be getting ugly,*" Washington's voice came over the comm. Rowan quirked an eyebrow and tapped his chin once for clarification.

"*Active hostile movement, with security forces and police clashing with some of the more active demonstrators. They're getting bad, Ripper.*"

"That's the last time I let her pick the codenames," Rowan muttered as he moved closer to the ambassador. The rest of the guests were beginning to make their way into the larger ballroom, where the formal reception for the Caledonian royal family awaited. Rowan already had the layout mapped in his head and had spotted three potentially threatened areas. He couldn't cover all three, but he could limit the ambassador's exposure to two of them.

He tensed as they passed through the first area he had previously marked as dangerous without incident. That was the first obstacle, and with the seating arrangements set up as they were, he would be able to cover the ambassador without exposing him to the server's entrance. He had subtly moved the ambassador to his left upon entering the ballroom and smiled politely as the *maître d'* frowned at the breach of protocol. Rowan gave him the biggest, cheesiest smile he could manage as he mashed himself up on the ambassador's side. The other man blushed and looked away.

Assumptions would be the death of many people one day, Rowan decided.

"Ripper, al–" the comm suddenly died. Rowan frowned and checked his sleeve phone.

Nothing. A quick glance around the room confirmed that all comms were down as security members he had picked out were tapping their ears or pressing their collars. None of the guests had realized what had happened, not yet in any case. Rowan wasn't sure if this was a real emergency or that they suffered a general comm failure.

Better safe than sorry, he thought as he moved even closer to the ambassador. To anyone else watching, it would appear to be an extremely intimate gesture. Kiem turned and gave him an inquisitive look, so Rowan began to explain.

He never got the chance.

"*Down with the patriarchy! Death to the false royals!*" a voice shrieked from the foyer near the entrance. An explosion ripped through the doorway, causing it to collapse and block the primary entrance. Rowan's head whipped around quickly and he spotted a small group of men running through the outer guards, firing compact pistols into the group as they passed. One guard stepped out to interpose himself between the group and the main ballroom but was cut down by two quick shots to his head. Small devices were tossed into the ballroom by the terrorists—there was no other group who would be both brazen and stupid, Rowan decided as he tracked everything going on around him—and bounced across the floor.

Rowan grabbed Ambassador Kiem and threw him to the ground, then covered him with his larger frame. The devices exploded, sending smoke and dust throughout the room. A secondary concussive blast ripped through the guards coming down to support him, taking most of them down in a flash of fire and black smoke. Rowan risked a peek around the room to take stock of the situation.

The terrorists were moving in toward the royal family and there was no one to stop them. No one that Rowan could readily identify, at least. The angles were wrong for the rapid response teams of the Royal Life Guards to cut the terrorists off before they reached the Royals.

Ears ringing, Rowan expertly searched the ambassador for any sign of wounds or injuries. After a moment of inspection he was satisfied. Other than having the wind knocked out of him from Rowan landing on top, the ambassador was uninjured. However, Rowan's hearing was shot from the explosion, which meant that the ambassador was probably suffering as well. Rowan figured that it couldn't hurt to check.

"Are you wounded, sir?" Rowan asked in a breathless tone as he lay down atop the ambassador. The ambassador's hearing wasn't as damaged as he had suspected. The smaller man shook his head. Both men turned their heads slightly and watched as the small group began to fire indiscriminately at the Life Guards, who were not firing back due to the royal family being in the field of fire.

The guards were moving but would not be able to do anything for the Royals in time. The three who'd been placed on this side were down. However, *his* path was clear. It took less than a second for him to analyze the situation and realize what he could do to eliminate the problem, even though it would mean abandoning the ambassador.

All of this analyzing occurred in less than a single heartbeat.

"Sir?" Rowan asked. The ambassador did not hesitate for a moment in his reply. He had seen it, too.

"Go. Save the Royals."

The Operative nodded and triggered the required mental commands for Boost, the most secret weapon in the entire FMF. As he boosted, his vision blurred, and the world seemed to slow down as the decidedly secret mix of adrenaline, oxygen, and sugars kicked into his bloodstream. His heart rate increased twofold and his hands shook as the initial shock of the Boost hit every single nerve in his body. He could taste the burnt ozone in the air, hear every single piece of rubble being kicked around by the terrorists. Every individual hair on his arm was standing on end.

His blade was out and had slashed across the bare throat of the first terrorist before his vision had even sharpened. The guy didn't stand a chance, his eyes looking elsewhere and ignoring the man who he thought had been on the ground a singular instant before. Momentum carried Rowan into the hostile, so he turned slightly and thrust his sword into the unprotected gut of the terrorist. Using his enhanced strength, he pulled the blade out the side of the dying man, coating the floor with intestines, blood, and spleen. The sword sang, and from the brutal cut came the *iaido*, pure and true. The instant was his, the *iaidoan* in his true element. It rang loudly in his ears.

Everything went still for the barest of moments as Rowan felt the natural order of the universe align itself upon his blade. His eyes locked onto blood which was still in the air, seemingly moving in slow motion as it fell back to the ground. The natural rhythm in the universe matched his perfectly, and he was one. This was a moment of clarity, his *iaido* reaching something that he thought that he had lacked. He could feel it hum, hear it trumpeting throughout every heartbeat. He would never achieve this level of awareness again.

The two terrorists who had been trailing the first had not even begun to register Rowan's attack on their dead comrade as his blade began to work on them. A virtuoso in the act, the katana removed first the left hand then the right arm of the nearest of the duo. The terrorist's mouth opened to scream in pain and fear, so Rowan shoved the tip of the blade home to silence him forever.

A solid kick shattered the man's ribs as Rowan yanked his sword out of his head and drove it straight through the heart of the second. The terrorist, a true believer from the look in his eyes, managed to raise his submachine gun and pull the trigger. The rounds impacted in Rowan's hip and lower ribs. Rowan felt them punch through the reinforced fabric of his dress uniform, slowed but not stopped at this close range. He ignored the flash of pain and twisted the katana in his hand. This destroyed the heart of the coward once and for all.

The song raged on, with Rowan conducting the finest of melodies with each beat of his heart.

Rowan spotted four other terrorists turning to see what was going on. One of them included the erstwhile server he had tagged previously. The distance was too far for him to cross without getting mowed down, so he did the next best thing. He dropped to one knee and ignored the screaming, burning pain in his hip as he grabbed the fallen weapon of the terrorist. He hefted the submachine gun (an idle part of his brain noticed that it was an Arsenal Shipka-11, a decent enough weapon if a bit inaccurate for modern weaponry) and took aim. Two quick shots showed that the gun was zeroed in at fifty yards and the round that he took in the ribs was affecting his aim a bit. Both of his shots struck true despite this, and two more terrorists were on their way to answer for their crimes.

Gunfire began to spackle the wall next to him. He felt two punches in his abdomen and grimaced. Special Warfare Operative Survival Training taught every single Operative to push through the pain and to not break under any circumstance, but it still hurt like a bastard whenever one was shot. Bullets tended to have that effect whenever they drove through the fleshy parts and into the vital organs.

He fired off three more shots and was rewarded with another failure of a human being falling to the formerly pristine marble floor, his blood seeping into the grooves between tiles, his soul on its way to whatever Hell the man had feared. Rowan sprinted forward, charging into the depths of the firefight as the two remaining terrorists split up. The first, the server who Rowan had pegged earlier, moved directly toward the princess. He was in the midst of the Royals, so Rowan didn't take the shot yet. The second was posturing, however, screaming at the top of his lungs and standing out in the open. The decision was easy to make.

"The Common People's Action Group has struck a blow against this cesspit of shite and outdated nobility on our world!" he shouted triumphantly. He had his weapon pointed at Rowan but was aiming from the hip. Rowan put even odds that the bastard wouldn't even get a round within a meter of him, so he shifted directions and sprinted, his Shipka-11 aimed with one hand, katana wielded in the other. The two men fired at the same time.

Rowan felt impacts before he heard the shots. He grunted in surprise as his left arm dropped and fell limply to his side. He clenched his hand as tight as he was able to in order to keep his sword from falling from his grip. Two more rounds punched into his chest, causing him to stagger slightly as his lungs began to fill with fluids. The fourth round destroyed his left shoulder, punching through the clavicle and tearing muscle and tendons apart as it fragmented while the fifth merely left a shallow, painful groove on his neck.

He was beginning to have difficulty breathing, thanks to the perforations in his chest. Lungs typically did not function well when they had holes in them. The terrorist wasn't quite so lucky, as both of Rowan's shots had removed the back of his head upon impact. He fell to the ground as Rowan pivoted and tossed the Shipka-11 aside, the chamber open. He was out of ammo, patience, and blood.

Time he still had, though it was not much. The song was nearing the end, but there was still one final piece of the *iaido* that he could perfect.

To avoid coughing up blood—which could interfere with everything and cause him to fail in his mission— Rowan simply held his breath. The waiter-terrorist had managed to grab the crown princess's arm and force her in front of him. He pressed his forearm against her throat while pointing his gun directly at Rowan. All the while he screamed at Rowan.

"I'll fucking kill the bitch! Stop or I'll kill her!"

Rowan computed the scene in his head and considered his angle. It was entirely probable that the terrorist was going to kill the princess anyway, whether he stayed in place or attacked. The man might not be the zealous fanatic that his fallen compatriots were, but he was still a dangerous threat to innocent lives. That made the decision easy. It made the notes flowing through his hand perfectly synchronized with everything around him. Sweet, undulating music erupted in his ears. He was fully in the *iaido* and he vowed to never leave it.

What had seemed like a long span to Rowan was barely a second in reality, his body nearly a blur as he poured the last amount of strength and energy into the sudden attack. Boost lasted for a hundred seconds or so, and he wanted to be certain that he would not run out of time before the chemical cocktail pumping in his blood wore off. He ignored the pain which coursed through his ravaged body and pushed through. The maneuver caught the perpetrator off guard, causing him to hesitate just long enough for Rowan to bring his katana up for the attack.

The terrorist fired once just as Rowan reached them. The round punched directly through his sternum and tore apart his manubrium and several major blood vessels in the process. It was a lethal shot, except that Rowan was far beyond caring about pain. He had the correct angle, the tip of the blade pointed precisely where he wanted to go. Nothing in the universe could stop him now. Like a cobra, he struck hard and fast.

The blade drove straight through bone and scraped along the inside of the skull. The terrorist jerked but his higher motor functions had been ruined by the singular thrust of the katana. The compact carbine had fallen out of his nerveless fingers, unable to commit one final act of terror.

The song reached the finale, a crescendo which would turn into the greatest symphony ever created. The notes had been perfect. The playing, masterful. Each piece of the orchestra had done its job, and the end result was that Rowan Moran, Operative, had managed to keep the entire Royal Family of Caledonia alive with minimal casualties to innocents around him. In fact, he—

Abruptly the music ceased.

> Her Majesty is graciously pleased to signify Her intention to confer the decoration of the Elizabeth Cross on the undermentioned...
>
> With respect for service to the Freehold, the Diplomatic Star is posthumously awarded to...

—◆—

These odd battles continued. That one had been among civilians, when those without honor had tried to harm them. She, or someone, had impressed on her bearer that a warrior should always be honorably armed. And oh, how he'd fought! His precision, his movement, so light and perfectly balanced. Not only was he a master, he had danced a dance of death with her.

It was exciting, and she hoped to do that again.

His family revered her, and held her close, before eventually exchanging her to another family, also warriors. They understood her and cared for her, until she was again presented to one who fought.

—◆—

Lovers

Tony Daniel

Dear Major Riggs and Mrs. Heaton,

My name is Warrant Leader Robert McKay of the Freehold Military Forces First Legion Air Wing. I'm a close support pilot with the FMF on Mtali. I am writing to you in regards to your daughter, Sergeant Lisa Riggs, Squad Leader of Seven Alfa Three Mobile Rifle Squad.

Lisa was my friend.

I have waited several days for you to have received official notice from the Civilian Liaison Office and an individual letter of condolence from Captain Arnando of 1st Battalion Alfa Company, as well as from Colonel Richard, commanding officer of Mtali Expeditionary Freehold Military Forces, who indicated to me he, too, was going to write to you expressing my gratitude toward Lisa.

I wanted to send you my own personal note to share what information I have so that you

*know as much as I know about Lisa and her days
on Mtali.*

Lisa was a fine soldier.

She was also a good woman. A good person.

I'm lucky to have known her.

"What the hell?" Sergeant Lisa Riggs muttered.

"They're...I dunno," said Corporal Alan Chambers.
"Sarge, what *are* they doing?"

Music blared from speakers somewhere in the huge
compound. A bone-shaking bass thundered, while a
keyboard-guitar combination screamed out a throbbing
wall of sound.

Pounding.

Danceable.

"I think it's some kind of...skating rink." Lisa
shrugged her shoulders, although her tactical vest
damped the gesture.

The compound they'd entered looked like the usual
Mtali concrete-polymer structure from the outside, but
instead of an inner courtyard, the place had a large
steel roof, and the ground was neither dirt nor the
sector's ubiquitous blue and white paving tiles, but was
coated with a smooth flooring that looked ceramic.

The militant they pursued had come through the
main entrance to the building. Vert-stat reported the
place was about a city block in size with three side exits.

She and Chambers were in what seemed to be a
lobby, outside what looked and sounded like an auditorium. The auditorium's main entrance's two large doors
were pulled back and latched open with small metal
hooks anchored on the wall. She immediately had two
members of her squad check behind the doors. Nothing.

The huge room they looked into had a floor set about a meter below street level with a polycrete ramp leading down from the doorway. Because of their elevation, Lisa had a view of the whole area. It was maybe fifty by fifty meters. The floors *and* walls were pure white.

People glided on the porcelain surface. They wore shoes that tapered beneath to what looked like a miniature boat keel. She couldn't tell if the keel touched the floor or hovered over it. But somehow or another, the shoes—the skates—supported the Believers who crowded the floor.

At least she thought they were Believers, since this was al Dura, which was the neighborhood that contained mostly evangelicals.

Many of the occupants moved around in a counterclockwise circle on the floor like fish circling in a tank. Some were doing leaping turns and other acrobatics in the air as they went.

"This is sooo freakin' weird," Griffin murmured into his throat mic. They all heard his comment over their earbuds.

"Can it," Lisa said. "We have a job to do."

"May I help you?" A woman approached from inside with a worried expression. She was middle-aged and wore a powder-blue dress. Her hair was what grabbed Lisa's attention, however. It hung down her back almost to her heels.

That must be hell to brush, Lisa thought.

The woman said, "I'm the head usher. It's in the paperwork. This is a peaceable assembly. We have our licenses in order. I have to say there are quite a lot of regulations, but we've met our obligations.

I can flash the permits to your pad if you'd like. We follow the diversity directives your people have put in place."

"*My* people?" Lisa said, perplexed.

"You are United Nations forces aren't you?" The woman was dark complected, probably originally of Mediterranean ancestry, although it was hard to tell on Mtali. The planet had been settled for nearly three centuries. Her face paled now, though, and she visibly trembled.

She's terrified, Lisa thought. She didn't blame the woman. All of Lisa's squad's weapons were shouldered for fast movement, but she knew they must still seem an imposing bunch.

"Ma'am, we're FMF troops. Freeholders. We have no intention of interrupting your gathering any more than we have to. We've pursued a terrorist here. We've entered the UN sector under their 'hot pursuit' edict, although we would have come anyway. The man was trying to blow up one of our transports."

The woman continued to tremble. "We don't profile entrants," she said. "It's a requirement of our diversity license for assembly."

"Like I said, we are not here to enforce UN rules," Lisa said.

"A man came in about ten minutes ago and asked to use the restroom. His clothes seemed very dusty."

"What about his accent? Did he sound like he was from around here? Do you think he might have been al-Wadi?"

"I wish I could answer you, but we will have our license revoked. We aren't allowed to profile. The UN sector administration sends whisper drones to ensure compliance." She nodded over her shoulder toward the auditorium. "They're too small to see, but they *are* here monitoring, I assure you."

"All right, thanks for your help. We're going to need to look around. This man is very dangerous."

It finally seemed to dawn on the woman that Lisa wasn't here to shut down the gathering.

"Please enter," the woman said, then leaned closer to Lisa and spoke in a low voice. "If you really are chasing one of those al-Wadi jackals, we want to help."

"We really are, ma'am," Lisa replied.

She turned to the squad behind her. She clicked a finger on the data-feed on her wrist. There was an aerial schematic of the compound they were in with all entry and exit points marked by blinking green dots. "Vert-stat Control has a positive determination that the bomber ran in here."

The vert-stat was a tethered hovering platform packed with cameras and other remote sensing gear. It was connected to the sector Combat Operations Center, and was the FMF's eye in the sky. The resolution was incredible. The capabilities immense. Without somebody on the ground to *do* something about all that wonderful information, it meant shit.

Also, the boots on the ground had to be *allowed* to actually do something about it.

"Please remain aware that the al Dura sector is UN battlespace, and we have to at least pretend to play by their rules," Lisa cautioned.

"Which nut should we cut off, Sarge?" asked Murphy, in Fireteam One. He had a Saltpan accent and had never been to a city, much less off his home planet of Grainne, a year ago. Now he was cracking jokes like

a . . . well, a grown man. Which he hadn't been a year
ago, either.

They were all so young. Twelve, thirteen Grainne
years old.

"Better cut off both to be safe," put in Chambers.
"It's the UN way."

"Yeah, okay," Lisa said. "We all want to limit CD.
That we can agree on." CD was collateral damage, as in
dead civilians. The UN forces down to the squad level
had to provide Collateral Damage Estimates, CDEs,
before engaging an enemy, even if an enemy was very
much engaging them. Fortunately, the Freehold military
depended on the judgment of its soldiers, and trained
them until they "reeked of trust," as Lisa's senior sergeant instructor once put it when she was going through
FMF NCO training. "Let's just track this guy down, vent
him, and leave these people to their . . . whatever it is."

They moved down the ramp and into the crowd
that surrounded the skaters. There were tables and
chairs spread around the central area of the rink. Many
people were seated at them drinking from clay cups
and watching the action on the rink. The unmistakable odor of almond milk and gingery-sweet tea let
Lisa know it was chai they were drinking.

As if it would be anything else, she thought. Chai
was the odor she associated with al Dura, and practically all of Mtali.

Well, the only *pleasant* odor she associated with it.
In a place where you were taking your life into your
hands if you drank water from a faucet, it was the
hot drink of choice, even in the scorching summer
months. Drinking chai was the one unifying element
of all of the warring factions of Mtali.

Those who weren't seated stood near the edge of the skating rink, waiting to go back to it. They balanced on the thin edges of their shoe soles. Closer up, Lisa could see that the blades did not fully touch the ground, but were suspended in the air a few millimeters above the floor.

From the little she knew about skating—which was one trip to a Freehold rink years ago—she thought they were called "gliders." They worked with phased magnetic fields. She knew about the principle from rail-gun applications she'd studied in NCO school. Two intersecting electromagnetic fields interacted with a very strong, very precise field in the skate. That insanely narrow edge served a purpose in keeping everything aligned.

The "blade" of a glider skate was almost molecularly thin and sharp. The field could be adjusted in height. She'd seen really good skaters gliding about on what looked like a meter of thin air.

Her briefings hadn't mentioned a thing about a big skating rink on Mtali. It was the last thing she'd expected to find here. Well, that and maybe competent local government.

But here it was. With the aid of the eagle-eyed cameras on the vert-stat platform, and the control crew that manned it and interpreted the imagery, Seven Alfa Three, her squad, had tracked the feck-head through the seemingly endless alleys of both the Sunni-majority Ta'izz Jadeed district to the Christian al Dura district tucked away inside the much larger Ta'izz Jadeed. He had been targeted by the vert-stat and rousted while planting an IED made with a Shia faction military demolition block. He'd worked too fast for an airstrike from a drone or vertol, but Lisa's squad was patrolling in the vicinity. They'd flushed the militant, and he'd run away surprisingly fast. But not faster than a vert-stat infrared camera.

The bastard had ducked in here.

She'd leave the weapons team in the lobby, the M-23 machine gunners, two marksmen, the missile gunners, to provide cover and reinforcement. The rest would go inside with her.

"Corporal Chambers, you'll take Fireteam Blue to the south entrance." She touched her data-pad and the green light lit up on all the squad's pads. She noticed with approval that a couple of the designated squad held to SOP and kept their heads up, looking around. If was tempting for an entire squad to engage in pad-stare when planning an operation. When it did, situational awareness went to hell. "Green, you guard the northwest exit. Red back-up remain at this doorway. The rest of Red team, you're with me."

That covers the ingress and egress routes, Lisa thought. *Now let's see how much china we can keep on the shelf.*

"Rifles at tactical." The squad positioned their rifles closer to firing position, but barrel-up. The M5s shot caseless cartridges. The slugs were fed to the firing apparatus in pre-stressed sections, sort of like a stapler—a stapler that flung out its staples at supersonic speeds with devastating effect.

Lisa and Red Team moved forward into the crowd. At first, they were only noticed by those nearby. Several of them had to be shouldered out of the way. Some turned, looking resentful and ready to push back—but were inhibited by the sight of a Freehold soldier in full kit staring back at them.

We're here to protect you, Lisa thought. *Now get your ass out of the way before we shoot it off.*

A vert-stat camera had gotten a decent frontal shot of the militant, if at a downward angle. She popped it up on her data-pad, ran it through her helmet feed, and compared faces.

Mtali denizens mostly dressed alike. At least the men did, and they were looking for a male. They ate the same food as far as she could tell, and *everybody* drank chai. Sunnis, Shia, Amala, Druze, the small community of Bah'ai'i ... and here in al Dura, the small community of evangelical Christians. She knew little about the evangelicals other than that they weren't Catholic and everybody called them Believers, even though the Believers was just one sect, and a minor one, among them.

She also vaguely recalled that, like the Muslims, there was some kind of evangelical reward in the afterlife for murdering the right sort of people. A jaw for a tooth, or something like that.

They all looked alike and everybody on the planet wanted to kill each other. At least that's the way it seemed to her.

That wasn't really true. She had noticed one other characteristic of evangelical men: not all of them had beards. From the vert-stat image, the bomber had a beard. Looking around, that left out about half of the men in the rink. Unless the feckhead had somehow hidden away a shaving kit in a bathroom, which she doubted. He'd been patterned by the vert-stat observation platform. The facial and somatic recognition tech in her data-pad was busy processing and analyzing the feed from her helmet cam and those of the rest of the squad.

"Fan out," Lisa said in a low tone, almost a whisper. The contact mic under her chin picked up the words and carried them to the rest of the squad's earbuds. "I want a visual sweep of this place."

She was taller than several of the men in the squad, so she didn't have any trouble looking over the heads of most of the crowd. Even though it appeared a bit like ice, the ceramic surface was not particularly slick. She moved forward toward the edge of the skating rink.

The skaters were both male and female. Some of the women wore headscarves. *Must be a custom they adopted to get along,* Lisa thought. But most of the women let their hair go free—and they grew it very, very long. Down their lower backs. Some of them, like the usher she'd talked with, past their butts, even. Was there some commandment in the Christian rule book that women weren't supposed to cut their hair?

It didn't seem so absurd when she saw it here. The long hair made a lovely effect. Some women spun as they skated, and their hair flew around them, cascading in flowing fans and arcs. The men were more acrobatic, jumping up, spinning in air. A couple even did flips, twists. Some skated entirely backward. And all at incredible speed. After a moment watching—how could she not?—she saw that the movements were in pattern. They were a wild dance.

It was kind of . . . beautiful.

"Okay, what the hell are the Believers *doing*?" asked Green Team leader Sabine Meyer's modulated voice in Lisa's earbud.

"I think it's a dance," Lisa answered.

"Ain't nobody dancing with anybody out there."

"Not a dance like that. Dance like . . . maybe it's

religious or something. How would I know?" She
nodded toward the chai drinkers at the tables. "All
of you, scan the crowd. I doubt the feckhead is out
there skating or dancing or whatever it is."

She gazed around.

Now they see us. Most of the eyes had fixed on
her and the squad.

They don't seem happy, Lisa thought. But the looks
were of irritation, not the outright hatred she so often
got in the Shia sector where COB Jackson was located.

After all, she was a woman. A soldier. In what they
thought of as a man's uniform. Shorn hair. No scarf.
Face fully visible.

She even used a little makeup, especially on days
she was scheduled for patrol. The thought of pissing
off the fanatical assholes who hid among the local
population helped break the monotony.

It was actually good that they had everyone's attention. It gave the FR program a frontal for comparison.

"Got him," said Chambers. "He's moving toward
the northeast door."

"Okay, let's go," she said. "Subsonic one, subsonic
one."

Subsonic One was a UN-mandated mod to the
rifles that bled pressure out of the barrels before the
projectile reached the muzzle. It also cause the barrel
section to get hot quickly. Subsonic One was low, but
it was still deadly. It was meant to prevent the slug
from cutting through a swath of bodies.

She'd also heard it unofficially called the "Uno
setting." *Not* because the UN troops on Mtali were
ordered to use lower velocity at all times, but because
most of their troops' rifles were that low by design.

"Damn it, he's got a backpack," Chambers shouted. "I say again, he's got a backpack and something in his hand, might be a detonator."

"Take the shot!" Lisa yelled as she sprinted ahead. The music throbbed. It was loud enough to drown even the muffled subsonic crackle of the M5.

Someone dropped to the floor as if their strings had been cut. It was a woman.

"Crap," Lisa said. Chambers had missed.

She leaped over the victim and shoved aside two men who were trying to get to the downed woman.

And there the dogfucker was.

She shot him in the chest.

The militant shuddered, took a step backward, so she knew she'd hit him. But he remained standing. He was wearing body armor—it looked like a UN-issued tactical vest. His eyes were wild from the pain, however.

He's got to be hopped up on stims, Lisa thought. *That's the only way he's still standing.*

It was well known that the UN was constantly getting their battle meds raided, and that some went missing seemingly all on their own.

The hostile raised his arm. There was something in his hand that was probably a detonator.

He's going to blow himself up. That's why he came in here.

There must be more than a hundred people in the gliding rink.

She needed a headshot. Instantly.

She couldn't move that fast. No way.

She pictured her father's dry, disappointed smile.

Catastrophic failure to anticipate the consequences of your actions, Lisa dear.

Not good enough. Like always.

Then something strange. Someone, a man, stepped up behind the feckhead. His arm moved in a sideways motion. As it did so, the Shia militant's head wobbled. First to one side, then another. Not natural.

Then it fell off his neck entirely. He'd been guillotined while standing.

Behind the militant stood a thin man—thin, but muscled. In his hand he held one of the skates.

Decapitated by a skate, Lisa thought. Well, decapitated by the molecularly thin blades of the repulsors.

The terrorist's body got the message a tic later that it was no longer needed. It collapsed.

Blood spurted from the severed arteries as it fell, some of it shooting a meter or more, enough to splash several of those nearby. The neck pumped itself out in a puddle on the floor.

The detonator trailed a wire that ran back into the rucksack. It fell from the body's lifeless hand and onto the floor beside a shoulder.

Lisa quickly stepped over the dead body. SOP would be to leave the body in place and call in a EOD team to defuse the rucksack . . . but no way she was going to do that. This situation was far from standard. She glanced down at her data-pad, which was telling her that the detonator was a simple switch. She gingerly picked it up.

"Thibodeaux, Nourse, let's get the body and the backpack out of here," she said. "Leave the head. Corporal Meyer call in medevac for her." She nodded toward the woman lying prone of the floor. She'd taken a shot to the chest in the left lung and who knew what other damage. The slug hadn't come out her back, and so had probably torn up her thorax.

Chambers grabbed a clot pack from his gear to try to staunch the flow of blood from the woman's wound.

"Permission to stay with her until medevac gets here, Sarge?" Chambers said. "She's still alive." His voice was plaintive.

Barely, Lisa thought. She didn't hold hope that the medics could do much when they arrived. But she'd seen them perform near miracles on minefield and IED victims before, so maybe.

And maybe she would forget this sight. An innocent woman, bleeding to death on a pure white floor.

Maybe not. Lisa felt a cold pit forming in her stomach. She wanted to vomit. Hell, she wanted to turn and run.

But couldn't.

"Yeah, permission granted, Chambers. Ling, you stay with him. The rest of you, let's go."

The other squad members jumped to it and they hooked arms under the shoulders and lifted the body. They moved toward the entrance.

"I'll help you," said a voice she didn't recognize. It was a voice speaking English, but in an accent with the cadence and fricative of Arabic. It was the man with the skate, only now he'd put it down and had hold of the insurgent's legs.

"Sir, I'd rather you didn't, for safety's sake..."

The man ignored her, and Lisa shrugged. He'd certainly earned the right to do whatever he wanted at the moment. Together they all walked the body and the presumed bomb to the entrance. The skater moved with a limp, but Lisa saw that this was because he still had a skate on one foot.

The door led to an alley. The rest of the squad

followed behind Lisa and she had them guard either entrance to the alley.

Her data-pad was telling her it was unsafe to cut the twisted wires leading from the detonator. She needed to secure it somehow.

Lisa looked around. There was a trash can near a door across the way. She dumped out its contents onto the ground and placed this carefully over the detonator.

"All right, we'll stand by until the EOD team arrives," she said. "Everybody be careful around the trash can." She examined the wire leading out from under the can. The twisted wires were red and black.

Easy colors so morons don't get confused and blow themselves up early.

"Can I help you up?" The man with one skate was standing close by. He was extending a hand toward Lisa.

The man had startling green eyes set against his copper-colored skin. Although he was thin, she could now see through the gauzy muslin shirt he wore that what there was of him was rock hard. On second look, he seemed young but not a teenager, maybe sixteen Grainne years or so.

About my age, Lisa thought.

"Sure," Lisa said. She took his hand in a palm grip and let him take some of her weight as she stood.

"Thank you," she said, drawing her hand away. "How did you do that in there?"

The man shrugged. "Acrobatic skates have higher settings," he said. "So they have a much finer edge. We use the setting for individual praise, not for group dance. Elevates you a meter over the arena." He smiled and seemed to blush, which reddened the

LOVERS   323

brown of his skin tone. "You have to be pretty good to do it, though."

"Watch out. Pride goeth before a fall, right?" She thought the old saying might be vaguely Christian in origin.

He smiled even wider. "Actually it's: pride goeth before destruction and a haughty spirit before a fall," he replied. "But yes."

He's handsome, Lisa thought. *For a skinny dude.*

Lisa allowed the tension within her to relax enough to smile back at him. "Well, you probably saved some lives in there. Including mine."

"And including mine," he replied. He held out his hand again. "I'm Jedidiah."

"You're kidding, right?"

"About what?"

She shook her head. "Nothing." She extended her hand again and took his hand. "I'm Sergeant Lisa Riggs."

"Pleased to meet you, Lisa."

"There's a . . . reward and restitution fund," she said. "We can definitely pay you back for the cost of the . . . acrobatic skates, did you call them?"

"Yes," he said. "But I don't think mine were damaged."

"You killed a man with them."

"I wouldn't call that"—he nodded down at the headless body—"a man."

"Okay, but the battalion has a reward fund. It's a lot of money, and you deserve it."

"I wouldn't feel right taking a reward from your government."

"My government?" Lisa chuckled. "I don't think

you understand how the Freehold works. Listen, it's a battalion reward. A contract. Voluntary. We all contribute."

"Hmm, since you put it that way," he said. "I'll take it on one condition."

"What's that?"

"That you personally deliver it," he replied.

"That I . . . what?"

"I'll flash you my comm code," he said.

She heard Edwards, who stood nearby, giggle.

"Hey, Sarge, he'll give you his digits," Meyer said with her best shit-eating grin. "So you can deliver his *reward*. You know, his reward."

Lisa turned savagely on the team leader. "Corporal Meyer, for that you get to go back in there and pick up this thing's head," she said, motioning to the body. "Bring it out here and bag it."

"Really, Sarge?"

She just stared at the trooper. After a moment Meyer's look of disgust turned into the emotionless stare all of them had learned to put on in Pipeline. Meyer went to do as she was told.

"Help her, Edwards," she said to the trooper who had giggled.

When both disappeared back inside, she pointed to her data-pad and smiled. The Believer, Jedidiah, sent over his personal comm code.

Then she gave him hers.

The woman who had been shot died. Chambers was devastated. He needed to work it out. He was still a boy. Sweat was usually the answer. She assigned him extra PT for a week and let him out of COB maintenance duties. But she requested of her warrant leader that Chambers go back on patrol immediately.

The evangelicals, for their part, seemed to understand. There was no uproar in al Dura, at least that she heard about.

But, of course, charges were brought against her and the squad by the UN.

Al Dura was *their* sector, after all. The captain of India Company agreed to an internal investigation. It was over in two days and exonerated the squad. The report did, however recommend peer counseling for Lisa, and her captain and warrant leader backed it up.

I guess I was as depressed as Chambers and didn't recognize it, she'd thought when she read the report.

The "peer" in this case was a warrant officer and vertol pilot named Robert McKay. He'd been through a very similar collateral kill experience. He'd made a call that led to the death of a civilian. More than one, as it turned out.

Major Riggs and Mrs. Heaton, I told your daughter what I'd found myself to be true. You never get over it. So you have to get through it.

Not exactly wisdom for the ages, but it did help me and I think it helped Lisa.

Normally she'd have been called back to the Combat Operations Center for counseling, but since I'm a vertol pilot, I requested and received permission to fly out to COB Jackson and talk to her several times over the course of a few weeks. She and I got along well, and spoke a great deal, and though I do not in any way claim to know

Lisa well, I believe we became friends during that time.

We spoke a great deal about you both. You may not be aware of how much Lisa respected you and longed for your approval. From what she told me, you both created some pretty big shoes for her to fill.

I'm probably not telling you anything you don't know, but Lisa was intimidated by you, her parents, and any time she made what she thought of as a mistake, she felt as if you both were looking over her shoulder.

She told me more than once that she believed you were disappointed when she enlisted. I cannot believe this is true. If anyone had a calling to be an NCO, it was Lisa.

Lisa also showed me the beautiful family sword you presented her after her graduation from NCO training. I understand the damaged blade I recovered was returned to you by Lisa's commanding officer along with her other effects.

I don't believe I've seen a more elegant and balanced o-wakizashi in my life. And I have seen and held a lot of swords.

I also learned of Lisa's growing interest in the young man who had taken out the militant in the gliding rink in al Dura. During her next down day, she arranged to go on a date with him.

This is uncommon. Even beyond fraternization issues, the people of Mtali are so extremely tribal and factional that they often have no desire to mix with us. Yes, there are shuras among battalion commanders and local leaders, and higher *headquarters meets with regional governors and powerbrokers.*

But to sit down and share a meal or a drink with the locals outside of a patrol? It isn't often done even by the FMF. It can be dangerous, for one thing. But mostly it's because the opportunity doesn't arise.

So Lisa's relationship with the man, whose name was Jedidiah Farmer, as I later discovered, was unusual.

Frankly, I'm not sure what the attraction was. But it was definitely strong.

The evangelicals, who outsiders collectively call Believers (they are part of the local Christian Coalition composed of several churches and sects) are one of the smaller factions. They've mostly been live-and-let-live people since they settled on Mtali over two centuries ago. Well, live and let live when it comes to war. Some of them do have peculiar and restrictive beliefs about abortion, homosexuality, and polygamy. If I got into the intricacies of these taboos, you may not be able to stop laughing.

Nevertheless, being noncombatant on a planet in turmoil only made them into the whipping boy for the larger factions, especially among the Shia and the Sunni tribes. The Sufis, the Amala, and the Bah'hai'i seemed to leave them alone. The Sufis are almost as few in number as the Believers, the Amala even poorer. No one defends Believers, and their militia is a pitiful group that spends more time arguing denominational doctrine than fighting.

Which brings up the question of what we, the FMF, are fighting for on Mtali.

I cannot tell you it is for liberty for all or anything as lofty as that. We have two goals. Mtali is a hotbed of interstellar terrorism. We hope to nip this in the bud. And if we can't get them all, which we can't, at least we'll put the fear of Freeholders in them so that they'll avoid Grainne like the plague.

The other reason we're here, and perhaps I should not be saying this, perhaps a censor will black it out, is that war with Earth seems inevitable.

Our military is on Mtali to gain experience. To train in a live-fire setting. I realize how callous this sounds to those who lose loved ones here, but it is necessary for the survival of our society.

I think Lisa believed in both of these reasons for fighting. The UN forces are waging a doomed and risible campaign to "win hearts and minds" on Mtali. Lisa and I both joked about the futility of this as a military objective more than once.

So it's maybe ironic that Lisa, through no plan of her own, went out and did exactly that.

"I can't believe I got picked up at a gods-damn skating rink," Lisa said.

"A praise rink," Jedidiah replied.

"Uh-huh."

"Worship brings men and women together. That's part of the reason for it. Jesus didn't call us to be celibate." Jedidiah rolled his eyes and smiled. "Although sometimes Paul did. But he's kind of harsh and it's not like he was the Son of God or anything."

"And your Jesus *was*?"

"He isn't just my Jesus, he's—"

"Oh, stuff it, Jed, will you?"

He looked down at their naked bodies lying together on the bed. "I kind of already did," he said.

"Isn't this a sin or something?"

"It's the opposite," Jedidiah replied. "It's impossible for me to believe the Lord could not want you and me to have this. But what about you, heathen woman?"

"Oh, the goddess approves," she said, and ran a finger down the line of his jaw. "In fact, I think the god and goddess want us to do it again."

"Right now?"

"Right now."

They met in the UN-controlled sector. It was a gray zone adjacent to al Dura. She had to sign out to visit the Uno base, which was a matter of a couple of minutes on the FMF side. Then she must endure at least an hour of UN bureaucracy to meet him in a café just outside the UN command base hard perimeter.

Above the café, there was a room that belonged to a friend of Jedidiah from the al Dura seminary, the same school Jedidiah attended.

Lisa knew where Jed lived in al Dura and had passed the building on patrols—in fact, she went out of her way to do so. She could never go there unaccompanied, however. Even here in the gray zone, in a quaint Mtali café, things were dangerous.

Jed was worth it.

He was even worth putting up with the odor of chai. She'd hated it before. She would never love it. She was, however, getting so she could tolerate it. The whole planet seemed to run on the drink.

Chai was one thing. She would *never* get used to

boiled cow's feet, however. Gelatinous. Jed's favorite meal when eating out.

In al Dura, it was considered a delicacy.

She'd spent most of her leave inside the COB wire during the first months of her deployment. Now she left Jackson every chance she got.

Mtali was dangerous. Al Dura was dangerous. The gray zone was dangerous. Although the evangelicals were tolerant of women going about unescorted and even having *jobs*, there was one thing most Believers couldn't tolerate.

Short hair.

Her pixie cut wasn't even that short by FMF standards. Plenty of women troopers had trimmed theirs down to fuzz for convenience. But most al Dura women had never cut their hair in their lives. It had to take hours to brush every night, Lisa figured.

One hundred strokes a night? Try a *thousand*.

At first, she dressed in civvies, but that did her not much good. Everyone knew she was from off-world—although most took her for a UN trooper, to Lisa's chagrin.

Things had gone hostile a few times, and she'd been spit on once. After that, she started wearing undress greens, a pistol, and her sword any time she left the Uno base's hard perimeter. Her sidearm and her concealed pistol and knife would be far more effective in an attack. The sword was just for down-right *intimidation*.

She'd lied to Rob McKay. Her father hadn't given her the sword.

He'd *sold* it to her, the bastard. With her mother's blessing, too.

He'd intended it as a gift when she got commissioned an officer. That had always been the plan. After she'd enlisted all bets were off.

Half a year's salary. That's what he'd charged her.

But she wanted the *wakizashi*. She knew she deserved it. It wasn't her fault her parents were being assholes about it, and she didn't intend to punish herself by denying it to herself.

So she'd contracted a loan to buy the sword. She'd never missed a payment. She even learned how to use the sword to some extent, although she was nowhere near getting a hand-to-hand weapons expert rating and probably never would. But nobody in the al Dura gray zone knew that. When they saw a lady with a sword, people mostly kept their distance.

Where else was she going to go if she wanted to meet Jed? Where else could she go if she wanted to have sex with him—which she very much did? To one of the escort trailers in the Central Operations Zone with the contract sex workers? Not likely.

Jed *would* probably go along with that. Despite his religious leanings (or, he would say, *because* of them) Jed seemed to be completely amenable to just about anything when it came to sex. He'd proved it to her several times in the tiny borrowed apartment above the gray zone café.

Another Believer stereotype shot down.

Others included the notion that Believers only did it in the missionary position. If they did, those must have been some adventurous and polymorphous missionaries.

After the sex, they had even begun to *hang out*. They talked about many things. They argued philosophy like a couple of amateur Aristotles.

One thing neither one of them talked about was the future. As far as Lisa could tell, there *wasn't* one on Mtali, not for anybody.

She would be leaving the planet soon enough—soon enough to make their lovemaking desperate.

Lisa took a sip of her chai. It was tepid, almost cold. Had they been sitting in the café and talking *that long*?

"I've passed my Greek exam," he said. "Now I have to get through the Hebrew exam next month. It's the hardest thing I've ever tried."

Lisa nodded sagely. "And when you finish, you'll be able to speak with all sorts of dead guys," she said.

"I'll be able to read the Bible in the original languages it was written in."

"There's that, I guess."

He leaned back in his chair and smiled. "You really don't like that I'm going into the ministry, do you?"

"Lots of things you could do seem *more* pointless," Lisa replied. "I can't think of a gods-damn one at the moment, however."

"You like the praise glides. You said you thought they were beautiful."

They'd attended a couple of the events—those held within the soft perimeter, the gray zone—since the fateful night of their meeting. She'd seen him skate.

He grew ecstatic.

And he was very, very good at it.

"Yes," she nodded. "Those I like. They're pretty."

"Skating got me a scholarship," he said in a more intense tone of voice. "It's the reason you and I met. God has a plan. I believe that."

"Oh, please."

"It's maybe like the military is for you." He straightened up, took a sip of chai. "Before God spoke to me and told me to praise skate ... and before I got to go to school because of it ... Lisa, things were ... I was bitter. I was full of hatred. I had shut God out."

He'd told her he was an orphan. He'd told her he had a brother who died. Beyond that, she knew nothing.

"I'm sorry." Her words felt flat, unequal to what he was attempting to say to her.

Sounds like I don't care at all, Lisa thought. *Not one gods-damn bit.* "I really am. Sorry, I mean."

"Thanks," Jed replied. He smiled his crinkled smile at her, the one that made her melt a little inside each time he did it. "What about you, Sergeant Riggs? Your parents okay with you putting your life on the line here?"

"Dad understands, I think. He gave me my sword." She patted the scabbard slung across her shoulder and under her arm.

Then she'd had enough of the charade. She told him how her parents had made her pay for it.

"But you're still close with them?"

"Yeah ... No, not really."

"Your brothers and sisters?"

"Just me," Lisa replied. "Hence the officer hang-up. Hence my ability to play piano. And shoot at a competitive level. And ride show horses."

"You play piano? That's great!"

"I'll play for you sometime," she said, but then realized where this was probably going. "Not in a church. I mean it."

"All right," Jed replied, obviously let down. She'd

guessed correctly. "Anyway, I think your parents are fools. You are perfect."

"Hardly."

"We all are perfect in God's eyes."

"Uh-huh. So you never did tell me. How did your brother die?"

Jed's body shook for a moment. Little ripples formed on the surface of the chai tea he was holding. He frowned. She'd never seen him frown so hard. She didn't like it.

"Look, you don't have to talk about it. I was just—"

"It's okay," he said. He set the chai down, then reached over and touched her hand. "Really, it is."

He leaned back, squeezed his eyes shut for a moment, then dabbed them quickly with his fingers. He looked at her again, and the scowl was gone. Or at least under control.

"Malachi was three years older than me. He took care of me when my parents...when they died. We were on the streets, but he took care of me. Got a job as a messenger. Worked for Sunnis a lot at the strip mall. Got into delivering aircars from dealerships to wholesalers. The Indonesians were big in that, and they really liked him. Can you believe a thirteen-year-old kid driving aircars all over the district? But that was Malachi. Quick. Smart. Trustworthy. And he made sure I learned to read."

"Sounds like a really good guy."

"Yeah, he was," Jedidiah said. He paused for a moment, gathering himself again. She waited. "Then when he was fourteen, which is like nine or ten to you, right?"

"More or less."

Suddenly Jed seemed far away.

"There was this truck. A land vehicle. It was the kind they use to haul stuff from the lift-port with one of those boxes on the back."

"A cargotainer?"

"Yeah, one of those. Anyway, they pulled into the middle of the shopping center parking lot. A bunch of guys dressed in black got out of the truck. They had guns. Like the one you have on duty."

"Rifles."

"Except some were little."

"Merrill carbines, maybe."

"Yeah. They went around the strip mall. Only talked to Muslims. Boediono, the rug seller Malachi worked for a lot, told them something they didn't like, and they knocked him down and rolled him up in one of his rugs. I found out later he suffocated."

"Dear gods." That wasn't as ugly as some other things, but bad enough.

"Yeah, it was bad. And the militia didn't come. Of course. Nobody came. Then the men with the rifles, they were Shia, I don't know what sect. They shot all the Christians. One by one they went around the units and shot them. The little gun was the worse." Jed drummed his fingers on the wooden table. "Rat-a-tat-tat. Rat-a-tat-tat."

"That's . . . I don't know what to say."

"The children they got hold of? The women? They rounded them up and put them in the box, in the container. Malachi saw what was going on and he hid me. He made me promise not to make a peep even if they took him away. He promised he would find a way to get back, so I had to stay quiet."

Lisa swallowed hard, dabbed at the tears forming in the corners of her eyes. "Where did you hide?" she asked.

"In a church across the street at first. In the baptismal tank up behind the altar. There wasn't any water in it. Huffman Assembly of God."

"Assembly of God. That's your denomination," she said, absurdly proud of herself for remembering.

"Yeah."

"And they didn't find you?"

"No," he said. "Because I didn't stay there. I snuck out. I thought I could save Malachi, I guess. I kept moving. I've always been fast, you know? Good at moving. And I saw. This really short guy. He was... light skinned. More like you. He was the one who grabbed Malachi and put him in the box. And you know where I hid?"

"Where?"

"Under the box."

"Gods."

"It was the one place they never looked," he said. "They burned the church. I think Malachi saw that. He probably thought I was still in there. I wanted to tell him I was okay, that I'd gotten away. But I stayed quiet. Like he told me. Then they closed up the box and...well, they drove away. Left me lying there exposed in the middle of the bazaar, but none of them saw me. They didn't look back, I guess."

"Did you...what happened to the container?"

"That one? Who knows? But that kind of thing goes on all the time. Sometimes they drop it in the sea. They like to leave them out in the desert, especially if it's summer. Sometimes they bury them. The thing is, they don't kill women and children directly, not even us Believers. Nobody can accuse them of that. They just . . . make them disappear."

"And they never let them go, even if it's just to make them slaves or whores or something?"

"I haven't heard of it," Jedidiah replied. A dreamy look came over him. "So I took Malachi's job. I became a messenger. I drove aircars from place to place. The Sunnis at the shopping center, they used me the most. I guess they felt sorry that they got to live and everybody else died. So they kind of took care of me, like a pet or something. A dog you like."

"How did you ever get out of there?"

"I knew how to read, so I read. A lot. Anything I could get my hands on. One day this guy named Terrence who owned a used data-pad shop—do not *ever* buy a personal info pad from him, by the way—told Brother Ronsesvalle about me. Brother Ron runs a skate school. You know, glide praise. It's how people get good at it. They pay for skating lessons. God helps those who help themselves."

"Okay."

"I told you I was fast, right?"

"Yep."

"I was more than fast. Nobody could make a delivery or take a message that wasn't suitable to send electronically as fast as I could. Nobody. Because I climbed walls. I ran along the roofs and jumped from building to building. You ever heard of parkour?"

"Yeah, it's actually part of our training. The special warfare guys get lots more of it."

"Brother Ronsesvalle saw me doing some of that stuff. Just a routine delivery of some medicine I ran for the pharmacy. He told me he would pay me to teach adults how to do it. Movement. Gymnastics. And I would get my own room—which never happened, but that's okay. It wasn't really his fault. The new place he built got blown up before we could move into it. And so I taught sacred dance. I learned to glide. I went to school. Now here I am."

"Studying to be a minister, like Brother...what's his name?"

"Ronsesvalle." Jed replied wistfully. "No, not like him, the poor guy. He has a strong calling. It's left him pretty broken down after all these years."

"Then what?"

Jedidiah seemed about to answer her. Then he shook his head and smiled. "Want to go up to Zebedee's place? I'm feeling a strong calling for something else right now."

"Sure do. But—"

"'But' nothing. Let's go."

"Listen, I'd like to ask you something. Something about us," Lisa said. "If there's one thing about Believers...they sure as hell don't believe in sex before marriage. Does the Assembly of God make some kind of exception?"

Jed grinned sheepishly. "No, not really."

"Then how are we even together?"

"Want to know the truth?"

"Uh, yeah."

"I like your hair," he said.

"What?"

"Your hair. I liked it when I first saw you. I followed you around the glide arena. I just wanted to look at it."

"Gods, I was wearing a *helmet*, Jed."

"I know. I knew your hair had to be *short* under it. I was kind of hoping...that you'd take it off. In front of me."

She laughed. "You were looking for a striptease with a *helmet*. Pervert!"

"I guess you could put it that way. Then when we got together that first time you had leave, and you came without it...and I saw...it was like lightning hit me or something. Like God spoke to me and said this would be okay, you and I would be okay."

"And my cute short hair was the reason you were there to decapitate the feckhead?"

"Yeah."

"So the rest is history."

"And prophecy."

Major Riggs and Mrs. Heaton, I believe that Lisa fell in love for the first time with Jedidiah Farmer. I think she found a good man. Would it have lasted?

They were very dissimilar. Lisa struck me as being only slightly religious. And she wasn't a Christian, of course. The young man was studying for the ministry or priesthood of one of those seemingly countless denominational divisions within their faction. I can't remember which it was.

Yet the relationship did work, at least for the time that they had together. It not only worked. It helped Lisa overcome her depression. This I experienced with my own eyes and ears. Although she was well liked by her troops, Lisa was a droll person, not given to much outward emotional expression. But it seemed to me whenever she talked about Jedidiah, she was very, very happy.

That evening Zebedee swapped apartments with Jed. They were free to stay in his place all night. They made love once in bed, and then took a blanket and did it again on the flat roof of the polycrete building that housed the apartment. The night was warm and comfortable, so after sex, they lay looking up at the stars—and at the occasional passing aircraft and shuttle.

She cuddled against Jedidiah, feeling his ropey muscles, running her fingers over his abdominals. She'd never been with a guy like him. Never expected to be. Her former boyfriends were split between beefy jocks and skinny nerds. He was like the perfect combination of both.

Who was she kidding?

Nothing had been like Jed. She'd never been in love before.

She was a Freeholder, so she'd had sex once she was of age, of course. But she was a virgin in one way. Jed was her first love.

And she was pretty sure she was Jed's first *anything*.

Who was this man she'd saved her feelings for? This one she'd waited to love?

A Christian. A killer.

"I was thinking," she said. "You took that Shia's head off with a skate blade."

"Yes. So what?"

"Aren't you Christians supposed to turn the other cheek and be pacifists?"

He said, "That's from Jesus' Sermon on the Mount.

The idea is not to overreact to small things. But you don't have to be a doormat."

"I can't even tell what people are fighting about on this stupid world. I mean, sorry to be so blunt, but your home planet is a worthless shithole in general."

He smiled. "We get good sunsets."

"You've never seen any others."

"True," he said. He leaned over and kissed her forehead. "Maybe I'll see Grainne's one day."

"Yeah, I'd like that." She sat up and the blanket fell away from her shoulders, revealing her bare form. Jed was instantly gazing at her. She smiled and put a hand on his arm. "What *is* your plan, Jed? You going to be a priest or pastor or whatever?"

"I don't know," he said after a moment's pause. "I think about . . . getting revenge. A lot."

"And this will help you *how*?"

"Not at all. I'm running from a, from a *lust* for it. Revenge. It is sin. It is selfish. My parents and brother are in heaven. They don't give a damn whether I get it."

"But you do?"

"School gives me something more important to think about." He gazed up at her with a wistful smile. "And so do you."

She touched his cheek. "Good," she said.

"And what about you?"

"I care about you." She pursed her lips, wanting to give him something more, maybe something true. "I care about my job. I want to be brave. I'm scared I'll screw up and let my troops down." She fingered the folds of the blanket. "Maybe I was a chickenshit not to go to Commissioned Officer School like Dad wanted. Maybe I'm just chickenshit in general."

"God has a plan for you."

"Look, I'm where I want to be *right now*." She pulled his arm around her and snuggled next to him. "I love you," she whispered. "Gods help me."

"You...do?"

"If it never gets better than loving you right here, right now, I'll be all right with that."

Jed kissed her hair. It tickled.

"Why do you like it being short so much?" she asked. "I guess it makes me different from the other women around here?"

"The reason's kind of embarrassing, actually," he answered. "Maybe even depraved."

"I can get into depraved."

He chuckled, then sighed. "Well, I *do* kind of remember my mom. I was real little, but I have this impression. She cut it like yours. Her hair. She was a Methodist. She just came here because of Dad."

"Don't you have any pictures?"

"There wasn't any virtual net back then, not in al Dura, especially. World-virt came after the Unos got here and set up their satellites. Back then you saved things on personal media. Nothing got mirrored to virtual. You had what you had."

"So?"

"All that stuff got blown up when the first UN occupation accidentally bombed our house," he said. "Malachi and I were playing over at our friend Jacob's." He swallowed, brushed fingers across his eyes. "I mean, they blasted our place to *ash*. It's a shame they never seem to be able to get it together and do that to the, how do you say it? The *gods-damn* feckheads."

"Hmm," Lisa said, but nothing more. She snuggled

closer until she could catch the scent of his skin. Not surprisingly perhaps, he smelled a bit like chai.

Above a shuttle streaked across the sky, rising, rising.

"Brother Ron says these are the end times," Jed murmured. "Revelations. The four horsemen. The Mark of the Beast."

He laughed softly.

"You believe that?"

"What I know is that God led me to you."

"Thank the god and goddess."

"Yes," he whispered. "It's all part of His plan."

She almost left her sword in the apartment when she headed back to the COB the next morning. She simply forgot, and had to double back from two blocks away to get it.

In the apartment, they'd fucked once more before she left. A quickie. Against a wall. Well, against all the walls. And not that quick.

When she returned to COB Jackson, there were rumors of something building. Blazers were in the area. The feckheads were restless. Lots of chatter on the command channels of the comm, and the vert-stat stationary observation platform was catching glimpses of larger groups of men flowing into the area. They kept themselves fairly well hidden.

Which meant they knew how to. Which meant they were dangerous.

In retrospect, everyone should have known where the Shia militants would strike first, even if it was a feint.

The soft spot. Al Dura. That night Jedidiah's apartment building was hit by a shoulder-fired rocket and it simply caved in. Crappy concrete. No polymer or even rebar for reinforcement. It had been essentially a mud hut made to look like a modern structure.

Which had to be an allegory for *something*, Lisa thought when she heard about the strike over the battalion feed. But she couldn't say quite what it might be allegory *for*. All of Mtali itself, maybe.

The rocket strike had happened past curfew. Everyone was in their beds when it hit.

Kid can't catch a break.

But he wasn't a kid anymore. Neither was she.

The man.

Her man.

She hoped he'd died quickly. She'd seen enough troopers hit by explosives to know that not everybody died instantly. Not by a long shot. Even when half your skull was blown off, you often flopped around for a second or two. Felt something horrible had swallowed your most primitive, basic self.

Or maybe not. Maybe all feeling, all care, was gone by then. What the hell did she know?

At least don't let him have suffocated. She thought it again, thought it as prayer directed at Jedidiah's Christian man-God.

Let it have been quick.

Then the war was on, and that was her business.

She wasn't going to be able to shut herself down emotionally. Lisa knew that. But she also knew she could and would put those feelings off, project them ahead so that she could do her suffering when there was time for grief.

She was only partly successful at this. It would have to do.

The UN was drawn into the al Dura firestorm, which made it a total clusterfuck for a while and lives were needlessly lost.

Then the real attack came on Ta'izz Jadeed. A Blazer unit was already in the vicinity, and so the FMF joined the battle.

Thankfully, the situation demanded all of her attention.

She did look up once and see that Mtali's star was setting. With all the smoke in the air, it was an even more beautiful sunset that usual.

Major Riggs and Mrs. Heaton, the battle was a massive push by a coalition of majority-Muslim factions to drive all offworld peacekeepers from Mtali. In terms of military history, it had similarities to the Tet offensive or even more closely, to the Tbilisi Police Action in more recent times.

The militants were experienced fighters. While they do not have the level of weaponry our military possesses, at that time they had assets we simply did not know existed.

We were caught by surprise.

Our intelligence, which mostly came from UN satellites and a laughable system of paid informants, was faulty.

One of those assets the militants acquired was a vehicle-mounted antiaircraft electrostatic rail gun and solid-fuel missile battery.

This battery was capable of taking down vertols, transports, drones, or even ballistic shuttlecraft. It was bad news on wheels.

It wasn't merely a danger to our pilots. Without

*air support, many more of our ground forces
would be killed.*

They were prepared to make us bleed.

As it happened, COB Jackson was the first to get
hit by the al Wadi faction attack. It came just after
sunset. Al Wadi was the largest of the Shia militias.
They'd made their reputation by blowing off prisoners'
limbs with detonators before beheading them. It was
practically a genre of vids on the networks.

They amputated with explosives if the prisoners
were men. Women got to live a little longer. This
wasn't a good thing. Those were another genre of vids.

At first the assault was with fire-and-forget rockets
and small-arms fire. Then a converted desert rover
drove up with a 20mm machine gun with explosive
projectiles quite capable of chewing its way through
Jackson's berms.

COC called for consolidation of FMF forces in
the sector.

A fallback by any other name should smell as sweet,
Lisa thought. But the decision was wise.

There were three other squads in COB Jackson
besides Lisa's. Seven Alfa One, Two, and Four.

Seven Alfa Three pulled rear guard.

She put the heavy weapons in back. There was a
mounted M-23 in a turret sticking out of one of the
GUVs and manned by Robins, a specialist on Chamber's fireteam. Providing coverage behind the line of
GUVs were her antiarmor section and machine guns,
with four M5-bearing troops to back them up.

The antiarmor proved their effectiveness. They
loaded white phosphorus antipersonnel instead.

After a wave of attackers was burned to a crisp—
the screams were terrible, but mercifully short—their
pursuers pulled back, biding their time.

They're hoping to surround us, and they just might,
Lisa thought.

The rear guard seemed to be the most dangerous
position until the GUV minerollers hit the mined
roadway ahead. There were stolen UN sensacles that
leapt for vehicles and personnel like evil spiders, and
IEDs made from the ancient recipe of homemade
ammonium nitrate and aluminum. ANAL, it was called.

It really sucked to have your legs blown off by a
hard-packed ANAL load.

Which was exactly what happened to the lieutenant
when he got out to inspect the damage to his GUV.

He might live and regenerate, but for the moment
he was a double amputee. Seven Alfa One stayed for
the medevac. That was not going to be easy. The faction forces weren't far behind and there was already
harassing fire.

It was hard to tell distance with her multispectrum
eyewear, but there was compensating software that
provided a range estimate in the upper-left-hand
peripheral vision. The enemy were half a klick away.

Vertols were going to have trouble landing, and it
might come down to a ground evac.

If that happened, Lisa didn't rate the lieutenant's
chances at surviving as very high. There was only so
much tourniquets and hemostasis could accomplish.

Lisa and Jack Woods, the Alfa Four sergeant,
dismounted from their GUVs and led their squads
onward. Each squad numbered twenty, including the
NCOs, a sergeant and two corporals. The going was

agonizingly slow as six troopers spread out in front of the vehicles and swept for explosives.

Clearly the factions had expected a pullback from the COB and had mined appropriately for it.

The enemy knew where the explosives were. Sooner or later, they would surge in, taking advantage of an explosion's aftermath.

She debated saying anything, but finally huffed up beside Woods.

"I think we should mix this up, Jack."

"What do you mean, Lisa?"

"Cut northwest. Alleys, side streets. I know Ta'izz Jadeed fairly well. You have to go through it to get to the UN sector perimeter from COB Jackson. I've been that way...a lot recently."

"We have orders to fall back to the COC."

"They didn't tell us *how* to do it, did they, Jack?" Lisa said. "Let's ask them."

She used a flick of her tongue to key up the COC frequency.

"Control, Seven Alfa Three."

"Control acknowledge. Seven Alfa Three."

"Situation Charlie Foxtrot, Control. Threat context may be unsafe with all units bunched together. Seven Alfa Three and Four request permission to disperse from Jazeer Boulevard and approach COC via side streets, Control."

There was silence on the other end for several segs. The squad GUVs crawled forward as the two sergeants waited for an answer. They'd doused the headlights and were running dark, with only infrared spots to navigate. Behind them the militants had flowed around the lieutenant's position with Squad

One and were gaining. They were almost in accurate
firing range. Projectiles whistled over the Freeholders'
heads and created miniature sonic cracks that they
felt as well as heard.

Finally a reply came.

"Negative, Seven Alfa Three. Seven Alfa Four,
continue on route to COC," said a gravelly voice.
Was that General Richard himself? It sure sounded
like him to Lisa. "Something else has come up. Seven
Alfa Three will divert to Ta'izz Jadeed quad five niner
seven. Acknowledge Seven Alfa Three."

What the hell? But it would get her off this boulevard of death, which was what Lisa most wanted.

"Ta'izz Jadeed quad five niner seven. Seven Alfa
Three acknowledge," Lisa said.

"Seven Alfa Three, link with Recon Three Zulu
One to provide fire support."

Gods, Lisa thought. A Blazer Black Ops unit. This
was getting interesting. Scary, but interesting.

"Link with Three Zulu One. Seven Alfa Three
acknowledge."

A shoulder-fired passed low over their heads and
impacted a brick-faced structure in front of them,
showering the squads with fragments.

She turned to Woods. "See you at the COC, Jack."

"Good luck, Lisa."

She nodded and clicked on the squad com. "Seven
Alfa Three we are on a mission diversion. Load GUVs.
We are Oscar Mike in two segs."

Her corporals acknowledged the orders. Both
sounded a bit stunned.

"Seven Alfa Three drivers, headlights. We *want*
them to know we're coming now."

Two segs later on the dot, they left the boulevard and headed into the maze of Ta'izz Jadeed.

It turned out she didn't need a map to find Three Zulu One. She'd walked these streets with Jed. In fact, the position wasn't that far from the shopping center where Jed had once made an orphan's living.

The GUVs' mirrors slapped the walls and folded against the body, but the vehicles fit down the alleys that they raced along. A smaller vehicle width was a requirement across the entire FMF planetary expeditionary force. This was why Freeholder vehicles on Mtali always seemed undersized in comparison to the UN transports. Today wouldn't be a good day to get your collective ass caught in a wide-load squeeze.

As they drew closer to the coordinates, Lisa saw flashes ahead through gaps in the buildings, and then could hear explosions and weapons fire even over the buzz of her GUV's surging powerplant.

Two more blocks and they were there. Wherever "there" was.

"Seven Alfa Three, weapons check."

She unslung her own M5 and checked once again that projectile and grenade launcher were loaded and off safe.

Meyer, who was driving, screeched around a corner and they rolled into hell itself.

Her comm buzzed on the COC frequency. "Three Zulu One—Control, unit approaching from your three hundred mil mark is friendly."

Control is talking about us, Lisa thought.

"Seven Alfa Three here," Lisa radioed. "Glad to meet you."

"Seven Alfa Three, Three Zulu One. Glad to meet you, sir."

Lisa chuckled. "Three Zulu One, negative on the 'sir.' My parents were married when they had me."

And he thinks I'm a boy.

There was laughter on the other end. "Correction acknowledged, squad leader."

"*Very* glad to meet you, Three Zulu One," Lisa said. "Tell us where you want us."

She keyed to the squad frequency.

"Corporal Chambers, covering fire to our right. Seven Alfa Three, prepare to dismount!"

Lisa was more scared than she'd ever been and exactly where she wanted to be.

She was fighting the assholes who had killed Jed. Murdered him. In his sleep.

Fuck them all.

They secured the GUVs behind a half-shattered polycrete wall. She ordered the encoding switches on the vehicles engaged, but Lisa had a feeling they wouldn't last long. The squad charged into a building the Blazer warrant leader had designated.

She stationed Meyer with a heavy MG and Green fireteam below, then led Red and Blue up the left-hand set of stairs.

IR headlamps and reticles flashed crazily in the stairwell as they charged upward.

The five-story building was infested with militants. Shots ricocheted down the well. She saw the thermal signature of the sniper, two floors up and leaning from a stairwell, zeroed in and returned fire.

She hit him immediately.

The militant's *face* disappeared and a smear of incandescent brain and blood sprayed onto the underside of the stairwell above him like an infrared abstract painting.

They cleared the building floor by floor. The thousand divs of training began to pay off. The squad moved like a well-oiled machine.

The heavy MG proved to be an excellent cover weapon for advance as well as an effective killer, just as she'd been taught. Effective, that was, if you avoided getting rattled by the two dirtbags who fell screaming down the stairwell. They looked like chunks of exploded meat. She wondered how they even managed to cry out as they fell.

But she *could* ignore it. For the moment at least, all they were for Lisa were two eliminated variables in the calculus of battle.

Seven grenades and nine dead hostiles later, Lisa and Red Team burst onto the roof.

The militants on the roof had heard the commotion below and taken cover. Fire roared from their weapons. Lisa leaped out the stairwell door and rolled right seeking cover. She found a vent outlet to crouch behind. Chambers, emerging behind her, moved left.

Ling, out next, wasn't so lucky. A slug smashed into his chest. There was no blood and it seemed his tactical armor had absorbed it. But another projectile hit him in the shin and his lower left leg exploded, leaving a stump below his knee.

"Oh shit," she heard him mumble.

"Red Team, remain behind that doorframe!" she shouted into her comm. No one else emerged.

Things were urgent now. She needed to clear this roof so they could tend to Ling.

"Moving up," she said to Chambers.

Chambers rose firing, slugs zipping past Lisa and into the militant positions. The one who had fired on Ling dropped, his chest an open, bloody cavern.

The tactical calculus raced through her mind. Six targets here. Four were concentrated near the skylight on the right.

Ah, there was a sixty-millimeter mortar there they were servicing. Now where the hell had they gotten *that*?

The two others were pinned down by Chambers' continuing fire—and his very frightening scream of rage that went on and on.

First the skylight. She burped a grenade in that direction, then another for good measure. After that, she hit the deck. The explosions were close and immense. When she looked up, the militants near the skylight were not merely dead. They were *gone*. All that was left was fragments of bone with bits of flesh clinging to them scattered across the rooftop. The mortar was nowhere to be seen.

Stiggs, her heavy gunner, looked chagrinned when he emerged on the roof. Nothing for him to do here anymore.

"Give me suppression, Red and Blue," she called out to her team as she painted the target on their visors.

The remainder of the troops charged onto the roof, and the cadre of militants who were left were caught between the crossfire of nine rifles each emptying eight fifty-round clips inside a seg. They were obliterated while trying to swing their weapons into position to fire.

The remaining assholes on the roof had been diced to pieces.

Ling's wound was tended.

Flares lit the urban night with a shadow-strewn, macabre light.

Down below, she could see that the faction had arms they weren't supposed to possess. High-explosive artillery was flying upward like a hailstorm in reverse. A flatbed V7 Bison pulled up with a mounted 11mm heavy.

She ordered an IR flare shot up, and the squad lowered their goggles. The urban scenery lit up for them, but the enemy, most lacking IR eyewear, would gain no advantage.

More fire erupted from hostiles positioned in the street, in doorways, and from windows across the street and above. There was no lack of targets for her squad. Lisa zeroed in on one militant who kept leaning over the shattered glass of a window to aim. The target was trying to be random, but it was hard not to take on a rhythm of firing in the midst of the action.

She timed him once. Twice. Her finger was on the trigger just before he emerged from cover the third time. She watched as he jerked back into the room behind him as if his body were attached to a spring coil. He didn't come to the window anymore.

Then there was the chuff of air and roar of down-facing jets that was the unmistakable signature sound of a Freeholder vertol, an aircraft lifted by thrust and not airfoil. Over the comm channel she learned which ones.

Hatchets. Attack vertols.

The dogfuckers were about to have a very bad night.

She couldn't risk glancing up, but the thruster roar grew ear-splittingly loud. A Hatchet was overhead. The pilot was coming in dark.

Fire concentrated toward her position. She ducked. When she risked a glance to the street again, she saw that the hostiles had driven up in a battered Zil utility vehicle covered with ceramic plates, scavenged, but no less effective at absorbing small-arms fire.

Two boxy missile batteries rose from the bed of the Zil on extending armatures. They looked very like UN four-pack LG-9200 Biter missile batteries.

Dark or not, from the downwash of air, they knew where the vertol was in the sky.

Gods damn it.

And where the hell had the faction gotten Biters? Militants were supposed to be completely lacking AA missile batteries on Mtali. There was guaranteed air superiority.

Obviously they had them. Obviously there wasn't.

There was a trailer attached to the Zil ute with a heavy machine gun mounted on it.

A Hatchet swerved in on approach.

A Biter launched.

It streaked upward, but the Hatchet pilot through some miracle of reflexes jogged the craft to avoid it. What he did not avoid was the machine gun fire. Tracers streaked up and their fiery paths disappeared into the ducted fans of the vertol.

Red and yellow flames burst from the nacelles.

Damn it.

The vertol began a wobbly plummet.

Get out of here while you can, she silently urged the pilot. Instead the pilot was headed straight down.

Almost like he *meant* to crash.

Then Lisa realized what was going on.

With a satisfying crunch, the attack vertol landed

directly on top of the missile launchers. Four or five militants fled in all directions. A couple were *thrown* willy-nilly when a missile exploded. Amazingly the Hatchet remained intact. She saw the pilot pop the hatch and climb out.

Something in his hand. What the hell was he carrying?

His sword. He'd managed to salvage it.

"All fireteams, cover that pilot!" she yelled into her comm. "Concentrate fire. Take out battery personnel. Suppress those lower window positions!"

The pilot crouched down at the eruption of firepower. After a stunned moment, he realized it was cover for *him*. He wasted no more time and charged across the street and into the building.

"I'm heading down," Lisa said. "Eckhard, you've got the roof."

"Roger, Sergeant."

Somehow she'd known the pilot would be Rob McKay. He'd turned a disaster into a tactical advantage and destroyed the AA battery.

"Thanks," Rob said. Then a weary smile spread over his face. "I'll be damned. If it isn't Sergeant Riggs."

"Yep. Nice flying, Warrant."

"Nice crashing, you mean."

"Isn't that basically what I said?"

Rob grinned. "Sometimes we get it wrong and actually land," he said. He glanced through a broken window. "Oh, hell."

From down the street another vehicle trundled.

This one was no converted civilian ute.

It was a Sysunion Mobile Air Defense platform. Had the UN told anyone that a multimillion-credit piece of equipment had gone missing on Mtali?

They had not.

Had it been smuggled in by other means?

Who knew?

Certainly not Uno intelligence.

Gods.

There was a cab and a flatbed. Four four-pack Biter cans and two Helborne long-range interceptor missiles. There were also two 11mm twin-mounted machine guns. And on the back of the flatbed was a swivel-mounted free-electron laser, tunable to slice through smoke, mist, clouds, and antilaser aerosols.

The SMAD took up a position behind the wreckage of the crashed Hatchet and the smaller battery.

The SMAD immediately sent a triple barrage of a Biter, laser and AA cannon fire into the sky. Lisa risked leaning out the window she was standing beside. She looked up in time to see a transport vertol take fire. It gyrated for a moment, then the pilot regained control and wisely got the hell out of there.

With the mangled metal and ceramic of the crash scene for cover, there was no way to get a shot in on the ground. She hoped they had a better angle from above.

But Eckhard said no. They were also exchanging heavy fire with hostiles on an opposite rooftop.

"Looks like it's going to be up to Alfa Three," she yelled into Rob's ear.

"And me," he replied instantly.

"Hell no!" she said. "Light body armor and no weapon. Not a chance."

"I have this," he said. He held up his scabbarded sword. "And this." He hefted his carbine with his other hand.

"You will not endanger the lives of my squad by foolish heroics."

Rob looked chagrinned. "Okay, Sergeant Riggs. You're right."

"Gods-damn right I am!"

She screamed into her comm for the entire squad to gather across the street from the new AA battery.

"Even the roof?" asked Corporal Eckhard.

"Especially the roof," said Lisa. "It's gonna take all of us."

"So what are you planning to do?" Rob asked, gazing worriedly out.

"Take down that position before it knocks any more of our people from the sky."

No more time for chatter. She spoke on the squad frequency again. "Fireteam Blue, advance in echelon, Green and Red to cover. After Red engages, Green, then Red to follow. Understood?"

She heard a chorus of acknowledgements over her earbud.

She turned to Rob. "Rocket destroyed Jedidiah's building last night," she said.

Rob had been grinning like a wild man, but now his expression turned to sorrow. "Oh gods. That's no good."

"Yeah," she said. She was about to go, but after a step turned back around. "You think there's anything to that Believer afterlife stuff?" she shouted to Rob.

"Probably not," he shouted back.

She felt a smile stretching out on her face. Maybe it was a skeleton's grimace, but it *was* a smile.

"How the hell do you know?" she said.

"Nobody knows."

"If I find him, Rob, I'm never gonna let him go."

"Absolutely not."

The squad was gathered and ready. There was nothing more to do but move out. "You stay here. I've told another unit about you." She keyed her comm, "Red team. Go, go, go!"

Iron hail from above, but there was also suppressing fire from the rooftop behind her.

Thanks, Three Zulu One, whoever you are.

Slugs slapped into solid surfaces to either side of her, and her rifle grew hot from firing.

She was shouting. No words. A long scream. Anger. Justice.

I'm coming for you, assholes!

They charged the battery. The SMAD crew seemed confused and unprepared.

Did you believe we wouldn't come? Lisa thought.

Maybe all those years dealing with the Unos, that's exactly what they thought.

Meet the Freehold Military Forces. We've come to kill you.

Then one of the militants got a clue and swung the defense laser in Seven Alfa Three's direction.

This was going to get messy.

"Rockets up!" she shouted. "Grenades, everybody else. Take your shots now!"

She fired her own and was watching its trajectory toward the battery when on the right the laser cut Meyer in half.

Closer.

A stream of slugs from the heavy licked over the edge of the trailer and a militant fell to the ground, his legs torn off. Then Red team was swarming up and over the destroyed battery wreckage, with Green and Blue curling around the sides.

They were charging into the spitting fire of the machine guns. More of her people fell, writhing, screaming.

Finally they were too close for the laser to be swiveled down.

At the flatbed—facing angry scum firing individual rifles. The return fire was more accurate. The enemies were blasted away. Not without casualties. She saw Eckhard grab at his guts, then fall with a melon-sized hole in his back.

Chambers knelt in front of her, making a step. With a running start she planted a boot on his back and leaped onto the platform.

The surviving enemy were back. They fired from behind the missile armature. Four or five. Daley climbed up beside her, but slugs took him and he flipped back over the edge of the flatbed and out of sight.

Lisa dove and rolled. Noticed movement overhead.

The Helborne can was rotating. Locking on a target. She fired a burst up at it. Nothing. The superceramic of the can was protecting the fragile missile within. Her M5 wasn't going to do it. What could?

Grenades? No, and she was out anyway.

The laser. That could do it.

She sprang back on her feet and charged for the rear of the flatbed. The operator saw her coming. He tried to swing the laser around to cut her down, but the mount did not permit more than 180 degrees of movement. Wise. You didn't want to accidentally spin around and cut through all the weapons on the platform in one swoop.

Lisa shot him in the face. His head disappeared in a spray of blood and bones, and he toppled over the edge. She reached the laser.

It was operated by a simple joystick with a firing button on top. Idiot-proof.

But what good would it do if she couldn't get its muzzle turned toward the missile can?

How was it anchored in? What was limiting its range of movement? She examined the mount.

Projectiles smashed into the floor and against the metal flash plating of the laser. Lisa felt a bite in her leg. She looked down.

Gods.

Half her left calf muscle was blown away. Bloody flesh splayed out from a ragged, gaping wound. The wave of pain that hit her was overwhelming. She almost blacked out. But it was a wave, and it subsided for a moment. Enough to allow her to think.

She gritted her teeth and felt around the undercarriage of the laser where it met its swivel stand. Was there a latch, a way to dismount it? Her hand closed on what felt like a handle.

A slug sped by her face, slicing her cheek open.

She yanked on the handle. Nothing. No movement. She put both hands on it and pulled as hard as she could. It moved. A millimeter.

The blood loss from her leg was already making her weak.

I need a way to apply more force. I need some kind of lever.

And I've got one.

If the side of her face wasn't shredded, she would have laughed.

She reached under her arm and drew her sword. Ducked down and jammed the tip of the blade behind the handle beneath where the laser met its mount.

Pulled on the sword grip.

The laser mount handle moved. She pulled harder. The handle clicked out of its seating.

Got it.

She slammed against the laser and it swung—past the safety stopper.

A slug blew apart her right shoulder. Her arm hung by a strip of muscle, tendon and flesh.

That was okay.

She could operate the joystick with one hand.

Gods, the leg was all right, but now the shoulder hurt like a mother. Like nothing she'd ever experienced before.

Pride goeth before destruction.

Will remained.

She pulled the joystick down, elevating the laser. Jogged it to the right. Looked up. The Helborne was locking into place. Firing solution acquired.

The laser's red targeting dot—itself a small laser—winked back from about halfway up the Helborne can.

She pressed the red button. Held it down.

Nothing happened for a moment.

Her shoulder screamed. Blood trickled around her teeth from the ruined cheek and pooled in her mouth. She spat so she could breath. Took another breath.

Had she broken her sword? She looked down. Couldn't see it in the darkness.

The night was getting to be so dark.

Looked back to where the laser was firing.

She saw smoke rising from the missile can, illuminated by the laser beam itself as it burned through the ceramic protection of the can.

A haughty spirit before a fall.

He was really handsome. For a skinny dude.

Will. And desire.

Also desire. Even at the end.

She hadn't expected that.

Then the beam was through the can to the solid-fuel rocket marrow within.

Lisa's world exploded.

Major Riggs and Mrs. Heaton, your daughter and her squad took out a well-defended SMAD antiaircraft platform. You, Major Riggs, will surely understand what that means, as well as the difficulty and importance of the deed.

The squad followed Lisa Riggs without question.

She was their leader.

All but the wounded Private Ling were killed.

I have personally recommended Lisa for a Valorous Service Medal. Commander Richard has seconded my recommendation, as has 3rd Mobile Assault Regiment Commander Naumann, the leader of our Special Warfare element.

We have begun to call the skirmish the Battle of the Rooftops. I think the name will stick.

I did look into the matter of Lisa's friend, Jedidiah Farmer. It took me a while to even discover his last name. Sector security confirmed that his effects were found in the rubble.

I visited the seminary. They said Farmer had not shown up for his classes at the seminary after the rocket attack, and could not be located.

At the seminary, they told me that on the morning after the rocket strike, Lisa had called there as a last hope for locating Jedidiah alive.

She had spoken with several staff members who had seen the destruction of the evening before. One had been a searcher in the rubble of Jedidiah's apartment building. He confirmed to her that no one had survived.

Did he find a body? Did anyone?

Could she speak to Jed's friend Zebedee, maybe he know something?

Zebedee was also missing. There were multiple strikes.

There were no bodies, only body parts. That was what the searcher told her.

In the past weeks, there have been rumors of a new Believer and Amala hybrid group that calls itself the Second Measure. The Christian Coalition and the Amala Shura Council have vehemently condemned the Second Measure as rabble-rousing troublemakers. Apparently the SM has taken the fight to the Shia factions in particular and destroyed several armories.

Information about the group is sketchy. The leader is supposed to be a young man who was formerly studying to be a minister of the Lord.

His name is Jedidiah.

This may be a nom de guerre. If not, Jedidiah is a fairly common name in al Dura, after all.

It may be merely a coincidence.

It may not.

The Second Measure leader is said to have a face that is the very image of sorrow.

He is also said to be an implacable killer.

Lisa noted once that Jedidiah didn't flinch or react much after he sliced the terrorist's head off.

No, thought Rob McKay. *I can't send this.*

He stared at the payment book in front of him.

There were fifteen payments remaining on the loan Lisa had taken out for her sword. Three thousand credits.

She'd paid her parents full value and then some.

I'll keep them up till we pay them off, Lisa, Rob thought. *Don't worry.*

Don't worry there in the afterlife.

Dear Major Riggs and Mrs. Heaton: screw you for making Lisa buy her sword from you. You didn't deserve her. Burn in hell.

Dear Major Riggs and Mrs. Heaton, I am so sorry for your recent loss. I write to say that I was a friend of your daughter. I was there when she attacked and destroyed the antiaircraft battery. I witnessed her bravery and resourcefulness firsthand. Sergeant Riggs not only saved the lives of several pilots, her actions also permitted close air support of our forces which saved many additional lives.

Lisa told me about the lineage of her family,

*and I promise you she did you and her ancestors
proud.*

   Sincerely, Warrant Leader Robert McKay.

"So there's most of the sword blade left," Rob said.
"Gods know what her parents will do with it. Probably
throw it out like they did their kid."

"It was a *wakizashi*?" the armorer asked.

"Yeah. A good sword," Rob said. The armorer was
an old and trusted acquaintance of his. "Possibly great."

"You saw it whole?"

"Oh, yeah."

"Must have been something," said the armorer.
"You know swords." He held a piece of tubular metal
Rob had given him. He turned it in his hands as he
examined it. "Let's talk about this now. Gun barrel?"

"Heirloom shotgun. Chemical propellant. The good
old days."

"Family piece?"

"Sort of. I acquired it some time back. I'm ... I
need a few extra credits. I'm paying off a debt."

The armorer held the barrel up to the light stream-
ing in through his shop window—the light of Grainne's
sun. He traced a finger along the pattern of the steel.

"Think you can use the metal?" asked Rob.

"Maybe," he shrugged. "But I doubt I'd even get
a dagger out of it."

"What about as a collector's item?"

"Yeah, okay." The armorer shook his head, "But
there's a lot of old weapons floating around. Pieces of
this and that families hang onto until they forget why,
then get what they can for them. You'd be surprised."

The armorer pulled out a long, felt-lined drawer

behind his shop counter and nodded toward it. Rob leaned over to see what was in it. Gun stocks, trigger actions, and yes, gun barrels and barrel pieces. "Market's kind of flooded."

"Two hundred credits," Rob said.

The armorer smiled. "I'll give you a hundred," he said, "because it's you."

"Done."

The man took the rifle remnant and carefully wrapped it in clean cloth.

"So, the owner of that *wakizashi*? Was she your girlfriend or something?"

"Just a friend."

"I'll be on the lookout. Things turn up. You never know."

Rob smiled sadly. "It'll end up in a landfill."

"Probably." The armorer put the shotgun remnant in the felt-lined drawer and slid the drawer closed. "Well, I'm sorry about your friend."

"She was brave. She lived well," Rob said after a pause. "Not long enough." He shrugged. "Or maybe it was."

The armorer shook his head. "You don't believe that."

"Nope."

"What was her name?"

"Lisa," Rob replied. "Lisa Riggs."

Posthumous Citation to accompany the award of the Valorous Service Medal...

This bearer had fought beyond what she thought mere flesh could endure. Even her metal was brutally broken and damaged. It might be her death, too, but she had no regrets. She had been honored to fight in so many battles, across so many lands. If this was her end, it was well earned.

But she felt the caresses of a smith, the fine handling of one who knew metal from its touch. She was placed in waiting, and could smell a forge nearby. It was a strange forge, but professional. Around her were other blades, most mere lumps of metal, but a few had their own thoughts.

Then she was taken to the fire with tongs and metal. The smith struck surely and easily, forcing her back to a straight shape, and reuniting her with her damaged half. Then he added new metal along her spine.

This was different. She had the metal of another sword, but no thoughts of it, and of parts of a gun. Gun metal in a sword was almost obscene, yet oddly satisfying.

This smith was an artist. At first she was terrified, with all the new mixed metals forged into her. Her soul was so small at this point, diffused throughout, but still in command.

But he knew metal. The soft and pretty went around

the ductile and tough, over the hard and sharp. No one had shaped her thusly in centuries, but she was certainly fit and strong.

He seemed unsure of what fittings to use, until she realized there were two sets. One for parade, in wood old enough to have its own thoughts, if wood could have beyond the simplest of impulses. The other was in a soulless but amazingly tough material that gripped her tang tightly. It would be hard to feel a bearer's spirit through that. She felt its matrix for a long time before she grasped how to reach through it.

Over the long centuries she could no longer track nor follow, styles and materials had changed. Still, she was a warrior once more, and named the War Bride. At first she thought it condescending, to refer to a warrior like some common bystander. However, she was made of a mix of cultures and styles. It did fit.

Several hands grasped her, and all appreciated her beauty, but none were enamored enough to take her. It was not many days though, before one female warrior drew her from the rack, and held onto her. She also was a product of melded cultures, from the old place before the new frontiers, and they fit perfectly, sisters in background if not quite in spirit.

—m—

The Reluctant Heroine

Michael Z. Williamson

Three years earlier, Kendra Pacelli had fled Earth. Now she was fresh from Recruit Training and Mobile Assault Training in the Freehold Military Forces.

She'd fled her home because of an embezzlement case in her UN Peacekeeping Force logistics unit. She'd been one of many secondary victims, accused of profiteering from the sale of military supplies. It was now probably understood that she and tens of others had been framed.

Probably.

With the cost of space travel, there wasn't much chance of going back. All her assets and indentured labor had got her here. It was a one way trip.

Anyway, Grainne was beautiful, once you adapted to the climate and gravity, and she'd made strong friendships. She was again surprised at how much she'd adapted to the planet and people. They were vital, intense and energetic.

Then there was her odd relationship with Rob and Marta. It had just sort of happened. She was involved with both, though much more with Rob than Marta. She cared deeply about each of them, though.

She wondered if Grainne could remain independent. The economy was slipping, which was part of how she'd wound up back in service. Though part of it was the sense of belonging, and both her lovers being veterans in 4th Legion (Landed Reserve).

There were significant differences between the two militaries. Her UN uniform had been a professional dress to identify her on duty, and not worn elsewhere because it drew unwanted attention. Her FMF uniform made her feel proud and respected. It was blatantly military, and had been hard to earn.

She wondered when the shine would wear off. It felt real this time, as though it was more than just service, but allegiance. Hopefully that allegiance wouldn't be tested. She knew where it lay, but Commander Naumann's predictions of an interstellar war scared her.

Marta was with her, and they were shopping for minerals and wood. She'd already arranged a gift delivery to Marta, without the other woman knowing about it.

It felt good to be on pass before yet more training and her permanent duty assignment. Iota Persei was bright, the weather was clear and refreshingly cool—about 23°C or so. She wanted to get out of the vehicle and enjoy it.

"One more stop," Marta insisted, and flew them a few kilometers to the outskirts of town. They stopped in front of a blocky building, removed from its neighbors. A simple painted sign outside proclaimed CARDIFF CUTLERY. They went inside.

Rustic was perhaps the word. The back of the building, visible through an opening, was equipped with bay doors for loading equipment and material. Inside, it resembled an archaic smithy crossed with a machine shop. The front contained racks and displays of exotic cutlery. She'd never imagined so many varieties of edged weapons.

Mike Cardiff was about Marta's height, stripped to the waist and showing knotty biceps He had a short, graying beard and mustache and a shaven head. "Well! Marta!" he said brightly in a resonant voice that belonged to a man twice his size. He grinned evilly and reached out his grimy hands.

She was still in uniform and squealed, "Don't even think it! Or I'll never kiss you again."

He wiped his hands off and held them at his sides while she leaned to kiss him chastely. "Who's your friend?" he asked as he leaned back. "Is she taken?" He leered comically at Kendra.

"Yes, by me and Rob. Mike, Kendra Pacelli. Kendra, Mike Cardiff," she introduced. Kendra took his hands and shook. He gave her a glance from head to toe that boosted her ego. His thoughts were obvious.

"You ladies look at the hardware, I have to check on one in the oven," he said and walked into the back again.

Kendra stared at the work. It was amazing. Some of the blades had grains and patterns like burled wood. She'd heard of pattern-welded and Damascus steel, but had only seen one small piece of Rob's. This was incredible.

Looking to Marta for assent, she lifted one from the rack. It was a standard kataghan pattern, chisel pointed, slightly S-curved, with a grip of nuggetwood set with silver pins. One nearby she didn't recognize by shape had a handle of malachite. She whistled in respect.

Cardiff returned with clean hands, wiping them on a rag, and asked, "Any questions?"

"Not yet, but I am impressed," Kendra said. Marta was scrutinizing a small knife.

"Your accent is familiar. You're from Earth?" he asked.

"Yes," she agreed. "Minneapolis."

"Oho! Do I have a piece for you!" he said, guiding her by her elbow to another rack. He drew the blade from its slot and handed it over. She took it from him, curious, and stopped suddenly. The balance was amazing. It floated in her hand, seemingly ready to swing in any direction she willed without physical effort. She raised it and marveled at the artistry of it.

It was a *wakizashi*, she recognized. The blade was about fifty centimeters, patterned with interlocking curls of the constituent metal writhing like a snake along the length of it, treated with some chemical to reveal it in shades of gold and tan. It seemed to have a depth, hypnotizing the eye into staring into it. The sides curved slightly into an edge so fine there was no glint of reflected light. Just back from the edge, there was what she knew was a temper line. It was wavy, crisp near the edge and clouding into nothingness toward the back. The guard was a circle of carved black iron with gold hammered into it in the shape of a rosebud. The hilt behind it was a golden-hued wood that was tiger-stripe grained and had a chatoyant depth of its own that shifted with the angle of the light. The scabbard Cardiff held was carved of the same wood.

"What *is* that wood? I've never seen it before," she asked, stunned at its beauty.

"That's actually quilted maple from Earth, salvaged

from an old piece of furniture. I forged the blade from two damaged pieces. One was an old family blade that was too trashed to reuse as was. The other was an absolutely archaic Damascus shotgun barrel, also worthless in the condition it was in. You'll see the weld pattern change from Persian twist to waterfall along the shinogi, which is this line here, where the bevel starts," he indicated the break and she could see a faint line where the two patterns met. "So all the materials are from Earth. The surface is treated with titanium nitride for the gold tones," he finished.

Kendra wanted it. No, she lusted after it. She didn't dare look at the price tag. This was an entirely hand-crafted work of art. She nodded and thanked Cardiff, putting it back on the rack. She turned to see Marta buying a small dagger, the grain of the blade twisted back on itself, hilted in Grainne amber and silver.

"Not getting it?" Marta asked.

"I want to, but I don't dare spend the money," she admitted.

"You need a sword for formal wear," Mar chided.

"But—"

"And it should be distinctive," she added.

"But—"

"And you'll never see that one again. Mike's stuff is magic that way. You come in and wait for one to call to you," she insisted.

"Marta, sto—"

"And you just finished your training, which calls for a special gift to yourself," she reasonably pointed out.

"Dammit, I—"

"And you want it," she finished.

Cardiff brought the sword over again and held out

the tag. Sighing, she took it and read it. It listed the materials, the date finished and gave the name of the piece as "The War Bride." Below that was the price. Cr3500. It was more than reasonable for the work involved, but she flinched anyway. Even with the bonuses she received for hazardous duty, that was almost two months' pay. But she did want it. And another one like it would never exist.

She hesitated a moment longer until Cardiff said, "If you're a friend of Marta's and just graduated, then let's say three even. And I owe Rob."

"Let me guess, he saved your life on Mtali," she said. It was becoming a running joke.

"Nooooo! I'm a civilian, thank you very much," he protested. "I just make the hardware for them. But he's referred a lot of people and does research for me."

She sighed and handed over her card. He scanned it and let the machine transact while he wiped the blade with a cloth and gave her a hardsheet of instructions. "Thank you!" she said, thrilled.

They left and Marta begged to handle it once. Kendra relented. She loved watching the light coruscate from the surfaces. She said so.

"That's all?" Marta replied. "It makes me wet to look at it."

"*Everything* makes you wet, dear," Kendra replied, laughing.

"Sure does. You want to?" Mar asked, running fingers down her shoulder.

"Umm...after lunch, you could probably talk me into it," Kendra agreed.

They parked at a downtown ramp and walked to a cafe. The sword thrust through Kendra's sash drew as many stares as the two women themselves did. It was a good afternoon.

Seventeen Freehold months later

Kendra really hadn't believed Commander Naumann when he spoke of war. The actual invasion made no sense at all, except that her new home was reduced to a shambles. Her base had been smashed, and she escaped on a craft intended for others. She'd dropped into the deep north woods and met up with local volunteer forces.

Months of guerilla operations had destroyed her compassion for people. She retained enough awareness to hate herself for that, and to hate the invaders who'd brought her to it. That they were her own people on both sides . . .

She had no nation.

She chose logistical targets and led small bands of militia to attack them. She didn't see it being of any use whatsoever, but her duty and standing orders were simple. "In the absence of other orders, locate the enemy and destroy them."

That made it very clear. The UNPF referred to "Opposition" or "resistance." The FMF referred to the "Enemy."

They sniped, set explosives, engaged hand to hand when they had to. She used her sword on legitimate targets, and on an element of prisoners who made it very clear they wouldn't act in good faith. She soiled herself and her sword with their deaths.

She was known as an immigrant, though, and eventually, the enemy, her former people, knew as well.

The old-style reward would have been amusing, if it didn't name her personally.

There was only so much tension a mind could take.

And then a vehicle and driver arrived, to escort her back to organized forces. The vehicle was a battered farm truck. The driver was a senior sergeant.

She was surprised to get an escort of that rank. "By the way, corporal," he said as they bumped away, "You are now a sergeant."

"Really?" she asked. "Thanks, I guess."

"Don't thank me. We're keeping the schedule going, and you'll probably be higher shortly. Naumann is keeping the chain of command filled. He's a colonel now, too."

"It sounds like he's going to go down fighting," she replied.

"Going down? You've really been out of the loop here, haven't you?" he asked, surprised. "We've got them out of the Halo, except for mopping up, and they'll be off the surface in a couple of weeks, tops. The habitats are sort of holding; no one wants to use the force necessary to win because of the risk of destroying them, so they'll surrender once they have no support. That leaves the gates, which we can blow if necessary. Actually, JP One is already blown."

Kendra was shocked. It was impossible! "We're winning?" she asked, wanting to hear it again.

"Not winning. We'll still be a mess, but they'll be gone. Best we can manage under the circumstances."

She resumed her mindless state. Victory, peace, were words. All that mattered was survival.

Within a day, she realized how huge the offensive actually was. Everything available was assigned to positions, even if it was only to have cooked rations ready.

She assisted with programming logistics at a frantic pace, constantly changing as new equipment was smuggled in. It was frustrating, endless revision, removing useless outdated blocks but not erasing them in case things changed yet again. The troops not involved griped nonstop, but relocated equipment as ordered. Most of the battle was being fought now, in detailed deployments and plans. The actual engagement would be of less relevance. While no battle ever went according to plan, proper preparation enabled a disciplined army to make the most of actual conditions.

"Kendra," Naumann said quietly behind her.

She turned and said "Yes, sir?"

"I want you on the ridgeline when we start. You'll have a platoon, and your own squad. Can you handle that?"

"I guess I have to, don't I?" she replied.

He nodded. "I need all the experience I can there. This isn't raiding, sniping, or ambush. This is going to be face-to-face, brutal warfare. If anyone breaks, we all die."

"Yes, sir, I understand."

"You'll have tac commo, all the ammo we can spare, and some tactical support weapons. Body armor we can't spare; it's needed for the assault troops. You will have explosives and emplaced weapons. Can you hold there, even if they come face to face? Even if your troops rout?"

She breathed deeply. "Yes, sir."

"I'm asking you because I trust you to understand what's at stake, and not flinch," he said.

You're asking me to die. "Yes, sir," she nodded, breathing again. "I'll do it."

He squeezed her shoulder and left. She turned back to the program at hand, and realized she couldn't work further on it now. She closed, secured, and stood. The actual engagement would be of less relevance, except to those who fought it.

Outside was warm and dry, thoroughly black to her vision. As her eyes adapted, she saw a few stubborn dapples from Gealeach pattering through the heavy cover. From the south came the muffled rumbles of fighting in Delph', as it was slowly being shredded into rubble. South of there, Jefferson was being systematically looted and raped, triaged as lost to the enemy...for now.

So here's where it ends, she thought. *I've made my decision on my home, and I'll die trying to save it. Can he really pull this off? Or is it just a defiant gesture?*

She sat there a long time, pondering what the future held. Until recently, she thought they'd lost already. Now she found that Naumann had cobbled together a regiment from the dregs available and the local farmers, and intended to fight an army over a hundred times his size. There was no way he could use infantry and light support against such odds, and the UN had support craft in space and more they could call. Every calculation she ran showed their task to be suicide, but he clearly had a plan. It hit her suddenly that she trusted her commander with her life, or her death, and wasn't at all afraid of not being able to follow his orders. She would do as he said, and believe he knew what he was doing.

Two days later, she became a heroine.

❖   ❖   ❖

"Now," Naumann ordered.

Drifting far overhead, in the total silence and serenity of orbit, was one of many intelligence satellites. This one was of UN origin, but there were others of local manufacture, recoded and in use to betray their owners. IS3-17, as it was known, was providing data on the firebase and its perimeter. It showed the lazy flow of the river, traffic on the roads and a few anomalies that would be investigated by armed reconnaissance teams. A well-placed charge punched through its casing, shattered the delicate instruments inside and damaged its orbit. Within seconds, others flashed into death. Further out, a manned relay station had already been breached. The crew had hurried into vacsuits as a second charge damaged its solar array. More charges demolished the antennae.

Across the system, intel and commo assets died. The ground forces were cut off from almost all their support, and were brought to technological equality with the defenders.

Below on Grainne, along the Drifting River, several dikes rumbled as deeply placed charges damaged the structure. Previously compacted dirt, now loosened, collapsed and was swept away by the current. The berms heeled over into the water, slumping until waves spilled over the top. Trickles became streams, then raging torrents.

A precious few artillery tubes fired time-on-target salvos, then attempted to evade counterfire.

Three vertols lifted out of the hills. They'd been hidden in caves, and slipped out of the trees unseen for now. Accelerating brutally, they angled toward the beginning carnage. One of the three was actually a cargo lifter with hastily improvised launch racks and munitions. It dragged slightly behind the other two, engines straining. It dropped lower for cover as the two Hatchets rose for tactical advantage.

Up on the ridge, the snipers and support weapon crews unloaded ordnance at a furious rate. Their targets were across the river, but were still within range. Mortar crews sighted in on defiladed positions. To the south, Blazer teams crept forward from the river and the trees.

The Combat Air Control team called coordinates to the two Hatchets and scouts drew further artillery down on selected equipment. Their first priority was the UN armor. No armor could stand against modern firepower, but it was virtually unstoppable by lightly armed civilians. Tanks were great tools of oppression. Also a threat were the particle-beam guns that could claw artillery shells from the sky. They could not be allowed to start shooting.

The cargo lifter dropped into the melee and furious supporting fire stirred the ground around it. The fire lifted as the aircraft did, leaving more Blazers and Mobile Assault troops behind. Peeling off in twos and threes, they got behind the enemy and cut them down. A handful of lunatics drove combat buggies across the bottom of the ridge Kendra and the other infantry were to hold. Their light vehicles were loaded with deployable mines that spread across the ground to make an additional obstacle. Kendra and her unit had already set several thousand kilograms of explosives in the trees.

✧   ✧   ✧

Naumann didn't like what he saw. They simply didn't have enough munitions to sustain the rate of fire needed.

"Cut half the tubes on the next five volleys, advance as planned, then cut to thirty-five percent fire after that. Keep them rotating to save force and make every fifth tube counterbattery. How is CAC coming?"

"CAC reports they will be designating targets in six segs," support control reported.

"Understood. Take care of the arty and armor first, then get them on the bluff," he ordered. He keyed his mike and said, "Infantry. Naumann. Air support will be there soonest. Hold position."

Buried in her hasty position, Kendra heard Naumann's advisory. *Hold how long?* she thought. There were a *lot* of UN troops down there, with a lot of vehicles. Most of those had crew served weapons. It would turn into a bloodbath if it became supported infantry attacking a numerically inferior force of grunt infantry.

Her position was a hollow dug in the earth, a cover of netting and twigs over a woven polymer mat and a layer of sandbags as rests and cover. The tiny portable monitors showed the automatic weapons arming and firing. The first echelon detonated, sending out hypervelocity shrapnel in an arc like a circular saw. Bodies cut in half collapsed in heaps, some wriggling in brief agony before finally dying. The UN forces momentarily stopped, then spread out to flow around her. "Station Three, this is One. Data sent," she advised as she dumped the video into the net. Incoming intelligence from other stations showed a huge force massing. There were far more enemy than anyone had anticipated and no air or arty support. She frowned and overrode automatic for the second echelon. She triggered the mines from outside in, to channel the dismounted troops for greater casualties. Gouts of mud erupted skyward and UN soldiers ran to avoid the carnage. Her reinforcing squad took aim at any vehicle and she ordered them to choose targets toward the outside first. "This is One. Engage automatics from the outside, say again, engage toward the middle of your position. Cut them into as many bits as possible," she ordered her other two squads. This was going to be unbelievably bloody.

She chose now to launch her three drones, laying a bisected V across the zone. The drones dropped sensor mines that armed on impact and split the approaching force into two pinned groups and two small groups of stragglers. She directed automatic fire and the drones over them. The drones sought movement and targeted. When they exhausted, they detonated, adding more bodies to the toll.

The forward elements hit her first perimeter, well up the slope and in the trees, and the M-67 Hellstorm system tore them to pieces. Fragmentation mines, direction-seeking concussion, and antiarmor mines blasted across the landscape in a dark gray pall of mindless death. She saw an Octopus mine trigger on one of her monitors, leaping through the air, sensacles waving until it brushed a horrified, retreating soldier and detonated. The screen went blank as the camera was destroyed by the blast. It cut to the second perimeter camera. "Left support, drop your loads and retreat to Line Two," she ordered. There was a flicker of confirming indicators and of charges arming, then her attention swung back. "Reserves reinforce the right," she ordered as she switched frequencies and continued. "This is

One. Go to manual and do as much damage as you can, then switch back to automatic. Prepare to engage on ground. Hold positions as long as you can. We will retreat toward the east and south as necessary."

Her screens turned to static. Someone in the UN had finally taken control and found some of the frequencies she was using. She had two wired feeds left. Quickly sketching in her mind her last recollection of the scene, she scramble transmitted, "Right, retreat on your own authority. Give me data soonest. All units ground and cover." She paused five seconds, then detonated the entire remaining first echelon of mines, setting the second one to individual automatic. It was not as effective as sequenced groups, but would last slightly longer. She was rapidly running out of explosives and still needed to hold as long as possible.

She swore as one of her remaining feeds died, hit by a stray shot. Right informed her they were retreating. She ordered Left to pull back as soon as they thought it advisable. This was not good. Any hole in the line would mean huge casualties and probable loss of the battle. One echelon of mines remained.

The last feed died. She set everything to automatic and grabbed her gear. With nothing left to do here, she might as well head out. That meant almost certain death, unless a miracle happened. It didn't occur to her to run and abandon her troops.

The bunker had tendrils of smoke, but outside was a scene from Hell itself. Dark night sky, pounding rain, howling wind through the trees. There was the steady cacophony of small arms, the occasional slam of explosives and distant, barely audible screams. A stench of blood, scorched meat, ozone, chemical residue and fresh earth assaulted her nostrils. "All elements retreat to second perimeter," she ordered over the noise. Flashes from weapons and illumination threw ghostly, cavorting shadows through the trees.

There was the scream of a light shell, probably mortar, she thought. She flattened and was grateful that it detonated in the treetops. She praised the thick forest and hoped it would hold. Then there was the basso chatter of cannon fire chewing into the ground. It wasn't well aimed; the weather and lack of intelligence forced the gunners to resort to eyeballs, but it was still potentially lethal. The *crakcrakcrak* sound set her ears to ringing. She cursed and ducked.

She slipped cautiously forward toward the battle, her tac giving her details of the horror below. The last echelon of minès, reinforced with a few hastily thrown scatterpacks, was detonating at the bottom of the slope. "All elements cover in the trees at one-ought-ought meters, line abreast," she ordered and picked a spot near a stout bluemaple. Rain trickled down her back and between her buttocks, cold and shivery. She stuffed her clips into pockets and pouches, readily accessible. This was going to be ugly.

The trees were thick enough and heavy enough to prevent even armor from entering, so the smaller vehicles wouldn't be a problem. Most of the heavy vehicles had been captured or destroyed, all but eliminating that threat, but there were undoubtedly more mortars and rockets available. Her element had three M-41 Dragonbreaths and a small mortar, two squad weapons and one last trap. That and Naumann's belief that they could hold until the UN broke and surrendered.

She heard an advisory from her left neighbor, whom she knew only as "Second Platoon," nodded to herself and ordered, "Inverted V position, elements at twenty-meter intervals, stand by on tubes." With the squads in V formation, she could have them retreat as they took casualties—and they *were* going to take casualties—and still have a line abreast formation with decent defense. It also gave better crossfire opportunities. She moved back ten meters behind the line she'd set. Thank God they all had modern helmets with tac and comm, if they could use them properly. She got a row of green acknowledgment lights and hunkered down to wait. Wet dead leaves plastered against her as the wind gusted past. She noted that the friendly artillery was decreasing. Either ammo was running low or they were taking casualties.

It wasn't a long wait. A probe in force moved quickly toward the ridge, one soldier carrying a sensor suite. "Squad leaders engage at will—break—First squad fire on my command," she ordered. Just a bit closer...

"Fire," she snapped. Three rounds took the bearer, four more the pack he carried. A volley dropped the rest of the probe, some covering, most dead. Sporadic fire returned and one light winked on her helmet. Casualty. Lethal. It was not someone she knew personally, just a name: Lowe.

There was a large, seething mass approaching, vehicles crawling to the edge of the woodline with ground troops among them. She could pick out darting figures on her visor and the signs of others behind them. They were waiting to determine where her troops were, then they'd rush. She had the one last area weapon left. She warned, "Fire in the hole," and coded for ignition, then closed her eyes and felt the actinic brightness against her face, right through the polarized visor. The improvised weapon was a string of white phosphorus and magburn canisters along the edge of the trees. It hurled white-hot flame into the troops dismounting from their vehicles, creating more disorder and casualties and a roaring fire to damage night vision and sensors.

There was a pause, then the rest swarmed forward as the initial flash died, desperately seeking cover in the same trees that protected the defenders. She raised her weapon and fired a string of fifteen grenades along the approaching front, the recoil hammering into her shoulder. There'd be bruises there tomorrow. She reloaded quickly as the second wave hit the dense cover of the trees. Her squad was taking shots at the attackers and she could see them falling. There were six directly ahead of her, less than a hundred meters away and closing at a run. Her rifle pointed almost of its own accord and she commenced careful, rapid single shots as they appeared through gaps between the boles. Six rounds, six hits, then three more as others appeared. Another light winked on her visor. "Eighteen, Two, fall back and fill in," she shouted to hear herself. "And fire the tubes!" Her own weapon was relatively quiet, but the simple mass of fire brought the volume up. There were explosions among the trees that threw sparks and debris across her vision and added to the din. She moved further to her left, the south, where the shooting was heavier. She scrolled through her vision options, but found nothing obvious to shoot at. A glance at the other two squads she commanded didn't offer much. On the other hand, the reservists leading them seemed to have their heads on straight. They were following her lead and keeping order.

The shrieking hiss of the Dragonbreaths startled her, even though she expected it. Three tongues of flame lashed into the approaching mob, the flash ruining night vision and momentarily blinding sensors. Men and women screamed as the chemical fire reacted with their skin to burn hotter still. They thrashed in agony as their squadmates recoiled in horror. The weapon was intended for bunkers, not open terrain. Temporarily stunned and illuminated, they dropped by the tens from desperately accurate rebel rifle fire from Kendra's platoon and the flanking units.

Movement. It was too high to be ground troops and too small and low to be an aircraft. It was a recon drone, hovering quietly on its impeller, guided through the trees by its robotic mind. She took careful aim, letting the grenade read the image, then squeezed the trigger. The small hyperexplosive charge smashed the pod, its turbine shattering at high revs, the pieces tearing chunks from nearby limbs.

Becoming resolute again as the incendiary brightness faded, the enemy advanced en masse. Kendra shot dry, reloaded quickly and tried to shoot back to her previous line of aim, now covered with incoming troops crashing through the underbrush. There was a brief pause and she switched to a fresh clip. She had two full clips of a hundred left and one of thirty-seven. After that, hand to hand. After that, she didn't want to consider. The war was lost, that was all.

Another casualty, only two spaces from her. "Fourteen, fall back and fill in," she ordered again and retreated one tree during a lull. It had a boulder next to it she could use as a better defensive position. She had barely reached it when another salvo of mortar bombs detonated. Before the firecracker pops of antipersonnel rounds finished, a second one of standard high-explosive hit, booming echoes through the trees. Illumination flares were glaring overhead, but the shadows confused what vision the light gave. She hoped that was true for the enemy, also. The occasional canopy fire they ignited was quickly doused by the rain, but hot cinders of twigs blew down here and there. She slapped at her neck and brushed off a glowing ember.

She could hear fire from the sides, indicating that the other sectors were still holding to some degree. How much longer? She wiped droplets from her sight screen. Water was running into her boots now and her pants were soaked and cold. Her breasts were tingling from the chill as they had in recruit training, a lifetime ago. Branches fell from the trees as cannon fire shattered them. The occasional trunk exploded in a shower of wooden needles. The forest was just one more casualty of the battle.

The enemy was well into the trees, crawling and darting through the weeds toward her position and shouting. She leaned across the rock, breathed and commenced firing. Pops and louder bangs sounded all around her and more of the enemy collapsed, some screaming for help, some silent and some wiggling closer. She set her grenades for minimum range, airburst, and fired three down the center. She had two hand grenades, but hoped it wouldn't get that close. She knew better.

The enemy was covering and creeping nearer. She sighted one figure as he shimmied forward and put a bullet through the top of his head. That earned her a torrent of return fire from his comrades, rock chips slashing and stinging across her face as she ducked. Time to move.

"Elements retreat twenty meters by leapfrog. Provide cover," she ordered her whole force. Then she slid low and lizard-crawled backward, rifle over her arms in case she needed it in a hurry. Another light blinked. Dead. An explosion shattered the ground next to her, spraying her with mud and stinging like a hard slap. Whatever it was, it was a thankfully small charge and the soft, wet ground had tamped it just enough to expend its force upwards. Her hearing dropped a level despite the helmet cushioning and a ringing sound drowned out much of what she could hear.

She hoped they retreated in an organized fashion. They were doing admirably well for predominantly untrained amateurs; only nine of sixty were veterans of active duty. Most had some experience, but guerrilla fighting was different from a stand-up battle. None of the guerrillas had ever used tac helmets, and she worried that the wealth of intelligence displayed would distract them.

As she slithered further, her hand brushed a mate to the bomb that had just missed her. This one was sunk into the dirt but had not hit hard enough to explode. Perhaps it had ricocheted off a tree. No matter, it was still live and she shied from it and worked her way around.

Clicking in her ears indicated a scrambled and burst message being decoded. "Pacelli, retreat at once to Zeta Three. Report when clear." Naumann's voice was barely audible in her ears. She boosted the gain.

Retreat? At once? How the hell do I do that? she thought. *If we cover, they'll kill us as they roll over us. If we run, we get shot in the back. If we retreat piecemeal, we get cut to shreds.* The only thing that came to mind was to let them roll through and attempt to surrender, then hope to survive whatever Naumann planned. That was suicidal, too. Zeta Three was the grid mark south of them along the ridge. So what was happening up north?

She forced herself to think. "Forward elements, fall back forty meters soonest. Report when done." Leapfrog them back a few meters at a time, covering each other as they did so? What would conserve troops and be effective? A click signaled another message.

"Pacelli. Retreat to Zeta Three immediately. We're—" it chopped off.

Her helmet was dead. More jamming. The sights on her weapon and the grenade controls were frozen, too. Directional EMP.

She realized now why the fire was so heavy—it was all concentrated at her position in an attempt to break through. Naumann was going to blow holy hell out of the area. If her troops were there, they'd be hamburger.

The problem was that the platoon on her right flank was no longer capable of holding. There was fire coming from that direction, indicating that they were either being forced to retreat or had been subdued. If she pulled back from the right flank, the UN troops would simply follow her. Some would die, but they'd be inside the perimeter. Naumann certainly had the temperament to kill his own troops to get them, but not enough soldiers to waste. If she retreated, they would be swarmed. If she held, they'd be under whatever Naumann was about to throw. Either way, her troops were dead. And she had no commo or night vision.

She stood and sprinted, tossing her helmet aside. Fire spattered the ground around her feet as she dodged trees. She counted paces through her rasping breath and angled downslope. She was working on eyeballs alone, assisted by flarelight, hindered by smoke and dark. A sharp pain burned across her left arm as a branch snagged her, but she kept running.

The end troop, whose name she didn't know, turned at her approach and fired. He yanked the weapon aside as he identified her, and missed. "INCOMING!" she shrieked, gasping for breath. "MOVE OUT NOW!"

He stood and ran, taking a supporting position behind a tree and waiting for her.

"GO NOW!" she screamed and pointed. "TWENTY METERS, THEN RIGHT AND KEEP GOING!"

A hum alerted her. She spun and saw another recon drone, hovering and scanning. She swung her weapon up and fired a grenade. It arced away, struck a limb and detonated. She cursed. Her weapon had been set to minimum airburst when the EMP hit them, but it had defaulted to contact fusing. It couldn't accept proximity fusing, as the sensors and controls were damaged. She took careful aim and fired again at the small pod. She missed as it easily evaded, and fired at it again. This time she hit and it exploded, metal and fiber confetti drifting out of the smoky cloud.

The damage was already done. The incoming fire was intensifying and seeker projos swarmed down. She ran back upslope obliquely, hearing them *ZIZZZZZ!*

behind her as they sought human body temperature. The enemy knew what line they were on now.

She had a repeat of her first warning, as the second woman in line almost wasted her, too. "INCOMING! RUN!" she repeated and staggered past. She ordered the next one to get the message to the other side and pull them back, then alert the next unit. He nodded and ran.

She ducked past a tree and another drone sat a bare two meters from her, drinking in data. She fired bullets at it as it tried to dodge. It thrust up then over and down again. Finally, a few shots grazed it and she caught the main probe panel with a lucky shot. It drifted away, weaving as it did and she downed it with two more shots. A distant series of thumps indicated another salvo of canisters full of seekers on the way from small mortars.

The squad was peeling back slowly, which was still dangerous, but might let some of the others survive. They'd have to clear a safe distance, then hold it against anything that came. If she could get a runner to the next platoon for support, they could keep the UN where it was until the artillery arrived. Seekers swarmed through the woods like angry hornets, seeking warmth to bury themselves in. The cold wetness of the trees made it easy for them to find the blazing heat of the defenders' bodies, but also interfered with their flights. Kendra heard a ZIZZZZZ! and a meaty *thunk* as one caught her in the calf.

She stumbled, rolled upright and kept limping, shrieking under her breath in tortured agony. It felt exactly as she'd been told it would to get shot—a freezing, burning, electric cramp through the muscles.

She reached the second man from her position, whose leg was shattered. He'd tied a tourniquet and stopped the bleeding, but couldn't possibly walk. He was barely conscious. She slung her rifle, pulled at his arm and began dragging him, fire lancing up her leg. Waving her left arm, she stumbled toward the last troop in line. He came running to help. "NO!" she shouted. "RETREAT!"

Through the roaring confusion she somehow detected death approaching from all sides. She spun and walked a burst of automatic fire into a disorganized gaggle of UN soldiers just coming through the trees, shooting offhand with her left hand, the weapon a heavy, kicking weight on her wrist, an ache in her arm. Sighting movement in the dying flicker of a flare, she lobbed three more grenades, still set to contact fuse, into an approaching knot from the right flank. The enemy were spilling through the gap to her right, pounding for the summit to hold the position and fight an attrition battle that they would surely win. She fired to her left again, then to the right, while backing away with her burden.

Her good ankle twisted on a branch, spilling her to the ground. She stifled a scream as her casualty groaned, still alive, and she forced herself to her knees and up under him. She muscled him into a rescue carry, more painful but faster. After nearly three hundred meters of sprinting through rough terrain, with a burden for the last fifty, she was seeing black spots. A hidden tactical part of her brain made her reach for, arm and throw her two hand grenades to keep the enemy's head down. They were small charges, but even with the cover of the trees they were close enough after her feeble throws that the blasts ripped at her.

She ate up one clip and let the weapon hang from its sling so she could reload with her single available hand, falling uphill and to the right.

Her last right-flank troop had either not heard her or ignored her. He dropped two clips at her feet, took the limp form from her shoulder and hefted it easily across his brawny back. "You have the rifle, you cover me! Back soon!" he shouted and took off at a sprint.

Kendra grabbed the clips and turned, throat too dry to talk or swallow, and pumped out her last nine grenades. There were figures darting all around her now and she wasn't sure if any were friendlies. There wasn't time to decide. She leaned against a tree for support, raised her rifle and used the iron sights. She had no idea how many she killed, but the barrel was hot enough to burn her hand by the time she finished the next clip. She reached for another as she retreated. Then her subconscious kicked in again. She threw herself flat.

The sky filled with the basso fabric-ripping sound of high-speed cannons. Hatchets made that sound, and nothing else. Wet splinters showered Kendra as the swath of death moved within meters of her and downslope. She stood quickly, surprising a Peacekeeper about to step on her. He staggered, confused and staring blankly and she kicked his kneecap, wondering why her calf no longer hurt. As he stumbled, she brought her leg up, knee in his face, and crashed her rifle on the back of his neck. She jerked a half step, knee searing, and shot again. The buddy of the last assailant appeared next to her, pointing the muzzle of his weapon into her face. She stared down the black hole for only a microsecond, then parried it and smashed him in the face with her muzzle as she shot. She swung around and fired at another trio stumbling into view. Her clip ran out and she reached for another. She had none. She buttstroked another soldier as he charged blindly past, kicked his ankle from under him and circled her foot over to crush his throat, feeling the gristly crunch up her leg. She grinned unconsciously. This was it. Time to die. A ripple ran up her spine.

Slinging the weapon and drawing her sword, she turned and ran uphill. Another drone sat in the crotch of a tree, trying to be inconspicuous. She jabbed the blade into the nacelle and the turbine shredded, throwing needlelike shards into her hand. They didn't do much damage, but her hand blazed with white-hot pain. As she ran past, the sky ripped again, level with her, as a pilot gunned along the bottom of the hill. Ahead of her, two UN troops were braced against a tree, shooting at someone from her squad. She slashed across the spine of one and thrust into the kidney of the second. The first one screamed and thrashed to the ground, half-paralyzed. The second simply collapsed. The keen blade had sliced through fabric designed to resist impact, not cutting.

Sheathing her sticky, gory blade, she grabbed the weapon and magazines from the dead one as she rolled for cover, bullets cracking past her. It was familiar from practice years past and Freehold training, and she retreated backward, shooting at anything that moved, starting with the one she'd wounded with her sword. The targets were backlit by the roiling fires below and she picked them out and picked them off. Fire. Aim. Fire. Aim. A round cracked past her ear, ignored in her current frame of mind. Shoot. Shoot again. Reload.

She saw movement, aimed toward it, then realized in the shifting light that the clothing was local hunting camouflage and the person wearing it was not in anything resembling cover. He was still moving, though. She fired three bursts to keep heads down and ran downslope. Her calf cramped with every jarring heelbeat and she winced, biting her lip. A few rounds made her flinch and she ducked lower, running hunched over.

The casualty was one of hers, but she had forgotten his name. Again she slung her weapon, heaved him up and around and over her shoulder and backed away, firing with her half aching, half tingling-numb left arm. Her bursts were fired for directional effect, not with any real hope of hitting anything. She stopped shooting as incoming rounds replied, aiming where her weapon had been when she fired. A part of her brain realized that meant that the UN helmets were nonfunctional, also. The pilot must have emped them as he tore overhead.

She chose her aim carefully and walked a series of bursts into the area in question. No further fire came from that one, but tens of others whipped past, cracking as they did. She stumbled, recovered and carefully lowered her burden behind a shattered stump. She crouched, rested her arm on her knee, and recalled where the last flashes had been. Returning to single shots to conserve ammo, she returned fire as fast as she could aim and squeeze. The enemy approaching seemed simply to materialize out of the flickering light and she swung back and forth, stopping the closest, taking any targets of opportunity between them. It was a losing proposition and she knew it. Fire. Fire again. Click! Curse and reload with one partial magazine. She quickly checked for her sword, realizing she would need it again soon.

Her shots spaced longer apart, then stopped. She could see UN troops throwing their weapons, scuttling behind trees and waving their arms. Cries of "Surrender!" and "Medic!" sounded all around, mingled with curses and screams.

The hillside was eerily quiet behind the voices, bereft of weapons fire. Smoke and steam drifted past in a nightmarish illusion of reality. She could hear ringing in her ears and wondered if she were deaf. There was smoky fire below and to her right. Running fingers through her hair, she waited for any sign of movement. Nothing. She crawled behind the tree, dragged her second casualty over her shoulder, turned and trudged, alert for danger, watching for her people. There they were. Eight of them and one wounded, anyway. And more fires behind them. She and her casualty made it eleven out of twenty.

Her hair was sticky, she thought. In a moment, she realized it was her hand. Blood. Probably from the victim she'd carried. Then she remembered the shower of shrapnel from the drone. Then she noticed the neat gouge in her arm, where she thought a branch had caught her. It was a bullet wound and suddenly hurt like hell. Her arm cramped up and she winced. Blood was running freely. Her leg turned rubbery, then tensed up, dropping her sideways.

She collapsed as hands reached for her.

Kendra sat at a UN medic's tent, now run by Freeholders. They'd patched her arm and leg and the flesh wound in her other leg she hadn't noticed and told her to wait for a scanner to become free. The surgeon in charge expressed the opinion that she'd lost thirty-five percent of her hearing, but that would have to wait for better facilities.

She sat silently, tired and sick and emotionless. Someone had told her she was a hero, and her force had held the brunt of the attack. The four-hundred-odd Freehold regulars and militia along the ridge had held against almost seven *thousand* UN infantry troops with local support units. She nodded, uncomprehending, and tried to ignore her ringing ears.

Reports were coming in across the system. The UN fleet had been captured or destroyed, mostly by converted mining craft and ore carriers using mining charges and beam weapons. Once command and control was lost, the UN forces had muddled about helplessly, individual commanders untrained and unwilling to take charge and give orders. The casualties had been horrifying on both sides. The SpecWar Regiments had captured or destroyed every fixed station that mattered and two cruisers at a cost of ninety percent casualties.

And there'd been biochemical attacks south of Kendra's position, an act of desperation by an artillery commander who had hoped to save his troops. There were tens of casualties, alive but raving from the vicious neural toxin. It occurred to her she was one of the lucky ones: alive, mostly intact and not screaming crazy from nanowar. She didn't feel lucky.

It wasn't her first battle. It wasn't her last. It was made notable by the words of others.

Citation to accompany the award of the Citizen's Medal . . .

---⚇---

She waited. Her bearer was a reluctant warrior, but most worthy. She recalled the damage, the abuse, the repairs. It was all worth it to serve with a bearer like this.

She not only had a fine stand to rest in, she had a shrine, laid in beautiful wood paneling and the delicious scents of fine oil. This culture understood war. It understood swords, and treated them as the partners in battle they were.

But she wanted more than weekly practice and a yearly parade, in the long, strange years this place had.

---⚇---

The Thin Green Line

Michael Z. Williamson

Captain Kendra Pacelli wondered why she was here. She understood the military conference wanted several heroic figures for a "roundtable." She had never felt heroic. She'd done what she needed to stay alive and support her home and comrades. Even sixteen years later, twenty-five Earth years, she didn't think she had any particular insight. She was far more interested in the historical fora. Even those could be done cheaper by presentation-response by network in a shorter time frame than transiting all these troops to a single location, especially one that had been at war longer than she'd been alive. The UN still had too much money to waste on outdated schemes and the perception of diplomacy. As far as she could tell, it was all aimed at grasping at credibility while clutching at straws.

She'd been invited, and the Freehold Diplomatic Corps paid transport and expenses for Rob and her, ostensibly for him to talk about battlefield aviation, which wasn't much of a thing anymore. War had changed dramatically in the last few years.

By any military's standards, she was an old lady pending retirement.

Mtali was much as she remembered it. This area was subtropical with odd plants, and the planet had shorter days and lighter G. It even had a fresh religious uprising. The Amala had spent the thirty Earth years since her tour evolving from barely literate, violent savages to highly educated violent savages. Educated, at least, in the means of violence.

On the trip from the spaceport, they'd passed several security cordons, physical barricades and technical interdiction. There were even antiaircraft mounts with both particle beams and old-fashioned projectiles. She wasn't sure if she should feel glad they weren't manned by the UN, but by local Coalition Forces—Sufis, Shia, Sunni and the Christian Unity, who had apparently settled most of their differences after killing enough of each other to populate another planet.

More likely, she thought, they just feared the Amala more and would revert to internecine warfare once, or if, they neutralized their common enemy. At least by having a mix of elements on patrol, the guests could expect some sort of backup if attacked. The locals would either compete with each other for the "privilege" or wipe out the attack with glee.

Rob had suggested, "They might all turn on each other and leave us holding the bag."

It wasn't a comforting thought. The only weapons they had were her rifle, his pistol and their swords. That made them more heavily armed than any of the non-Freehold elements.

Their room at the Caravanserai was modern and

clean, but the view of the city showed raw wounds of bomb blasts and the Hesco and sandbag perimeter around the entrance.

Lieutenant Aisha Rahal felt an odd mix of familiarity and strangeness. Mtali was an entirely different world from Ramadan. Lower G, thinner air, different climate zones even here in the subtropics, different growth and a different star. On the other hand, most of the locals in this area spoke Arabic, though the dialect was different and their accent was atrocious.

It was hard enough being female in a mostly male military. As a visiting junior attache here, she was out of place among groups who were offended by even the notion of women in the military.

It wasn't a comfortable party. All the rest of her element were male, and talking to local males. It wasn't that they intentionally ostracized her, but they had more in common with each other, and wanted to avoid awkward conversations, so she was shut out.

She made her way over to another group, with several women, who were laughing and animated and seemed much more relaxed. Freeholders.

As she approached, one of them turned her way, nodded marginally, and stepped to make a slight space in the group. He was fit, about fifty, in business dress, not uniform. He wore an open-fronted jacket with hip flares over belted pants, and had polished boots. On the belt he had a short sword and appeared to have a pistol in a shoulder holster.

He said, "Welcome," squinted and added, "Lieutenant Rahel?"

"Correct, Rahal," she said. His pronunciation wasn't

great, but he was educated enough to read her uniform and the Arabic nameplate.

"I'm Robert McKay, Pilot Captain Retired. This is Ken Chinran, also Captain Retired, Reconnaissance. That's Lieutenant Jelling, Third Blazer Regiment, Reconnaissance. This is my wife, Logistics Captain Kendra Pacelli."

That name was passingly familiar, and then she saw the plain green ribbon and platinum medal around the tall woman's neck. The Citizen's Medal for extreme bravery during the Separation War with Earth. She almost saluted, then remembered they were inside.

"Ma'am, a pleasure to meet you," she said, and offered her hand.

Pacelli looked slightly uncomfortable as she shook hands firmly. "Thank you. And the same. It looks like you're separate from your own contingent."

"Yes. Well, Mtalis . . ."

Lieutenant Jelling said, "And women." She gave a nod, with an amused glint in her eye.

If Aisha had to guess, Jelling, from a high-G planet, with that build, and the Blazer tab and a couple of other qualification badges, could probably break most of the men in the room in unarmed combat.

Three others came into the group, along with two Caledonians, and there were shakes, hugs and friendly punches. She didn't catch their names. They accepted her though, all with a quick glance over her own sparse ribbons. In her case, she hadn't served long enough to earn much. In the Freeholders' case, any decoration meant combat or some other kind of engagement—disaster, extreme training. It was apparent from their age most had served in the War with Earth.

They hadn't earned those medals for writing reports.

Captain Pacelli said, "If you drink, we're enjoying Silver Birch. Our national liquor."

"A half shot will be fine, thank you," she said.

She accepted the offered glass. It was an actual glass, tiny in size, with cut facets and a green and black textured twist. Handmade.

"To absent companions," McKay offered, and raised his glass.

She watched to see how they drank. They sipped, rather than tossing it back. She wasn't sure which would be better. She knew it was a cherished liquor, hand produced, and had subtle nuances of flavor and scent. She also knew that all liquor tasted like turpentine to her. She took a sip, then another, swallowed and felt the burn, and waited for it to pass.

"Thank you for your hospitality," she said.

"You're welcome." Pacelli took the empty glass back and placed it on a tray. Aisha noticed the ring on her left hand.

She said, "That ring is amazing. Your wedding ring?"

Pacelli held it forward. "Yes. The olive gold is for Rob, the yellow gold for me, and the rose gold for Marta."

"Marta?" she asked.

"Our wife."

It was said so casually, and had been a thing in Arabian history, and still was on Mtali. It wasn't prohibited in Ramadan, but certainly uncommon and frowned upon.

The ring was reticulated and woven into a complex knot of strands and ropes, an optical illusion in heavy metal.

"Is she here with you?"

Pacelli shook her head. "She is not. She retired as a medic lieutenant from Third Reserve, and is home with our children."

Pacelli moved next to Aisha and flashed an image from the phone on her wrist, of herself and her husband with a beautiful dark-skinned woman who looked mixed Asian and Hispanic, and two boys and a girl in their teens.

"A striking family," Aisha said. The girl and one boy had faint olive hints with high cheeks and light hair. The other boy was dark and had bronze tones.

Pacelli said, "Thank you. I haven't been away from them for years." She obviously missed them.

"You should be back soon, though. Your transport is phase drive, yes?"

"It is. They keep improving that technology. My trip from Earth to Grainne was almost a month, with the jump point and transit times in system. This trip was just over a week."

Aisha said, "Ours took the jump point here, but the Novaja Rossia delegation has offered to detour and take us back with their ship."

"Oh, excellent," Pacelli said. Then she added, "Well, if you're going to socialize with us, please do take a seat."

Aisha sat, and while they paid her little attention, it was better than the nonattention elsewhere. It was only because she wasn't known.

"What is your field, Lieutenant Rahal?" Mr. Chinran asked. He was a bit older, but very solidly built with good muscle tone.

"I am in security investigations," she said. "I came... was sent here to attend the seminars."

He nodded, "Interesting. I'll be presenting one of those at the end of the week."

"I look forward to it," she said. "Did you move into that after reconnaissance?"

"What I reconned was security procedures and methods," he said. "Among other things."

She noticed McKay almost snickered. She missed the joke but didn't think it was critical. She guessed he was likely some sort of counterintrusion type.

A few moments later, he stood, said, "Pardon me, there is a matter that requires my attention," and left at a brisk stride. Jelling was a moment behind. McKay was obviously looking at something on the glasses he'd just donned.

She realized Major al Hani was approaching, and rose to meet him.

"Good evening, Lieutenant," he said.

"Good evening, sir." She wondered if a dressing-down was coming.

"I am sorry you were not more included, but I see you found worthy company."

"Very worthy, sir. May I introduce you?"

He turned to the table. "I would very much like to meet you all, but we must return to our embassy. It seems the Amala's Mahdi Brotherhood are burning the business district. There are concerns it will spread."

Everyone at the table was suddenly attentive, and their phones started dinging messages, too.

"Thank you very much, Major," McKay said. "Do you have transport home?"

"We do, with the Sufis. They have sent a convoy for everyone."

With slightly widened eyes, McKay asked, "And if

you'll pardon the paranoia, is the attack confirmed by your own people?"

"Yes, and by Novaja Rossia."

He nodded. "Thank you." He looked across at Pacelli. "We should leave, too."

"Agreed," she said as she stood. "Lieutenant Rahal, Major al Hani, a pleasure to meet you. Hopefully we will again this week."

Kendra sat in the back of an armored limo that drove behind some sort of local gun truck that looked crude but effective. The limo was decent but obviously well used. She scanned updates.

"The riot is a solid three clicks from here," she said. There was an aerial map, but only a few overhead images. The rioters were shooting down drones.

Rob said, "Three districts would be better."

"Yeah. Didn't the locals insist this area was pacified?"

He muttered, "Including our hosts."

She wasn't sure if he meant the Sufi society or the UN. Either way...

It wasn't a small riot, either. Even in darkness, she could see smoke illuminated by the flames underneath it.

"Have they determined how big the movement is?" she asked.

Rob said, "The last report was ten thousand. This morning they said that was an underestimate and raised it to twenty-five."

He turned to look out his window and said, "I think they may still be optimistic."

Back in their room at the Caravanserai, the news load on the big screen said another thousand troops had been ordered in to secure the conference.

Rob coded on his phone. He tapped to make the image public for Kendra.

"Yes?" Chinran answered.

"It's your field, sir. Should we leave?"

Chinran looked tense.

"We don't really have that option. Our ship continued on the dip run. There's nothing nearby with available space. We can probably get an old tramper, and that would have been easier when this dump had an orbital station. Now, it's got direct spaceports and the Oort docks."

Rob said, "I'd rather sit in any orbital or the habitats than here."

"That's the problem," Chinran replied. "We can't guarantee those are secure. There's been vandalism damage and threats. If there's an uprising there, we breathe vacuum. At least here we have air and somewhere to run."

Rob asked, "You were on this dump about the same time I was. Is there anywhere worthwhile to run to?"

Chinran shook his head, but said, "Worst case, my daughter and I can guide everyone to a position I know, and some friends. We'd be stuck there until proper response."

"Response from the UN? In other words, we'd be underground until the Mahdi burned out or finished takeover."

With raised eyebrows, Chinran said, "I did officially advise against this venture."

Rob said, "Yeah, we got that message en route. That was our military's screw up. Well, the third, after trusting these idiots and the UN."

"I wish I had better news. The Sufi are professional

now, and do have a good military. I can't guarantee they weren't compromised and infiltrated. We may have to hope for massive fratricide among local forces."

"Just what I need to help me sleep. Thanks for the update, sir."

"You're welcome. I'm sorry it's not more reassuring."

By morning, the riot had subsided, but three square blocks were too badly destroyed to save. In the city, one of the larger bank buildings had been demolished by fire and explosives working through the superstructure until it fell and destroyed everything in its arc.

En route to the conference, Kendra heard occasional extinguisher bombs blowing off, and there was still smoke, and heat shimmers from the damage.

She muttered, "Can we black market some additional weapons?"

Rob murmured back, "Mr. Chinran and Senior Isman are working on that."

She said, "I think we should stay in our own embassy if we can."

"We probably can. I'll arrange it."

There were more guards at the venue, including UN forces. She was actually glad to see them for once. She wondered if any of them knew who she was, and if it mattered to them.

The day was grueling. Her official events included a brunch acknowledging the status of a number of heroes, a round table on how heroes felt about their battles, and a fairly interesting presentation on how risk factors had changed for both soldiers and civilians over three thousand years of warfare.

The intent was for it to show that even the war

between Earth and Freehold, and the political fallout space-wide, were not hindrances to good relations. Kendra didn't think that was an issue. The issue was politicians grabbing for power and not being able to let go.

Everyone presented as a hero said much the same as she did. She noted Corporal Macklin, Royal Caledonian Army (retired), with regenned arms, several organs and right eye. Here on Mtali a decade before, he'd secured an escape route from a torched building by charging through a fire, running an extinguisher back inside to quell the flames, then leading his element out, providing supporting fire while they secured weapons from their arms shack. He'd been shot fifteen times in addition to the burns. More than half of his body was regenned and without modern medicine, he would never have lived through evac, nevermind surgery.

"Well, shit, excuse me," he said. "Someone had to do it. We were all going to die anyway. I figured if I got anyone out it was a plus. I just reached a point where I couldn't care anymore."

Her own comment had been, "We really didn't have any choice, and it was 'we.' My entire element fought bravely. I got noted for the circumstances, but I wasn't paying attention at the time. I was trying to . . ." she didn't want to say, "*kill as many UNOs as possible before I died.*" This was about the brotherhood of the military, how people were similar and didn't need to fight. So she deferred to ". . . hold my position as long as I could. None of us expected to survive."

Really, it was humbling to meet other people who'd seen that side of death, but it wasn't something she cared to dwell on, and there wasn't a need for face to face. Though if the media attention made people think about what all these "minor" wars, and the big one, had cost humanity...

No, they were still going to do it again. The thought was nice, but pointless.

In between discussions, she was constantly being sidelined for interviews from every agency who could reach her, for as long as she'd agree to talk. She signed a hundred or more autographs for younger soldiers and some escorted children, mostly cadets.

The latter were so young, and so determined. She was still patriotic herself, but with age came a recognition of human limitation. Even if one survived, there were only so many kilometers the body could take, so many jumps, falls, adrenaline rushes. Eventually it stopped being exhilarating and just became tiresome.

"...I hope I can be as heroic, if I'm called," the cadet in front of her was saying.

Right. Autographs, attention, respect.

"Hopefully, you won't need to be. A great many who were never went home. But I wish you well in your career and hope you excel." She signed another image of herself across his book screen. Then she motioned him next to her and smiled enough to make a good image without looking weird. Marta had taught her that from her vast repertoire of modeling.

She realized she was getting irritated. It wasn't the awe and respect. It was the self-brainwashing that being a hero was a desirable career move.

Next to her, Rob muttered, "Downtime, love?"

She realized she was wound up from the discussions and the attention. Yes, downtime, definitely. They had an evening coffee reception to attend in a couple of hours.

She looked around and said, "I'm very sorry, but I need a break before my next engagement. Thank you all very much for your presence and interest." She stood.

Rob led the way slightly in front, and his body language and brisk movement kept people from pestering her. They found the elevators. The security guards—mixed NovRos and Caledonian troops, not locals—checked their IDs and cleared them through.

In lieu of space at the embassy, already overfull, they were now assigned to the venue hotel. It wasn't quite as nice as the Caravanserai, which was still plenty, but it made security easier for everyone.

They were alone in the elevator and she leaned against Rob, eyes closed, able to not be everyone's hero for a few moments.

Neither said anything until they were in their room.

As the door clicked, he said, "I could tell you were getting overloaded. Too much adoration."

She nodded, sighed and hugged him close, enjoying his strength.

She said, "I guess part of it is I'm ashamed on your behalf. You were as heroic, ass out in the sky and visible from orbit. Your wounds were worse than mine. I had my hearing reconstructed and some minor surgery. You lost your biointerface and can't fly. The trip here was murder on you. But my silly ribbon is green, while yours is black, green and purple, so you don't rate highly enough."

He shrugged with a smile. "It's fine. Everyone who matters knows what I did. I did it for them, not for the medal. And I was very glad to know you survived. Then you helped put me back together. And Marta."

She asked, "How was your day? When you weren't around me?"

He tilted his head and said. "I listened to a lecture that didn't name me, but was clearly about our battle and told me everything I did wrong while outnumbered thirty to one with short munitions and minimal superiority capability. The lecturer has the benefit of four years of detailed study, fifteen years of hindsight and the arrogance of youth."

"Damn, I'm sorry."

He shrugged. "Again, it doesn't matter."

He always said that, but it did matter to her, and she could tell it mattered to him. He never was jealous of her, though. Possibly he saw what a chore it was. He was also a hell of man, though, so it could just be him.

She said, "So, I'm on a low-G planet with my husband, and this suite has a plunge tub that can be filled with a scented, high-specific gravity mix that won't let us submerge without serious effort. It also has a cloud mist shower enclosure."

"Want me to wash your hair?" he asked, smiling.

"I do," she said. "Eventually."

The next day the security at the plaza was at least double, and armored vehicles with machine guns and web projectors guarded entryways and patrolled the perimeter.

There had been another attack, in another district. There'd also been violence on the other coast of the continent at the UN Commerce Envoy office there.

Rob said, "They need to stop pretending the cease fire is an actual treaty, or even a truce."

"We can go to the embassy if we need to, at least," she said. Ambassador Manley personally had authorized everyone to lodge there, *with the understanding that amenities may be lacking and conditions may be sparse*. Which was fine. Pillows on an office floor behind their own Blazers was safer than a hotel with guards of questionable quality and loyalty.

She glanced at the news. It had a recorded message from the "Mahdi," whose name she couldn't recall. His expression was creepily amused. The scrolling translation into English said, "... the righteous ones will control the planet. From the planet, the system, from the system the universe as God wills. Do not weep for the dead, for they are already with God the Merciful."

Kendra was sure she'd heard similar rants from history. They always ended badly.

Aisha watched the report while eating breakfast and felt a streak of shame. These people were largely Muslim, at least nominally. They represented everything bad about the history of the faith. They were violent, primitive, self-serving, corrupt and conniving. Not all of them, not even half, but enough that the entire society never actually became a society. They'd spent three hundred years reaching a state almost as good as they'd had on Earth before they left. Ramadan was a jewel of art, science and culture. Mtali was a sewer.

The refectory was full of people, including troops, diplomatic staff, families and children and trade representatives. The Aswani family, billionaires, were here this morning. She'd found them charming and the children delightful. They were very approachable and down to earth. Mr. Aswani looked nervous, and clutched his youngest daughter to reassure her. She obviously recognized the insanity in that man.

Major al Hani was across from her. She said, "I'm available in any capacity needed, sir. There are serious concerns about embassies being attacked."

He replied, "That is very professional of you. I expect, though, that the best elements of the local forces can keep the rabble down. The Amala are loud and angry, but they've never held up against professional forces."

"Yes, sir," she agreed, "but there's a lot of them."

"There are indeed. They seem to have called in from other parts of the system. Ambassador Haroun suggested lowering the visibility of the forum. The promoters don't want to do that. They think if they can pull through despite this, the political impact will be greater."

"I see, sir," she said, not wanting to argue. "I hope they are right."

"So do I."

He didn't sound convinced.

That evening, a lifter transporting people from the Alsacien embassy to the Caledonian embassy was shot down by antiaircraft fire.

Kendra's remaining obligation was to take part in a "handshake" ceremony. Representatives from Freehold and UN, Earth proper and NovRos, five of the major Mtali factions and two from Salin would publicly acknowledge each other. On the one hand, it was a nice gesture for the purpose they planned. On the other, it didn't mean anything. Groups that had settled their differences probably wouldn't resume fighting. Ones that hadn't might blow up at any moment. None of the individuals spoke for their nations officially.

She sat in formal uniform, Rob as her escort again, and listened to a presenter drone on about the "misunderstanding" of the war. She had a bit of a grudge against some of the UN troops, who had not been the top quality and had committed their share of atrocities. She had no reason to hate any particular current UN troop or civilian. She bore plenty of animosity for her old nation's government. They owned the war, plain and simple.

The lecture was too long and would bore people, and it wasn't as if everyone in both Earth and Grainne systems wasn't well aware of the war. The body count and infrastructure damage had been staggering for both. Earth still bore craters from that error. Grainne was still recovering economically and socially.

". . . we therefore present a soldier of each side, both of whom fought in the Battle of Braided Bluff. From Earth, Joshua Norris, awarded the Meritorious Star for exemplary courage under fire. From Grainne, Kendra Pacelli, awarded the Citizen's Medal for bravery beyond that normally expected."

They were seated across from each other on purpose. Their rank had not been mentioned. She'd been promoted since then. He'd left service. She rose, walked out as he did, met at the podium, and graciously shook hands. He smiled a bit awkwardly, she did too, and that was it. They held it for a five count for images and video, then dropped it. She returned to her seat, trying to ignore the camera pans.

The Mtali one was complicated. There'd been

several changes of alliance and allegiance. The final conclusion was for them each to shake hands with all the others. They turned in a circle, each shaking hands. The Amala were notably absent.

The handshakes in total took about four minutes. The rest of two hours before and after was all talk. She couldn't sleep, couldn't use a phone, so she tuned it out and focused on happy memories of herself with Rob, Marta, Alex, Leonidas and Kate. The small amount of bonus pay and service points for this were nice, but she'd come here from a sense of duty. That duty felt discharged at this point.

Finally the talking stopped and they moved to a private hall for lunch.

As they rode a ped dolly, Rob said, "We're approved to move to the embassy. They asked about sending someone for our possessions. I said yes. So we're going directly there after this. So is everyone."

"Understood," she said. That was a mix of concerning and a relief.

At the hall, they were escorted to tables immediately. The hosts seated Mr. Norris across from her, and he was quite a charming man.

"Captain," he said. "It's interesting to meet you."

"And you," she said. "This is my husband, Rob, who was actually flying CAS above the battle."

"Ah," Norris said, looking thoughtful. "Were you the one who ripped overhead and cordsanned right down the north side?"

"I was," Rob admitted.

They paused to be served their roasted guinea fowl. It did look tasty. The organizers had spent money on good chefs.

Norris continued, "Damned good flying. I hate to say it. I lost a bunch of friends there, but that run was surgical."

Rob said, "Thank you. I'm sorry it was personal for you."

Norris shrugged. "It's alright. We all did what we had to, and no animosity now, eh? That's why we're here."

Kendra noticed he couldn't make eye contact while saying that.

"We are," she agreed.

"And it must have been doubly tough on you, being from Earth and all, if I may say so."

"It was," she said. "That was the worst part. I felt caught in the middle, and I got distrust from my own people."

"Which ones?"

"Exactly," she said, with a covering chuckle. "I mean the ones I was serving with."

"Right," he agreed. "Do you still fly, Rob?"

Rob stiffened just enough for Kendra to notice and said, "No. I was injured by a nanovirus. It destroyed the neural connections to my flight interface and... other things."

It had wrecked his brain. His recovery had taken weeks physically, months emotionally, and he was still angry at not being able to fly.

"In fact, I get sick when I fly, or even ride amusement rides. The trip here took a lot of balance-dulling drugs and booze."

"I'm sorry."

It was Rob's turn to shrug. "It certainly wasn't your fault. As you said, we did what we had to."

They were all lying to some degree.

A table away, even the Mtalis seemed to manage okay. The Salinates didn't speak much, but didn't appear to have any issues.

People generally weren't the problem.

Bang!

The explosion was outside. The walls shook and dishes clattered.

Except for some people.

There was the sound of support gunfire with shouts, then there were other yells, then small arms and more shouts with agonized wails.

She watched Rob stuff two big mouthfuls in, and take a huge bite of the pie. She grabbed a couple herself, and got ready to move.

The noise outside dulled down and the gunfire ceased. With a barely visible shrug, Rob resumed eating normally.

Norris said, "If we need to run, count me with you."

"Understood, and thank you," she said.

Some people weren't the problem.

They finished dessert, acting as if nothing had happened. She and Norris had coffee. Rob had Freeholder chocolate, dark, bittersweet and strong.

Norris said, "It was frustrating that nothing changed from the war."

She said, "Well, not from a political perspective, no."

"That's what I meant," he said. "We beat the crap out of each other, and then went back to what we'd been. Stupid."

Rob said, "That's tragically common in history. Though not as common as someone getting wiped out, for good or bad."

After the lunch, she and Rob took transport immediately back to the embassy.

On the way out the venue exit there were barricades with an overhead shield. Over the blascrete, she could see a stun fence. Outside *that* were cordons and armed police. Outside that, a chanting mob.

She didn't know much Arabic, and the accent here wasn't classical. They were chanting and shaking fists, and looked crazed or drugged. The night before, they'd scorched three city blocks, and now they were here.

The Freehold Embassy was only two blocks distant, on a low-G planet. They took an armored car. Not a limo; a military vehicle.

"Tomorrow our vehicles are going to be driving directly into the loading bay," Rob said, looking at his phone. "It looks like both Salin contingents have regretfully withdrawn from the conference. They're hiding in their embassy."

His tone didn't blame them for "hiding." It seemed like a good idea.

At their embassy, they locked through a triple gate, with ID checks inside both locks. The soldier who came aboard wore Blazer and Mobile Assault badges. He checked her ID, compared her face and bioscan, then said, "If I may, ma'am," and saluted her. It was her medal.

He obviously held her in respect, and she returned it, a bit awkwardly while sitting on a troop bench.

"Thank you very much, Sergeant," she replied.

He checked Rob's ID, nodded and said, "Thank you very much for your service, sir," and departed.

They were checked again inside the next gate.

The crawler rolled under the awning at the front,

which was decorative but convoluted and reinforced. It would withstand most small explosive weapons, and it would be a challenge to get a bank shot inside.

The vehicle ramp dropped, they debarked and walked inside.

She popped her tunic collar the moment she was in the entrance, and shivered to let the sweat and tension out. She ignored the staff and guests walking by.

She said, "So, I have three days until closing ceremonies. I think I'll watch the drill presentations and ignore the work." The Best Soldier combat competitions had been "regretfully cancelled." The area it was to be held in was ironically unsafe for trained combat troops.

"I think that's wise," Rob said. "I'll find out where we're lodging here. Apparently, the buildings against the outer wall are closed, even with armor reinforcement."

"That's probably a good idea," she said.

Right then, the ambassador personally arrived.

"Captain Pacelli, Captain McKay, Ambassador Keith Manley. I've been wanting to personally greet you, but schedule hasn't allowed it."

"Perfectly understandable, sir," she said, shaking hands. "Please forgive my uniform."

Manley said, "Oh, that's fine. War zone. Stressful conference. I completely understand. I know you'll understand room is tight, but I did find you both a small private room. It's actually my security chief's room. He insisted on vacating it and will sleep in his office."

She said, "He doesn't have to, but we certainly appreciate the gesture." Though for an unescorted member to clear space for a couple wasn't unexpected.

"I'll take you there," Manley said. "This way, please."

The embassy was packed, and they passed two Blazers en route to security duties. She saw four of them outside, one on a skimmer, two in all-terrain buggies. The grounds weren't large, but seconds might matter.

Most people were fully dressed and had packs with them. Casual nudity was common at home, but wasn't a thing on a planet where you might get raped and killed for it, male or female, especially with active hostiles rampaging around.

"This isn't looking good," she said, nervous and frustrated. There was nothing to do but wait for transport.

Manley said, "We are keeping on top of it, and coordinating with other embassies. Ironically, pretty much everyone has settled any remaining differences they might have had in the face of these 'disadvantaged' people, as the press refers to them."

Rob said, "They have plenty of numbers, and look decently fed for 'disadvantaged people.'"

Manley said, "Yes, we're not sure what their network looks like, but it has reasonably professional logistics, and we expect they have more and better weapons than they've shown so far. Here is your room."

The bed was big enough, looked comfortable enough. They had a single dresser, a small private bathroom, and good comm equipment. It was about the size of a budget lodge. That made it far better than a hole in the ground under a cloak, a squat in a corner of a bombed-out building, or the musty, pest-filled crawlspace under a farmhouse. For emergency accommodations, it was a palace.

"We are very grateful," she said. "Please relay our thanks until we can do so personally. And thank you also, sir."

"My privilege, Captain and Captain. Please avail yourself of any facilities."

He closed the door as he stepped out.

She poured a drink. Gunn and Patrick Malt Whisky, straight. Discussion of *that* battle, followed by a screaming mob of lunatics barely restrained by military barriers had her on edge.

"Keep our weapons next to the bed," she said.

Rob was already sprawled on it, with his pistol on the night stand. "Yeah. No word on additional ones. The black market is apparently bought dry."

"By whom?"

"Everyone."

She shook her head. "How long have they been trying to pacify this dump?"

"Since five segs after the first landing."

Their phones buzzed. She glanced at her wrist.

Rob said, "Senior Isman wants us to meet in the conference room."

"Oh?" she said and grabbed her tunic. They took the stairs right outside their room.

Everyone military and veteran was in that room or arriving as they did.

Senior Sergeant Isman was talking as they entered. "As you may have heard, the NovRos embassy was attacked a few segs ago. They have some damage to their walls, scorched greenery, copious graffiti and some random UXOs to take care of. The Alsacien embassy was hit at dawn. No casualties inside, but the damage was severe enough they've relocated to the Caledonian embassy and are withdrawing. They're going to leave a token rep at both Caledonia and UN-Earth and have advised all their people to evacuate."

Mr. Chinran stepped forward.

"My assessment here is that our embassy could be stronger, but should be strong enough to hold off that mob no matter how large. That doesn't prevent them besieging us. On my recommendation we're canceling our participation in the conference, recalling our trade and other delegations from around the planet to here, and from around the system to their Jump Point Three to Novaja Rossia. The embassy is going to minimum staff and maximum security, and in a few months we'll reassess. Honestly, I'd advise anyone against doing business here. It might be best for the UN to administrate it alone."

Wow. Chinran just said that.

"So, everyone get comfortable, and we'll be loading out as soon as we can, hopefully on our own military vessels. I request that all military and veterans let us assign space to civilian families first. After that, military families and those with families, then single civilians, then single military. Essential staff and security will remain to the end. I will remain with them."

There was buzzing conversation all over, but no argument.

"I wonder if we'll fight from the rooftops here," Rob asked quietly over the noise. "I guess we should message Mar that we're going to be late."

She said, "I almost feel guilty about being second out. But we have to think of the kids."

"Right. This isn't about our nation. This is about one element. I'm glad Chinran is here. If anyone would handle this, he will."

She was no fan of the man or his methods. He'd personally wiped out her hometown. Knowing it was militarily necessary didn't make it comfortable. But the man was flawlessly logical and brilliant. She didn't like him, but she respected him.

"I guess we get comfortable in our room," she said. "At least it's private, and we do have access to a good shower."

Rob cocked his head. "That and food and a way home. The luxuries in life for this place."

Aisha alternated between excitement and fear. With the Alsaciens evacuated to the Caledonia embassy, NovRos and Caledonia were strongly considering leaving outright. Then word came across the Freeholders were actually leaving. There wasn't much that scared them. They'd beaten Earth outnumbered a hundred to one, and had shambled this place last time they were here. They genuinely expected the collapse to be complete.

She spent frequent intervals in the security office, allowed updates that were not embassy-critical, for the major only, though the staff acted put upon. It wasn't her sex, either. She was lurking in their work space. Still, she needed intel for professional reasons, and reassurance. Not knowing would feel worse than the threats. She watched the panorama of screens with news, private feeds, intel reports and their own camera views.

The latest was that almost a half-million insane, violent Amala were overrunning the city. Transportation was almost entirely shut down. Sewage and power were overloaded, where they hadn't been destroyed.

Al Hani came in. At least he would talk to her. The other officers and most of the enlisted ignored her presence as much as possible. She had private quarters, no regular assigned duties, and was supernumerary and treated that way.

Without greeting, he said, "It's been decided that we, too, are leaving. May God show mercy on everyone here."

"We are," she acknowledged.

"You will travel with the families on first available transport."

"I understand," she said. *Typical*, she thought.

The major said, "This was my idea. It's not at all to denigrate you. They need a military escort, and two others will be with you. I have cautioned them that you are an officer and they must obey you. You're trained in security operations. That will be relevant."

That was a bit better, then.

"I see. Thank you, sir. Though I wish I could remain to the end."

"I understand that," he said. "But you can best serve as a trained intermediary for the noncombatants."

She nodded. "Yes, sir. I'll start planning now."

"Did you hear about the valuable artifacts at the Alsacien embassy?"

"I know several were there for an upcoming museum exhibit, and were believed stolen. Have they been found?"

"Only in that they were seen on casts, being destroyed and burned as idolatrous."

"Fucking savages," she muttered. "Sorry, sir."

"No, I share the sentiment." He sighed. "The Islamic culture on Earth accomplished many great things, then stagnated, then turned on itself and others, because we failed to heed the Prophet's message. We were the last major faith to be accepted as social equals. Even the retro-heathens who went to Grainne were acknowledged before us. Now we have a modern, peaceful society in our system, and this complete... farce. It is a lie built on mindless hate, mindless breeding, and false faith."

"No one has held it against us," she said.

"Not yet," he noted. "It's happened before. The mid-twenty-first century wasn't good for Muslims."

"Do you think it will get that bad?" Could it?

"I don't know. The irony is the moderate Muslims were too peaceful and in-focused to eliminate the extremists. But of course, we'd have sunk to their level doing so. This is how Allah tests us."

"While I love His guidance and presence, I could wish for an easier ordeal."

Kendra watched two seminars on vid then stopped. The theories were very pretty on screen. They failed when one had to run them live, in combat, by intuition. She wasn't even primarily a combatant, other than a few weeks when everyone was a combatant.

"We should just go home," she muttered.

Rob said, "We are, as soon as we can."

"Yeah. And faster than my first interstellar."

An alarm blatted. She looked at her wrist while Rob looked at his glasses.

"Molotov over the wall, scorched some flowers."

Rob said, "The engineers are already running a taller mesh with shock points."

"I always wondered what it was like to fight here. I mostly sat in the Logistics Function and sorted stuff across the service line."

Rob said, "It was confusing, with groups constantly changing allegiances. Parliamentary Warfare, if that's not a phrase it should be. If it comes to actual fighting for us, Mar will be pissed at missing it, pissed at us for being here, and pissed at the military for letting us be here."

He shrugged. "Let's get dinner," he said.

"Sure."

At the dining hall, the food was plain in presentation but plentiful. There were skewers of meat, veggies for salads, soups, cheeses, drinks and dessert. A couple of civilian spouses muttered, but no one else complained at all. Apparently, local shopping was curtailed, so everyone would be eating here as the supplies in their apartments ran out.

She and Rob grabbed food on trays, found a table for two and sat.

The five troops on patrol came in, their reliefs out in their place. They were in full kit with armor, sensors, visors, and two of them had combat exoskeletons. They barely fit through the door.

She took a bite of venison and buffalo charstick and said, "Honestly, this is fine. I've paid for worse."

Rob nodded, swallowed and said, "Hopefully they got enough, even if it's dry or stasis, so we don't run short."

They ate fast, cleared space for others to use, and headed back up to their room.

Their phones chimed again.

"Goddess," Rob muttered. "All military to third-floor conference east."

They walked through the halls and joined others in and out of uniform, and some obvious veterans all headed that way.

Isman was there, and Ambassador Manley.

Manley said, "Thank you all for coming. Senior Isman has a quick update."

The wall turned into a map of the city. Animated flames and black splotches appeared. Red Xs showed.

"Attacks and damage," Isman said. "Now, watch the timeline presentation."

The image rolled across, the attacks becoming more numerous.

"There's another big one due, and it's pretty obviously there"—he pointed—"at the Ramadani embassy. They're beseiged by people and barricades and taking light, for now, weapon fire. The local forces can't disperse it. It outnumbers them."

A troop in front raised his hand and asked, "Senior, just how hopped up are these freaks?"

"Enough that they ignore stunners and even blunt instruments, and occasionally ignore small-arms wounds."

"Thank you. How many are present there?"

"The local police estimated a couple of thousand. We estimate about seven thousand. There's more over here at NovRos and Caledonia. They haven't come for us, yet."

Someone asked, "What is their point in doing this?"

"Drive the infidels off the planet, secure it for their particular branch of crazy, force the rest to convert, by torture if necessary."

"The local army can't handle them?"

"The problem is the local army is heavily infiltrated. The staff are reluctant to deploy in case their own forces take hits. Of course, it could be the leadership are infiltrated and are sitting it out to let it happen. Either way, the embassies have some police patrols of questionable reliability, some Salin mercenaries of questionable quality, and our own details."

Manley stood up and said, "I wish we had better news. We're confident we can hold them off for a week, and we have food and water. If they cut power, we have enough backup for necessary functions. If they cut plumbing, it gets nasty but we can survive."

Isman stood alongside the ambassador and said, "So, the second reason you're all here is that Ramadan needs backup. Their troops aren't bad, but they have fewer than fifteen, not the forty we have. That includes their regular security. I told them up front I wasn't letting any of our assigned personnel leave except as escorts for ours. I've gotten volunteers from our veterans to help with battle management, secure any of our nationals who are inbound and may need rescue. Pretty much every embassy is doing the same. NovRos is covering Salin, Caledonia is supporting Alsace, Chersonessus basically abandoned theirs and is split among others to support them. We're the only ones close enough to try to support Ramadan. It'll have to be by air. No vehicles are leaving."

He pointed at Rob and Kendra, Chinran and his daughter, and three others.

"You're supernumeraries or guests, and if you volunteer, I can let you go."

Chinran said, "I'll do it."

His daughter was a moment behind. "In."

Kendra watched the senior Chinran. He gritted his teeth for a moment, but didn't protest. Yes, she was risking her life. Yes, that's what they'd both signed up for. Yes, they might die together, but would they want to die apart?

Rob said, "I can probably fly well enough to get a craft over there. I'm not sure about getting back. So if you don't have a pilot, I'm in."

Kendra would rather fight here, with her own people, but it was reasonably certain a squad of Blazers and Black Ops could hold this place against anything short of a full Mobile Reaction Force. The Ramadani embassy was much more open and less sturdy.

"I have to go with you," she said.

"You don't have to," Rob replied. "But I understand."

Why? she thought to herself. Why? It was stupid to be here, it was stupid to hold an event like this that was provocative to idiots who wanted to be provoked and had a couple of centuries of violence as their notable cultural achievement. Why do it? Now she was compelled to help others avoid being slaughtered by them.

All three of the Operatives nodded simultaneously. Jeff Crandall spoke, "We can't leave them to be pillaged."

Rob asked, "What craft do I take?"

Isman said, "The V-Nine."

Rob nodded. "That's archaic enough I might be able to manage." He looked determined but nervous.

"I'll make the call," Manley said.

"We'll message our family," Rob said to Kendra.

"She'll understand," Kendra said.

"It's not Mar I'm worried about."

"Yeah."

"Mar, love, things are getting bad here. We're assisting another embassy who's being overrun. They don't have any way to evacuate as it stands. They need Rob, and Kendra can't just stand by. We hope you understand. With luck, we'll be on a ship home in a few days. Love to you and Alex, Leonidas and Kate."

They hugged and kissed in front of the screen, then cut the recording.

Rob said, "I feel less confident now."

Kendra replied, "Yeah, but it had to be done."

With security manning the walls and reinforcing entrances, it fell to Lieutenant Rahal to manage the security operations room. While waiting desperately for a return call, she watched vidlinks of buttresses and barricades being slid into position on all the gates on the outer wall, especially the construction and supply entrance.

Aisha slapped the phone on the moment it lit, before the chime sounded.

"Ramadan... hello, sir," she said as she recognized the Freehold security chief.

"Hello, ma'am," he said. "I have seven volunteers I can spare. They're flying over. Is your landing apron clear?"

"Yes, it's on the roof." She gave grid coordinates. "I will disable the defensive battery."

"Understood. Keep it clear. The available pilot has function problems."

"Function problems?"

"He's not promising he can land gently."

She didn't ask. Beggars were not choosers.

He said, "They're outbound from here, inbound your way. Arrival in five minutes."

"Understood." At least they were nearby.

"If the pilot is fit enough, he'll attempt as many extraction runs as he can. He can carry six adults or nine children to our embassy per flight."

She felt a wash of relief. "Oh, thank you."

"You're welcome. Stand by."

Seven. It was infinitely more than none, and not a token, given the small size of the element at their embassy. But numerically, it was seven troops.

Which effectively almost doubled their effectives, she thought.

Possible extraction as well.

Hopefully it would all blow over soon.

Hopefully she'd convince herself of that.

He'd called her "ma'am."

She called at once to al Hani as she left the office. There was little she could do there. The craft would be landing on their roof pad, and thank Allah the locals weren't using air transport. They'd probably crashed it all by now.

To al Hani, she said, "Major, the Freeholders say they can extract six adults or nine children per flight, as long as their craft and pilot allow."

"Understood, stand by...I will send six children and two adults on each flight. I will send them up now."

"Yes, sir."

She waited, hand on sidearm, twitchy to do something and knowing she had to remain.

The thrumming roar was one of the Freehold small cargo lifters. She looked west and found it. It wobbled as it approached, slowed and hovered, turned a quarter turn, then settled a bit unevenly, as if the pilot were inexperienced and nursing it down. Wind whipped her briefly, then gusted away. It was warm and pleasant outside otherwise. It was gaily lit by burning buildings around the panorama.

The impeller notes dropped as the engines were cut, and troops started debarking with large cases. The pilot stumbled out, fell to all fours and vomited. Someone jumped out and slapped a patch against his neck. He staggered up and joined the rest.

She waved, and they sprinted toward her and inside

the gallery as some kind of projectile whistled overhead. It would be a beautiful night if those were fireworks, not rockets.

The arrivals might only be seven, but they brought a pile of weapons. They each had a rifle, a sidearm, a sword. Two had shotguns as well. One had a machine gun. Another had some sort of projector. There was another bag of mixed pistols and carbines.

The four she'd met that first night were here. McKay and Pacelli, Chinran and Jelling. With them were three others, young and very fit. They were all in uniform with armor and harness, bristling with ammo, gear and blades.

"Blazer Jeff Crandall."

"Blazer Creigh Tompkins."

"Blazer Adam Newton."

She shook hands. "Lieutenant Aisha Rahal. Welcome and thank you."

McKay said, "I can make at least one flight out. Is anyone ready?"

"Yes, here they come," she said and pointed. Two of the trade delegation women were herding four children out the patio. Two of the "children" were teens, and carrying others' babies. The other two children were toddlers.

McKay planted a very passionate kiss on his wife, and staggered back to the aircraft. He pointed and gestured for the passengers to load. He reached in to help settle them, then heaved himself into the cockpit. A moment later the engines were spooling.

Lieutenant Jelling asked, "Lieutenant, is our current map of your facilities accurate?"

Aisha said, "I think so. What is the date and title?"

Jelling flashed the info on her wrist com. Aisha glanced at it and said, "Yes."

"Who's present?"

"Quite a few people including families. Several of our legal and immigration staff found shelter off site. The ambassador wanted to keep the families here. There are several single staffers. All male."

"Where is your security detail?"

She answered, "All ten are at the perimeter, armed. The five reserve are operating equipment to reinforce the wall and gates."

Jelling kept asking questions. "Any veterans among the others?"

"Some."

"If they will fight, we have two more shotguns and some pistols in that bag."

She said, "They might, and I will take one also."

"Have the noncombatants relocated to a safe area?"

"Yes, we have a secret vault room."

"I assume it's at the bottom of those stairs." Jelling pointed to the blueprint. Aisha blanched. Jelling said, "The structure and architecture makes that a logical location. If we can figure it out, so can the Mahdi's nutjobs. They're insane, not necessarily stupid."

Jelling scrolled the map around and said, "It looks like the Grand Atrium is a good place to start from. Good, clear fields of fire, and several options for repositioning or retreat."

Aisha asked, "You're not going to try to defend the gate?"

Jelling was wide-eyed for a moment. "You haven't seen the update then. Fifteen thousand screaming fanatics with breaching ladders, small arms and some explosives. Your wall is three meters. Even the wire won't stop them. There's already been incidents elsewhere of a hopped-up whacko throwing himself over the wire so his buddies can use him as a step."

"Yes, Grand Atrium is a good plan," Aisha agreed. "Should I advise the perimeter to retreat? Major al Hani is actually in charge."

"I'd recommend it. Want me to make the call?"

She hated to do that, but they were much more likely to listen to Jelling. Part of it was the combat experience and rank. Part of it was that a foreign woman was less of an affront.

"Please."

Jelling adjusted her earpiece and throat mic, tapped her wrist comm, and spoke.

"Major al Hani...this is Lieutenant Jelling, Freehold Forces Third Blazer Regiment. Our element has arrived with additional weapons and compatible ammo...You are most welcome, sir. Have you seen the recent aerial views?...Yes. I strongly advise retreating to your Grand Atrium. We can construct a better defense here...Understood."

She turned and said, "They're inbound. Tompkins and Crandall, get grid on the wall, if they start breaching we'll take what we can right there, offer them a direct route in lieu of actually channeling them. Is there time to emplace charges on the approach?"

Tompkins said, "I can at least improvise a fougasse outside the stairs."

"Do it now."

"Yes, ma'am." He nodded and sprinted with a pack of something.

Allah, they were disciplined. Thirty seconds on site,

and they had a plan. It involved blowing the walls to let a mob in, but it sounded like they intended to engage on their own terms, no matter how poor the choices.

Jelling said, "Lieutenant, brief me further, please, before the major arrives."

She stuttered and responded, "Ma'am, you have the grasp of it. The wall is surrounded, our local security has abandoned us, and we have very few combatants."

Major al Hani arrived then, glanced at her, turned to Jelling, hesitated a second, and identified himself.

Jelling saluted. "Sorry to meet you under these circumstances, sir. I have planned, if you approve, to enfilade them when they try to breach the wall, choose our own breach to invite them into our fixed defenses and established points, and kill as many as we can outside the building. If that is acceptable, I would like your counsel on how you wish to defend the building."

Al Hani paused a moment, probably over the language, and said, "I think that may be the best we can wish for. I'd hoped to defend the whole building, but it's probably impossible. I'd rather not retreat to our safe vault, though, because it gives them unrestricted knowledge and time to attack it."

Jelling nodded. "Right, so where should we post?"

Kendra listened. Jelling/Chinran was definitely a seasoned expert, and al Hani sounded competent. That was good. Given the numbers, though, their survival seemed unlikely. She hadn't thought about death in a number of years. That battle on the ridge all came flashing back now.

I survived that one, she thought. Of course, every one you survived led toward the one you wouldn't.

Al Hani said, "We have a good field of fire from the lower gallery. We can retreat to the upper gallery, hopefully drawing their attention, then to the underfloors by the rear stairs."

Jelling said, "And we can enfilade the fuck out of them in there. Is there an organic way to seal those side corridors?"

"A...ah, I understand," al Hani said. "No, nothing built in. You may modify the building as you see fit."

"Thank you. Crandall, drop those stairs on the left and try to rubble that corridor."

"Will do," he said. He swung his rifle, glanced at the map, glanced at his optic, shifted slightly and fired, then shifted and fired again.

The first grenade blew a three-meter gap in the stairs that should slow them down at least. The second rubbled the top of those stairs, which proceeded to creak and bend and obstruct most of the hall. He fired one more shot into the stairs above that, which bent, broke and finished blocking the passage. That left a single stairway at front right of the lower atrium, and the rear stairs that descended to private offices and the vault, with no direct connection to the front.

"Of course," he said, "Sealing them out also seals us in."

Jelling grinned. "We have them right where they want us." She paused a moment and spoke into her mic. "Jelling, understood." She turned to Kendra. "McKay is inbound again."

"Good," she said.

Aisha turned and looked as back behind the patio, the lifter settled again, backlit by glare from an entire district aflame. It wobbled a lot, dropped the last meter, and the pilot tumbled out and lay on the ground. Someone else hopped out deliberately, sprinted around the craft, rolled McKay over, and started dragging him back. One of the others ran to assist.

He was twitching and shaking as they brought him close.

"I ca..." he stopped and puked. It was mostly a dry heave with some slippery fluid.

After a deep breath and some spitting, he tried again. "I can't. Reflexes shot. Complete overload. I landed hard there, landed hard here. If you have a pilot, take over."

Al Hani said, "I don't think we even have anyone trained on a private flyer rather than centrally controlled. There are no military personnel who are rated."

"Sorry," McKay said. "I can't. Also, I took some damage as I got low over the wall. Small arms but big enough. I think one impeller is damaged. Whoever does it will have to do high trajectory approach and a drop landing."

Pacelli was alongside him, trying to help him relax.

"There isn't anyone, love."

"Then I'll try to do one more," he said, and got to his knees. He was weeping through the nausea and pain. "We can spare a pilot."

The new arrival, a woman, said, "The hell you will. Not even if we were in hell." She fumbled in her pack then slapped a patch on his neck. She was in uniform with no insignia at all and no armor.

He screwed up his eyes and nodded.

Al Hani said, "You saved six children and two women. Thank you."

Jelling said, "If you recover, we can use you here. Take your time, I need you fit. You've already done more than your share."

The woman turned to Jelling.

"Ma'am, Maureen Vaughan, trauma nurse. I grew up hunting in the Dragontooth range. I can provide supporting fire and treat wounded."

Jelling didn't even have to give orders. One of her troops ran up and handed a carbine to Vaughan. The nurse cleared the action, checked the loading, and nodded. She had no armor, did have a knife, and looked grim and focused. She was a civilian, and she'd volunteered for battle.

Crandall grabbed a crate from the craft, that contained field rations and more ammo. How precious it seemed.

With doors closed and barricaded, elevators cut, staircases blocked and collapsed, and a few portable folding shields, they had a redoubt. Once their outer force withdrew up those stairs, those could be dropped as well.

Aisha wasn't going to kid herself it wouldn't come to that.

She now understood what being a hero entailed.

"Captain Pacelli, Captain McKay, thank you very much for coming. I know how significant it is. You're guests, after all."

Sitting up, McKay said, "You're welcome. Guests should help with the chores, including taking out the trash."

He looked better and seemed to have his neural control back. Good.

"Lieutenant, thank you, and your troops."

"It is a privilege to serve," Jelling said with a serious expression. She looked eager, though. Blazers were shock and clandestine troops. She almost certainly hadn't chosen that career because she wanted to watch screens. She was in her element.

Then she said, "Mr. Chinran, thank you. If it's not rude to ask, why are you here?"

Without looking up from setting his gear, Chinran said, "I was consulting on embassy security. My report was that ours was reasonably secure but could benefit from some improvements, and most of the others were far too dependent on host-nation forces with poor discipline, reliability and training. It appears I was correct."

"Yes, but why are you *here*? You'd be safer in your embassy."

Chinran shrugged, turned and said, "I've seen enough children die. I don't plan to watch any more if I can do anything about it."

The expression on his face was so serious and deadly it scared her. She took it he hadn't been watching them die on vid.

"That, and I knew my daughter would come." He indicated Jelling.

Aisha looked over as Jelling said, "Yeah, real name Chinran. We try not to ever use them in public. But at this point . . ." she shrugged.

The elder Chinran looked the other way and said, "Captain Pacelli, I've wanted to say this for a while. I apologize for Minneapolis."

Pacelli sighed with a broad gesture. "It was a long time ago. It was war. The Freehold is my home now. My parents survived. But I accept your apology."

Was he saying he'd been part of the team that wrecked Earth during their war? One battalion of their elite troops had destroyed entire cities. He was apparently one of those, and, she guessed, one of the officers.

She wasn't sure how to feel about that. It had been war. It had also been horrific. But if he had those skills, possibly he could help hold back this wave? If there was time?

While she mused, Lieutenant Chinran said, "I see public latrines down the hall. Everyone go in turn. You'll fight better if you're comfortable."

Aisha went when the other women indicated she was first. She hurried, rinsed her hands and sprinted back, passing Vaughan on the way. Two of the males sprinted past each other as well.

Someone had flavored water out, and some candy. She wasn't hungry, in fact the thought of sweets made her feel ill, but she did drink.

The female Chinran was staring at a tac display on her goggles.

"It just passed estimated twenty K locally, and the entire city is swarmed. They're literally killing people in their homes and others are either retreating or joining the movement, at least temporarily. They probably think it's the only way they'll survive. Assume most of them won't be actively hostile, but will be happy to loot and burn."

"This is nuts," her father said. "And I wouldn't count on them not talking themselves into some action just to prove their worth. Or because underneath they're jealous of something."

Al Hani said, "The men at the walls report rocks

and vehicle rams. I must join them." He walked forward and down the outer stone stairs, carrying a carbine and with his pistol holstered.

McKay, Pacelli and Tompkins unsheathed their blades, muttered something, then drew the flats across their hands before returning the weapons to scabbards.

"And our honorable allies," McKay added, loudly enough for her to hear.

Nearby, Newton knelt with his right knee down, left knee up, and a weapon grounded in each hand. She could just hear some of his recital.

"... legs are my foundation, on which my strength is built. My left arm my shield, for myself and my brother. My right arm is my sword, all my foe shall feel. My mind is my weapon, and I will keep it clear and sharp. I will not waver, for it is my honor to serve..."

She looked up, and Mr. Chinran whispered, "Religious creed of the Temple of the Warrior."

"Ah," she nodded. It was something she'd vaguely heard of, but it was obviously sincere and powerful to Newton. He stood, and his expression was a unique combination of eager and deadly calm. He didn't shake; he was motionless, and seemed to draw energy from the space around him.

It was then that something rammed the gate hard enough to loosen the hinge pillars. They were rated to stop a tank, but someone with a large vehicle had found the right angle and the ground under the pillar was breaking loose.

It was suddenly irrelevant. Men started leaping over the tops of the wall. Her compatriots started shooting at them.

Major al Hani reported, "They are breaching the

gate, and the wall next to it past the south pillar."
She heard his weapon through his commlink.

"That was quick," Jelling said with a raised eyebrow.
She was actually smiling. "Newton, Crandall, can you
do something about that, please?"

She sounded so conversational.

Both of them raised their weapons, adjusted slightly
and fired. Bang! Bang! Bang! Bang! Bang! There were
air ripples in front of their grenade launchers.

A moment after the last shot, the first rounds hit.
Whoom! Whoom! Whoom! Whoom! Whoom!

The mob had just broken the gate and took a
frontal impact of fragments and splinters of metal,
polymer and concrete.

Jelling said, "Dad, can you . . . ?"

"On it," he said. He already had a rocket launcher
out of the pod, raised it to his shoulder and fired.
Steam and dust erupted from the exhaust, the rocket
made an odd banging whiz, and a streak zipped into
the breach at the wall. That explosion threw bodies
and pieces of them. She watched a head and connected
arm tumble through the air and down.

Lieutenant Chinran said, "Crandall, Tompkins, Newton, you may shoot when you have targets. Conserve
your ammo."

The three started shooting with precise but surprisingly even shots, as did the Chinrans. The range wasn't
great, but the targets were moving. It seemed though,
that as many bodies fell as shots were fired. Each of
them seemed to have picked one of the Ramadani
troops to provide covering fire to.

Sure enough, she heard that on her buds a moment
later.

The men were encouraged and kept shooting into the mob that didn't reach them, though it piled around them in semicircles of bodies.

Chinran said, "By sequence, retreat to the stairs. Maintain cover fire. Rest of element, provide cover during transition."

Aisha leaned over the decorative wall, raised her own carbine and searched. There. Sergeant Asfan was being covered by Crandall.

"I have him, sir," she said, not knowing his rank.

"Moving!" he announced, and sprinted.

She started firing into the crowd, cognizant that she was killing people, and not all of them men. There were women, teens, even some children who she refused to target. They shouted, waved weapons, threw rocks, raised hands in dramatic prayer. It was grotesque. One of her bullets hit a man in the upper shoulder, ripping his arm nearly off and dropping him to thrash under the crowd.

Allah be merciful to them, she prayed silently.

"Perimeter, you should retreat steadily," Chinran instructed, and Aisha saw they did.

Then Chinran said, "Rahal, Crandall has resumed, advance to the stairs."

She stepped back from her position and ran for the stairs and behind the improvised barricade.

Ahead of her, she watched the men back toward the lower atrium, shooting as they moved. Then one of them stumbled, and the crowd engulfed him even as some of them continued to die.

"Shifting my targets," Blazer Newton said.

"Shifting mine," Crandall added. Another of her fellows was down.

Mr. Chinran loudly said, "Ramadanis retreat. Free-holders, fire in the hole."

A massive concussion cracked like thunder and rumbled. She jumped, felt her pulse stutter, and realized it was several explosions of directional mines, and a huge explosion from a dug-in position that blasted into the mob at an angle. She watched rock, cable, brick and whirling chain shred bodies. Momentarily, the screams were louder than the chants.

Major al Hani appeared with two soldiers. They had four police from the inner gate with them. The other eight soldiers lay dead in and under the mob.

As the screaming rioters reached the outer steps, the stun fields and static fence seemed to hold the mass back. The nearest swayed under the sonic emanations, then convulsed back from the blue shocks in the air. Behind them, others screamed at thermal induction, but they were replaced by more.

She looked out at the results of the explosions.

"If anything, that's angered them more," she said.

Lieutenant Chinran said, "It has."

To punctuate that, a fusillade of small-arms fire cracked among them, and the utility room near the entrance below exploded as a rocket hit it. Someone was trying to find the field generator. It wasn't there, but the room had flammables and bellowed smoke.

Lieutenant Chinran said, "You need to get below with your people." She pointed behind them.

"What?" Aisha replied. "I stay here to fight." Everyone wanted to get rid of her.

Al Hani said, "Lieutenant, that is where you can best serve."

Aisha wouldn't have argued with the major, in

insubordination, if she didn't expect they were all going to die.

Before she opened her mouth, Mr. Chinran said, "No, you must join them. They need to see your uniform for reassurance and authority. And if we can't hold the goobrains, you need to take as many as you can if they breach the door. Last line of defense. All of us have experience or are more expendable. Your charges need your presence."

She burned in impotent rage. He was absolutely correct, and that was her duty.

She wanted to do anything but her duty, but she could not.

She nodded, near tears. "You're correct."

Mr. Chinran handed her a rifle and another pistol.

"If you need to, share with anyone who can shoot, or just set up a redoubt inside and lay down fire. Good luck."

"Good luck to you, Soldiers." She snapped her hand in salute, and they snapped their fists back. It was the first time she'd seen their salute in person.

Even Mr. Chinran took it seriously.

She turned and strode slowly up to the landing, then toward the rear stairs and down toward the vault. She would not be seen to retreat in haste, and she needed to control her damp eyes before she arrived.

She spoke at the door. "This is Lieutenant Rahal. I am undistressed. I have been posted here. Please open the door."

The outer vault door opened, and closed behind her, then the inner. It seemed impossible anyone could breach those, but somewhere in that mob were explosives and flammables. The inboard oxygen supply was limited, and the blastic and concrete could be defeated with enough impact. It was made more for natural disasters or fire than for deliberate assault, and it served as a vault for confidential personal effects and information that were not of national importance. With this many people, it would last a few hours at most.

Everyone stared as she entered, and she felt compelled to report.

"The insurgents have breached the gate and the wall. Our element has returned fire with rockets and grenades. There are emplaced defenses, and they are prepared to enfilade the approach with fire. Major al Hani has posted me here to monitor and report movements to them, and to ensure the vault is reinforced to its maximum."

She paused for a moment. She actually did have those duties. She was in support, but she was not useless.

She pointed and said, "I would like those two tables placed directly in front of the inner door, to jam it if it opens. The water tank and anything else heavy should be behind them. The furniture should be placed there"—she pointed—"and the blast fabric layered across it to create a berm. If necessary, we will retreat behind it."

They understood she was giving orders, and they actually responded. None of the men quibbled, they just complied. Even Ambassador Haroun helped stack the blockade.

"I see a fire axe, a wrecking bar and I assume there are things in the tool crate in the corner. Everyone arm yourself with anything you can use in an emergency. That includes the women and juveniles. If it comes down to that, they won't show any mercy, so we can't. After that, I would like everyone to pray. It will be as God wills, and we will hope He is merciful."

Several people touched their foreheads and said, "As God wills."

She carefully placed the rifle, pistol and her carbine against the comm station. The ambassador brought over a hunting shotgun he used with the local chiefs, and a presentation pistol that seemed functional.

"You should keep your shotgun, sir," she said. "If you need it, use it."

He took it back and nodded.

"Please relay my good luck to them, Lieutenant."

"I will," she said.

It took a few moments to link channels so she could talk to al Hani directly, and to the Freehold embassy operator, who opened a direct channel to their troops.

"Vau—Rahal, requesting communication check." She'd almost said "vault." If anyone was listening, that would be a useful hint.

"Al Hani acknowledges received, Rahal."

"Jelling: MR. That is to say, signal is clear and I understand."

The screen transcription tagged them blue and green on the glass in front of her.

"Ambassador Haroun and myself offer good luck and thanks."

She watched via camera as other soldiers fought on her behalf. It was her right and duty to fight for her people, but here she was, locked into a vault.

It was her right and duty to remain here with them, as a last line of defense, and to be witness to the bravery of others.

The three Blazers nearest the stairs stood relaxed back against pillars in the atrium. She understood they were far from the windows to present harder targets, while being clear to shoot out. They fired almost casually, as if on the range. But the outside view showed bodies hit and erupting blood and brain. Sometimes they fell, occasionally the mass of rioters held them in place against the crowd. It was macabre.

The bullets would rip through the target, and sometimes through a second, splashing them with blood from the first, and often ripping and tumbling into the second, or tearing into them as fragments. Tens of them were down, and surely they must flee in fear?

Some at the front probably would, if they weren't crushed by the mob behind, who likely couldn't even hear any gunfire. A big enough wave was a capital weapon all by itself.

Then the power failed. Emergency lights came on, her system had batteries, as did the cameras, but the protective field failed and the mob surged up the outer steps.

The three Blazers didn't retreat. They advanced.

No, they *charged*. She'd never seen anyone move so fast. With sword, axe and hammer, and rifle, they charged down the stairs, waded through the incoming mob, leaving swaths of twitching and writhing bodies. They swung with perfect precision and control, every movement ripping someone open and laying them on the ground to scream or die. Guts, skulls and limbs were split and butchered.

It was disgusting, but it was awesome.

Nor was it a suicidal charge. They crossed paths several times to support each other, then turned and cut across the mass to the low wall on the edge of the lawn. From there, they bounded up onto the roof over the patio, and clattered across.

She recalled their unofficial unit motto: Outnumbered, always. Outgunned, frequently. Outclassed, never. If three of them could inflict this carnage, it wasn't an idle boast.

They were back inside through the Trade Office window, down the back stairs by skipping down the railing, and falling back into formation with the four inside.

Al Hani and the remaining soldiers shot straight down the stairs, then backed up as those collapsed to hold off the attackers. One of the men was hit in the arm, and shouted in pain.

Vaughan ran up, and under fire, sprayed wound sealant into his tricep while he shot across her shoulder left-handed. She had him step back as they did so, and positioned him behind the ballistic shield. One of the others helped him up to the second floor. They could shoot down from there.

The Mahdi's legion were insane if they kept coming. Anyone with any sense or training would retreat and plan for heavier weapons. Drugged out on God knew what, false faith and mindless hate, they came anyway.

They strode into the foyer slowly and purposefully. Stomp stomp chant. Stomp stomp chant. Stomp stomp—

A terrifying wave of fire swept across from the Ambassador's Hall. It spanned the entire width of the entrance, and drenched bodies in flame that clung like wrap. Even massive doses of psychedelics and stimulants couldn't numb one against that.

Rioters screamed, howled, squirmed and kicked in agony, clutching and ripping at themselves, trying to extinguish flame that kept going.

She realized Newton's other weapon was a primitive flamethrower, like that used centuries before. It was a pressurized tank of fuel and that projector wand she'd seen, and thought was a hose for sticky web or such, and may have been at one point. Now it spewed thick, black, oily fire that turned the mob into shrieking, thrashing elementals.

She had no idea how someone could stand behind that wave of flame and watch people die in horror. Then she remembered they wanted her, the diplomatic staff, and the children, dead.

The fuel ran out, and Newton dropped the harness and retreated. She wondered where, with the stairs demolished, but there was a rope waiting for him.

There was a pause that stretched out. Nothing moved inside, the rioters milled about outside but didn't enter further into the building. It was full of choking fumes and lingering flame, even with the fireproof construction. She saw one attacker, his fat body sputtering flame with his clothes as wicking. It was horrifying.

They'd done it. They'd forced the mob to back off...

No, they came forward again now, even more aggressively.

The Mahdi's men had courage born of insanity. The Freeholders resumed shooting, and the attackers died in waves.

Kendra disconnected her feelings and shot. Combat cold, it was called. She'd learned the hard way how painful it was to empathize with your enemy, especially since in her previous war she'd been from the same culture as the enemy. She could shake and cry and rage later. Now was time for shooting.

This was different. It was like shooting rabid dogs. Their expressions were mindless, hateful and barely conscious. They weren't really from any of the local cultures; they were self-exiled predators.

She was scoring about eighty percent hits in the mass. Shooting them wasn't the problem. The problem was there was no end to them. They rolled forward in a tide without pauses.

Lieutenant Chinran opened up from her position, with one of the machine guns. She chewed a hole through the mass, which would have stopped any military element and forced them to divert or regroup. This bunch of lunatics just flowed around the pile, or clambered over it, like ants.

Grenades flew, the other machine gun opened up and another pile of them died.

The pile was immediately used as cover by the advancing armed members.

She glanced over to her left. Her lover, best friend, and decade-long partner looked as focused as she felt, as he calmly ran out the clip in his rifle, stuck a full one in the tractor feed, and hit the release. To her right, Mr. Chinran shot faster than she thought possible, but every round seemed to hit.

The seven of them and the five Ramadanis had to have killed a hundred and fifty or more of the wave by now. Then there'd been the explosives.

It was too loud to talk, but she shouted, "I really did expect them to quit by now!"

"Same here!" Rob shouted back. "At least I'm with you!"

They'd figured they could hold the wave back, with enough firepower.

Her comm sounded. It was their own intel.

"Detachment, this is Eyeball. Intel estimates total engagement of four-five thousand. Your area approximately one-two thousand. I wish we had better news. Good luck. Over."

She heard Lieutenant Chinran respond, "Eyeball, this is Detachment. Any more support available? Rocket volley? Anything? Over."

"Detachment, this is Eyeball. Nothing here. Caledonia has an element, but no transport. NovRos may have transport in two-zero segs. If they can refuel and repair after it returns. If it returns. Over."

"Eyeball, this is Detachment. It's a long time but send them if you can. We'll hold here. Listening, out."

It wasn't the first time Kendra had stared death in the face, but this was particularly gruesome.

Chinran said, "In sequence, retreat to middle landing."

There was a momentarily lull in shooting as they repositioned for better cover. Kendra backed up the steps, weapon at ready. Next to her, Rob said, "They can't have us alive. If anyone gets overrun...do them a favor."

"Yeah," she rasped. What a fucked-up planet.

He said, "I wish we had more explosives we could fall back to. At least take a few more with us."

"It's not over yet," she said.

"Not yet."

The crowd surged again. At the top of the damaged

stairs, Operative Newton was hit and stumbled. He fell forward and down into the rubble, breaking his fall with a grab at a tangle of railing. The expression on his face was calm and cool as he raised pistol and sword and faced the attackers. He must have already run his rifle dry.

"Cover my sector," she called to Rob. She shot around Newton, trying to clear a dead zone. She managed to clear space about three bodies back in the crush. In front of that, he used a pistol and a sword and cut, stabbed, punched, kicked and shot his way into her gap. He was climbing over the bodies, at least a meter up.

Then he stumbled and pitched face forward into the mob.

There was nothing she could do other than wish him a clean death.

One of the machine gunners chewed into the pile, hopefully ending it.

Lieutenant Chinran said, "Fall back, second floor, that includes you, Dad."

She noticed Mr. Chinran didn't argue. He retreated while firing, moved behind Rob and her and indicated he would cover. They fell back the same way, took station at the top of the stairs. Operative Crandall bounded past them and secured the top balcony, followed by Tompkins. Lieutenant Chinran slid in alongside Kendra. The Ramadanis were positioned along the railing shooting down into the mob. One of them staggered back, a hole in his neck. Dead.

The problem was that the safest place for the civilians was deep in the bottom of the building, farthest from rescue. The roof would have made extraction easier, but was easier to breech.

The mob had bodies, debris and ladders, probably

from the lawn shed, and were swarming up the building and the stairs. An explosion crashed the air and the stairwell collapsed, at least.

The atrium was too broad. One of the Ramadanis charged forward, shooting and shouting and smashing his attackers. He died heroically, but he still died. The remaining pair, one wounded, with Major al Hani, formed an arc and shot and shot. Crandall and Tompkins moved alongside them. The volley of fire kept the area around the element clear at least.

Chinran said, "We'll have to use the rear stairs, top and bottom. Blazers and locals top. Guests, we're down below. Move."

Kendra backed up while shooting past the front echelon, then turned and bounded down the stairs.

Next to her, Rob said, "I'm out of ammo." He punched the action pin on his rifle, snapped it open, pulled out the bolt and scattered the pins and springs. He dropped the empty weapon. "Thirty-five in the pistol," he said, "and one spare mag."

She lifted the mag cover on her weapon and glanced at the prestressed clip of cartridges. There were about twenty left. Once the follower clicked shut, she was out, too. She'd fired 780 rounds already.

"No pistol," she said, and clutched reassuringly at her sword.

It wasn't the first time she'd used that in combat, either.

Vaughan half stumbled down next to her, turned with her carbine and aimed up the stairs, shaking but looking determined. There wouldn't be any treatment for casualties until this was over.

❖   ❖   ❖

Aisha saw the retreat on her monitors. Allah, how they'd fought! She thought about opening the vault, for just a moment, to let at least the closest in.

Echoing her, the ambassador said, "Let them in!"

It was agonizing to say what she said next.

"Sir, we cannot," she insisted. "They were specific in their instructions, and my duty here is clear. You, and the families and children must be kept safe. I need everyone to retreat behind our berm."

"I . . ."

It seemed he would argue, but he suddenly stopped and stared at her.

She realized her hand was on her sidearm.

He gestured and pointed, and the civilians moved back.

She said, "Sidi Koury, you are a veteran."

"Yes, Lieutenant!" he agreed.

She handed him the rifle.

"Take position at that corner of the barricade. If they breech the door, lay down fire until you are empty. You will do this even if I am in the way. Is that clear?"

"Yes . . . Sayida." He nodded gravely and she saw respect in them. *Finally*, she thought bitterly.

"Sidi Abbas, you are a police officer." She drew her pistol and cocked it, then handed it to him. That gave him a second pistol. "Take the right side. Your orders are the same."

"Yes, Sayida."

"Sidi Masour." She handed him the spare pistol from the ambassador.

She turned to Ambassador Haroun. "Sir, you will protect the families from there. If I am killed, you will be able to cross-fire until the attackers reach the barricade. Everyone will then engage with hand weapons."

Assuming they don't blow the door open, blow a wall open, or just fire the building atop us and wait for heat to cook us as our oxygen runs out. It was already stuffy, muggy and warm. She could smell sweat and the air was thick. The building was probably already partly demolished.

She lifted the carbine, checked the loading, and stood at her station, hoping not to have to stand at the door, and furious at being denied the right to stand outside.

She resumed watching the monitors as foreign allies stood and died in her place.

Kendra stood ready, focused. At the top of the stairs, Crandall and Tompkins had stopped firing, and there had been explosions. She assumed that was intentional. There was no sign of the remaining Ramadanis. They'd died defending their position and not retreated.

On either side, the Chinrans stood with carbines resting over swords, and quivered in tension. She figured they were both running on the synthetic neurostimulant they were implanted with. They moved so fast they blurred, but with perfect control.

The mob started down the stairs above. She leaned into the core of the well and shot up. There were screams and tumbling intruders. If only it were narrower, they might actually block it with bodies.

Enraged, obsessed maniacs poured down, heedless of fire. After all, they'd made it this far.

The rifle slapped her shoulder until it clicked, and she dropped it and stepped back.

Next to her, Rob's pistol clacked empty, and he threw it at a man struggling over the wounded and dead to reach the bottom flight. Vaughan ran dry, shrugged and hefted the weapon like a club. Rob had his seax, she had the War Bride. She drew the sword, wondering how many more nicks it would acquire, and if it would even survive. It was a shame that Cardiff's work so often wound up being destroyed.

Then she thought that the whole point of his skill was so his tools were strong enough for combat. She twisted her hands slightly, and rubbed her thumbs along the grip, feeling instinctively for the right balance. After all these years, she knew the sword and it knew her.

A round slapped her armor. She'd thought the rioters were out of ammo, but someone had acquired another weapon somewhere.

"We need to close on the stairs," she shouted.

"Yes!" Rob and Lieutenant Chinran said together.

Chinran walked up two steps toward the assault and dumped her weapon's full load. It left another pile of bodies. She smashed the muzzle into someone's face as he climbed over, and used it as a block as she started slicing with her left hand. Then she tumbled backward down the stairs.

Mr. Chinran seemed to be trying to injure them as fast as possible as he moved into their mass. Whatever was exposed, he cut. Hands, faces, arms, torsos. He shoved them aside as he waded through. He fell but his position suggested he was alive, just buried for now.

Four of them charged down at her, one with a machete, two with large knives, one with a club. She

swung up in oct, across in hex, back in tri, and thrust
at the one in front.

Behind them were four more...

Vaughan brained one with her carbine butt, grunting as she did so.

Up top was another explosion.

All she could do was poke into the tumbling mass,
feeling flesh shear and tear. They'd been slowed, and
were clambering over the bodies of their own to reach
her, but she was alone, with Rob somewhere nearby.
She felt a searing pain as someone sliced down her
arm. The tough fabric deflected it along the limb, but
it tore off a strip of skin that continued to burn and
jolt as it brushed anything, even air.

She stabbed at another man as he loomed over
her, ripping out his bicep as he swung a large kitchen
knife with the other hand. It bit into the side of her
head and burned. She felt blood cascade over her ear.
Her second thrust got him in the neck.

"Always with you, my love!" she shouted through
a dry throat, and stabbed, and stabbed. She thought,
Marta, take care of the kids. We love you.

For a moment she ran out of bodies. The nearest
were just on the landing. Nothing moved in her reach,
and she saw Rob trying to free himself, and hoped the
bodies pinning him were dead. She started to wade
across to him as a crimson drip obscured her right eye.

Another explosion blew concrete shards around the
landing and rattled her brain.

Aisha stared. Someone had finally brought in air
support and chewed the crowd with rapid-fire cannon
and thermobarics. Every window above had to be

broken. The shock wave had been palpable through the hardened door. She wondered if that request had been approved from Earth, from some UN BuState rep in system, or if someone local had finally made the call to declare it an actual war.

All was quiet. That last blast had done something, and no one else had come down the stairs. That left only forty or so in the atrium outside. They were the most drugged, and hacked at bodies long since dead. The mob had broken here, and run off. Hopefully it wasn't to another nation's embassy.

"I think we can shortly stand down," she said.

Her head reeled. She'd fought the battle by hiding behind steel and ceramic, while others died for her.

No, they died for the civilians.

There were duties as morally tough as fighting, but one couldn't ever say it.

The phone flashed. She slapped the key.

"Ramadan Embassy, Lieutenant Rahal on duty. How may..." she stopped.

The other party said, "Captain Rustov, Novaja Rossia National Army. I lead a relief force and request permission to enter your territory."

"Please," she said. She wasn't sure if that was within her duties, or the ambassador's, but she took it.

She was safe, and regretted it. But the civilians were safe, and she was joyous.

After the National Army Engineers had run up a field ladder across the destroyed front stairs, it took three soldiers ten minutes to clear the top of the rear stairwell. A directional mine had clogged it with debris, bodies and body parts.

"*Bozhemoi*," the sergeant muttered. "This place was a slaughterhouse."

"Which side?" Captain Rustov asked. There'd been a handful of Ramadani uniforms on the way in. They'd fought bravely even in this meatgrinder.

"No uniforms. Near as I can tell, all Mahdi madmen."

The squad stepped gingerly around bodies, then gave up and just stepped on them. There were hundreds of them. They'd been shot, blown apart, sliced and chopped. It was so bloody it was surreal. One soldier grabbed an arm to dislodge a body. The arm came off. It had been sheared nearly through.

The sergeant said, "Wait, there's one in uniform. Freeholder, from the embassy. Damn."

Rustov noted, "Another over there, at the rear stairs."

It was a wave of dead and critically injured lunatics, broken all the way down the stairwell.

"Damn." He looked at the lifeless faces with wounds in the bodies below. As long as it had been, there was no point in any kind of stasis field, even if they could get an ambulance in here.

"Damn," he repeated.

Down below there was banging.

He said, "There's the vault. Sounds like where they're holed up."

The sergeant replied, "I'd surely like to see some live civilians after this butchery."

"I think they lucked out."

He pointed. Halfway down the bottom flight to the cellar, the wave of bodies ended. There was clear space there and down.

The sergeant said, "More troops there."

Rustov looked. Yes, there were more uniforms, under the edge of a literal heap of bodies, or parts of them. The Freeholders loved their swords, insisted on them in dress uniform, and carried them on duty. They'd put them to use here. He'd seen less blood and chopped bone in butcher shops.

There were five more Freeholders half buried under the pile of meat.

The sergeant scrambled over the corpses. He didn't waste time fumbling for a probe. He reached out and felt for a carotid pulse.

Rustov asked, "Alive?"

"Maybe. MEDIC! Emergency!"

Rustov turned to the corporal behind him.

"Get down there and open the vault. Stay inside with the civilians and reassure them, but don't let them see this. We'll need some time to clear it."

He reached down to haul a body out of the way. Alive or dead, the Freeholders deserved to have a clean extraction, not dragged over these filth.

Citation to accompany the award of the Valorous Service Medal...

Citation to accompany the award of the Humane Action Medal....

With respect for service to the Freehold, the Diplomatic Star is awarded...

The Grateful Nation of Ramadan is honored to present the decoration of the Golden Crescent, for personal sacrifice in battle...

—⚯—

It was one of her prouder moments. Her bearer had again fought to save noncombatants and children, and done so with courage and honor. To the warrior, she had offered comfort and encouragement, then fought as she should. There should be more of this in her existence.

They returned home, and her previous smith, though old and tired, refreshed her edge and dress. She returned to her place of honor, waiting for the next generation of warriors.

They didn't come.

It was frustrating that warriors could go so long without fighting. She enjoyed the care and attention, but she needed the fight. That was her purpose. She was a weapon, not a sculpture.

Time passed, and she was willed to another, and then another. She slept restlessly, waiting to serve.

—⚯—

family Over Blood

Kacey Ezell

What the fuck am I doing here?

I remember specifically thinking that question, right about the time that our stealthed boarding pod made contact with the skin of the Cutter ship. I felt the reverb through my seat as the grav grapples engaged, and took a quick look around at the faces of the company.

Assholes all looked calm and collected. My hands shook and I wanted to throw up in order to get the damn flutterbugs out of my gut. But when Corporal Hyan opened his eyes and caught me looking, I managed to conjure up a suitably manly bland expression. This was supposed to be an easy mission, as such things went. Simple cargo ship, board and capture. No sweat. But for some reason, I had the proverbial "bad feeling." Hyan blinked slowly back at me, his own neutral expression belied by the beads of sweat I could see glistening through the face shield of his helmet. Maybe I wasn't the only one.

"O Two," Captain Aiella ordered, her voice crisp

and calm. I reached up and toggled the switch that disconnected my combat helmet from the capsule's oxygen to my suit's integrated bottle. The suit itself was a combination of conventional armor, pressure suit, and an additional exoskeleton that had been beefed up to withstand Cutter energy fire, all worn over a composite undersuit that fit like a second skin. The whole setup was bulkier than any of us would have liked, but it might keep us alive. The Cutter ship would have atmosphere that we could breathe, and the suit would allow for that, but tragic mistakes in the past had taught us that discretion was the better part of not getting killed. In the event that any of us found ourselves on an unexpected EVA, we'd have air for a short time . . . hopefully enough for rescue, anyway. A series of clicks and a burst of metallic-tasting air told me that my suit was working properly. Oddly enough, focusing on that simple series of motions calmed the flutterbugs, and I felt my tension start to drain away. Maybe it was just relief that the wait was nearly over.

Below my feet, the boarding capsule gave a shudder and a jerk, indicating that the breaching sequence was complete. The dim red light overhead turned to green, and our restraints tightened as our stations began to slide toward the captain.

"Breach seal established! Time to go, boys and girls!" Aiella said. She reached out and punched a key next to her station, and the floor of the capsule opened up under her feet. I saw her bring her rifle to ready as the capsule's mechanism shot her "down" through the open airlock and into the Cutter ship.

My station jerked into motion as the capsule spat us in rapid-fire sequence down through the breach.

I barely had time to pull my own energy rifle to the ready position before I felt my body drop and my stomach rise up into my throat. There was a wave of disorienting nausea as the ship's artificial grav took hold. Then my boots hit the deck of the Cutter ship, and a blast of energy sizzled by my head, knocking me flat on my ass.

Cutter energy fire. Despite all my training, fear stabbed icy fingers deep into my chest. When humanity first encountered the Cutter race, no one had ever seen anything like the weapons they had. Roughly the size of a rifle, but they packed an energy punch that rivaled our biggest, beefiest kinetic weapons. We couldn't stop them, couldn't shield from them. Even our laser ablatives did nothing. It wasn't until we captured one of their rifles and reverse engineered it that we learned how to counter it. In essence, we beefed our laser ablative materials up, combined them with reactive materials that would absorb some of the godawful punch, and strengthened the whole thing against impact. The result wasn't pretty, but it worked well enough ... unless the fire was unusually intense, and the range particularly short.

Like right now.

I barely had time to roll out of the way before Hyan's big feet came down on top of me. With his size, that would have killed me just as quickly as the energy bolt would have done. I rolled free and came to my feet ... and froze. I wasn't prepared for the noise, or the smell. Even filtered through my suit's oxygen apparatus, the entire place reeked of something warm and musky, punctuated with the hot-metal scent of energy fire. The fear that had pierced my chest now reached up to wrap around my throat and squeeze. I felt my eyes pop wide, and I couldn't do anything about it.

"Carreon!" Aiella yelled in my earbuds, "Clear the breach site! Cover high, left!" As she did so, another bolt came from that direction, searing the air and stinking of ozone. Her voice jolted me into moving, finally. I turned as ordered and fired what was supposed to be a three-round burst, but was probably more like a ten- or twenty-round burst. *What the fuck was going on? This was supposed to be a stealth board!* I forced myself to take a shaky breath and try again as more of my platoon came dropping into the ship. The Cutter fire intensified, and I felt sick as I watched more and more of my buddies being shot as they landed.

Hyan came up hard on my right side, making me stagger to the left. "Get down!" he shouted, pulling me down with him behind what looked like an overturned table. I remember thinking that it seemed oddly shaped, like it was made for people whose legs were too long. "We got fucking Cutters coming in from three directions," he growled as he took more shots. "Looks like we dropped into some kind of rec room. Intel said this was supposed to be a maintenance passage! Figures!" He slammed a fresh power pack home into his rifle and started firing again. I followed suit, until the universe exploded into brilliant streaks of light. I heard Hyan gasp, saw him slump over the newly created hole where his chest had been. The stink of burnt meat wrapped around me, and then I got swallowed up by a rising darkness.

❖   ❖   ❖

I woke up when my head bounced against something.

The salty copper tang of blood filled my mouth, and I gagged, spat, and tried to raise the rifle that I no longer held. At that point, I realized that I was being dragged, and I started to try and fight my way free.

"Thank the Gods," Aiella said. "I was afraid I'd lose you, too." Her voice sounded weird: hoarse and broken. I couldn't see, my faceshield was blackened, and I struggled to breathe. Something was wrong with my O2 system. I didn't have either bottle or ambient air. I reached up and twisted viciously at the helmet, trying to get it to disengage. It came free with an audible *pop* and I flung it away, sucking in air like a drowning man.

"Where are we?" I asked. My own voice sounded pretty terrible as well. I swallowed hard, and immediately missed the water tube in my helmet.

"Some passageway. I don't know. Intel on the ship's interior was all jacked up. The Cutters..." she broke off, swallowed hard. I fought to sit up. My armor's power assist was dead, apparently.

"Here," Aiella said. "Let's get you out of that," she said.

"My armor?" I asked, startled. Why in seven hells would she want me out of my armor. I mean, I'd be lying if I said that I hadn't had thoughts. Aiella was a bit more muscular than I liked my women, even for being from Grainne, but...well...she *was* female. And the whole officer thing gave her a certain mystique. But we were in the middle of a boarding action! On a hostile ship that had *way* more Cutters than we'd expected, as far as I could tell. Truth be told, it was all a confusing mix of images in my head. But still...now?

Captain Aiella looked at me and then reached out and slapped the back of my head, hard.

"Shit!" I hissed, unable to hold it back.

"Don't be an idiot, Carreon," she said. "Your suit's dead. The armor's only as good as the materials at this point. No energy assist, and it's bulky enough to slow you down. Ditch it. Your best bet is to move quickly and hope the composite underneath is enough to stop their damn cutting arms."

I felt my face flush as I nodded. She looked narrowly at me and then began helping me out of the bulky power armor suit. She had lost hers, too, I realized abruptly as I watched her. Without the power armor, she moved like a hunting Ripper. I let my eyes trail down the line of her back . . . then jerked them down to my armor and the latches that held me in. Now may not have been the time, but I was still a guy, all right? Once I started thinking about sex, it was hard to let it go. Sue me.

My rifle was nowhere to be found, much to my shame. I climbed out of the carcass of my armor and tried to look casually around. Aiella noticed, however. Of course. She snorted and shoved her own weapon toward me. I just looked up at her.

"Take it," she said, her voice impatient.

"But . . ."

She shoved it at me again, so that it hit my chest and I reached up to take it by instinct. She started to turn away, muttering something about getting more power packs.

"Captain," I said, trying to make my voice sound much less scared and lost than I felt. "Ma'am, I can't take your weapon! What are you going to use?"

She turned back to me and looked at me for a long moment. I realized that she was probably debating whether or not to snap my head off for implying that she needed the weapon more than I did. That wasn't what I meant, of course. She could kick my ass completely unarmed. It was just that...well...she *deserved* her weapon. *She* wasn't the one who'd lost it, after all.

"I'll be fine," Aiella said finally. For some insane reason, a tiny smile curved her lips. She reached back under her shoulder and drew out a sword.

A sword.

Don't get me wrong, it was a beautiful weapon. I'm no expert, but it *seemed* old...old and expensive. But at the end of the day, it was a freaking edged weapon. I carried my duty knife like everyone else, and was trained in its use...but these were Cutters we were talking about. Was my captain really planning on bringing a sword to an energy rifle fight?

"Listen," she said briskly, interrupting my incredulity. "Something's off here. There were too damn many of the Cutters at the breach site, especially for a cargo ship. Even for our intel being wrong. It was too organized...like an ambush."

My eyes widened. "Ambush?" I asked, sounding brilliant.

Aiella nodded. "That's all I can come up with. They knew we were coming, they knew where. Which indicates that they might have known that our intel was bad. In any case, something's not right about this situation. Which means that you've got to get back to our people to tell them about it."

"Me?" I asked. My voice might have squeaked, just a little bit. I tried to ignore it. "What about you?"

She turned and looked straight at me, that crazy little smile growing just a bit. "We were given a mission. Take the ship."

"You can't take the whole godsdamned ship by yourself!" I said, aghast. I probably shouldn't have spoken that way to my captain. But shit just kept getting weirder and weirder, and I just didn't think about protocol at that particular moment.

"I never said I meant to take it *intact*," she said. She opened her mouth to say more, but right at that moment, another energy bolt came sizzling down the passageway at us. I dove for the nearest cover...which happened to be the pile of my armor. I landed flat on my stomach, took a deep breath, then raised up and squeezed off a few rounds of my own. An ear-splitting howl-screech echoed down the passageway, followed by a distinctly human laugh. I felt the wind of her passage as Captain Aiella sprinted past me, blade first, right into the teeth of the enemy.

"Wha—shit!" I spat, and before I could think too hard, got to my feet and sprinted after her. I don't know how they didn't take us out during that wild run, but they didn't. In fact, they stopped firing, and their howl-screechy noise took on a different tone. If I didn't know better, I'd have said it sounded approving. Perhaps they admired our craziness. Who knows?

The captain impacted them first, her sword flashing in the ship's lights. That blade must have been ridiculously sharp, because she sliced through the Cutters like they were semiliquid. And the way she moved! Before I could even manage to fire a bolt of my own, she'd spun and lunged and managed to decapitate or impale every member of the fireteam that had found us. One of the Cutters' severed heads rolled past me, leaving a trail of red in its wake. I always found that odd, that the Cutters bled red just like us. I suppose it made sense, considering that they breathed oxygen as well, but it just seemed...wrong.

"Let's go," Aiella said, snapping me back to reality. I swallowed hard, forcing back the nausea that threatened to erupt from me, and started to walk through the carnage she'd left behind.

"Where are we going?" I asked her, a few steps later.

She shrugged one shoulder without looking back at me. "Intel's layout suggested that the life support pods would be back this way. Intel may have been completely jacked up, but it makes sense that they'd be near the living quarters. And that's where we dropped in, so..."

I jogged after her. "Captain," I said, feeling a bit of desperation. "Isn't that where we were ambushed? And you want to go back there? With all due respect, ma'am, are you fucking crazy?"

She turned and shoved me up against the bulkhead, then leaned in and put her face inches from mine. For the first time, I got a good look at her blue eyes, and fear curled through me. Madness waited there, in her gaze. Madness tangled with the kind of rage that made my hackles stand up on end. Then she did something I never would have expected or predicted. She smiled.

"Wayne," she said, using my first name. I hadn't even realized that she'd known my first name. "I've just watched every single member of my command, save one, be slaughtered before my eyes. We took a few of them out, and gave a good account of ourselves, but that doesn't change the fact that *all of my people are dead*. Except you. So, yeah. I guess you could say that I. *am*. fucking. crazy."

I took a deep, slow breath, trying to calm the sphincter-puckering fear she inspired. I opened my mouth to say something, though I had no idea what, but she shook her head and laid one finger over my lips, like a mother shushing her child.

"But that's good news for you, Private Carreon. Wayne. Because that means that you will survive. You're getting off this ship, because *you've* got to get word back about the increase in the Cutters' troop strength. And because if *you* survive to do that, then I can rest knowing that at least *one* of my people made it out."

She leaned in close enough that I could feel her breath on my ear. "So for fuck's sake, stop asking me stupid questions, keep your mouth shut, and follow my orders, is that understood?"

I swallowed hard and sternly told my body that it was absolutely *not* to react to the disturbingly close proximity of this clearly very crazy bitch. My body didn't listen, but thankfully, Aiella didn't seem to notice. She just backed up and pinned my eyes with her icy blues again. I gave her a tiny nod, and that did the trick. She nodded back and, finally, let me go.

"So," she said, her tone conversational. "Now that we've got that sorted out, I believe we were headed this way?"

So here's a thing or two you might not know about the Cutters. Most everyone knows we call them that because they have this really disconcerting practice of grafting a huge, wickedly sharp blade onto one or more of their various appendages. Cutters are, of course, bipedal, and vaguely humanoid shaped because of it, but the size and shape of these cutting blades meant that they didn't necessarily *look* humanoid all the time.

What we found on that hellish trek through the bowels of the Cutter ship was that they really seemed to *like* using those blades. In fact, they preferred melee combat to shooting. To be honest, that worked in our favor more than once, as they tended to put down their own energy weapons in order to watch Aiella and wait for their opportunity to match blades with her. Part of the reason for that might have been the tight confines of the ship's passages, but it really did seem like they were queuing up for their turn. I started holding my fire and just basically covering her, keeping them from picking us off from the rear. Not that they seemed inclined to do that. They could have taken us out ten times over, but the ones I saw just watched us, their six-eyed stare bright as she moved like a scythe through the ranks of challengers.

I don't speak Cutter, but damn me if they didn't sound like they enjoyed watching her. You might almost say that they *admired* her. Me? She scared the living piss out of me...but she was on my side.

At one point, several of them were awaiting us in an open area that served as a large junction. For the first time, two of the Cutters attacked at once. Aiella severed one of their bladed forearms. Like something you'd see in a holo, it fell in front of me while a spray of apparently arterial blood made a perfect arc through the air. I kicked the limb out of the way and felt the hot patter of the blood on my face. Perfect. Disgust roiled through me, and when one of the waiting Cutters managed to slide by Aiella without getting sliced open, I struck more by instinct than anything else. I brought the butt of my energy rifle up and smashed it roughly in the direction of the creature's face. It reeled backward, tripped on the severed blade arm, and fell to the ground. It let out a howl of pain, and I looked down to see that the blade arm had cut the back of its leg, just above the foot. On a human, it would have caught the Achilles tendon. Essentially, the Cutter had just hamstrung himself on his buddy's severed arm. Apparently they kept those blade arms insanely sharp. I'd been lucky not to have severed my toes!

Howler at my feet wasn't done, though, despite being flat on its back. It swung its own blade arm up over his head to try and tangle in Aiella's dancing footwork. I may have let out a howl of my own as I reacted. I lunged forward and stomped down on its already battered face. That was probably a mistake, because that made him turn his blade arm to *me*. I managed to use the butt of my energy rifle to block his first strike, and then turned the rifle to shoot him in the face. The stink of ozone and burnt meat exploded all around us.

"Shit!" Aiella yelled. "What the fuck did you do that for?" I heard the Cutters let out something that sounded like screams of rage, and one of them lunged at Aiella again. She spun out of reach, then grabbed the back of my jumpsuit and hauled me along with her. The Cutters watching from the crossing passages started bringing their own energy rifles to bear. We were rats in a godsdamned barrel until she shoved me sideways into an opening in the hallway.

I fell through it, stumbling on the raised lip of the floor beyond. Aiella stepped on me, then over me and kicked my ribs to get me to move out of the way. I curled up in a ball, not knowing what else to do, and she smashed her fist into some kind of control panel on the bulkhead, causing a thick panel to slide shut behind us.

"Get up!" she yelled at me. I didn't say anything back, partly because her kick had knocked the wind out of me, and partly because I didn't know what to say. She was mad at me, I could see that, but I had no idea why.

I struggled to my hands and knees, then up to my feet, just in time to see her knife hand as she jammed it into my chest.

"You bleeding moron!" she screamed, shoving me back against the bulkhead. "I *had* them! Didn't you even bother to read *any* of the intel reports on the Cutters' culture? They're a warrior-caste people. They *revere* melee combat, and they would have let us cut our way to wherever we wanted to go if you hadn't cocked it all up and *cheated by shooting!*"

"What? Are you kidding me?" I said, my voice rising with my temper. "What the hell else was I going to do? Watch it hamstring you and cut you down? I'm not a damn baby, Captain! I'll shoot when I damn well feel the need! I don't need your permission to save your *life*. For gods' sake, *we came in shooting!*"

"Yeah, but that was when we thought we'd be doing a simple board and capture, remember? This is a small support ship, not a troop carrier. There's no godsdamned reason for all of these warriors to be on board, and yet they are. So when we got shot up all to hell, it made *sense* to switch to melee combat. Until you had to go all guns blazing on me!"

I snapped. "Well excuse the *shit* out of me!" I shouted back. I leaned forward and got in her face. She didn't move a millimeter, but she did cross her arms over her chest and stare at me. "I would have known that if you'd have fucking *said something!* But nooo, you just go acting all ninja on me and start running down the hall with a godsdamned *sword.* And you *gave* me your rifle. What the hell was I supposed to do?"

She stared at me with those icy blue eyes for a moment, and then smiled slowly. "All right," she said, in a normal tone. "You're right, I should have said something. You're a soldier, after all. I should have expected you'd be inclined to 'shoot first, ask later.'"

I leaned back a little bit, my chest heaving and my face flushed. I took a deep breath and forced it slowly out my nose before I responded. "Well, maybe not, but I *am* going to shoot if it looks like the best way to keep us alive," I said, feeling somewhat mollified.

Her smile grew slightly, and she shook her head. "Unfortunately, that still leaves us stuck in what looks like a maintenance locker, with very few options."

I perked up, looked around.

"Maintenance locker?" I echoed her. I got to my feet and stood up on my tiptoes. At 191 cm, I was tall enough for a human. Cutters, however, were on average a fair bit taller. Consequently, the majority of displays were just above my head, right at Cutter eye level.

"Yeah, don't you think?" Aiella asked, stepping closer to me and craning her neck to look up as well. "Why? Do you see something helpful?"

"I don't know," I answered. I didn't read Cutter.

What I did know, however, were some of the basic principles of ship engineering and design. Cutters were bipedal oxygen breathers who lived on a planet with gravity roughly similar to Grainne's own. That meant that a lot of things were going to be similar. Or should be similar, anyway. A man can hope, right?

"Give me a hand with this," I said. When she didn't move, I looked over at her. She was looking at me with one raised eyebrow. Shit.

"Sorry," I said, meaning it. "Give me a hand with this, please, ma'am?" I said. I'm sure I sounded sarcastic, even though I was genuine. She was my superior officer. Being a dead man walking was no excuse for forgetting my military discipline.

She gave a short laugh and shook her head, then stepped forward. I pulled out my service knife and began working at a seam in the panel in front of us. Aiella caught on and went to work with her own knife, and before long, we'd managed to pry the panel loose.

Inside lay the typical tangled nest of cables and lines. I don't know what I'd expected to see, but disappointment suddenly crushed my insides. I couldn't make heads nor tails of this mess. I guess I'd hoped for...a component that I recognized, or something. All I got was a mess of a Gordian knot. I felt, more than saw, Aiella look expectantly at me. "Well?" she thought. "Any ideas?"

"Kinda," I said. When in doubt, apply brute force, right? I took my knife and made a sweeping slash from left to right, cutting through as many of the wires and hoses as I could.

As you can imagine, this wasn't the smartest thing I could have done.

The first thing that happened was that I got electrocuted. It felt like liquid pain shooting through me, riding along each of my veins as I flew through the air and slammed into the panel that Aiella had closed. My ears rang and my vision went dark. For a moment I thought I was dead, and I remember hoping that I hadn't killed Aiella too.

Hearing returned first. Sort of. It took me a moment to realize that the bizarre, warbling shriek that I heard was, in fact, some alarm and not the tinnitus of my poor abused eardrums. Well, some alarm and Aiella calling my name.

"Carreon!" she said, sharply. She followed up with an even sharper *smacking* sound as she slapped me, hard.

"Ow!" I said in protest. Or tried to say, rather. It came out sounding like a half-strangled cough. Though my eyelids felt like they weighed a ton each, I forced them open.

Aiella's own eyes widened, and she let out her own half-strangled laugh. Then she did the damnedest thing. She hugged me. Hard. Like iron-thewed arms hard around my shoulders, forcing my face into her chest kind of hard. I might have enjoyed it, had she been wearing a lot less. As it was, it just kinda hurt.

Then she let me go, and my head fell back against the wall again. The lights flickered off and then on again. At first I thought it was because of the repeated impacts to the back of my throbbing, abused skull. But Aiella grinned and got to her feet, hauling me up a second later.

"I don't know what you did, but you certainly managed to get someone's attention." Aiella said. Her voice still held an edge of laughter. Or maybe madness. It was hard to tell.

"Is that funny?" I asked.

"Not in the slightest," she replied with a grin. The lights went dark again, for longer this time, and an ominous hissing started to fill the air, along with the scent of smoke. Acridly sweet smoke. Like the kind that occurs when you have an electrical fire. When the lights came back on, Aiella's mad grin had disappeared.

"I have no idea what that is, but it doesn't smell good," she said.

"Electrical fire," I supplied. "We should probably go. I think that's a life-support module, given the HVAC tubes or whatever they are that are branching off. We're going to have smoke in a minute."

She looked at me for another half second, and frowned.

"An electrical fire isn't going to cripple the whole ship," she said. "Get up, I have an idea."

While I struggled to push myself back to my feet, I watched Aiella reach inside her composite shirt. Apparently, she'd stashed one of the breaching charges from either her armor or mine in there, which had to have been damned uncomfortable. For half a second, I wondered what else she had shoved down in there.

She primed the charge and set the delay with a twist of her wrist and tossed it into the sparking, smoky mess I'd left. Then she turned back to me with that crazy grin.

"Let's go," she said, and turned and slammed her hand down on the control panel and the door slid open to reveal an empty (thank the gods!) passage. Outside, lights flashed in various colors in time with the blaring klaxon that still thrummed through my head. I was certain that they were meant to convey some critical information ... but again, I had no clue as to what.

Aiella brushed past me, her sword out and ready. I brought up my rifle and followed close behind. Despite her explanation of Cutter cultural mores, I wasn't ready to abandon the only weapon I had. I wouldn't go in shooting, but I'd be ready to shoot if I had to do so.

The lights dimmed a final time, and then went out completely. The klaxon went on, blaring through the continued ringing in my ears. I couldn't get the sweet-burnt smell of electrical fire out of my nose, and for a moment I considered throwing up. But instead I reached out a hand and brushed my fingertips across the back of Captain Aiella's shoulder. How long had she set that timer for?

"Stay close, moving forward," she said in a low tone. Not that anyone else could have heard her, what with the klaxon and all. The darkness was disorienting, but that was all right. Part of our training had been in darkness. I saw, more than heard, Aiella crack the seal on the emergency chemical lights we all carried. She kept it shielded in her off hand and started to move quickly forward along the bulkhead of the passageway.

It didn't take long before we found them.

It was awkward as hell, but we managed to work out a system. Cutters can't see in the dark any better than we can. In fact, their visible range tends toward the higher frequencies of the electromagnetic spectrum. This meant that their dark vision was, in fact, *worse* than ours, so they all tended to have bright lights that they swept around in front of them as they searched for the problem with their ship.

Aiella handed her chem light back to me, and I flipped the shield closed and stuffed it in a pocket before bringing my energy rifle up to ready. My eyes were already starting to dark-adapt. If things started to go badly for Aiella and her sword, I'd shoot at the lights and keep moving. What could go wrong?

I tried to stay pretty close on her tail, but *damn*, the woman moved like water. She stalked them like a Ripper in the night and then attacked from the darkness. The Cutters, blinded by their lights, never seemed to see her coming. She'd leap, or lunge, or turn, and a Cutter would cry out, and a light would drop to the ground. I'd kick it to the side, shoving it under whatever body lay closest, so that the glare wouldn't hamper her vision.

I had to give it to them. Even with fluid death moving through them like a hot wind, they didn't panic. They'd shine their lights in the direction of the last cry, and sometimes catch a glimpse of Aiella as she whirled away like a shadow disappearing in the dark. They'd attack with their bladed limbs raised, but as often as not they hit each other, because she was just that damn fast. All I had to do was stay out of the way and not die.

Then, before I realized it, we were alone in that junction of the ship. The last Cutter died choking on its own blood as Aiella ran her sword through the creature's thick, squat neck. I'd just dodged another severed Cutter arm when the punishing noise of the klaxon cut off.

"It's me," I said into the sudden silence, while I

bent to retrieve the dead Cutter's light. I lifted it and shined it over Aiella's body, making a quick check to ensure she was unhurt. She stood there like the Morrigan, her chest heaving, her eyes glassy. I stepped slowly forward.

"Captain?" I asked softly, snapping my fingers in front of her eyes. She blinked and annoyance replaced the battle trance in her eyes and she turned to me.

"Wha—?" she started to say. But then the deck raised up about a meter, and listed hard to starboard. A massive wall of sound and pressure slammed into us, knocking the wind out of my abused lungs and making my head pound and my ears ring even harder. Then, of course, my head hit the deck, because I'd been completely knocked off of my feet and barely managed to avoid landing on a bladed Cutter carcass. The deck pitched again, rolling back to port.

A bright white smoke started to snake along the ceiling of the passage. I probably wouldn't have noticed it, except that I had to lie still for a moment and force my body to remember how to breathe, and my light was shining directly up. Eventually, I sucked in a lungful of air and coughed as I tasted that sweet, acrid electrical taint. I somehow managed to force my battered body to roll over, and promptly sliced open my knee on a downed Cutter.

I hissed a curse just as Aiella got to her feet next to me. She shook her head sharply, like she was trying to dispel her own disorientation and knelt next to me.

"Don't you ever look where you're going, Carreon?" she asked, her voice ragged but firm.

"Was looking for you, ma'am," I managed to say. She snorted and turned to cut a piece off of the dead

Cutter's uniform. Fabric or some kind of leather, I couldn't have really said, but it parted easily enough for her blade. As any number of also-dead Cutters could testify. She examined my wound, and then smiled.

"It's shallow," she said. As she spoke, she wrapped her makeshift bandage around my knee and tied it off. It hurt, but then again, so did everything else by this point. I let her help me up (again, damnit!) and managed to work out a sort of hobble that didn't make it bleed too much. The deck pitched under us again, and I stumbled into the bulkhead.

"Nice work," Aiella said. I looked at her, uncomprehending. She snorted a little bit and shook her head, presumably at my ignorance. She reached out to grab my arm and pulled me along after her as she started to move.

"Back in the locker. Opening up that maintenance hatch and finding the life-support module. Could be we've crippled this ship. Maybe destroyed her. Nicely done. That *was* your intent, right?" she asked. We'd left the Cutter light back with the bodies, so I could only guess that she was turning her head toward me with a sardonic grin, but I felt my face heat up anyway.

"Uh, yeah," I said. I didn't sound convincing at all. I heard her laugh softly, and my face flamed even more. In truth, I'd only been thinking of getting out alive when I slashed up the locker. I'd thought that maybe I could create some kind of diversion to let us get past the hordes of Cutter warriors that apparently inhabited this ship. I probably watched too many holos.

We kept moving. Eventually, we found more Cutters. As before, they died quickly in the darkness. Their behavior seemed different, however. Instead of roving as full patrols in search of something (us, perhaps?), we were encountering them in twos and threes, occasionally singly. They weren't organized, but they all seemed to be moving in roughly the same direction. Which was helpful, actually, because I, at least, was completely lost by this point. Even with the advantage of human eyes, fighting our way through an alien ship in the dark was a difficult task. Keeping a sense of direction? Impossible.

"The escape pods must be this way. That's got to be why they're all flocking here," Aiella said, after we'd come up behind the third small group. They'd turned and fought, and they'd all died well, if such things counted for anything. By now, the smoke had infiltrated the interior of the ship to the point where it fogged through the thin beams cast by the Cutters' lights. My nose burned from it, and I feared I'd never get rid of that scorched-sweet taste in the back of my throat. I grunted something that sounded vaguely like agreement and continued. Following close behind her meant me trying not to trip over the dismembered bodies she was leaving in her wake. It took a fair amount of concentration, especially in the dark.

It seemed that she was right, though. That was the good news. The bad news was that as we got closer and closer to the possibility of actually making it out of this clusterfuck, we were running into more and more Cutters. Support personnel, too. I could tell because of the lack of wicked blade monstrosities growing out of their limbs. The nonwarrior Cutters looked significantly smaller without the blades. Or maybe it was their body language. They seemed to shrink back from the cyclone of edged death that was my company commander. In fact, if I'm not mistaken, they actually started to give way and bow down to her, as if she were some kind of legendary figure. Who knows, maybe she was. These guys certainly did seem to revere edged combat... and she definitely *looked* like a goddess of the sword.

"There!" she cried out as she ran yet another Cutter warrior through. The smaller support Cutter that had been with the warrior backed away and folded itself into a curiously still bow. I tore my eyes from the bowing alien to look where Aiella's dripping blade pointed.

Down the hallway a few meters was an open hatch, just large enough for me to walk through without stooping. It would have been small for a Cutter, but it looked like it opened into a dimly lit capsulelike space with a contraption that looked a lot like a grav-couch.

An escape pod. We'd made it.

Or very nearly. Right then, an ear-splitting, screeching yowl echoed down the passage from a crossing passageway. That sound made my skin crawl with foreboding. I'd heard it before, in that first hallway, before we killed the lights and lit this place on fire. It was the sound of a Cutter attack.

"Go!" Aiella shouted at me. She reached out, grabbed my free arm and slung me, hard, toward the glowing beacon of the pod's soft light. I stumbled, willing myself to fall toward the pod as I fought to keep my battered, unsteady body upright. I felt her let go and turn to face the onslaught of enraged Cutter warriors as they charged down the crossing passage to try and cut us off.

Let me just get to the pod, I thought, forcing my legs to keep fighting forward. *Let me get there, and I can turn and cover her retreat.*

I don't know what God or Goddess was listening to me...maybe all of them, because despite everything else going wrong on this royal goatfuck of a mission, I made it. My shoulder slammed against the frame of the hatch, rendering my left arm numb, but it didn't matter. I turned, braced against the hatch frame, raised my energy rifle and fired.

"Aiella! Let's go!" I shouted over the sound of the Cutters' battle rage. The deck bucked again, and I fell hard against the opposite side of the frame, then landed flat on my ass inside the pod itself.

"Fuck!" I shouted as I struggled to get back to my feet. My knee throbbed, and my pant leg was wet through. I couldn't hear Aiella's words, but I heard her voice shouting something. With my teeth shredding my lower lip bloody, I used my rifle as a crutch to lever myself up. Every moment I wasn't firing at the Cutters was a moment lost, and I cursed every aching muscle, every battered joint that made me move so godsdamned *slow*!

Right foot first, then left, and I managed to get myself upright just in time to see Aiella in a flat sprint for the pod. The Cutter horde was hard on her heels, their bladed limbs scything through the smoke and darkness toward her. She reached out her hand. Our fingertips just touched...

And she coughed. Then looked down.

A double hand length of alien steel protruded from her chest.

I screamed something. I still don't know what. It may not have even been words. Somehow, I had her blade in my hand, and I was bringing it down on the limb that had pierced her from behind. Her blade shattered, but so did the Cutter's limb, and the ship bucked upward violently enough to throw Aiella and me hard to the deck of the pod as the hatches slammed shut. I tried to catch her, but the angles were wrong. I just couldn't get all the way there, and she impacted the deck of the pod face down on top of my right arm.

The giant, invisible hand of massive acceleration held us down as the auto-launch mechanism of the Cutter pod ignited, spitting us out into the serene void of space. I struggled to move under Aiella, but her slim, powerful body suddenly had exponentially more weight, and I might as well have tried to move a mountain off of myself.

The pod launcher must have put a bit of spin on us, however, because I could slowly start to see the familiar shape of the Cutter ship drift into view above me. It convulsed like a wounded animal as explosions peppered one side of it. I felt a savage satisfaction at that. They'd killed us, sure... but we'd killed a lot of them, too; and crippled their ship as well.

"Wayne?" Aiella whispered, her face close to mine. I nearly choked. She was alive?

"Yes, ma'am?" I said. My voice sounded broken.

"You okay?"

I didn't know whether to laugh or cry. I started to do both. "Yeah," I said. "I'm fine. A little banged up, but you did it, ma'am. You got me out. Thanks."

"It's... cause I'm... sexy... ninja..." she whispered. She opened her mouth again as if she would say something else, but nothing came out. Instead she just smiled and let her eyes fall closed as she bled out all over me.

✧   ✧   ✧

I had her sword reforged.

In the end, it was the option that made the most sense. Especially after I decided to incorporate the blade from the Cutter arm that killed her. It was steel, after all, albeit some kind of weird alloy that was found only on the Cutter homeworld.

I figured I'd have it reforged and give it to her next of kin as a remembrance. It seemed like a nice gesture, and I felt like I owed her that, at least. Her next of kin turned out to be a brother, older, but just by a year and change. He was a plumber who lived in Jefferson City.

I'd tried to contact him before her funeral, but it hadn't worked out that way. I'd been in the hospital for a while with my injuries, and then there were the inevitable debriefings and admin actions before I was able to take my time off. It turned out that some more members of my company had survived the initial slaughter and been taken prisoner. Leadership and intel both were all over me for anything I could remember about the interior of the ship. It sounded like they were contemplating another attack to get my buddies back. It stung that I wouldn't be invited to the party, but I'd be lying if I said that a part of me wasn't relieved. And then there was the blade itself. It took me a while to find a bladesmith who would or could do what I wanted, but eventually I managed.

So on the day that Captain Aiella, Freehold Military Forces, was honored along with the others who'd died in the initial offensive, I was there in my uniform, her sword sheathed at my side.

After the service, I approached her brother. The man looked completely out of his depth, clutching the folded flag of the Freehold that had been presented to him. His casualty notification officer was somewhere nearby, but everyone involved knew me, and knew that I was the last person to see Aiella alive. Everyone figured I'd want to talk to her brother.

"Mr. Aiella," I said. The plumber looked up at me with eyes that were haunted and sad, and more than a little confused. He looked like her, only softer. I felt myself smile.

"I'm Space Combat Specialist Wayne Carreon," I said. "Captain Aiella was my company commander. She...she saved my life, multiple times, sir. It was my honor to know her."

The plumber smiled too, sadly. "Naomy was like that," he said. "Even when we were kids. She was always protecting me, even though I was older."

I nodded and swallowed hard. My eyes were starting to burn, and my throat threatened to close down. I forced air in through my nose and out again, then spoke.

"Sir, I have her sword. It was damaged in the battle, but I took the liberty of having it repaired. It...it now contains the alien steel that killed her."

I have no idea why I added that last part, except that I knew she would have enjoyed knowing it. I looked away from the plumber's eyes (gods, he looked like her!) and focused on unbuckling my baldric that held the sword and scabbard.

His hand covered mine. I stilled, and looked back up at Aiella's eyes in her brother's face. "Keep it," he said, his voice uneven.

"No," I said, my own voice cracking. "I can't...I..."

"Keep it," he said. "She was my sister by birth, but

she died to keep you alive. That makes you family, and family takes precedence over blood. She'd want you to have it. Keep it." He let out a harsh, broken laugh. "I'm a fucking plumber, for the sake of all the gods. What the hell am I going to do with a warrior's sword?"

I let my hand drop from the buckle, and instead moved to draw the sword and hold it high.

The reforged blade was a work of art, I must say. It still had Aiella's hilt and guard, but the blade itself seemed to glimmer with a faintly blue reflection. The bladesmith had said that the alien steel was an interesting alloy, heavy on the cobalt. I had only a vague idea what that meant, but it certainly made a striking weapon. I watched the afternoon Iolight ripple down the length of the blade.

I felt my lips curve in a smile, and I brought the hilt to my chin to render a salute to her brother, then lowered the blade with a ringing *swish* as it sliced through the air.

"Thank you," I said to the brother of the woman I could never thank, but to whom I owed my life. With the greatest of reverence, I sheathed her blade and reached out to shake her brother's hand. A faint breeze ruffled my hair, and I could almost hear Aiella's wild laugh.

This presentation confirms the award of the Galactic Whorl...

—⁂—

The battle had been glorious, sword against sword, as was always meant to be. Her bearer had fought desperately, precisely, deftly. Her bearer was dead, she was broken, and she could only hope for future preservation. At least she remained in a culture that appreciated her.

Again she was bent and dulled, torqued and hurt. She was disconnected from herself, then welded in an odd environment with tickling, stinging needles that sewed her fracture together. Then heat moved oddly along the break, healing it so she could barely tell herself. Well, then.

After that, she panicked as utter outrage was forced on her. He was chiseling open her spine. What was the purpose of this torture? He was clearly skilled, but he was brutalizing her.

New metal. New metal was laid into the wound along her back, and then the heat rose high, higher than ever before. She did not burn. The atmosphere around her was odd and low in oxygen. She glowed to where she should spit sparks, but didn't, and became almost liquid.

... and the hammer fell.

Oh, my. That was exquisite.

The hammer beat, thumped, caressed her length, and the new metal flowed into her.

It was strong, flexible, powerful. And now she knew why she'd been sliced open. The smith closed it all with expert blows, then massaged her sides around her new spine.

Being opened in front was ... odd. First he crushed her edge blunt, and thickened her. Then he started chiseling again, with that strange tool that was so fine. It was almost obscene, but she trusted him.

She had no worries, and expected the new metal.

Yet another alloy. This one with more strange ores. But it was mythically hard and tough. The smith beat and beat to get it to stick. She felt sorry for him having to labor so much for a single sword. He seemed unbothered. In fact, she could sense his thrill at this task.

Then he refined her bevels again, and she felt stronger than she ever had. She was a gleaming arc of death, or would be, she was sure.

The clay betrayed her and fell away, but the curve it left in her was a compound of true beauty. Never had she had an edge that hard, either.

He polished with surety, using yet new tools she'd never encountered. They felt like soft sponges, but smoothed away metal.

The fittings again were of materials made by man, soft enough for grip, and completely unadorned. But she also had a formal dress, and it was real rayskin, silk and mokume gane.

Her new metal was old, and strange. It didn't quite feel like iron, and it wasn't quite like the nickel she tasted occasionally. There were other strange tastes, too. She was strong, though, heavier than she'd been in some time, with a thick spine and shapely bevels.

She was named The Captain, after her bearer's commander. That was fitting, and honorable.

—⟁—

Choices and Consequences

Michael Z. Williamson

One never knew what would be in the Bazaar. Most of it wasn't remarkable, but there was the unusual, the artistic, the clever.

In the evening dusk and warmth, Sergeant Drustan Arnoy wandered, looking for anything interesting.

The first blade vendor had nothing of note. Further along, there was an actual smith with some decent quality knives, and he checked them over.

"Shopping for a new one?" the smith asked.

"Always," he said. "But not always buying. I do like your work, however. Good quality, especially for the price."

"Thank you, Sergeant."

He moved on. The second seller was less remarkable than the first, and two more smiths were apprentices. He appreciated their attempts, but really, they'd do better in time.

He passed some jewelers with neat stuff he had no use for, and someone who hand made historical mechanical clocks. Fascinating, but not what he wanted.

Illumination started coming on as the dusk grew, chains and bulbs of light throughout the awnings and plexidomes. It was still warm and pleasant, but not too warm for his uniform blouse.

The third seller had actual swords, some of them used. He assumed they'd be overpriced, but it was worth a look.

One was a kataghan, but with an old production number. About two centuries old. That was neat. You could see the change in style from then to now.

"I wonder what stories that has in it," he said.

The dealer said, "If I knew, I'd say. I can't guarantee it predates the Separation War. Or that it was used. But it is from that era, quite closely."

"Very nice."

He handled a straight sword. The craftsmanship was excellent, but he'd never cared for the movement. They'd been developed for use with a shield. Even a tonfa-held rifle wasn't really a shield.

"Tell me about the katana," he asked while pointing.

"Estate sale," the vendor said. "They said it came back from the Second Encounter."

With the Cutters?

"How likely is that?" he asked.

The man shrugged. "Certainly possible, but nothing will really prove it. The age and style seem to fit. It's been very well maintained." The man handed him the sword.

He drew the blade. "I see some practice wear," he agreed. Then he paused.

"Gods, this thing balances by itself."

The seller smiled. "That's what I was going to mention."

"Sheez, I could decapitate a room full of hostiles and barely up my pulse. It floats."

He handled it a bit more.

Musing, he said, "Huh. Well, it might actually get

to go to the Third Encounter. If so, I'll log the details. How much?"

The man showed him the tag. He flinched.

Whew. That wasn't cheap. But it was an amazing sword. Of all the ones he'd seen today, or even this year, it spoke to him.

He hefted it and let it balance and sing. At the merchant's invitation, he stepped into the space and tried some tentative blocks and cuts.

This was his sword. There was no doubt.

"Well, it's not like I'm going to buy furniture or a flashy car," he said, rationalizing it to himself. "Ten percent off for active military?"

"I can do that," the seller agreed. "And good luck to you, Sergeant."

—⁓—

Her new bearer was young.

He took her. And how was he for her? A student? An apprentice?

He held her surely enough. He was trained. She'd see.

His first cut was straight, and she sang through the mat. It was some strange material, but it acted like rice straw.

He wasn't quite on target, but it was a clean cut.

The second one was better. Then the third.

After that, a side of beef fell to her perfect edge. After that was a block of something else that resisted like flesh and bone. Her newest metal sheared through it all effortlessly.

The cuts were straight, and each more accurate than the last. It would take some practice, with her older, bulkier body with its strange splints. Her balance was excellent, just different than before. But her bearer would learn. He was a skilled journeyman.

One day, she could tell, he would be a master.

Then she was taken to what was obviously a place of learning, and many hands touched her, with the most honorable and serious of intentions.

Dr. Christopher French came out to meet the soldier who wanted his sword examined. In most of these cases, what they had was unremarkable, just an unusual limited production piece from some smith or other. Frequently, he had to gently break the news that what they had was no better, and sometimes inferior, to their issue blade. Sometimes they had something unusual from a smith of note. Occasionally, he could trace one back to an early system family.

The soldier, a Sergeant Arnoy by his uniform, shook hands.

"Good day, sir."

"Good day. I'm Dr. French."

"Well, sir, I acquired a sword in the City Bazaar, and it seems unusual. I doubt the story I heard about it was true, but it certainly handles better than most."

His uniform had the devices for Unarmed Combat Expert and Hand to Hand Weapons Expert, so he likely had some idea what he was talking about.

"Well, let's go to my office and take a look."

Arnoy followed his lead and they walked through the isolation field in the doorway. At once, but carefully, Arnoy drew the scabbarded weapon from his sash and handed it over.

French took it respectfully, drew it, laid the scabbard

on the desk, and used a cloth to support the blade so he didn't mar it. His cameras viewed it from all sides and showed him closeups.

It certainly was unusual. The texture was vivid and complex. It definitely had several patterns to it, rolling in and out of the surface. There were some abrasions and minor practice nicks that hadn't been polished out.

The balance was exquisite.

"Whoever made it knew their craft," he admitted. "The layering is very unusual, almost as if several patterns are fighting each other."

Arnoy said, "Yes, sir, I noticed that myself."

"Can you leave it with me for a few days? I'll send when I've had a chance to research it."

"I can. I'm lifting in less than a month, though. We've got an intercept with the Cutters."

"I heard. I should be done by then. I'll wish you good luck."

"Thank you. We're fairly confident."

He nodded. "There's much better intel than the first couple of encounters."

"That, and we have allies. Earth, Caledonia, NovRos, and even the Ishkul."

"Aliens in our midst. Their technology is fascinating. Or was, I should say, now that they're adopting modern metals and plastics."

"Yes. Very capable warriors, though, and amazingly astute strategists. They're the ones who predicted where we'd find the Cutters this time."

French said, "I'll have this checked thoroughly. But I can authoritatively say it's strong enough for combat."

The soldier smiled. "Excellent. I'll await your call."

❖　　❖　　❖

French looked up the maker's mark. Morlock. One of the better smiths in system. He placed a call.

Douglas Morlock explained what he'd done. "That was a long time ago, but I have the notes here. It was after the Second Encounter. I got the sword in two pieces from the customer, and he requested I incorporate some of the Cutter metal into it. I straightened the parts, forcebeam and diffusion welded the break. Then I induction heated and upset the repair, and forged it back to shape, then did a local migration heat. I electroimpact chiseled the spine and edge and incorporated the Cutter metal, then used an inert atmosphere and waldo-hammer to get the rough bevel back. After that, I did a lot of hand hammering—that stuff is tough—then standard surface polish. Do you need the metal analysis?"

"I'll take any details you have, Master Smith. And this was from Captain Aiella?"

Morlock looked off screen, presumably at his notes. "That's the name he gave, yes. Her family gave it to him."

Thank gods for a craftsman who kept records.

French said, "I have her bio, and her brother's. It appears he died four years ago, and his family sold most of his possessions."

"Sad when that happens," Morlock said. "More artifacts get lost that way."

"And because people don't document their own things," French noted. "Thank you very much for your help."

"Glad I was able to."

Naomy Aiella. There were good military records on her. Family history was less detailed, but they'd bought her sword from the Weyer company. Did the auction house have any details?

They did.

A div later, long after he'd missed dinner, he sent his compiled information, all two centuries of it, over to Moleculab.

He told the tech, "Yasmin, I think I'm going to need your services to confirm some of these findings."

"We can fit you in next Berday," she said. "Odd one, is it?"

"It could be," he agreed. "A couple of generations tracked, and an award." Then he called the senior curator and left a message.

"This may require some budget," he said.

Eight days later, he arrived at Moleculab with the sword. Yasmin Ridenour placed it very carefully in a shielded cage, and fiddled with controls to zero them. Then, in complete silence, the machine displayed a layered image on the clear screen of the cage.

She looked at it with wide eyes.

"What do you see?" he asked.

She said, "There are several intermixed layers here. I'm getting odd alloy readings. You mentioned Cutter metal, but there's more than one human metal, too. It's an ugly blend."

That seemed odd. "Really? I gathered it was well made before the repair."

She said, "I've heard of people just forging whatever was handy into a core, just to get some patterning. This could be that."

"Hmm. I don't get the impression that's so. I could ask the last smith again, but he didn't mention finding anything specific."

She traced a finger along the image in the air. "It's faint. He wouldn't without this gear. It was done long enough previously that there's been carbon diffusion."

"So it was reforged before that, then?"

She half frowned. "I'd guess so. It will take more scans to be sure."

"Then I want to do them."

"So, how much more do you want to invest?" she asked.

That was a good question. "I think I need to call the curator. I can approve one other scan now."

It was another week before he called and said, "Sergeant Arnoy, I have your sword."

"Thanks. What can you tell me?"

"I think you should come in here to see the documentation."

A div later, he escorted Arnoy into a conference room behind the offices. The chief curator and Yasmin were already present. They nodded.

"Curator Barth," his boss said in introduction. "Good to see you today, Sergeant."

"Thank you, sir."

Yasmin said, "A pleasure to meet you. I did the initial scan. It's a unique piece."

Arnoy said, "And you, lady. I'm excited to hear what this is."

"It's a very interesting piece," French said. He had to lead into this gently. "Lots of stuff has a story, not many pan out, but we always do some sort of check on request, even if it's just a visual. Since yours is very definitely a quality blade, we did a quick scan and found it was quite unusual inside."

"It's a multiple billet piece, then?" Arnoy looked hopeful.

French smiled. The man was in for the same shock he'd had.

"Yes, and there were irregularities that led us to do a further scan, and then finally we contacted East Bay University's physics lab and had them do a detailed metallurgical scan at the molecule level."

"How is that done?"

"It's a combination of things, and I don't know how it works, but everything from sonogram to X-ray to neutrino deflection. I've got images, and the experts told me what they mean. It's not cheap, but we've never seen a piece like this. Don't worry, you're not being billed."

He had Arnoy's attention with that. But the soldier's reply was one word.

"Okay."

French pulled up the overall scan and let it rotate in 3D between them, while letting the other images scroll underneath it.

"So, here's the forging done by Morlock with the Cutter metal in it. That edge is still technically steel, but very high alloy compared to the rest. They like cobalt and nickel and vanadium. Around that, you can see this layering here, which was done by a smith known as Mike Cardiff. I don't know if you know of Kendra Pacelli?"

"Vaguely. I've heard the name."

"Awarded the old Citizen's Medal during the Separation War, and then some other awards for a battle protecting the Ramadani embassy on Mtali."

"Awesome. So it does have real history. A long one."

Arnoy was going to be amazed.

"That was forged from what appears to be a recycled

Turkish shotgun barrel from old Earth, and pieces left from Mtali from a sword owned by a Sergeant Lisa Riggs. Also awarded the Valorous Service Medal after our operation on Mtali. Again. Or previously."

"Damn."

"We don't know who had it before that. But this metal, this thin line here, was forged in the twenty-second century."

"What? Really?"

"This alloy in the tang is twentieth century, and there's residue from a common flux used at the time, as well as fractured carbon chains from an oil used then."

"How far back does it go?"

He pointed. "This seems to be a steel from Central Asia. Eighteenth or nineteenth century. We can't even guess how that got there."

He kept going from his notes. "This bit they highlighted here and here is from the Bizen school of bladesmithing, sixteenth-century Japan."

Arnoy stared and waited, so he continued.

"This is probably thirteenth century. And this line running inside it, where metal was forged around an old core, is probably eighth century, Korean.

"And this small bit here in the rear core, has a very distinctive chemical trace. That's ancient steel we only rarely see even in museums. It was called 'damascus' because of the city where it was sold, but the source was in India on Earth, where it was called 'wootz.' That line glowing there, dates from Earth third century *BCE*."

"It can't go much further back, can it?"

"No, that's about when iron started."

"Damn." Arnoy said. "Just, damn."

They both stared down at the sword between them.

It was a fine-looking piece as it was. Knowing some of the history made it almost come alive. It felt as if the sword wanted him to pick it up and look for a fight. Arnoy had said the same when he'd first brought it.

"So what I got isn't just valuable, it's an insanely rare artifact. But without the scan, just a good-quality sword."

"Yes." He let that sit for a moment before he continued. "Our funds aren't unlimited. We generally prefer donations to purchasing artifacts, but what you have is unique and would certainly sell for a high price at auction. So I'm authorized to offer you a hundred thousand if you place it on ten-year loan with us, or a million if you can sell outright."

Arnoy sat staring at the sword but didn't touch it. French remained silent. Offering money for a piece with sentimental and intrinsic value was a delicate matter. He was prepared to wait long segs for a response, and possibly months for a decision.

But it was a matter of only moments before Arnoy spoke.

"Thank you very much for the information and the offer, sir, but I think I'm going to have it cleaned up by a professional so I can use it. We don't know exactly what the Cutters want or why we're fighting over space, but I know they're not immune to steel."

He'd expected a loan, would have been ecstatic with a sale, but that response wasn't even one he'd thought of. Yasmin and Curator Barth both gasped and muttered.

He had trouble framing his reply. "You want to take a three-thousand-year-old artifact into combat?"

Arnoy stared into his eyes. "Sure. You'd rather stick it in a display case?" He stood and offered his hand.

French shook the offered hand, sat back and stared at the young man.

There really was no answer to that.

———※———

The previous smith took her, but he had little enough to do. He tightened her dress hilt and gave it a fresh wrap. He peened two deflections in her edge and trued them, then worked down her length with feathery hammer blows that removed a few small warps in her form. It was so well done that sharpening and polishing barely scraped her skin at all.

Sharpening was more laborious with the alien metal. She still didn't understand its voices, but its feelings were clear, and in line with her own: to fight well and with courage.

The smith placed her in an oven, and low heat combined with some odd vapor furnished her with a coating over her steel. It was harder than anything she'd ever encountered, and shimmered in spectral waves. It tasted funny, and had no feelings she could detect.

That done, her scabbard was replaced. The new one was a perfect fit, magnolia wood inside, with the shell of another ridiculously tough material that had no thoughts but was a near indestructible tool.

She had a name again, too, and she was embarrassed.

The Empress.

Certainly she had been an honorable weapon, and perhaps would be again. This smith was a master, in ways she'd never known. But Empress?

She hoped to be worthy of it.

———※———

Two Freehold months later

Battle never changed.

The Cutters were pounding on the radius shield with something. He could easily see where they were attacking. That area glowed, and indented. From what he understood, the shield could only form a perfect spherical section. They were managing to force a deflection into it.

An entire section of perimeter wall disappeared into plasma, and debris exploded from the fractured and super-heated silicate. His mask flicked across his face to filter out the molecular particulates that would have choked him to death.

They'd shot right through the shield, which still shimmered. Whatever they fired ignored it entirely.

The shield slowed the Cutters, who waded through as if in deep water, but they came forward.

He read the tactical display's symbols in his field of vision. In near space, the ships had each other pinioned. Up above, the aircraft struggled to stay alive through a crossfire of near-light-speed missiles and bolts of energy. Once again the fight came down to armed men and women willing to engage up close.

The shield still held, and those Cutters had to haul each other through, before forming a small, tight perimeter. Their weapons were appalling, but at this moment the beings were vulnerable, for as long as it might take. Their shields stopped energy, but didn't stop solid matter, he noticed, as a chunk of vitrolith frag ripped one's side open.

In that moment, he was face to face with the enemy,

510 Michael Z. Williamson

destiny, history and himself. Everything focused on this instant.

In one hand, he had his photon rifle, tuned to fit his balance and neural responses. The projected sighting image flickered in his field of view. It was art-state for human tech. Unless the Cutter shields could be bypassed, it was useless.

In the other hand, he had what he knew to be the finest sword in the universe, unadorned steel with his hands as the only interface. It would cut.

The sword seemed to speak through his flesh. In the bottom of his mind, he heard whispers in languages known and strange.

"செல்."

"頑張れ"

"Алга!"

"Пошли!"

"Do it."

"Ayo."

"Saldır!"

"افعلها"

"Gah sssk."

There was only one possible, terrifying, course of action, but with the Empress as his ally, he found the strength to take it.

He ordered, "Third element, with me, advance to contact! Engage in direct combat!"

He shouted and charged.

TESTIMONIAL FOR THE AWARD OF
THE FREEHOLD MEDAL...

About the Authors

Zachary Hill

Zach loved life. He took every opportunity to experience it. He traveled to every country that he could, just to experience how the people there lived and to take part in it. He made friends all around the world and was the most loyal friend anyone could ask for. He was simply the best, most honest, loving and supportive man I ever knew. I could tout his accomplishments, like his two tours to Iraq or his two bachelor degrees, but if we could ask him what his greatest accomplishment was, he'd say marrying his soul mate. Tragically, Zach died on January 15, 2016. The best way to remember him is to read what he wrote. That's all he would ask for. RIP brother.

—by Joshua Hill

Larry Correia

Larry Correia is the award-winning, *New York Times* bestselling author of the Monster Hunter International series, the Saga of the Forgotten Warrior epic fantasy series, the Grimnoir Chronicles trilogy, the Dead Six thrillers (with Mike Kupari), the Monster Hunter Memoirs series (with John Ringo), and several novels in the Warmachine universe. A former accountant, machine gun dealer, and firearms instructor, Larry lives in the mountains of northern Utah with his wife and children.

Mike Massa

Mike Massa has lived an adventurous life, including stints as Navy SEAL officer, an investment banker and a technologist. He lived outside the US for several years, plus the usual deployments. Newly published, Mike is married with three sons, who check daily to see if today is the day they can pull down the old lion. Not yet . . .

John F. Holmes

John F. Holmes is a retired Sergeant First Class, having served in the Army and Army National Guard for twenty-two years. He took a vacation in Iraq in 2005. After accumulating numerous aches and pains and realizing he was way too old for this Army crap, retirement led to career change to cartoonist and writer. He is widely known for the *Powerpoint Ranger* comic.

His work can be found at: http://www.amazon.com/John-Holmes/e/B00C3NDAXQ/

Rob Reed

Rob Reed inherited his love of reading from his parents. He loves SF, fantasy, mysteries, thrillers, and military history. He's been an ER clerk, reporter, magazine staff writer, and firearms instructor. As a self-described "professional projectile launcher enthusiast" he writes about guns and shooting for a variety of publications and websites. He lives with his wife Marie and their three cats in the Metro Detroit area.

Dale C. Flowers

Dale C. Flowers always wanted to be called by his middle name when he was a kid but is glad it never took hold with his friends. C for Clinton, after the man who dug the Erie Canal. Who wants the moniker of a ditch digger? Dale enlisted in the Navy in 1965 at age seventeen and retired in 1991 as a Naval Surface Warfare Officer. He is a Vietnam and Desert Storm veteran. He spent most of his career on ships and after retirement worked as a cowboy, in construction, managing a feed store and as a County Construction Inspector for road building and asphalt paving. He lives in extreme Northwest Florida.

Tom Kratman

Tom Kratman is a defector from the People's Republic of Massachusetts, having enlisted into the Army in 1974, age seventeen. He served tours as an enlisted grunt with both the 101st Airborne and the 193rd Infantry Brigade. At that point the Army gave Kratman a scholarship and sent him off to Boston College to finish his degree and obtain a commission. Commissioned, he served again in Panama, then with the 24th Infantry Division, and with Recruiting Command. Saddam Hussein (UHBP) rescued Tom from the last by invading Kuwait.

Tom got out in 1992 and went to law school. He became a lawyer in 1995 but stayed in the reserves, taking the odd short tour and a bit of white collar mercenary work to retain his sanity and avoid practicing law.

In 2003 the Army called him up to participate in the invasion of Iraq. As it turned out he had a 100% blockage in his right coronary artery and wasn't going anywhere fun anytime soon. Instead, he languished here and there, before finally being sent on to be Director, Rule of Law, for the US Army Peacekeeping and Stability Operations Institute. Keep in mind the divine sense of humor.

Retired in 2006, he's returned to Virginia to write. His books published to date include the Countdown series, the Desert Called Peace series, three in John Ringo's Posleen universe, plus *Caliphate* and *A State of Disobedience*. Tom's married to a (really beautiful) girl from rural western Panama. Yoli and Tom make their home in Virginia.

Leo Champion

Leo Champion grew up in Sydney, Australia, but came to the US when he was nineteen. There, he mostly lived in Boston and around Silicon Valley, where he ran a local newspaper and worked for startups. He's the author of seven published novels, including the Legion series.

After sixteen years he's now back in Australia, where he's writing, running a small-press publishing house and working toward a computer science degree.

Peter Grant

Peter Grant was born and raised in Cape Town, South Africa. Between military service, the information-technology industry, and humanitarian involvement, he traveled throughout sub-Saharan Africa before being ordained as a pastor. He later emigrated to the USA, where he worked as a pastor and prison chaplain until an injury forced his retirement. He is now a full-time writer, and married to a pilot from Alaska. He and Dorothy currently live in Texas.

Christopher L. Smith

A native Texan by birth (if not geography), Chris moved "home" as soon as he could. Attending Texas A&M, he learned quickly that there was more to college than drinking beer and going to football games. He relocated to San Antonio, attended SAC and UTSA, and graduated in late 2000 with a BA in Lit. While there, he also met a wonderful lady who somehow found him to be funny, charming, and worth marrying. (She has since changed her mind on the funny and charming.) Chris began writing in 2012.

His short stories have appeared in several anthologies: "Bad Blood and Old Silver" (*Luna's Children: Stranger Worlds* anthology, Dark Oak Press); "Isaac Crane and the Ancient Hunger" (*Dark Corners* anthology, Fantom Enterprises); "200 miles to Huntsville" (*Black Tide Rising*,

Baen Books); and "What Manner of Fool" (*Sha'Daa: Inked*, Copper Dog Publishing).

His two cats allow him, his wife, their three kids, and two dogs to reside outside of San Antonio.

Jason Cordova

A 2015 John W. Campbell Award finalist, US Navy veteran Jason Cordova has traveled extensively throughout the US and the world. He has multiple novels and short stories currently in print. He also coaches high school varsity basketball and loves the outdoors.

He currently resides in Virginia with his wonder mutt, Odin.

Tony Daniel

Tony Daniel is a senior editor at Baen Books. He is also the author of ten science fiction novels, the latest of which is *Guardian of Night*, as well as short story collection, *The Robot's Twilight Companion*. He's a Hugo finalist and a winner of the *Asimov's* Reader's Choice Award for short story. Daniel is also the author of the young adult high-fantasy novels *The Dragon Hammer* and *The Amber Arrow*. Other Daniel novels include *Metaplanetary*, *Superluminal*, *Warpath*, and *Earthling*. Daniel is the coauthor of two books with David Drake in the long-running General series, *The Heretic* and *The Savior*. He is also the author of original series Star Trek novels *Devil's Bargain* and *Savage Trade*.

Kacey Ezell

Kacey Ezell is an active duty USAF helicopter pilot. When not beating the air into submission, she writes mil SF, SF, fantasy, and horror fiction. She lives with her husband, two daughters, and an ever growing number of cats.

About the Editor: Michael Z. Williamson

Michael Z. Williamson is variously an immigrant from the UK and Canada; a veteran of the US Army and US Air Force; a consultant on disaster preparedness and military matters to private clients, manufacturers, TV and movie productions and occasionally DoD elements; a bladesmith; and an author. His lifelong fascination with weapons often leads to buying, collecting, fondling and anthropomorphizing weapons, or else taking them to the range or pell for practice.